GATEWAY TO FORTUNE

Books by Peter Bourne

DRUMS OF DESTINY

FLAMES OF EMPIRE

THE GOLDEN ROAD

GATEWAY TO FORTUNE

PETER BOURNE

Gateway to Fortune

G. P. PUTNAM'S SONS · NEW YORK

GATEWAY TO FORTUNE

ALL NAMES, CHARACTERS, AND EVENTS IN THIS BOOK ARE FICTIONAL,
AND ANY RESEMBLANCE TO REAL PERSONS WHICH MAY SEEM TO
EXIST IS PURELY COINCIDENTAL.

1

THE OLD MAN rocked slowly to and fro; and the monotonous creak of the rockers as they pressed down upon the dry veranda boards was the only sound in the house, though the surrounding jungle was mysterious with noise. Near at hand sat his daughter, Marie, for old man Perrigot insisted upon company even while he slept. There were some who maintained that his conscience was haunted, and that he was afraid of solitude. Marie was needle working, mending in succession stockings, shirts, and underwear which had been washed that morning.

"Two people come," he announced unexpectedly. "On horseback. Men." He spoke in French.

The sound of his voice neither surprised nor startled her, although she had assumed that he was asleep. But then it was always difficult to be certain. Awake or asleep he always faced the east, and stared through half-shut eyelids into the steamy distance where lay the land of his birth, neither speaking nor moving save to maintain the steady rock—rock—rock. Perhaps the slight movement lulled his uneasy spirit. If he had a spirit! And if it were uneasy!

The prospect of visitors excited Marie. She raised her head, and eagerly stared down the hill at the narrow black trail of hardened soil which threaded its way through the jungle from the Perrigot house to infinity. In spite of her concentration she saw nothing but familiar landmarks which had long since grown hateful to her in their unchangeableness. The story was always the same. Her eyes were young; her father's, old and sunken from exposure; but always he could see farther and more clearly than anyone else in the household.

She continued to gaze down the trail, and with her hand shaded her eyes from the glare of the sun which was sinking swiftly toward the mountains. At last she saw what her father had seen: two small objects moving slowly along the trail toward the foot of the hill. She marveled once again at the keenness of his sight. She could not be certain that the two objects were necessarily human, and male.

The two men disappeared beneath the obstructing plume of a sentinel tree, appeared again, then were again concealed from her sight by the spreading foliage of an umbrella tree. They continued to reappear and

3

disappear, all the while growing larger. At last she could contain her excitement no longer.

"Anne! Anne! Visitors!"

Anne quickly joined her sister. Anne was seventeen, and older by two years than Marie, but the difference in ages was at first glance scarcely noticeable. Facially, they might almost have been twins, so alike were they. Their hair was raven black and dressed in long curls; their eyes were as dark as sloes; their complexion, darkly olive. Besides, they always dressed alike. In build they were different, for Marie had not yet lost her puppy fat. She was plump and still unshapely; she had no waist to speak of, and her prominent breasts threatened to burst through her print frock. Anne, on the other hand, was slim and appeared taller than Marie. She carried herself with an air of assurance and gave promise of a maturing beauty.

She rested her hands on the rail of the veranda, and gazed down into the valley. She was no less excited than her sister, but she was trying hard to conceal the fact.

Impatience overcame her pose of indifference. "Where are they? I cannot see anyone. How many?"

"Two. Men, Papa says. Look! You can see them now, this side of Papa's sentinel." There were five outstanding sentinel trees bordering the trail, which the sisters long ago had named for identification purposes.

"I see them." Anne glanced at the sun, and grew tense. "It's getting too late for them to reach anywhere tonight. Do you think they will ask to stay the night here, Papa?"

"Probably." Rock—rock—rock— "You're unusually interested, girl," he commented. His voice was casual, but his sideways glance was sharp and angry.

"It's so long since we've seen anyone, Papa. It's so lonely—" She began to falter. "At times—"

"Lonely! What nonsense! You have me and Marie and Dolores to talk to. What else should you ask for, at your age? You need more work to occupy your thoughts—"

"Please, Papa—" Pleadingly, she turned a sad face toward him. "Don't be cross with me. Not just now, please. I want to look my best—"

"Yes, my girl, that's the trouble," he muttered. He said nothing more, from which forbearance Anne deduced that for once he intended to abstain from the inevitable, interminable homily. With restrained eagerness she turned her attention on the approaching visitors.

They were not far off Marie's sentinel, at the foot of the slope which led up to the hilltop veranda, and through the occasional gaps in the green canopy which overhung the trail it was possible to distinguish details of their clothing. They were dressed in suits of white drill, leather

4

gauntlets and leggings, and wide-rimmed felt hats. Bulky saddlebags straddled the rumps of their animals.

There was a strangeness about their clothes, and their stiff posture, which made Anne catch hold of Marie's hand. Perrigot did not miss the impulsive movement.

"Well, Anne?" he demanded.

"I don't think they are Panamanians, Papa."

"Not Panamanians—" Perrigot leaned forward and stared over the wooden rail. The two men had disappeared from sight, so there was silence on the veranda for several seconds, until the visitors reappeared again.

"I believe you are right," Perrigot exclaimed sharply. "What the devil!"

The visitors reached the slope proper. Their progress slackened as their animals took the strain of the ascent.

"Shall I go down—" Anne began.

"No." He rose to his feet and moved heavily along the veranda toward the short flight of wooden stairs at the far end. Behind him the chair rocked in uneven momentum. Pausing only to pick up a frayed Panama hat and a walking stick he moved down the stairs until he reached the ground. The reflected heat of the baked earth rasped against his face as he awaited the coming of the two riders.

In a short while they emerged from the edge of the jungle and moved slowly across the clearing which surrounded the house. They halted their animals a few yards from him, and he noticed that their necks were shining with perspiration and that their faces were caked with dirt which beads of sweat had in places transformed into muddy smears.

One of the men raised his hat. *"Buenas tardes, señor."*

Perrigot raised his hat in response. "Good afternoon, gentlemen," he replied, speaking in English. He smiled at the comical expression which passed across the face of the man who had first spoken. "You are Americans, are you not?"

"Yes, sir. Is our nationality so obvious?"

"Two such fresh complexions could only have come from a nontropical country, gentlemen, so the United States was my first guess." He spoke fluently, but with a marked French accent. "Welcome to the home of Felix Perrigot. Won't you dismount, gentlemen?"

The men on horseback looked embarrassed. "My name is Wesley Adam, sir, and my companion here is Olaf Ericson. We've a favor to ask you, sir—"

"To stay the night here?"

Wesley nodded. "If it's not too much trouble, sir. Any place that we can bunk in for a few hours, an outhouse or the stable—"

"The stable by all means, gentlemen—for the horses! For yourselves,

5

there is a spare bedroom that it will give me and my family much pleasure to have you occupy. Shall we dispose of the animals first?"

"At your service, sir." The two men dismounted stiffly and, leading their horses, followed Perrigot around to the rear of the house, where they stabled the animals underneath the kitchen quarters, for the house was built on stilts. Having unpacked their personal belongings and fed and watered the animals they joined the Frenchman.

"It's mighty good of you, sir, to receive a couple of perfect strangers—" Wesley began.

"Not another word, Mr. Adam." Perrigot led the way back to the veranda. "It is not the first time we have been asked to accommodate strangers for a night. It is a pleasure one looks forward to when one lives so many miles from the nearest white settlement."

"Don't you find it lonely, sir, being so faraway from people of your own color?" The speaker this time was Olaf Ericson. As did his name, his appearance clearly revealed his Scandinavian ancestry. His hair was thick, unruly, and a warm shade of ripened corn; his eyes were the blue of polar seas. His shoulders were massive, but without being disproportionate to his height. His clipped accent similarly betrayed his origin.

"Not at all," Perrigot sharply denied. "We are sufficient unto ourselves, my daughters and I. We work, read, and talk; we are never bored." As the three men ascended the last stair he called to his family.

"Anne! Marie!"

The two girls moved forward to greet their guests; Anne, with demure poise; Marie with an ungainly lolloping action. He made the introductions in English. To the surprise of the two men the girls spoke in their own language. Wesley was overjoyed.

"It's lucky for us you can all speak English. My French doesn't get me any further than asking the time, and Olaf here can't do that much."

"We speak Spanish too," Marie told him.

He grinned. "I'm not much better at Spanish."

When Wesley smiled his face was transformed. In normal repose, his long lean face was somber in expression, almost hungry looking, for he had high cheekbones and a complexion which was becoming coppered by constant exposure to all types of weather. But in smiling his entire face crinkled; his eyes glowed with a warm humor that no one could suspect of insincerity; and the set of his hard chin was softened.

"Shall we go in?" Perrigot suggested. "I am sure you gentlemen would like to wash after your journey. Anne will take you up to your room. Anne!"

Anne led the way into a narrow passage and up a flight of stairs. On the floor above she turned left and entered a room at the far end of the passage. By the time the two men had followed her in, she had half raised the Venetian blinds so they were able to see something of the room which was

6

to be theirs for the next few hours. It was spotlessly clean, and every square foot of its polished woodwork reflected the last minutes of daylight. Otherwise it was furnished with the utmost simplicity and contained no more than the essentials for a night's rest: a double bed, a night table with candlestick and candle, a chair, a chest of drawers, and a washstand.

Anne smiled at the men as they unconsciously sighed with the pleasure of entering a cool, shady room. "I will bring you water," she said as she moved toward the door.

Wesley protested. "That's a man's job. Let me—"

But she shook her head with prim disapproval. "Papa would be cross. Besides, you must be glad to rest and get cool." Before he could argue further she went out, closing the door behind her.

"By Jimminy! She's right about wanting to get cool." Ericson peeled off his jacket and exposed a shirt that was wet with perspiration. "If I haven't lost twenty-eight pounds during the past few days—"

Wesley was unfeeling. "You can afford to, you big gorilla." He removed his own jacket and showed his own shirt, which was equally soaked. "Which I can't." He rubbed his seat with a rueful grimace. "Toss you who has the chair."

"Who has it? Winner or loser?"

"Don't you want to sit down?"

"Not on that chair," Ericson groaned. "Winner has the bed."

He won, and sank down upon its springy softness with a rapturous sigh. Wesley gingerly lowered himself on to the chair. A few moments of contented silence followed.

"Quite a little lady, that girl," he remarked.

"Anne?"

"Yes."

"Beginning to realize her sex. Bet she's putting on an act for our benefit. It's the age. You should see my kid sister, when the boys come around."

"She's going to be a good-looker."

"Sure, but not so good as her sister."

"Marie! That tubby little barrel?"

Ericson nodded. "In a few years' time she'll make your hair curl, or my name isn't Olaf. Did you see her eyes?"

"Nothing to them. Just excited—"

"You'll see."

Wesley chuckled. "All the way from Providence? I'll need a mighty powerful telescope."

A knock on the door interrupted the conversation.

"Come in."

Anne re-entered the bedroom. She carried a large pitcher of water in one hand, towels in the other. Ignoring Wesley's hasty movement to help her, she poured some of the water into the basin and arranged the towels on the rail. Her studied, graceful movements made Wesley's eyes twinkle. When she had finished she turned.

"Is there anything else I may bring you, please? Soap—shaving paper—"

"Not a thing, thanks." Wesley pointed to a small bag on the floor. "We're hardened campaigners, and carry everything we can possibly need."

"Papa says will you come down as soon as you are ready?"

"In about fifteen minutes—Miss Perrigot," Wesley added, as an afterthought. His impulse was richly rewarded, for a delightful smile passed across her lips and was reflected in her deep, lustrous eyes. With added self-confidence she moved toward the door. Just as she was passing through she turned again.

"The toilet is at the other end of the passage, on the left," she told them, and left.

"That's what I like about the French," Wesley said with a grin. "They're realistic." He took a nickel from his pocket. "Who washes first?"

Olaf won again, and plunged his face into the cool water. "Ah!" he exclaimed in ecstasy as he came up for air and poked his forefingers into his ears.

Just after the promised fifteen minutes the two men descended the stairs. An open door with a soft glow of light streaming through showed them a sitting room. As with their bedroom, it was furnished with the minimum requirements, but four lighted candles made it look cosy, and a tray with glasses and a bottle which reposed on a small table, was a welcome sight. Perrigot stood up, with his back to a wall, but Anne and Marie each sat stiff backed on a small chair, doing needlework.

"Ah! There you are, gentlemen. Will you join me in drinking vermouth? I have no whisky, I regret to say."

"Vermouth sounds good, Mr. Perrigot."

The Frenchman filled three glasses to the brim; two others he quarter-filled for his daughters. The five glasses were quickly offered by Anne. Perrigot raised his with a courteous gesture.

"Welcome to the Isthmus of Panama."

They drank to the welcome. "Have you been here long?" he added.

"Four days." With a grin, "Four days too many for Olaf here."

"Do you not like the country, Mr. Ericson? Or the people, maybe?"

"It's the climate I don't like, sir. Is it always as hot as it has been for the last four days?"

"Always, except during the rainy season."

"Ah! And then—"

"It seems even hotter. But one grows accustomed to it, even to like it. Isn't that so, my girls?"

"Yes, Papa," they answered obediently.

"Have they lived here long?" Wesley asked.

8

"All their lives. They were born here." There was a sharp bite in Perrigot's voice.

Wesley quickly changed the subject. "How do you find the Indians, sir? Reliable?"

Perrigot looked puzzled. "As workers?"

"I meant, as guides."

The Frenchman shrugged. "As reliable as any other people of color. Are you needing some?"

"For some weeks. Do you know of any you can recommend?"

"That depends on which direction you are making for, and for what purpose. Hunting—exploring—"

Wesley laughed. "We are not here on vacation, sir."

"No!" Perrigot tried, not very successfully, to mask his intense curiosity. "Forgive me, gentlemen. I jumped to conclusions. One does not see many American businessmen in this country, except railroad and shipping companies' staff."

"We are surveying the country on behalf of Mr. William Nelson Cromwell, attorney for the New Panama Canal Company."

"The Canal Company—" Perrigot's expression became bleak.

"Papa!"

"Quiet, child," he harshly ordered. "For what purpose, gentlemen?"

"In the hope of persuading Uncle Sam to build the canal."

"No," the Frenchman gasped. "Never, never, never!"

2

THE EFFECT OF Perrigot's outburst on his visitors was too marked for him not to realize that he had startled them. He made an effort to recover his composure.

"Again I have to express my apologies, gentlemen. My indiscretion is unforgivable." He wiped his forehead with his handkerchief. "This tropical heat is apt to affect us foreigners until we are not always responsible for our acts."

"But, Papa, you are the same whenever the canal is mentioned."

He turned angrily to face his younger daughter. In doing so he turned his back on the two men, who did not see his face. Marie shrank back as he half lifted his hand to strike her. Then he let it fall, shrugged, and turned to face his guests.

"It was wrong of the girl to expose her father, but what she says is true. I cannot bear to speak of the canal, or even to think about it, because to me the project was accursed from its inception, and always will be. I am not a religious man, but I agree with the sixteenth-century priests who advised Philip of Spain against the project of a canal. 'What therefore God hath joined together,' they told him, 'let no man put asunder.'"

The story was a familiar one to the Americans. Wesley made a slight gesture of dissent. "There was also the chaplain who said of the mountains which separate the two oceans, 'But if there be mountains there are also hands.'"

"The canal is accursed," Perrigot repeated obstinately. "It was never intended by the Creator that it should be built, and it never will be."

"*Never* is a strong word, sir," Wesley dryly commented.

"Yes, of course. You are a young man. Youth has neither fears nor doubts. I am an old man, with years of wisdom and experience behind me. I know the pitfalls of building a canal across the Isthmus; the treachery, the malignity, the unconquerable defenses of nature."

"The marvels of modern engineering have defeated nature before now, sir."

Perrigot laughed. "Perhaps you think I know nothing of modern engineering, Mr. Adam. I am—I was an engineer. I landed at Colón with De Lesseps on the thirtieth of December, eighteen years ago. I worked on the canal for ten years, until the old company went bankrupt."

Though Wesley regretted any suggestion of arrogance on his part, he gazed challengingly at his host. "That is all the more reason, sir, why you should agree with me that it is possible to build a canal here."

"Sea-level or lock type?"

"I can't answer that question yet. We are surveying the possibilities of both."

"No matter. Both are impossible." Perrigot drained his glass with an air of finality which seemed to suggest a subconscious medium of emphasis. Before his guests could speak he turned to his daughters. "Anne, go and tell *cook* to have dinner ready for seven o'clock sharp."

Wesley did not miss the significant look which accompanied the order, but as Anne rose to obey the command the Frenchman refilled the glasses. Having done so he sat down and stared at his visitors with an aggressiveness which embarrassed them.

"Is this your first visit to the Isthmus, gentlemen?"

Wesley answered for them both with a nod.

"And you landed at Colón five days ago?"

"Yes, sir, from the *Seguranca*."

"Since when you have visited what places? I do not wish to be impertinent, or to pry into private affairs, you understand—"

Wesley felt nettled. "There is no secret about our movements. We stayed at Colón for the remainder of the first day, that night, and also the next day; to complete arrangements and purchase horses and other necessities for our trip across the Isthmus and into the interior. The third day we spent examining the existing French canal, and we stayed the night at Mindi. Yesterday we made Gatun our headquarters. Today, Bohio. We were on our way to Alhajuela when we realized that we had underestimated the time. We asked an Indian how long it would take us to get there. He told us not before dark and advised us to come to you."

"He did right." After this aside, Perrigot went on. "You have seen no more than a few miles of the Isthmus. What you have not seen, in this country at any rate, are the mountain peaks of the Great Divide, which separates the Atlantic from the Pacific, and forms the backbone of two continents, from Alaska to the Strait of Magellan. If you had a thousand thousand pairs of hands at your command, gentlemen, you could do no more than scratch away the surface of that mighty obstacle."

"A steam shovel takes the place of many pairs of hands, sir," Ericson pointed out.

"You would need giant shovels to tear a path through even the smallest peak, which French surveyors estimated at one hundred and sixty feet above sea level. Do you think it possible to cut a slice of volcanic mountain one hundred and sixty feet in depth, three or four hundred feet in width, probably eight or nine miles in length?"

The two Americans glanced at each other, but before they could comment on these figures Perrigot continued.

"On your way here you have seen, and probably crossed, the Chagres River; shallow, sluggish, often fordable. Perhaps you have seen the Indians poling their *cayucos* along its placid surface, and look upon it as a benevolent, kindly river. That is because you have seen it in early May, after three months' dry season. In the past two weeks no more than a cupful of rain has fallen. The picture will be different next month, when the rainy season begins."

Wesley resented Perrigot's assumption that his visitors had come to the country completely ignorant of its natural features.

"The habits of the Chagres are not unknown to us, sir. We are aware that the average precipitation here is greater than in almost any other country in the world, that this must obviously affect the speed of the river—"

"Words—statistics—what can they mean in comparison with what the native of Panama sees with his own eyes? In twenty-four hours your placid, benevolent Chagres can rise forty feet and be transformed into a torrent that annihilates everything in its path. And the Chagres is only one of several rivers, gentlemen. Scarcely less important are its tributaries, the Pequeni, the Trinidad, and the Gatun, to mention only three; there are a host of smaller streams that help to carry away the rain which has been known to fall at the rate of two inches in five minutes."

Ericson whistled. "By Jimminy! That's a cloudburst!"

"A cloudburst which can last up to three days, Mr. Ericson, and make the water, in the narrower canyons, climb fifty feet in three hours. How do you propose to deal with water that races down into the main watershed in waves? What is going to happen to your ships when your canal rises twenty, thirty, forty feet in half as many hours? Can you dig a fifty-foot canyon through the Isthmus?"

He drained his glass again, this time as if to soothe his resentment. Yet the vermouth seemed rather to inflame his passion. He leaned forward and pointed a shaking forefinger at Wesley.

"On your way here did you see the thousands of graves in the cemetery at Monkey Hill—"

"The cemetery for the men who lost their lives while building the railroad?"

"Many buried there died while building the railroad, Mr. Adam, but also there are the thousands who lost their lives when work started on the French canal. I came out here with a party of seventeen others, mostly young Frenchmen, all attached to my particular section of the project. Eighteen strong healthy men, fired by their enthusiasm to add to the prestige of France by building a second, greater Suez; ambitious and with an eye to their own future. Within one month of landing, every man save one was dead. I was the exception, perhaps because I was older and inured to the tropics. Or maybe I was a harder liver."

Ericson looked troubled. "Seventeen out of eighteen. Jimminy!"

Perrigot turned his unblinking gaze upon the blond American. "You cannot make a proper survey of the Isthmus without visiting the upper reaches of the Chagres, Mr. Ericson. I can tell you what happened to a French survey party of twenty-two who visited that region. They were stricken with a disease which killed ten of them. The mother superior of the French hospital at Ancon came out here with twenty-four sisters to nurse the sick and the injured. Of that number twenty-one died of yellow fever."

His voice faltered, and a silence followed his impassioned words. Their embarrassment was not relieved by observing the tear which slowly trickled down each leathery cheek.

"Of all my countrymen who came out to build that accursed canal, more than four fifths are buried here," he muttered. "What provision does a set of blueprints make for a loss of life on that scale? What makes you Americans believe that your workmen would be more immune than the French to yellow fever and malaria?"

Wesley glanced at the two girls. He could not decide whether Perrigot was sincere; he was not used to meeting men who displayed emotion so easily and suspected that the Frenchman was being dramatic for effect. The expression on the two young faces convinced him that he was not misjudging his host; there was a repugnance in Anne's eyes which made him believe she was ashamed on their father's behalf.

Before he could comment on Perrigot's last remarks, Ericson spoke. "Then you don't think a canal can be built across the Isthmus—by Americans, French, or anyone else?"

"No."

"But you must have thought it possible when you came here eighteen years ago."

"I continued to think it possible for three years."

"Not after that?"

"No."

"But you continued to work on for another seven years?"

"Of course." Perrigot shrugged. "What would you? It was my livelihood."

"What made you change your opinion?"

"I had got to know Panama, Mr. Ericson. By then I had seen money flow like water, without serving any useful purpose. I had seen all my friends, all my acquaintances, and hundreds of others whom I didn't know, die before my eyes of one disease or another. Even more depressing, from an engineer's point of view, I had seen what little progress had been made toward completing the canal. I had seen ten thousand employees excavate a daily average of twenty thousand cubic yards—considerably short of the estimated one hundred and three million yards which had to be excavated in nine years. It does not require a mathematician to work out that one million yards would have to be excavated each month to keep up to schedule. And the figure of one hundred and three million yards was, after all, only an estimate in which no allowance was made for slides."

"Slides, sir?"

"Yes, Mr. Adam. In one day at Culebra, where we excavated in all eighteen million yards, I saw one slide that took us nearly a week to remove. The deeper the cut the more such slides would develop." He snapped his fingers with a contemptuous gesture. "So much for your estimates."

The two Americans exchanged glances. Wesley thought that Ericson was looking depressed and wondered why. He had found Perrigot's remarks interesting, but not gloomy. Any constructional engineer who was able to complete a job without meeting unanticipated obstacles would consider himself one of the world's lucky men. He was glad to hear about the slides. In the event of his believing in the possibility of a canal he would emphasize in his report the necessity of estimating for the excavation and removal of additional material.

He gave his attention to the Frenchman. "Is the subject of the canal too painful for discussion, sir?"

The Frenchman considered the question before replying. "It is painful to the pride of any Frenchman to discuss the canal, Mr. Adam. It is still more so to me, who has witnessed the passing of so many young Frenchmen, some of them personal friends. Besides, I lost my life's savings in the *Compagnie Universelle du Canal Interocéanique de Panama*. I have both relatives and friends who lost money in the company. How could the subject be anything other than painful? But I will discuss it with you. What do you want to know?"

"In eighteen eighty-one, when work first started, the project was for a sea-level canal. Six years later it was decided to substitute a lock canal. Why?"

"I have already answered that question, indirectly. After six years' working, during which time less than a quarter of the canal had been built, it was realized that it would be impossible ever to build a sea-level canal within a reasonable economic period of time—still less within the period of twelve years allowed for its construction by the terms of the lease with the Colombian government.

"Then there was the question of finance, Mr. Adam. The original estimated cost of construction was—to speak in terms of your American currency—two hundred and eight millions dollars. By eighteen eighty-seven the greater part of this money had already been spent. Do I need to tell you on what?"

Wesley felt uncomfortable. "I am a surveyor, sir, not a financier."

"The more honorable profession." Perrigot laughed sardonically. "Very well, let us ignore the sad scandal of corruption, bribery, extravagance which resulted in less than one hundred million dollars being expended on the construction of the canal out of the capital of two hundred and sixty-two million dollars subscribed by the French public. The newspapers of the world have lately exposed the ineptitude of the first Panama Canal Company, which, as you know, was declared bankrupt eight years ago, a receiver having been appointed to take charge of its affairs. A new company was formed three years ago, which is still scratching about with a view to keeping the concession in force—no doubt you saw work proceeding at Gatun?"

"Yes, sir, we did. But this lock canal now. When it was decided to change over from the sea-level canal the new company decided to dam the Chagres at Bohio and Alhajuela—"

Although the Frenchman's eyes smoldered with anger, his voice remained studiously polite. "You are a persistent young man, Mr. Adam. That plan is even more fantastic than the idea of the sea-level canal. Do you realize that the damming of the Chagres at the two points you mention would create an inland lake with a summit of one hundred and one feet above sea level?"

Wesley shrugged. "The plan was not mine, sir. According to reports I have read it is proposed to reach that height in four stages. To lock a vessel twenty-five feet at each stage is far from being an insuperable engineering problem."

"On paper the problem is simple," Perrigot sneered, "but you are reckoning without nature and finance. The board of the new company which proposed the plan estimated the additional cost at another hundred million dollars. Since they have less than a tenth of that capital available, I leave to your common sense what value to place on such a wildcat scheme.

"But tell me, Mr. Adam," in a less contentious voice he addressed himself specifically to Wesley, "how you come to be here on this survey? I trust you will not think me impertinent if I remark on your apparent youthfulness. You cannot be long out of college?"

"Three years, sir."

"Three!" He did not indicate in so many words that he could not understand why so young a man had been given such important work, but the inflection of his voice was revealing.

"It's only an exploratory survey, sir. Of course, though I was lucky to get the appointment, they had to have someone ready to put up with the rough going and the climate."

"Of course!"

The slight ironic note produced an amiable grin from Wesley. "That must sound silly to you, living your life here. But back home the old covered-wagon spirit is disappearing. Life's become too easy for most folk, and every year sees it growing easier."

"But not for you, young man?"

"Not yet. When I heard that Mr. Cromwell was looking for someone to survey the Isthmus of Panama I moved heaven and earth to get the job."

"Was it the country rather than the job which interested you?" Curiosity, this time.

"Yes. I was brought up on a diet of Panama ever since I was old enough to sit on my grandfather's knee and listen to him telling stories of the place."

"Ah! So your grandfather knew Panama. And made it sound romantic!" A disagreeable laugh succeeded the last, clipped word.

Wesley flushed. "Adventurous is the word." His correction was sulky. He did not much care for his host's jibes. He added proudly, "He helped build the railroad."

"So!" Interest was succeeded by a puzzled frown. "The name isn't familiar to me, Mr. Adam."

An eager smile. "Were you here then as well as later?"

"I also worked on the railroad for a time. At the age of seventeen. Afterward, I left for California before returning to France."

Wesley was delighted. "Then you must have heard of Grandfather, even if you didn't meet him. His name wasn't Adam. It was Henry Stewart.

He married Jean Martin of Boston, and their first child, Elizabeth, was my mother. If you had been brought up on the stories of Panama Grandfather used to tell, you would have wanted to come—"

His words came to a stumbling halt when he saw the expression which settled on the face of the Frenchman. Above a body that bore the appearance of having fallen into the first stage of *rigor mortis,* his sunken cheeks had turned ashen and his eyes staring. He looked shocked, and much older.

He must be ill, a stroke or something, thought Wesley, startled by the sudden change in the Frenchman. He half rose from the chair, then glanced at the two girls. To his astonishment neither of them moved. They stared at Perrigot with frightened eyes.

"Is anything the matter? Is your father ill? Is there anything we can do?"

Before they could answer Perrigot waved a hand in protest. "Don't move, anyone," he muttered. "It is nothing. It is passing." His eyes slowly cleared, and the ashen look passed away. Soon he was able to speak normally again. "There are times when one is made to realize that the body is older than the mind. You were speaking of your grandfather, Monsieur Wesley. Was he the Henry Stewart who assisted Ran Runnels in stopping bandit raids on the gold trains?"

"Yes," Wesley proudly confessed. "I know the story by heart. So does Olaf here, I've told it so often. Then you did hear of him, sir, when you were working on the railroad?"

"Impossible not to. Everyone on the Isthmus spoke of his methods in combating banditry."

Ericson chuckled. "Not surprising, sir. There can't have been many people in history who could order more than thirty people to be hanged."

"It was not Grandfather who gave the order," Wesley sharply corrected. "Runnels did that. Grandfather had to obey. Runnels was chief of the police."

"One understands that," the old man admitted. "So your grandfather's stories of Panama have indirectly brought you here. Are you disappointed?"

"Well!" The exclamation lingered on in doubt. "It is far more civilized than I believed it would be. Grandfather spoke of jungle that no white man had ever explored; and made it sound savage and dangerous."

"Instead of which you've traveled along the railroad which your grandfather helped to build, and seen a countryside not so very different from parts of Florida," Perrigot stated dryly.

"More or less."

"That's because you've probably never left the Chagres valley. The valley is dominated by the railroad, which is run by your countrymen. Wherever Americans go they take with them the amenities of civilized life. Do you really want to see jungle country?"

16

"Yes. Don't we, Olaf?"

Olaf nodded.

The Frenchman regarded his guests with mocking eyes. "Earlier you spoke of a visit to Alhajuela."

"Yes, sir. I was waiting to ask you the best route to get there."

"You can go by way of the Chagres, by employing Indians to pole you upriver in a cayuco. Or you can go through the jungle."

"Which is the quicker route? And the easier?"

"You Americans! Always thinking of time!" Before answering the question he glanced at his daughters. "Go and give cook a hand with the meal, my cabbages. It is time we ate." He watched the two girls leave before turning back to Wesley.

"The easier route to Alhajuela, Mr. Adam? The Chagres, by all means. But there is a trail through the jungle which would save you several days on the double journey."

"Should we need a guide?"

"Not necessarily. The trail is well marked. Return along the trail by which you reached this house, take the first cross trail on your left, and continue along until you come to another cross trail that is marked by an old wayside shrine nailed on a tree. If you again take the trail on your left it will lead you directly to Alhajuela. By leaving here soon after dawn tomorrow you should reach there by early afternoon."

"What do you say, Olaf?"

Ericson nodded. "I'm for saving time, Wesley."

"Then that is settled, gentlemen. I will call you at four tomorrow morning."

Anne entered the room. "Dinner is served, Papa."

Perrigot rose. "Come, gentlemen," he said with a courteous gesture.

3

THE MEAL PASSED more pleasantly than the two Americans had anticipated. As if to make amends for his contentious attitude, Perrigot exerted the traditional charm and courtesy of a cultured Frenchman. The cooking was neither characteristic of the country, nor of France, but reminded Wesley of New Orleans, where he had once stayed for several months.

Taking their cue from their father, the two girls kept the table cheerful with their laughter. Marie was exuberant, boisterous almost, which seemed to please Ericson, and several times produced a responding guffaw from him. But Anne continued to maintain a queer restraint, which was not completely successful, for sometimes her eyes betrayed a bubbling humor of which the rest of her face gave only the most formal hint. In spite of Marie's boisterousness and Anne's twinkling eyes, both girls were careful, Wesley noticed, never to allow too long an interval between quick, inquiring glances at their father, as if anxious to detect the first sign of any sudden change in his mood. There was something about those questioning looks which made him believe that they were afraid of their father.

They spoke of and discussed several subjects of interest, ranging from the latest book by Robert W. Chambers, to the art of Frederic Remington; from the music of Victor Herbert to the milk baths of Anna Held. Before long Wesley was feeling embarrassed by his own lack of culture. Even allowing for the many extra years of life, the Frenchman's learning amazed him, especially when the eighteen years' stay in Panama was taken into consideration. Perrigot's worldly knowledge made him appear uncomfortably provincial.

The one subject which all carefully avoided was that of the canal. But they did speak of France and especially of Paris; and whenever Perrigot spoke there was regret in his voice and a faraway look in his eyes—his was the expression of an exile, and Wesley felt sorry for his host. He tried to imagine what he would feel if he were exiled from the States, from New England in particular, and realized that life in such circumstances would lose much of its savor.

Ericson broke into the conversation. "But there's something about Panama, too, sir—I've been here only a few days, and sometimes I think I don't want to see it again. And yet—"

"It begins to fascinate you?"

"Fascinate!" Ericson looked doubtful. "That is scarcely the description I had in mind."

Perrigot smiled. "Fascinate will be the right word if you stay here long enough. The tropics do something to a foreigner after a time. They work upon his spirit as leprosy does on his body. Life here first saps a white man's ambition, his will to work, his moral standards; then turns him rotten by decomposing his mental stability and making him powerless to exist without its narcotic draft."

He translated Ericson's expression. "I am no exception. On the contrary. If I have one desire left it is to spend the rest of my life in Paris. But I haven't the courage to cope with the problems involved. Life here in Panama is too easy; I have become too mentally and physically indolent to face the hurly-burly of civilized life." He frowned. "You look puzzled. Are you wondering how many years of life are left to me?"

When neither visitor answered, he laughed scornfully at their embarrassment. "I was forty-five when I arrived at Colón with De Lesseps; I am now sixty-three. Most people regard me as an old man. I look old. The

18

tropics are to blame. That's another effect which they have on people."
He regarded each man in turn with a stern paternal air. "Take the advice
of an older man and do not stay in Panama a day longer than you have to.
Get away, while you still can."

Wesley chuckled. "No fear of that where I'm concerned, sir. I have a
wife to take me back to Providence."

He thought he detected a suggestion of relief in the expression which
passed quickly across the Frenchman's face.

"A wife!" Perrigot made a clucking noise in reproof. "You are a young
man to be married, Mr. Adam. In my country young men are discouraged
from marrying early."

"To give them a chance to sow wild oats?"

"Perhaps."

"I never wanted to sow any wild oats, sir. Especially after I'd met Dulcie.
We were married the night of my graduation. That was three years ago."

"Then I must confine my warning to your companion—"

But Ericson had become bored with his host's pompous warnings. He
and Marie were enjoying some private joke. The blond young giant seemed
quite at ease talking to the younger girl.

With the end of the meal, which immediately followed Perrigot's remarks about tropical life, the pleasure of the evening vanished. Perrigot
was depressed by his recollections of France. He turned moody and somber,
and responded to his guests' advances in monosyllables. Perversely, Anne
followed her father's example. The smile left her eyes, and her demure
reserve changed to a sulky boredom, on which Wesley could make no
impression. Only Ericson and Marie remained cheerful, and even they
were eventually affected by the general atmosphere of gloom. As soon as
he could reasonably do so without appearing discourteous, Wesley suggested bed. The idea met with immediate and unflattering approval from
Perrigot. A few minutes later the two Americans entered their bedroom.

Wesley stripped off his jacket, sat down on the bed, and began unlacing
his boots. Ericson joined him there.

"A nice girl that, Wesley," he said, gazing at the ceiling as he lay back
on the bed and cupped the back of his head between his clasped hands.
"In another few years—" He whistled. "If I'm anywhere in this part of
the world—" His voice tailed off.

Wesley finished unlacing his boots. "It's a funny household. Did you
see the way Perrigot looked at Anne when he spoke about the cook? He
appeared to underline the word."

Ericson was not especially interested in the problem of the cook. "I
noticed," he agreed casually. "Probably she's just a helper, and he wanted
to impress us."

"He stopped working for the old Canal Company when it was made bankrupt. Why did he stay on in Panama—"

"He told you why. Tropical fever."

"I don't believe that fairy tale. Life may be easy here, but he needs some money to live as he does. What's his present job, nearly a day's journey from the nearest town of any size?"

"He hasn't one. Marie told me. He goes to Colón twice a year, and to Panama once every quarter, and takes the two kids along. That's almost the only time they see anyone except their father and Dolores, the cook. That's why they were so pleased to see us. Well, that and—" He sat up, and rubbed his fingers through his hair. His face expressed smug self-satisfaction.

"Anything else she told you?"

Ericson nodded. "He always takes a sack into town full and brings it back empty."

"Full of what?"

"Your guess is as good as mine."

Wesley stared at the candle flame, which danced to the slight draft from the window. "Selling surplus produce wouldn't keep him for three months."

"It's my opinion that he made enough from the canal scheme to keep him the rest of his life."

"Not by work, he didn't."

Ericson began to unlace his boots. "There are other ways of making money—" He added with regret, "But my Pop didn't teach them to me."

The two men were soon asleep. Sometime later Wesley awoke. The echo of an unusual sound was still ringing in his ears, but it was too vague for him to identify it. It might have been a knocking noise, he reflected. The slam of a door, for instance. On the other hand, he had a feeling that it had come from outside rather than inside the house.

He listened. By his side Ericson was snoring lustily, otherwise the house was silent. He heard no repetition of the sound which had awakened him. The only other noise he heard was a full-throated roar from the jungle, and that, faraway. The menace of it made him thankful that he was inside four walls.

As there seemed no special reason for having awakened he settled himself for sleep, but without immediate success. He began to think of Perrigot. There was something about the household that mystified him. The sort of hermit's life led by the Frenchman was unnatural, and not in keeping with the warmth of his reception of two strangers. He had welcomed their coming and enjoyed their company. Why, then, did he shun more regular visitors?

His perplexity was not of long duration. He fell asleep just as he began

20

to wonder about Dolores, the cook, and when next he awoke his ears were ringing with the sound of knocking. But this time it continued, and was accompanied by a voice calling to them in Spanish that it was time to get up. He did not recognize the voice, but the broadness of the lisped vowels made him conclude that the caller was Dolores.

The two men washed and dressed, but decided to shave later when the noonday heat would oblige them to rest awhile. When they were ready they descended the uncarpeted stairs as quietly as they could, anxious not to disturb anyone, but as they reached the lower floor the dining-room door opened and they were greeted by the family. Breakfast was already on the table.

The meal was not cheerful. Although Perrigot was in a sparkling mood, the two girls did not this time respond to his lead. They were amiable, and Anne showed no signs of her post-dinner sulks; but both were distrait and looked sad.

Breakfast was soon over. A short while afterward the two men were leading their saddled animals back to the veranda steps, where their host and his daughters waited.

Wesley swept off his hat with a courteous gesture. "Thank you, sir, for your generous welcome." His lean hand gripped the Frenchman's soft fingers. "I won't say good-by, sir, but rather au revoir. If I return in a year or two's time, as I may well do, I shall call on you again, if I may."

"Of course. Always glad to see you."

Wesley looked at the girls. "Au revoir, mesdemoiselles. Thank you, too, for all you have done for us."

"Me, too," Ericson echoed.

The girls looked downcast. "Come back soon," Marie urged.

Her father chuckled. "Don't expect them to come back, my girl."

"Why shouldn't we?" Wesley challenged.

"Because you will never be able to build a canal across the Isthmus, Mr. Adam. Your businessmen in America are not fools. They will not throw good money after bad."

Wesley saw no object in pursuing the subject. "Come along, Olaf." He mounted his horse and wheeled it into movement. "Good-by, folks, and thanks a lot." He headed toward the trail, followed by Ericson.

"Turn left at the shrine," Perrigot called out as the jungle closed in upon them. "And good luck."

In silence the two men followed the clearly marked trail; its dry mud surface was bounded by well-brushed-back green walls, and a canopy of interlaced boughs. They rode in single file, Wesley in the lead; there was no room to ride abreast.

Some time later he broke the silence. "I woke up sometime during the night, Olaf."

21

"You did!"

It was apparent from Ericson's voice that he was not interested, but Wesley persisted, for he now felt in the mood for conversation.

"I thought I heard a knock on the door, but I couldn't be sure. You know how one imagines noises during the night. Did you hear anything?"

"Not until someone shouted that it was time to get up. That was soon enough for me. You must have dreamed the noise."

"Maybe!" Wesley felt almost inclined to agree with his companion. "I still say he's a darned strange man. He and his 'You can't build a canal'—"

A short, reflective silence. "I suppose he can't be right?" Ericson presently commented.

"How can we judge that so soon? I haven't seen anything against it so far."

"You haven't seen yellow fever, Wesley."

"No!" A few paces later, "That's true enough, but we're surveyors, not doctors. It's their business to check yellow fever."

"You haven't seen the Chagres in flood. That's our business, isn't it, to tame and use it for a lock canal, or divert it if we recommend a sea-level canal?"

Silence again. Wesley visualized the brown, placid river he had already crossed twice, and found it hard to see it as the destructive torrent Perrigot had described so graphically. Could the Frenchman have exaggerated?

They plodded along the trail at an easy pace. In spite of being many miles from the nearest human settlement, the morning was noisy with a variety of sounds; some strange to the two men, and some with which the past few days had already made them familiar: the strange choruslike calls of the chachalaca, the scolding chatter of small troops of monkeys which sometimes accompanied them for quite a distance, swinging along from tree to tree with a speed and agility which the two Americans envied.

The monkeys were not alone in giving voice to their resentment. Parrots and parakeets shrieked at them and angrily fluffed gay plumage. Once or twice they were startled by spasmodic explosive noises which sounded like gunshots; only when they heard the angry squeal of a peccary as it charged destructively through the undergrowth did they realize that snapping branches were the cause. There were but few moments when the jungle did not give some indication of the wildlife which teemed in its depths.

They reached a small clearing where a second trail crossed theirs, but they continued ahead as Perrigot had told them. They mutually maintained silence, for they had already spent two weeks in each other's company, and would spend several more together. There could be few matters to talk about that they had not already discussed, so now they spoke only when there was reason to do so.

Half an hour after they had left the first cross trail they reached a second clearing. In the middle was a single espavé tree. On this had been hung a small shrine, a carved oak canopy over a figure which exposure had weathered beyond all recognition.

"Here's where we branch left." Wesley gazed at the cross trail with doubtful eyes. It was narrower than the one they had so far traveled that morning, and less cared for. The voracious jungle, ever striving to wrest from man's grasp even the least portion of his laborious clearing, had already tentatively stretched out thorny creepers and whipping twigs.

"We'll have to keep our machetes handy," he told Olaf. "Doesn't look as though it's used much."

Ericson glanced at his compass, then back at the trail. "It's facing northeast, which is our direction. He said turn left at the shrine. Besides, he said we would see something of the real jungle going this way."

"All right. Let's get moving. We'd best take turns at leading."

"Of course," Ericson agreed. "I'll take the lead for the first half hour."

Progress was slower, but not quite so difficult as they had anticipated. The jungle had encroached only here and there, they found, and one flick of the machete was usually sufficient to deal with the protruding tentacles. So, in actual fact, Ericson continued in the lead for rather more than thirty minutes before he halted to change places with Wesley.

"All right—" he began.

His words were interrupted by a loud bellow from behind the green wall on his right. Both men swung round; their hands instinctively reached for the rifle which each carried in a saddle holster. The noise was repeated; a deep, throaty roar which rose and fell in a torrent of guttural notes.

"By Jimminy!" Ericson pointed his rifle in the direction from which the bellow had come. Before he could fire the roar was taken up from another quarter, this time just above their heads. They crouched, hunching their shoulders against an expected attack. But suddenly Wesley laughed.

"Don't tell! A darned monkey!"

Ericson nodded. He, too, had seen the black form which leaped across their path from right to left, then disappeared behind a screen of foliage.

"What's all that about?"

Wesley remembered having read about the black monkeys of Panama. "You'll find out," he muttered grimly. "Get ready for rain."

The warning was too late. Rain fell from the sky in a white foaming sheet which all but hid the men from each other, close as they were.

4

WITHIN SECONDS both men were soaked to the skin; the water ran down inside their shirt collars and filled out their underclothes, that were tightly belted round the waist, until their shirts ballooned out like automobile tires and they had to undo buttons to let the accumulation escape. Their boots likewise filled, and their gun holsters and the saddlebags which contained their personal belongings. And still the rain teemed down, hushing the jungle into an uneasy quiet in which the padding noise of the rain alone was to be heard. It beat on the ground and churned into mud which splashed up on to the underbellies of their horses.

"This can't last long—" Ericson began, but his voice did not rise above the noise of the rain. He repeated what he had said in a shout, and this time Wesley nodded.

"Must be a cloudburst," he yelled back, as his glance moved from the rain that cascaded from the brim of his hat to the water which was already flowing along the trail. In his imagination he multiplied the water falling from his hat tenfold, and the water lapping against the horses' hoofs a hundredfold, and could understand how a confined river could turn into a raging torrent within a matter of hours. No soil, however thirsty, could absorb such stupendous drafts.

After five minutes of rain there was still no sign of its ceasing. Above, the sky was black with cloud. There seemed no object in their waiting any longer, so Wesley shouted, "How about moving on?" He pushed by and took the lead when Ericson nodded agreement. They plodded onward, sweating profusely in spite of the rain.

Ericson's conviction that the rain could not last was not justified. It continued to fall, now steadily, now in a dense white mass. Ten, twenty, thirty minutes it continued, by which time the water was rushing down the trail with force enough to make heavy going for the horses.

As unexpectedly as it had begun the rain ceased. The clouds moved away, and the sun blazed down upon a drenched world. Soon both men and horses were enveloped in a haze of steam.

"That was something," Ericson muttered in an awed voice. "I didn't know there was that much water in the world."

"It'll be a problem to deal with it, Olaf."

"A problem—" Ericson shrugged.

They rode on, and soon reached a clearing of sorts.

"Let's dry off," Wesley suggested.

"Suits me."

They halted their animals in a patch of sunshine, stripped off their outer

24

clothing, and spread it over their saddles. While they waited for their clothes to dry, they smoked pipes, a waterproofed bag having successfully kept tobacco pouch and matches dry. They leaned against their animals and daydreamed. Wesley thought of Dulcie, and hated the job he was doing. He had been away little more than two weeks, but the time had seemed more like two months and he ached to rejoin her. Life wasn't the same without her; it was cheerless without her teasing smile, and the way she had of saying, "Hello, husband Wes," when he returned home in the evening, and the trick she had of nibbling the lobe of his ear whenever she wanted to coax him.

He thought of the months which must elapse before he could envelope her unyielding body in his arms once more and kiss her into submitting to his love—for Dulcie still insisted upon being wooed. She was determined not to be taken for granted. The reflection made him feel glad that he was not a sailor. It was bad enough to be parted from one's wife for two or three months in a lifetime, but to spend perhaps only two weeks with her every six months—it was unthinkable!

He scowled at the surrounding wall of jungle, then up at the sky almost white with heat. Old Perrigot was certainly right in one thing he had said. The tropics did something to a man—filled him with a primeval urge that wasn't easy to hold in check, heated the blood to explosion point—

His reflections were disturbed by an exclamation from Ericson.

"What's that?"

He turned. Ericson was pointing toward the jungle.

Wesley could see nothing unusual. "Where? What?"

"A flame—just behind that big tree, on the left—" Ericson did not wait for Wesley's comment. He moved across the clearing and thrust his broad shoulders through the green curtain of undergrowth. When he emerged he carried something which gleamed in the sunlight.

"Gold, or my name isn't Ericson!" he stuttered with excitement as he passed the object over.

Wesley examined it. Crudely fashioned, badly rubbed and scratched, yet its purpose was unmistakable. It had the shape of an amphora, its curved handles still possessed an air of barbaric elegance. As for the metal of which it was made, where parts of its surface had been rubbed it certainly had the deep red gleam of gold.

"Well?"

"Looks like gold," he admitted.

"How did it get there?" Ericson demanded.

"Probably washed out of a grave. Gold ornaments were often buried with their owners. The Indians of Central and South America were smothered in gold. You've read your history—"

"I haven't. I was too busy helping to support my Pop and my kid sister when I was young. He was injured in an accident like I told you. Is this a gold country?"

"It was, before the Spaniards arrived in the sixteenth century."

"Tell me about it, Wesley."

Wesley glanced with curiosity at his companion. He had never seen Ericson in a state of excitement. Until now the other man had accepted everything, good and bad alike, with an enviable phlegm. In an indefinite way he was, with his lumbering walk, blond hair, and placid nature, rather like an amiable bear ready to dance to anybody's tune.

For the moment, however, he was transfigured. The light blue eyes vibrated with impatience, and the flesh seemed tightly drawn over the high cheekbones.

"There was a time when gold was mined in the Chagres valley. So much gold that the Spaniards named Panama City Castilla del Oro—"

"Castle of gold?"

"No. Castle is *castillo*. Castilla is the name of the region we call Castile. Gold Castile. It didn't remain Golden Castile for long. The Spaniards saw to that. They seized every gold article they found, and sent it back to the original Castile in Spain. Then they stole the raw material. They enslaved the local populations, forced them into the mines, until the Indians were killed off by the hundreds and the mines worked out."

"Every one? Every gold mine in Panama?"

Wesley shrugged. "It is believed there are still gold mines in the interior, but no white man knows where. The Indians fear the consequences of telling the whites. Anyway, the rape of the Isthmus didn't end its connection with gold. When the Spaniards conquered South America they found a fabulous gold treasure. Much of it was shipped back to Spain, from Peru to Panama, then, by way of the Chagres valley, to Nombre de Dios. So much gold flowed across the Isthmus that the trail became known as the Camino del Oro. The Golden Road." He turned the jug over in his hand and gazed thoughtfully at its tarnished pattern. "Now I come to think about it, Olaf, the Camino del Oro can't have been a hundred miles from this spot, for Cruces became an important transshipment station. The treasure was transferred from mule trains onto canoes and rafts so that it could be floated downriver to the sea, and then along the coast to the harbor."

He passed the jug back to Ericson. "Maybe that didn't come from a grave, but was dropped by one of the mule trains from Peru. Or maybe it was lost during one of Morgan's raids."

"Morgan?"

Wesley's face crinkled up in one of his amiable grins. "Yes. Henry Morgan. As bloodthirsty a scoundrel as Wales has ever produced. But he had spunk, the old ruffian, and in his own way was as good a man as any of the conquistadores who fought with armor and cannon against naked

26

Indians armed with bows and arrows. Set a thief to catch a thief. Morgan stole the gold the Spaniards had stolen from the Inca Empire, and good luck to him, I say, for long odds never frightened him. I'll bet if Morgan were given the job of building a canal across the Isthmus he'd build it by fair means or foul! Probably foul!" He pointed to the jug which Ericson was caressing. "That should sell for a few dollars in New York."

Ericson nodded. "Do you think there might be other gold pieces to be found? Hadn't we better look? You might find one—"

"And I might not. Think yourself lucky you've found that. Other men have spent years looking for gold without finding any." He felt his clothes. They were already dry. "Let's get going."

Ericson's expression turned mutinous. For a moment or two Wesley anticipated trouble. Then the other man shrugged.

"All right," he sulkily agreed.

They dressed, mounted their animals, and in silence resumed their journey. Before long they were wet through again, this time with sweat. The steamy heat enveloped them like a hot blanket, and made them feel limp and weak. Wesley grew mentally apathetic. His thoughts dreamily returned to Dulcie. He wondered what she was doing at that moment, and tried to picture her in their small home on the outskirts of Providence. She might still be in bed, yawning and stretching with the lazy grace of a sleepy kitten, for she loathed rising too early in the morning, and would surely take advantage of his absence to indulge herself with an extra hour or two in bed. He smiled wistfully, wishing that he could be there to wake her up by sliding his long, strong arms beneath her thistledown form and lifting her bodily into the air, bedclothes and all. Just as he had done on some past occasions, when he was feeling specially cheerful: the warmth of her soft body, and the lightness of it always gave him a feeling of exhilaration. Of course, she would pout her pretty lips, and pretend to scold him, but their play always finished with her gladly paying the ransom of three kisses, which was his price for restoring her to her feet.

Then he grew miserable, realizing how long it would be before he could again hold her for ransom. He was a darn fool, he told himself, for having allowed himself to be persuaded into undertaking the survey. If it had not been for Dulcie, who had urged him to accept— Of course, she had been one hundred per cent right to do so. Besides the good pay that Mr. Cromwell had offered for a few weeks' work, his future was rosier now. The survey would make a good talking point when it came to applying for a partnership in the H. C. Ackermann Company, where he had received his training. In fact, Ackermann had practically given his word—

Surely an assured future was worth the parting? But when he faced the prospect of having to spend night after night with Ericson, instead of Dulcie, to share his room—and even his bed, sometimes—he glanced at the

27

thick green wall of jungle and felt less sure that the brighter prospects were worth the parting.

Damn this mood! he reflected angrily. What started it? Not just the fact of having spent a few hours in the company of two kid girls? Well, one kid girl! Anne was almost a young woman— In shape, though not in looks, rather like Dulcie. Similar slim, rounded limbs; an equally attractive waistline and bust—

"Funny to think that that Indian who told us about Perrigot might be able to make our fortunes," Ericson said unexpectedly.

"What did you say?" Wesley asked absently, with his thoughts still dwelling on Anne.

"I said that perhaps that Indian yesterday afternoon could make our fortunes, if he wanted to."

"How?"

"I am thinking of the gold mines."

"Then you're wasting your time. The Indians haven't talked for more than three hundred years. Why should they do so now?"

"Gold means more in these days—"

The trail rose in a gentle gradient; sometimes diverging for a while, and occasionally crossing another trail. In spite of the altitude, the heat seemed no less. On the contrary, it appeared constantly to increase until their heads were swimming with the high humidity. After temporary halts to give their animals a rest, they decided to break their journey for the noonday siesta. Having chosen a shady spot beside a river, they dismounted, and unpacked their provisions. Wesley sat down and rested his shoulders against a magnificent mahogany tree.

But Ericson asked, "How about a swim first, Adam?"

Wesley looked at the river. It was moderately wide, and in midstream floating objects betrayed the existence of a swift-flowing current. Closer to the bank, however, the water looked quieter, and reasonably safe for a good swimmer. In spite of its muddy appearance it looked invitingly cool, and the idea of plunging his wet, sticky body in it was too attractive to resist. He began to unbutton his shirt.

"Oh-huh!"

Ericson's exclamation warned Wesley that something was wrong. He turned. Ericson had already stripped to the waist, but instead of completing the job he was staring upstream. Wesley followed the direction of his companion's gaze and saw in the dark shadows beneath the overhanging roots of a mangrove tree the small, evil eyes, and long brown snout of a large alligator.

"Not for me, thanks," he said as he rebuttoned his shirt.

"Nor me!" Ericson pulled on his shirt. "This is the darndest country—"

They ate in silence, shaved, then dozed uneasily while the jungle slept.

28

with them. The world seemed hushed; and was still quiet when Wesley roused. Ericson was still asleep: he could always sleep, anywhere, at any time. Wesley sometimes envied him that facility, though not at this moment. For the first time he appreciated the barbaric magnificence of the jungle. Despite its malevolence—which it was impossible to ignore— he was impressed with its beauty and grandeur. Although the prevailing color was green of every shade, this was relieved by masses of epiphytic orchids which sprayed the older trees with exquisite rainbows of color; the white bell of lady of the night making dark shadows starry; rampageous bougainvillaea in crimson curtains; and a solitary lignum vitae tree with its crown of yellow blossom. Elsewhere a gorgeous macaw supplied a splash of living color; and two ospreys fluttered among the brown leaves of a wild mango.

Perhaps the primeval savagery of the jungle impressed him more than its beauty, for he was a dour fighter himself when the occasion demanded. He could sense the bitter warfare that was being silently waged about him; the never-ceasing struggle for survival, the battle for breathing space. For in the jungle every living thing, he realized, had half a dozen enemies to contend with; and the most persistent of all enemies, the brush, which in parts matted so thickly that a reptile alone could penetrate it.

Ericson stirred. "I wonder if Morgan ever sat here," he mumbled in his sleep. "The Golden Road!"

Wesley believed that his companion's mind still dwelled on the gold beaker stowed away in the baggage. He glanced scornfully at the blond head. Hadn't Ericson a soul above gold—and young girls? One mustn't forget girls in thinking of Ericson. First the girl Joan on board the *Seguranca,* and then Marie—

"Olaf!"

The other man opened his eyes. "Yes?"

"If we're to reach Alhajuela before dark—"

"Alhajuela—you mean where Morgan—" His thoughts cleared. "Oh, sure!" He rose clumsily to his feet—sometimes his heavy frame was a nuisance to him.

They moved on up the trail. Up and ever up. Frequent rests became necessary for the sake of their laboring animals. The black monkey howled again, and again they were drenched to the skin. This time the storm was of short duration. But though the rain ceased gloomy clouds continued to hide the sun.

"This damned jungle!" Ericson exploded. "Doesn't it ever stop?"

Wesley did not reply, for he had been thinking along the same lines for the past few minutes. Not one human being had they seen since they left Perrigot's home. Nor one human habitation. They had faithfully followed the Frenchman's directions, and yet—yet to see nothing of civilization all day long—

29

There was something else, too—the existence of which he tried not to acknowledge. For some time past he had been affected by an eerie sensation of being spied upon, of feeling that every movement was being watched by human eyes which lurked somewhere behind the unending green curtain. Twice he had heard the rustling of a body moving through the brush, and only by exercising common sense had he forced himself to realize that their own movements had probably disturbed a tapir, or a large boa constrictor.

"We'd better get a move on," he told Ericson.

He was in front of Ericson, so he could not see his face. But there was something about the tone of his voice when he answered. "Sure we ought," which made Wesley realize that his companion was equally uneasy.

"Early afternoon be damned!" Ericson added. "You don't think Perrigot could have—"

"No." Wesley heeled his horse, but the tired animal did not respond. The trail was still ascending.

"It's colder this past hour."

"What do you expect with these clouds?"

"You don't think it might be higher altitude?"

Wesley would not allow himself to think. It wouldn't do to become panicky, he told himself.

"We ought to have seen Alhajuela an hour or more ago," Ericson continued. "Early afternoon—"

"Shut up!"

They plodded on in anxious silence. On and still upward, with the precious minutes rushing by. Early afternoon, Perrigot had said. Wesley looked at his watch. It was already late afternoon! And no signs yet that they might be within reach of a settlement. No scattered homesteads, no evidence of a machete having been recently used, no clearings, no cultivation of any sort—

He stared anxiously up at the gloomy sky. The clouds were not so sharply clear as they had been. In less than thirty minutes daylight would have gone. He stopped his horse, half turned.

Ericson said, "Don't tell me! We're lost, aren't we?"

Wesley nodded, and thought of the noise he had heard during the previous night.

5

"WE'LL HAVE TO make the best of it," Wesley added, dismounting. "If you tie up the animals I'll collect wood for a fire." He was beginning his search when a shout from Ericson halted him.

"Better take your rifle, Wesley. Looks like a cat's been around lately." He pointed to a clearly marked spoor which even a novice could recognize as belonging to one of the cat tribe.

"Jaguar or ocelot," Wesley muttered grimly. "Drake said to keep a sharp eye open for them in the jungle." He pulled the weapon from its holster, and slung it across his shoulders. Then he moved along the trail in search of fallen wood. He was lucky, and did not have to look far afield. Soon he had assembled enough to keep a fire burning until daylight.

They sat down near the fire, and found its warmth as welcome as its cheerful flames. They ate their supper in silence, for they were hungry and tired. Too tired for Wesley's peace of mind.

"We shall have to take turns in keeping watch, Olaf."

"Why?"

He pointed to the spoor. "Cats."

"The fire will keep them away."

"As long as the fire burns. How is it to be fed if we are both asleep?"

"By Jimminy! I could sleep for the next twenty-four hours. I'll smoke a pipe, then we'll toss who sleeps first." Presently, after he had lit his pipe, "Look here, Wesley, how and where do you reckon we got off the trail?"

"I don't know. I've been trying to work it out for the past thirty minutes."

"Perrigot said for us to turn left at the old shrine, and follow the trail which leads directly to Alhajuela, didn't he?"

"Yes."

"Well, that's what we did, and where's Alhajuela? You don't think the old scoundrel told us wrong, do you?"

"Why should he?"

"I don't know, but—"

"Besides, he told us in front of the girls. Wouldn't they have known he was wrong?"

"He sent them out of the room when you asked the easiest route to Alhajuela. Don't you remember?"

Wesley did. The horrible suspicion that Ericson was right was not easy to dispel, although he tried to. He felt relieved when he remembered another circumstance, which he hastened to point out to his companion.

31

"They were there when he called out to us to turn left at the old shrine."

"Yes." Ericson nodded thoughtfully. "Yes, they were, weren't they? And Marie wouldn't let him—she took a fancy to me—" His words trailed off.

Wesley's expression turned grim. He snapped a dead branch between his hands. The sound of it startled Ericson.

"By golly!" Then he glanced at Wesley's face. "What's the matter?"

"Olaf! That noise I told you about—the one that woke me during the night—"

Ericson grew impatient when Wesley paused. "What about it?"

"It's a fantastic idea, but do you think Perrigot could have changed the shrine during the night to make sure of our being lost?"

In the reflected light from the leaping flames the two men gazed at each other in startled doubt.

"By Jimminy!" Ericson exclaimed. He sucked furiously at his pipe. "But why should he want us to lose our way to Alhajuela?"

"Look, Olaf! It's no use closing our eyes to facts. We'll be lucky to get out of this jungle alive."

Ericson snorted his contempt. "You read too much—"

"I've read enough to know what it means to be lost in the Panama jungle. In the fifties a naval expedition of twenty-eight men left Caledonia Bay to trek across the Isthmus, and make a canal survey. They carried ten days' provisions and forty rounds of ball cartridge per man.

"You wouldn't think twenty-eight men could lose themselves, would you? But they did. It wasn't until two months later that they were rescued. By then nine were dead. The rest were dying. Of the few who lived, none ever regained strength."

Ericson knocked out his pipe. He had lost his taste for smoking. "Good God!" he muttered. He looked about him, at the green wall which almost surrounded the two men. In the darkness it was black, impenetrable, frightening, and restless with the scurry and rustle of animals and birds that the leaping flames had attracted to the spot.

"We can find our way back to the Perrigot's," he muttered thickly. "Straight back till we reach the shrine—"

"Do you think he wouldn't have taken the precaution of restoring the shrine to its original place? We might go on and on, never knowing at which cross trail to turn right."

"But what's he got against us? We've done nothing to hurt him."

"That's what I can't understand. That's why I can't quite believe—" He threw another log on to the fire. A shiver of sparks flew into the air; one fell on his knee and was already scorching the material when he brushed it off.

After a long uneasy silence Ericson exclaimed, "My God!"

Wesley looked up, startled. "What's the thought?"

"Do you remember my telling you of those quarterly journeys to the city? You know, when he always took a sack of something in, and brought it back empty?"

"What of them?"

"Do you think it could have been full of gold?"

"You've gold on the brain," Wesley exclaimed impatiently.

"Maybe, but it makes sense to me. What's he been living on all these years? Suppose he found a gold mine, and has been working it all these years in secret."

"Suppose he has! Is that any reason for trying to get us lost in the jungle?"

"It could be," Ericson argued. "What do you reckon the elevation of his home, even though it is on a hill?"

"Not much, but—"

"Suppose the mine isn't far off, what would happen to it if a lock canal were to be built, and the Chagres dammed at Bohio? The valley would be flooded to that level, wouldn't it?"

Wesley stared, grim faced, into the heart of the fire. Ericson's theory was not one that could be lightly dismissed. That the existence of gold mines within reach of the Chagres valley was a possibility he was prepared to accept, for past history made it a reasonable one. Granted that premise, he saw no good reason for not believing that Perrigot might have had the good fortune to stumble upon one.

Ericson saw that his remarks had impressed his companion. "It mightn't even have been a mine he found, Wesley. It might have been a cache. Morgan's perhaps. Or a graveyard. You said before that gold ornaments used to be buried with the Indians."

Still Wesley did not speak. He recalled Perrigot's contemptuous confidence that neither of his visitors would return. Such confidence could well have been founded on the near certainty that his guests would die in the jungle.

In quick succession the recollection of other circumstances deepened Wesley's suspicions of the Frenchman. The persistence of Perrigot's contention that a canal could never be built across the Isthmus; his lack of friends or casual acquaintances; the unusual desire to live at a fairly considerable distance from the nearest white settlement.

"Let's sleep on it," he suggested at last.

"Pah! You're too idealistic, Wesley. You don't want to believe he would like to see us die, just to save his gold. If the tropics do something to a man, so does gold. The two in combination—"

"Call," Wesley snapped, flipping a coin into the air.

Ericson won again. He settled himself for sleep. "I'll settle accounts with that two-faced Frenchman if it's the last thing I do," he muttered.

33

Before long the sound of deep-throated snoring advised Wesley that his companion had fallen asleep. He hoped that he would be able to do the same when the time arrived, for he had never felt less like sleep. He was troubled by a recurrence of the sensation that had afflicted him earlier on, and stared with anxious eyes into the wall of blackness to reassure himself that Ericson and he were alone. The piteous shriek of an animal in its death agony increased his uneasiness, for he believed he was hearing the final stages of a jaguar's kill, and thought it likely that the victim was a deer. He imagined the silent approach, the crouch, the angry swish of the tail, the slavering twitch of the tight-drawn muzzle, and lastly, the pounce —and was glad that he had his back to a tree. And he tightened his grip on the weapon lying across his knees.

Because his senses were keyed up he became aware of many trifles which he might not otherwise have noticed—the cloying scent of the lady-of-the-night orchid, which only exhales its fragrance at night; the antics of a pair of small owl monkeys whom he occasionally saw leaping from tree to tree in apparent terror of the fire, yet fascinated by its brilliance; the spectacular dive of a goatsucker hawk; the scurry of an opossum across the clearing.

But though he saw and heard and smelled these things, none of them helped to dispel his sense of insecurity. He felt naked, unarmed, and insignificant. Again he was envious of his stolid companion who knowing less of the dangers surrounding them, feared less. In any case discomfort was more likely to be of immediate importance to Ericson than the chance of being killed from any one of half a dozen horrible causes, each death more horrible than its predecessor in the list.

Determined not to dwell on such morbid matters he tried to fix his attention on Dulcie. The result was not wholly a happy one, for his heated imagination became distorted; he saw her dressed in a diaphanous night-gown which should have revealed much to his hungry gaze and yet failed to do so because of her restlessness: she would not stand still long enough for the material to fall into natural folds. This hallucination was extraordinary, because Dulcie was extremely sensitive on the question of modesty. Her long cambric nightdresses were invariably high around the neck, and tied daintily with pink ribbon; the sleeves, wrist long, were similarly adorned. She would have died, he believed, rather than be seen by him dressed in any transparent garment. In spite of this he saw himself, in his imagination, trying to tempt her to his side so that he might encircle her slim waist with his arms and bury his face in the warm valley between her small breasts. Then, as he drifted dangerously close to genuine sleep, it seemed to him that there was a miraculous change in her attitude to-wards him. Instead of resisting his advances, as she usually did, she yielded to them: he felt soft arms steal round his neck, and warm lips press against it with an ardent response which both delighted and surprised him, for he had not believed her capable of such passion. Moved strangely by her changed mood he gazed adoringly up into her face—but the face was not Dulcie's, but Anne's; the yielding body not Dulcie's, but Anne's—

Disgust with the unnatural trend of his thoughts restored him to full wakefulness. He grew rigid with alarm, intuition warned him that danger was near. So strong was this impression that he was tempted to wake the blissfully sleeping Ericson, whose snores had grown louder. But he resisted, for common sense derided his fears: he must have fallen asleep, and in waking—

He felt his back thrust forward, his arms grasped and wrenched behind his back. A stinking smelly hand covered his mouth. For the vital first second surprise deadened his wits, but not the instinct for self-preservation. He tried to free his arms from the imprisoning hands. He jerked his body from side to side, and endeavored to open his jaw wide enough to bite the fingers which brutally held his mouth. But his attackers gave him no chance. Ropes of liana were wound round his arms, pinioning them together. Then his feet, likewise. He saw dark shadows integrate and steal upon his sleeping companion; six stocky men, clad only in loincloths, who pounced upon the recumbent form in a body. In a moment Ericson was helpless enough for them to pull him to his feet. Then the hand was removed from Wesley's mouth. The two Americans looked at each other.

"I'm sorry, Olaf—they never made a sound—"

Ericson began to struggle. His captors though stocky were short, and the blond giant was contemptuous of them. He raised his knee with a powerful thrust, caught one of the Indians in the pit of the stomach. With a guttural groan of pain the man released his hold of Ericson and doubled up. Then the American jerked his head backward into the face of another Indian. The sound of skull against skull was like a pistol shot. The man behind dropped to the ground, temporarily unconscious. Ericson's arms began to thrash about. Another Indian went hurtling to the ground, his hand falling into the fire. He jumped to his feet, shrieking with pain, and ran off into the brush.

Unfortunately there were dark shadows in reserve. They threw themselves upon Ericson, bore him to the ground, and held him there while others trussed him with liana ropes. Then both men were propped up against a tree. An Indian placed himself before them, bowlegged. His dank hair was long, and hung down well below his shoulders; his round simian face was painted yellow and red.

He spoke to the Americans in slow, guttural Spanish.

"What does he say?" Ericson asked.

"I only caught a word here and there."

"Can you ask him to say it again?"

"I'll try. *No le comprendo á usted,*" he told his captor.

35

The Indian spoke again. Wesley understood a few more words, but did not immediately translate them. Ericson grew impatient.

"Well? Did you understand what he said then?"

"I think so, Olaf. He said that white men are not allowed in Indian country after dark."

"How the hell did we know we were in Indian country? Besides, who gave him the right to say white men aren't allowed here? He's not the President of Colombia, is he? Damn his nerve! Is that all he said?"

"No."

"Then, for God's sake, what? Why are you so mysterious?"

"I'm not trying to be. He said—he said that any man found in Indian country after dark is—is killed, Olaf!"

"Good God!" But the imaginative Ericson shook his head. "You didn't understand him, or else he's stringing you along. Damn it, Wesley! This isn't the eighteenth century. It's almost the twentieth. Indians don't kill palefaces in these days. Besides, we're scarcely a day's walk from the railroad track—"

The Indian interrupted. Ericson could not understand a word, but there was a note of command in the guttural voice that was unmistakable.

"What's he telling us to do?"

"Say our prayers, Olaf. He's allowing us about five minutes, and no more."

Ericson had to believe. He strained at the lianas which fettered his arms, but all his bull strength failed to part them.

"Damn their copper hides!" he burst out. "They can't kill us off just like that. Tell him we're not lousy Panamanians or Colombians, but American citizens. Tell him what Uncle Sam will have to say—" There was desperation in his voice, but not fear.

"I'll try," Wesley huskily agreed. In halting Spanish he said to the Indian, "We are Americans, not Panamanians. If you kill American Big Chief will send army to punish you."

The Indian made a sound at the back of his throat suggestive of scornful amusement. This the copper-skinned man followed up with a few words.

"They have been following us all the afternoon," Wesley translated. "If we had tried to turn back they would not have attacked us."

"Tell him we were trying to reach Alhajuela."

Wesley did so, with unfortunate results. The Indian turned angry.

"That was the wrong thing to say, Olaf. As far as I can make out Alhajuela is two days' march away to the south. Now he's convinced we're lying, and mean evil to his people."

"That swine Perrigot—"

"Best say your prayers if you want to," Wesley swallowed. "I'm afraid he means every word he says."

Silence followed. Wesley tried to say a prayer, but his brain refused to string the words together. His only clear thought was one of astonishment at the contrast between the comparative civilization of the Chagres valley with its railroad, its canal workshops, its rusting dredgers and steam shovels, its settled hamlets, its trade, its contacts with the outside world—and the primeval jungle with its naked, savage Indians, its own rigid tribal laws.

The idea of building a canal across the Isthmus now seemed like an improbable fantasy. Even apart from the insuperable, physical obstacles which might well stand in the way of its being built, it seemed to him now that the jungle would never allow its privacy to be invaded without striking back; it would always remain a menace to the canal's existence; it would fight on to time's end; it would always have to be held in check; at the first sign of weakness it would flow effortlessly back to the water's edge, swallowing up man's puny handiwork in its way, just as it had swallowed up alike the old town of Panama and a large part of the machinery the French had brought to the Isthmus and worked until less than a decade ago. Man could never build a canal, he reflected pessimistically.

"Are you ready?" the Indian asked.

6

TIME TO DIE! Wesley could not believe in the reality of the scene in which he had so unenviable a role. It was a nightmare. It must be a nightmare. Only a nightmare could overtake one so quickly without reason, without justification, without warning. He looked about him, doubting; at the black curtain of jungle, at the naked Indians vaguely reflected in the flickering light cast by the burning logs, and was almost convinced that he was dreaming. For they were nightmarish enough, with their long hair, their coppered faces, and their spears. So were the goatsucker bats that swept restlessly about within the orbit of firelight.

Ericson guessed what the Indian had said.

"God!" he exclaimed. "I'm not ready to die. Especially like a rat in a trap. Tell the devils something—make them understand—Jesus Christ! if only my arms were free."

"We're Americans," Wesley shouted desperately at the Indians who were pulling the two men to their feet. "Can't you understand, damn you? Americans—"

"You not Indian," the spokesman answered scornfully. "Only tribal

Indians allowed here at night. You must die. It is tribal law." He waved his hand. Spearmen raised their weapons—

Something whined through the air above their heads. The noise was followed by the short, sharp bark of gunfire. A second shot was fired. Again, above the heads of the party clustered about the two Americans. Warning shots. The Indians whirled round as a party of eight men on horseback galloped toward them: three were white men; the others were Negroes. All carried guns, and three of them oil lanterns.

"You, there!" the foremost man called out in Spanish. "Let those men free or we fire."

The Indian chief faced the newcomers, scowling. "They must die. They have broken our laws."

"They were trying to make Alhajuela, and lost their way."

Wesley was astounded that a complete stranger should know so much, but he was more interested, meanwhile, to see what the effect would be on the Indian. The man's impassive countenance, burnished by the red glow from the burning logs, revealed nothing of his thoughts as he stood, bowlegged, and stared unblinkingly at the newcomers. Behind him his men held their spears in readiness either to kill their captives or to throw at the newcomers, as their leader ordered. Wesley could sense their nearness, and his back tingled with apprehension.

At last the Indian spoke. "We are many marches from Alhajuela."

"They are strangers to Panama, they left the trail by mistake. They come from over the waters and have been here only a few days."

Again the Indian took time to consider the newcomer's words. Presently he nodded. "I think you tell truth, señor. They may go free this time. But if they come again, they die."

He turned, and addressed his men in their own language. The liana ropes were loosed from the arms of the Americans. Before circulation was properly restored, the Indians had silently vanished behind the jungle curtain.

"Phew!" Ericson exclaimed.

"Guess you're the luckiest two guys this side of the forty-ninth parallel," a bluff American voice told them, as the man who had been speaking to the Indians alighted from his horse. "You're Adam and Ericson, aren't you?"

Wesley nodded. "How did you know? And how did you know we were on our way to Alhajuela?"

"Thompson's the name; Jim Thompson. Meet Sparks and Riley." He indicated the other two white men. Sparks and Riley nodded. "We're railroad staff, stationed at Frijoles. I had word from Colón three days ago that you were on your way to Alhajuela. How the hell did you get to this spot?"

"How the hell did you—thank God!"

38

Thompson grinned. He was a smallish man, with a wiry frame, a broad smile, and a pair of thick gingery mustaches. "Thank George Washington Macdonald over there." George Washington Macdonald smiled from ear to ear. "He was in the jungle hunting new orchids for some crazy professor in Panama, and saw you heading hell-bent for the Indian country. When he got back to Frijoles at midday and told me he had seen you I kinder put two and two together, and organized a rescue party."

He dismissed the rest of the story with a wave of his calloused hand. "Didn't your Ma's never tell you the jungle ain't a healthy place to get lost in? If it hadn't been for George Washington knowing this part of the jungle like the back of his hand, and the boys not minding giving up an afternoon and evening to ride hell for leather, the ants would have been picking your bones by sun-up."

"Do you know Perrigot?"

"Sure. Everybody knows him. Or of him," he added significantly.

"We stayed all night with him. He said the easiest way from his place to Alhajuela was by trail through the jungle. He said if we turned left by the shrine, and carried straight on we'd reach the place by afternoon."

"Dat's right, Mr. Thompson, sir," George Washington broke in. "I took a gennelman dat way once."

"Then you must've gone wrong somewhere." Thompson nodded at the two horses beyond the fire. "We'd best get moving before them Indians change their minds about killing you. And us as well, come to that. 'Sides, we've a fair distance to go before any of us sees bed tonight."

So Wesley and Ericson repacked their saddlebags, kicked out the fire, and mounted. At a wordless signal from Thompson they fell into single file and started off down the trail: George Washington Macdonald in the lead, carrying a lantern, then Thompson himself, followed by Wesley and Ericson, and the rest of the party.

After a while Ericson called out, "It's time the Indians around here were taught a lesson, by Jimminy! I don't suppose everyone losing his way in the jungle is lucky enough to be seen by a George Washington."

"I wouldn't quite say that about the Indians, mister," Thompson drawled. "It is their country, and if they don't want white men in it at nighttime I reckon they're entitled to say so."

"You said *night*time," Wesley interrupted. "Does that mean they don't mind a white man entering their country during the day?"

"I don't know that it means quite that. The Indians don't like the white man at any time. But they don't forcibly stop him entering their territory during the day, and if he leaves before night they don't attack him."

"Why not?"

Thompson chuckled. "Because the reason for the law is the preservation of their race, and they reckon there isn't so much risk during the day.

39

They have long memories, the Indians. They mistrust white men on account of what the Spaniards did to them four hundred years ago."

"What was that?" Ericson asked.

"Murdered the Indians so they could steal gold and women. If them's the only two things white men are interested in, they say, we'll hide them away in the future. And, by golly, that's what they've done."

"Do you think there's gold still to be found in the Isthmus?" Ericson continued.

"Of course I do. The darned stuff is washed down by every river. But it would need a regiment of troops to guard men working any mines."

The party reached Frijoles well after 2 A.M., and after the rescuers had suffered the embarrassment of being warmly thanked by the rescued, dispersed for their respective homes. The generous-hearted Thompson insisted upon taking Wesley and Ericson back to his place: there was a spare bed, and they had to sleep somewhere, didn't they? Too tired to argue, and thankful not to have to search at that time of the morning for somewhere to rest, the two men gladly accompanied their host to the wooden bungalow he and his family occupied. Within a few minutes of entering the house all three men were soundly asleep.

Wesley was the first to wake. Looking at his watch he saw that it was past nine o'clock. He stretched with a satisfied sigh, rose from the bed, and crossed to the window, where he found himself looking out at the busiest part of the small town. Close at hand was the railroad station. Its only entrance door was closed, but evidently it was soon due to open, for clustered around about it was a small crowd of colored people of all ages. One or two of the men were dressed in blue jeans, shirt, and brimless felt hat; others wore just shirt and trousers. The women were equally varied in the matter of costume; some of them being dressed in a low blouse, and a short gathered pettitcoat; some, apparently in Sunday-best, in a ground-length, flounced skirt, and white blouse protected by a dark *rebozo* flung across the shoulders. None of the women wore a hat. The group was completed by a handful of barefooted, bareheaded children who ran among the patient travelers with high-pitched shrieks of excited laughter that should have made conversation almost impossible, but apparently merely spurred the older people on, for their chatter resounded loudly.

Opposite the station was a row of stores; run, it seemed, by Chinese; for two of the doorways were occupied by short, yellow-faced men with long pigtails, who stood with folded hands and blandly surveyed the passers-by with Oriental patience. Beyond the stores was a motley group of houses, irregularly situated and spaced, and varying in design from small, four-roomed bungalows to two-storied buildings with shingle roofs, wide verandas and balconies. Beyond these houses he could see the homes of the natives, constructed of a palm thatch resting on bamboo poles, with walls of bamboo sticks plastered with mud. Beyond these houses, in the near distance, he saw the brown surface of the Chagres River, and where it curved round toward the railroad tracks, a shallow pool at which a number of white-clad women were industriously washing clothes by pounding them on flat stones. On his right he saw a large brick-built building, which he guessed was the rum distillery for which an old Frenchman had made Frijoles famous.

Immediately beyond the outpost dwellings he saw the fringes of the jungle from which Ericson and he had been rescued the night before. It stretched as far as his vision, rising in gradual stages to the clouded mountain peaks of the Great Divide. In no direction was it possible to distinguish a break in the green carpet except to his left, in the Chagres valley, where three centuries of trans-Isthmus traffic had gradually cleared a broad strip of land on either side of the river.

The sound of carriage wheels below attracted his attention, and he saw a canvas-topped buggy drive up to one of the stores. The contrast between the scene immediately below him—in essence not dissimilar to any one of the smaller Louisiana villages which he had driven through during his stay there—and the unbroken belt of jungle beyond was so extreme that he began to reflect on old Perrigot's conviction that it would never be possible to complete a canal across the Isthmus. Toward the north the clouds had passed away, to expose sun-drenched mountain peaks, etched black against the white sky beyond. They looked massive, tremendous, and forbidding; giants which the puny hand of man might never hope to cleave asunder. So vivid was this impression of unassailable majesty that he had to remind himself there were lower peaks than the ones at which he was looking.

The sight of the distant range, the foothills no doubt of the Cordillera de San Blas, reminded him of Perrigot. He could not think why, unless it was simply that the memory of the Frenchman and his family would keep obtruding into his thoughts. He reflected on Perrigot's insistence that the canal would and could never be built. Ericson was quite possibly justified in believing there was a reason behind that reiterated statement. Nevertheless, there had been an underlying note of sincerity in his voice which could not wisely be ignored. Whatever his reason for wanting to make sure that the canal should never be built, he was honestly convinced that any second attempt would end no less disastrously than the first. A strange man, Perrigot.

The survey continued, as Wesley and Ericson slowly made their way toward the Pacific, having decided to leave Alhajeula for their return trip. From Frijoles they went on to Tabernilla. Here they found more evidence of the first attempt to build a canal, for the French had established the small village as one of their centers, by building a field repair shop there;

also quarters for the labor force. The village was depressing. The works had been abandoned, and now stood empty and disintegrating; the living quarters were occupied by squatters, colored immigrants, many of them, who had been attracted to the Isthmus by French offers of employment. Since the failure of the first company, and the cessation of all but token work to keep the concession alive, these people had been unemployed—no great hardship to them, for there was free food for the picking; and free quarters. What sane colored man would want to work in those circumstances?

On to Barbacoas, where the railroad crossed the Chagres; to San Pablo, where they saw the remains of a French labor camp; on to Gorgona—a larger town this, and surrounded by cultivated farms. Here, too, the French had established shops in which the machinery was rusting. On to Matachin, where there were signs of French excavation work, and near by, more shops. Thence by way of other small hamlets, varying to no great extent one from the other, to Empire, the most important of them all, for here the French had established the headquarters of the divisional engineer. Here, too, was begun the first excavation, in 1882, in the Culebra Cut.

They reached Empire by way of a track up the north slope of a small hill. For most of the ascent the view beyond the summit was limited by a sky line of trees; but as they neared the top, breaks in the screen gave them a glimpse of scattered houses, larger than most of those erected by the French. On nearing these they saw evidence of their occupancy; not by colored squatters this time, but by white people whose paler skin bore evidence that they were foreigners to the tropics.

They reached the summit. Before them spread a panorama that brought both men to an impulsive halt, the better to appreciate and digest their first glimpse of the Culebra Cut. To the eye of an ordinary traveler, it might well have lacked impressiveness; for the scene was less picturesque, less awe inspiring, less majestic than many in their home country, consisting as it did of little more than a narrow, curving valley set in a ring of encircling green-topped mountains. But looked at with the eyes of a surveyor it assumed quite a different aspect; for the north end of the valley was closed by twin peaks that thrust upward not perhaps with majesty, for they were dwarfed into comparative insignificance by their background of vaster peaks which lapped away toward a horizon beyond human vision, but with almost a scornful gesture, a rude, defiant gesture, like two sentinels of nature saying mischievously, "Thou shalt not pass."

"That can't be Culebra," Ericson said.

But it was. The evidence was below and before them: the labor camp, the line of workshops, and more importantly, the deep scar which had already deepened the cleft between the two peaks, and the tiny figures

42

which dotted the serrated walls of the canyon, like flies crawling up and down a wall of corrugated iron.

Wesley looked at the Cut with professional interest. The French had bitten deeply into the Cut, but its deepest point was still far above the level of the valley. As Perrigot had rightly said, the French had, comparatively speaking, no more than scratched away the surface dirt. Not only would the Cut have to be at least as deep again, but it would have to be wider, too, to compensate for the greater depth.

"By Jimminy! Sixteen years' work! Old man Perrigot was right, Wesley. A million pairs of hands couldn't dig that Cut deep enough this side of Judgment Day."

Although he was appalled by his preliminary inspection, Wesley felt annoyed with Ericson for voicing doubts. It was frightening to contemplate the stupendous odds against the completing of such a gigantic undertaking—at the same time it was inspiring to contemplate the possibility of success. The twin sentinel peaks were nature's challenge to man, daring him to join the two great oceans of the world, to cleave the chain of mountains which she had raised to keep the oceans apart.

The lean hungry face grew leaner and more hungry looking. What if the French had been working a large part of sixteen years on the Cut, without achieving more than that? His sight was long; the day was clear enough for him to observe the nearer teams at work. Even at a distance he could see no sign of urgency in their movements; yet they should be working with a will, he reflected. The work was urgent: any work which could lead to the betterment of world conditions was a matter of urgency. He examined the machinery that was being used: excavators that worked on the principle of a dredger; dump cars only eighteen feet long; excavated material carried away in cable cars—

The sight made him feel sympathy for the unfortunate French investors. The science of engineering had made vast progress in the past decade: most of the French machinery was hopelessly out of date. Modern excavators of the grab type, and larger dump cars would shift the material several hundred per cent faster. More efficient signaling would further speed up the work—and compressed air drills—

He filled the valley with people and machinery of his dreams—a score of teams to every one at present working—a score of steam shovels to every one of the antiquated type there below—a score of locomotive cranes with clamshell buckets—a score of mechanical scrapers—a score of tripod drills—

The battle would be man against nature. Since when had man been able to resist that challenge?

7

THE TWO SURVEYORS made Empire their headquarters for the next three days. Inspired by the immensity of the cut which would have to be made between the twin peaks if ships were one day to sail between them, Wesley worked himself and his companion with an unflagging energy which soon irked Ericson. They were reloading their equipment on the pack mule, preparatory to moving forward for a new collimation level, when he first openly expressed his disapproval of Wesley's enthusiasm.

He handed over a Trotter's curve ranger for packing. "This man-against-nature stuff sounds good in books, Wesley, but it has its limits," he grumbled. "By Jimminy! it's against nature for men to work as hard as we are in this sort of climate, ain't it? Ninety-three in the sun—" He mopped his forehead.

"It's hot," Wesley agreed. He packed a Dumpy level in beside the curve ranger. "It'll be hotter still for the poor devils who have to work the steam shovels."

"Look, Wesley—" There was a rasp in Ericson's voice. "We've started this preliminary survey, and we'll finish it. We're no quitters, either of us. But if you think it's going to lead to a digging party—"

"Why not?"

The question exasperated Ericson. "Look at your level book, man. There's your answer—and that's not allowing for all other obstacles against building a canal across the Isthmus." He waved his hand at the cut below them, where a French party were at work. "There's ten years' work for you, and not a third of the total excavation necessary."

"The ten years' work would save us plenty."

"The French have done the easiest work. The hard part's to come. How many times will ten have to be multiplied by us?"

Wesley turned to face his companion. "You read extracts from the French surveys before you left New York, and didn't seem to be frightened by them. There's nothing new about the depth of the Cut."

"Not in a civilized country, maybe, where there's no yellow fever or malaria. Besides, what would you do with the Chagres flood water; where are you going to dump the material excavated from the cut—"

"Colón needs a breakwater."

"How long do you expect the railroad to stand up to the weight of material that must be transported if the canal is to be built in our lifetime? Jimminy! The Black Swamp has swallowed enough track already."

"The railroad could be strengthened, relocated where necessary."

Ericson made an impatient gesture. "Where's the food coming from to feed the workers? There's not enough grown in the country to feed the Panamanians."

"The French found no difficulty in importing enough food."

"Because the workers died off like flies. This climate isn't fit for a man to work in."

Wesley lost patience. "Our job is to survey the canal, not build it," he snapped. "If it had been pie to build, the French would be finishing about now; and Uncle Sam wouldn't have an opportunity of undertaking one of the biggest jobs of engineering in history. Pass me that tachymeter."

This brush between the two men, slight as it was, spoiled the easy relationship between them. For some days afterward they were reserved; Wesley because he resented Ericson's pessimism; Ericson, because his heart was no longer in the project. His nature was too practical to be swayed by idealistic fancies, or by a patriotic fervor for the greater glory of a country in which his people had been settled for scarcely a generation. Subconsciously, his ambitions were directed toward the one object of returning to a mother country which he knew only at second-hand, as it were: through the nostalgic eyes of parents condemned by circumstances to perpetual banishment; through the eager voice of his father describing the beauties of a country which the threat of starvation had forced the family to leave.

So Ericson the realist scoffed at Wesley's ideals, but he did so in secret because he had no wish to hurt his companion. Meanwhile, conscience prevented his trying to shirk. Having undertaken to help with the survey he would see it through to the end. Besides, he had his pride, and was not prepared to see his slimmer, slighter companion outwork him. And when he grumbled about the climate he did so without reference to the canal, and so kept the peace.

In due course they finished their work at the Cut, but when Wesley worked out the contours from his level book even he was appalled by the magnitude of the cut which would have to be excavated for a sea-level canal. He studied his contour map, and his expression turned grim. The lowest curve was more than three fundred feet above sea level.

By slow degrees they moved on toward the southern limit of their field of survey, Panama City. As they neared the town both men relaxed, and something of their earlier comradeship returned.

"Looks good to see a real town again," Ericson commented. "How long are we stopping there, Wesley?"

"I feel three or four days' rest would not hurt us any."

"Hurt us!" Ericson laughed. "Four weeks' rest wouldn't hurt any! Am I planning to have a hot time in the old town! Just you watch what I'll

45

do to a Milwaukee beer." He grew suddenly worried. "You think we'll find a bar someplace?"

"If we don't, it'll be because we're blind, deaf, and dumb. And with no sense of smell. Panama City has more bars and women than a mangy dog has fleas."

Ericson spurred his animal. "Have I a thirst! And that's only half the story."

Soon they reached the outskirts of the town, and presently they were riding along an earth road, bordered by a number of dilapidated frame houses that teemed indiscriminately with Negroes and Chinese. The smell was unbearable, for nobody appeared to have even a rudimentary conception of sanitation. All around the houses the ground was a quagmire of refuse and slops in which dogs, chickens, and even an occasional pig rooted for scraps. Men and boys sprawled on the ground on the shady side of the buildings, and either slept or stared at the passers-by with vague eyes. The womenfolk sat inside the windows, gossiping or nursing babies, often both. As there was no attempt at privacy the insides of many of the small rooms were visible; they were incredibly dirty, and so filled with masses of broken furniture that it was scarcely possible to move about; a double bed, a bare table, two or three stools, a primitive charcoal or wood-burning stove, a pail for all washing purposes, and a line across the room for the washing.

Ericson, in whom cleanliness was a virtue inherited from generations of clean-living people, wrinkled his nose in disgust.

"Good grief! No wonder fevers and plagues flourish here. The place is a cesspool. Why hasn't the whole population been wiped out before now?"

"The children become inoculated by mild attacks."

"If I had my way I'd burn the place down. It needs cleaning up."

Wesley laughed. "The place has been burned down so often it's a habit."

But as they advanced into the heart of the city, the character of the streets changed. The frame houses gave way to brick buildings of Spanish architecture; and the Chinese and Negroes to people of a lighter hue. Here only the main street was wide enough for cabs to drive through; in the side streets there was barely enough room for three people to walk abreast. But, deeply shadowed by the buildings on either side, they appeared temptingly cool, and Wesley looked forward to exploring them.

There were many small hotels to be seen, but none of them seemed inviting, for the woodwork was crumbling for want of paint, and the plastered exteriors were yellow and crumbling. This would not have mattered to the travelers had the interiors looked reasonably clean; but they smelled and the open doorways revealed glimpses of dingy halls and blowsy women.

Warned by one of the French engineers at Culebra that the only hotel worth stopping at was the Hotel Central, the two men continued along

46

Avenida Central, and were glad to see that they were approaching the business quarter, where the population was predominantly white. Here the streets were cobbled, and the houses still Spanish in style but of sounder construction and mostly three stories high. The lower floors were mostly stores, with living quarters above. Here, too, there were private carriages, decked out in fine colors and drawn by animals which, unlike the cab horses, did not have every rib bone protruding. Here were handsome señoras dressed in rich silks, and dark-eyed señores with beetling eyebrows, and exuberant gesticulations. There were whiter faces, too, unmistakably American or unmistakably French; and men in seafaring clothes; and Hindus; and slippered Chinese.

The two Americans felt they were entering a different, and an exotic world; a world both old and new, for though it was part and parcel of the new world, every cobblestone suggested history, Spanish conquest, mule trains laden with gold, pirates and buccaneers, and bloody skirmishes —an impression that was not entirely true, for they were in a new Panama, that had arisen, many miles from the ashes of the old Panama which Henry Morgan had sacked. But old or new it was a romantic world for the two young men, and fully compensated for all their hard labors of the past weeks. In fact, Wesley was inclined to agree with Ericson, that four weeks in Panama City might not prove too long for a vacation.

They reached Cathedral Park; a small square, green and cool in the shade of luxuriant foliage railed round, and surrounded by a cobbled road, which separated it from encircling buildings. Chief among these was the Cathedral, with its towers of pearl shells, which the Spaniards had completed in 1751; and the offices of the Pacific Steam Navigation Company; and, next to a German saloon, a money-changer, and some offices, the hotel they sought. The two men eagerly dismounted, and leaving their horses and the pack mule in charge of a Negro porter, they hurried into the welcome shade of the hotel lobby.

The dark-skinned señor who received them with smooth courtesy spoke enough English to make them understand that they could have a choice of rooms on the top floor, at four dollars a day each, overlooking either the street or the patio. Upon Wesley's inquiring whether they might view the rooms, the clerk bowed gracefully, stepped out into the shady patio and struck a gong three times. A second or so later the sound of a boyish voice answered from high above.

"Yes, señor?"

"Two señores want to see the rooms," the clerk shouted back.

"Yes, señor."

The clerk returned to the office. "If you will go up to the third floor the boy will show you the rooms, señores."

They went on up to the top floor by way of a staircase which landed

47

them on a veranda overlooking the patio, where they were met by a young cheeky-faced imp. His English was worse than Wesley's Spanish; but he insisted upon conducting the conversation in that tongue. He showed them first the rooms overlooking the patio, which the Americans immediately refused, for they were windowless, and had for their only means of ventilation folding doors opening inward from the veranda, or a single door opening inward from a dark, windowless corridor. They were relieved to find that across the corridor each of the rooms had a window.

"Thes a better room, señores, yes?" the imp inquired with a grin as he opened another door.

It was a better room, because of the window, but it still left much to be desired, for though it was amply furnished, with two single beds, table and chair, rocker and bureau, and an inadequate washstand, the mattresses were stained, the rest of the furniture was falling to pieces from old age, and there was neither closet, nor wardrobe, nor even clothes pegs.

The boy could judge from their expressions that they were scarcely impressed, but his bright eyes danced with mischief.

"I see you like, señores. I tell Señor Castro to send baggage up." He was halfway to the veranda before a shout from Wesley halted him.

The boy reluctantly turned.

"What's your name, boy?"

"Eugenio, señor."

"Just you wait, Eugenio." Wesley turned to Ericson. "Well?"

"It's better than the Colón hotel."

"Señor." Eugenio returned and plucked at Wesley's shirt sleeve. "If you take room, me show you street Americans call Coco-nut Grove, after nine."

Ericson patted him on the head. "We've seen coco-nuts before, son. Go on, scat."

Eugenio grinned; which made his whole face sparkle with diabolic mischief. "You not seen coco-nuts like ours, señor. Thin, fat, tall, little— and small or big, as you like—" He gestured with his hands, and Ericson grew taut. "Very cheap, too—You like jig-a-jig?"

"He's talking about women, Wesley."

"Filthy little brat." Wesley was disgusted. Twisting the boy around he gave Eugenio's seat a slap which propelled the boy several yards along the corridor. "Get out and stay out, do you understand?"

But Eugenio just grinned. "Me know all the best girls, señores. All Americans like see Coco-nut Grove. Me come back after nine—"

After a long siesta the two Americans left the hotel to explore the city. Their first visit was to a bar, where Ericson ordered two Milwaukee beers

48

with a heartfelt sigh that made plain how long his thoughts had dwelled upon that moment. Even the price of one Panamanian dollar did not stagger him, for the stay at Colón had taught the two men that imported beer was the highest-priced beverage on the Isthmus—nearly twice the cost of a highball!

The beer tasted like nectar, so Wesley paid for a second round, and shuddered at the sirupy drinks which the local inhabitants swallowed in prodigious quantities. This second bottle temporarily slaked their thirsts, so they left the cool bar, and began to stroll through the crowded streets.

By this time the heat was tempered by a cooling breeze which at least made the streets bearable. With the pleasant feeling of being completely free and unfettered, they meandered hither and thither as their mood dictated. They wandered in and out of the various stores and bazaars—Indian, Chinese, French, and Panamanian—and bought a trifle here, a memento there, and reveled in the utter relaxation of having time to spare in an amusing and romantic spot.

Presently the novelty wore off—for Wesley, at any rate. A puzzling restlessness inspired his critical faculties: he saw that one store was very much like another; that the prices of goods were not so very much cheaper than they were at home; that most of them would be useless in the normal life of an American man or woman; that some were shoddy beneath their exotic decoration. His New England blood begrudged the idea of paying hard-earned money for fripperies, so he lost interest in them.

Later, he realized that his restlessness was not wholly due to economic causes. With guilty embarrassment he found himself staring at every pretty face he passed, with a tantalizing regret that it belonged to a stranger. He grew impatient with Ericson's childish delight in trying to buy goods at half the price asked, and thought how much more fun he would be having if only he were with Dulcie—or Anne—or almost any woman—

As the hours passed the feeling of loneliness grew more acute. He had another drink with Ericson, then another; and promised himself to go to bed as soon as the night was cool enough. But there were always women in the bars; women with firm breasts and seductive hips, women with crimsoned lips and mascara'd eyebrows, women with bold, inviting eyes. At last he admitted that Eugenio would not knock on the bedroom door in vain.

"You come, señores?" The broad, impish grin was confident; and the dark eyes danced with sly mischief. "Have friend below—he take us in cab, yes? He quite cheap—"

"What do you say, Olaf?" Wesley tried to deceive himself that his own mind was not already made up.

"Why not? We only need to drive there and back."

49

"Well, just there and straight back—" Wesley swallowed. "We can have a beer, someplace. My throat's dry—"

So they went, the three of them, in an open carriage which clip-clopped along electrically lit cobbled roads at an ambling pace. Then they passed out of the region of electricity, and buildings of Spanish design, into a neighborhood cloaked in the mystery of velvet darkness that was relieved only by the light of candles behind curtained windows. Later they passed cemeteries where the tombstones looked weird and unsubstantial in the luminous glow cast by the rising moon.

So to a street in the restricted district, where the rooms on either side were uncurtained and occupied each by a woman who flaunted her charms in competition with her neighbors, and invited custom with voice and gesture. Women, as Eugenio had promised, to suit every taste: fat, tall, slim; blonde, brunette; Chinese, mestiza, Caucasian, Negro—

Wesley stared through the windows, and was no longer interested. He was not free, like Ericson. He was married. He owed a duty to Dulcie.

"You want?" Eugenio anxiously inquired. "Me bargain special price—"

So Wesley clipped the boy's ear; and, wondering what his companion would do, studied Ericson. To his surprise the blond giant seemed little affected by the eager offers from either side. There was a grin on Ericson's face, but it was more one of tolerant amusement than anything else. Certainly it was not salacious.

They reached the far end of the street, where the reflection of candlelight was lost in the fringe of darkness. Outside the last house a young girl of fifteen played with a kitten by the side of the road.

Ericson stood up. "Hey there, girlie!" he called out. As the girl turned a naïve, unembarrassed, and pretty face toward the carriage and smiled, Ericson leaped out—

THE S.S. *Seguranca* slowly nosed past the Statue of Liberty. No more than the lower half of the bronze figure was visible from the deck because of a thick heat haze that overhung the bay and restricted visibility. Nevertheless the rising sun was fast dispersing the mist, and by the time the ship drew level with the Battery only sinuous trailers were left clinging to the masts and spars and ratlines of the many vessels alongside the wharves: barques and ships and steamers in disorderly ranks.

Wesley and Ericson stood in the bow of the *Seguranca* as fussy little tugs closed in upon her to nose her into the company's dock. Although the two men had been away from the city less than three months, both felt it had been far longer; so they gazed with nostalgic affection at the be-wharfed water front along which a line of ponderous two- and four-horse drays were already rumbling, and at the solid mass of masonry behind.

"Makes one feel proud," Wesley muttered. "It's worth going abroad sometimes just for the pleasure of returning."

Ericson nodded, but said nothing.

"Don't you agree?" insisted Wesley, who had been too interested in scanning the small groups of people on the wharf to notice that his companion had nodded.

"Yes," Ericson agreed, nodding again. "It will be strange to find oneself working in civilized places again, keeping regular hours, and having a boss."

"But good?"

"Easier," Ericson retorted, with an emphasis that made Wesley grin.

"There's our reward for hard work—a quicker return to this." He waved his hand at the city, but he was misunderstood.

"You've seen Mrs. Adam?"

"Not yet. She's probably someplace in the shade. She can't stand the sun."

"Then she wouldn't care much for Panama?"

"No."

"Then it's lucky we're not returning. I suppose you'll be a partner of H. C. Ackermann any day now?"

"Hope so. And you, Olaf?"

Ericson shrugged.

This time Wesley was paying attention. In a mood of good will toward the man who had worked by his side for nearly three months he said, impulsively, "Why not come up to Providence with me? I'll have a word with Ackermann when he's in the right mood—"

"No, thanks." The sharpness of the reply startled Wesley, and apparently Ericson himself, for he went on, apologetically, "I'd be a fish out of water working anyplace else but New York. I'll land on my feet here, especially after the Panama job."

"Sure." On second thought Wesley was relieved that Ericson hadn't jumped at his offer. The man had worked well enough in a way, but— "You're still set on advising against the canal?"

"I'm sorry, Wesley—"

"You don't have to apologize. You've got a right to your own opinion. That's what you were paid for. But I'm sorry you don't see it the way I do. It'll need courage, determination, imagination, but if the valley was to be dammed some place—at Gatun, maybe, which is ideal for a spillway—"

"No. The scheme's immoral. With a summit level of eighty above you would be turning the valley into an inland lake more than thirty miles wide in places. What about all the towns and villages below that altitude? Empire—Matachin—Gorgona—"

"There's plenty of room for resettlement."

"It's no use. You won't persuade me to change my mind. I'd settle for a sea-level canal if the Culebra Cut didn't have to be so deep, but it would, and you can't shift a whole mountain."

The same old discussion. It had been going on for many weeks, neither man having influenced the other in the slightest degree. So Wesley changed the subject.

"I'll get Dulcie to take our baggage to the hotel and wait for us there. You'll join us for lunch to celebrate our return, won't you?"

"If I'll not be intruding—"

In spite of the early hour more and more people congregated about the spot where the gangways would presently rest, but Wesley failed to pick out Dulcie's trim, neat figure. He smiled wistfully. He shouldn't, he knew, really expect to see her on the dockside at such a ridiculously early hour, but he was disappointed just the same. He longed so much to hug her that every minute's delay was torture. So much so that he felt sorry for Ericson, who was not being met by anyone: his family lived in North Dakota, and could not afford the journey. Then Wesley reflected, with some contempt, his companion probably wouldn't be lonely for long. He would find some young girl—

Shouts and whistles were heard along the length of the wharf as the space between ship and dockside slowly lessened. Ropes went hurtling through the air, to be hastily slipped over bollards: the stern winch began noisily to chuff-chuff as it took the strain of the tautened rope; then the bow—

The vessel rubbed softly against the dock fenders, and was still. An infuriating interval of a minute, even less. A whistle, a wave, the thud of clanging iron against iron—and at last the welcome sight of the gangway crew in action. A few more minutes, and the gangways were in place.

Wesley and Ericson were among the first to land. They had waited on deck nearly an hour for that privilege—but among the crowd of officials, dock staff, police, customs officers, and welcoming friends there was no sign of Dulcie.

Ericson sensed his companion's hurt. "She'll be at the hotel," he consoled. "I wouldn't blame anyone for not wanting to hang around in this heat."

It was hot. Walls and buildings shimmered in the heat which the cobbled roads first collected and then reflected. They might almost be arriving at Colón, Wesley thought, instead of New York. But the heat was more bearable: it didn't make one perspire even to breathe, as it did at Panama.

The customs examination was soon over. The few bits and pieces they had been able to afford aroused no excitement in the breast of the bored officer. He did no more than glance casually through the baggage before motioning for it to be closed up again. So, after some last halfhearted good-bys to shipboard acquaintances who were standing about awaiting their turn, the two men followed the porter out on to the water front, where a line of cabs jostled for fares.

They engaged two; one to take the luggage uptown to the Waldorf Hotel; the second to take them to 48 Wall Street, where the firm of Sullivan and Cromwell had their offices. With a sigh of relief that the most irksome part of their trip was over they leaned against the leather back, and surveyed the world of New York, a world of iron and steel, of unceasing movement and noise, a world of hacks, and private cabs, and belt-line cars—in spite of the heat, a bustling, busy, alert world. And as their iron-shod wheels rumbled over cobbles and steel rails; as they were deafened by the thunder of the elevated trains passing along above their heads; as they saw helmeted men in white coats watering the roads from hydrants; and other sweating men holding buckets of water up to the drooping heads of the animals which drew the dilapidated street cars; then Wesley compared this world with the one they had recently left, where haste was unknown, and work something in which only foolish foreigners indulged. New York emerged cleaner and more wholesome.

In contrast with the busy water front, Wall Street was only just beginning to awaken to the work of a new day. Junior clerks on their way to prepare offices for the day's work passed night watchmen and cleaners on their way home, and the atmosphere of the narrow street was curiously peaceful and unreal.

"What about a cup of coffee, Wesley? Mr. Cromwell won't be here yet."

"He won't be long. He's a busy man, our Mr. C. I'll bet you he will be here within ten minutes of the last junior. Still, that's time enough."

They walked into Broadway, and turned right to look for a restaurant. They found one, and frittered away thirty minutes before returning to Wall Street. In that short time the street had already undergone a transformation. Now the sidewalks were crowded with older men, and the roadway with a succession of private carriages setting down top-hatted and frock-coated presidents, and vice-presidents. Western Union boys and bank guards were present in abundance.

"Fools!" Ericson unexpectedly exclaimed.

Wesley was startled. "Huh?"

Ericson waved his thick, muscled arm. "These people. Rabbits in a warren. What sort of a life is it, coming here to work day after day? Always the same place, always the same work." His emotion intensified his harsh accent.

Wesley chuckled. "It pays them, doesn't it? There are more rich people working in this street than in the rest of America. If your name was

53

Carnegie, or Rockefeller or Morgan—Pierpont, not Henry—you wouldn't despise little old Wall Street." He expected Ericson to explain the strange outburst, but the other man remained silent and did not trouble to explain what had prompted his remark. Extraordinary fellow, Ericson, he reflected. He had changed of late; seemed quite different from the happy-go-lucky, amiable giant of the outward voyage. Had the tropics done something to him?

Nothing more was said until they reached the offices of the law firm. Both men had visited them twice before, but they were still amazed by their atmosphere of concentrated activity. One could sense from the effortless efficiency, which seemed to be a hallmark, that the firm was directed by a man of superb organizing ability and stupendous drive.

A young man in strictly formal office clothes inquired their business in a polite but strictly formal manner. At the mention of Mr. Cromwell's name he looked doubtful.

"Mr. Cromwell is an extremely busy man," he began with tactful regret. "Perhaps Mr. Clarkson—"

"Mr. Cromwell is expecting us."

"Oh!" The fact surprised the young man. "At any precise time?"

"We were to report as soon as possible after our arrival," Wesley firmly told him. "If you will send our names in to him—Mr. Ericson and Mr. Adam—"

"Yes, sir," the young man agreed, and passed through a nearby door. He soon reappeared, looking impressed.

"Mr. Cromwell will see you immediately, sir."

Ericson placed his hand on the young man's shoulder. "You new here, son?"

"Yes, sir. Four weeks ago."

"I thought so." He patted the curly head. "You must learn to recognize important people when you see them. Lead on, son."

Thomas Nelson Cromwell, senior partner of Sullivan and Cromwell, looked rather older than his forty-three years, which was not surprising for he was one of the astutest lawyers in New York, and as such had a finger in too many pies, to allow himself any real relaxation or repose. Above prominently marked cheekbones his eyes were an outstanding feature; shrewd and commanding, of an indeterminate, dark shade, they seemed to represent the pivot around which the rest of the face had been built in casual fashion. His lips were firm; his hair graying round the ears.

"Mr. Adam, Mr. Ericson." He gave each man a cool handclasp. "Welcome back to New York. Thank you for reporting so promptly." He sat down, and indicated two chairs. "Sit down, gentlemen."

They did so, feeling not a little self-conscious and out of place in an office whose furnishing and decoration had been subordinated to severity.

54

Cromwell continued, "I have received your reports from time to time, Mr. Adam, but would appreciate hearing from you, briefly, in your own words, a summary of your opinion." He leaned forward. "First, what are the prospects of building a canal?"

"A sea-level or lock canal, sir?"

"Either—both—" The attorney tapped impatiently on the table. "Tell me in simple language any ordinary citizen who knows nothing of surveying could understand."

"To do that, sir, I must begin at the beginning and describe the Isthmus."

"Very well."

"The Isthmus of Panama, as it is known in this country, is that part of Colombia which stretches from Colón on the Atlantic coast to Panama City on the Pacific. At that point it is thirty-five miles wide, the second narrowest crossing from ocean to ocean—"

"The second, Mr. Adam? I have always believed it to be the narrowest."

"No, sir. It's narrower, by four miles, from the Gulf of San Blas in the Caribbean Sea to the Pacific near the mouth of the Chepo River. But the great obstacle in the building of a canal between the two oceans is the Continental Divide, the mountain range that stretches almost the entire length of the Americas from north to south. The lowest point of the Divide on the Isthmus of Panama is at Culebra, but it is still three hundred and twelve feet above sea level."

"Which means that a cut of that depth would have to be made for a sea-level canal?"

"No, sir, the cut would have to be at least forty-five feet more, to allow for the draught of ships passing through it."

"Of course." Cromwell smiled wryly. "But would such a cut be impossible?"

"Probably not impossible, but it would take many years to complete, and the cost would reach astronomical figures."

"Besides, what could be done with the excavated material?" Ericson interrupted.

"Done with it!" Cromwell looked confused. "I do not understand."

Wesley smiled. "Mr. Ericson means that a mountain cannot be removed merely by excavation, sir. It costs more to transport a ton of rock than it does to blow it up. And, of course, the farther one moves it, the greater the cost. As it is, much of the material excavated and removed by the French will probably have to be shifted for a second time."

"Why?"

"Because it would probably be in the way of further operations."

"I see. Is the problem of the cut the only obstacle in the way of a sea-level canal?"

"It is not the only one, and it would be simpler to deal with than the

55

problem of controlling flood water. The route between Colón and Panama City follows the valley of the Chagres River, which drains more than one thousand squares miles. A sea-level canal would have to follow the course of the main river, the Chagres, from the Caribbean Sea as far as Matachin, a distance of roughly twenty-five miles. There the river takes a sharp bend to the north, so a canal would have to be dug from that point to the Pacific Ocean at Panama."

"A distance of ten miles or so, but through the Culebra Cut?"

"Yes, sir."

The attorney looked perplexed. "But if the Chagres flowed directly into a sea-level canal wouldn't the canal carry the flood water directly out to sea?"

"No, sir. In Panama the rainfall is so heavy that the Chagres has been known to rise as much as forty feet in twenty-four hours. If the canal were to flood to anything like the same extent it is conceivable that it could float an ocean-going ship many miles from the canal course and deposit it high and dry in the middle of a jungle."

"Then the river would have to be diverted, I take it?"

Wesley nodded. "That was De Lesseps' idea. He proposed to divert the Chagres and its tributaries so that they could not affect the canal. To do that would have meant excavation work as extensive as that necessary for the canal itself."

The thin lips tightened. "Then you believe that a sea-level canal is out of the question, Mr. Adam?"

"I do, sir."

"I believe that any canal is out of the question, Mr. Cromwell," Ericson slipped in.

"What!" Cromwell was annoyed. "What is that you say, Mr. Ericson? Any canal—"

"We disagree," Wesley interrupted quickly, not liking the ominous note in the attorney's voice. "I suggest we each give you our views."

"Certainly. You first, Mr. Adam. You think a lock-canal could be built?"

"I do, sir."

"But wouldn't the cost of building locks be infinitely greater than that of mere excavation?"

"I cannot give you an expert opinion on the question of costs, sir. I am not a costing or quantitative surveyor, but I feel tolerably certain they would be considerably less."

"But how would a lock-type canal operate? You would still have to excavate a canal right across the Isthmus. Why should it be cheaper to build one at a higher elevation than at sea level?"

"This map will explain, sir. We prepared it aboard ship on the way

56

home." Wesley took a large map from his dispatch case, which he unrolled and spread on the desk before the attorney. "This is a contour map of the Chagres valley. The wavy lines in red represent the elevation of the rising ground either side of the course of the river, which is in black. Now, sir, if a dam were built here, at Bohio, right across the river, at an elevation of fifty feet above sea level, this would result in all this area, which we have shaded brown, being transformed into an inland lake stretching across a considerable part of the Isthmus. It would then only be necessary to excavate a canal at either end of the lake. The additional area shaded gray would be added to the lake if elevation were sixty instead of fifty, mauve for an elevation of seventy, dark green for an elevation of eighty, and light green for an elevation of ninety."

Cromwell contemplated the map in silence which, after a long interval, he was the first to break. He banged the top of the desk with a sharp slap of his hand.

"By God! sir, it could be done," he exclaimed enthusiastically.

9

IT WAS ERICSON'S turn to speak. He began, enunciating each word with care in an effort to express his dispassionate disbelief in the feasibility of a Panama canal. But as he warmed up to his subject he speeded up, and spoke with so marked an accent that his hearers found difficulty in understanding all he said. Nevertheless, his meaning was plain enough, and Cromwell's mouth grew steadily tighter. Long before Ericson had finished Wesley realized that the attorney was intensely angry, and was impatient with the pessimistic forecast that no machinery was capable of cutting through the Great Divide, certainly not within the time limit of the Colombian lease; that slides would upset any calculation; that an army of additional men would be necessary to prevent the jungle from reclaiming its own; that malaria and yellow fever would constantly deplete the ranks of the laborers; that it would be immoral to flood thousands of square miles, towns, villages, and settlements in order to create an inland lake— The arguments were familiar to Wesley, but he had to admit that Ericson was marshaling his facts well, and putting forward a convincing argument.

As soon as Ericson had finished, Cromwell turned to Wesley.

"Well?" he snapped. "What's your reply to that damning indictment?"

"I cannot contradict it, sir, if that is what you mean—"

"Of course it is what I mean. You led me to understand that a lock-canal could be built."

"I still say so, sir, although I believe that the difficulties of building it would be so great, and the obstacles so alarming, there is only one man in the world likely to make a success of the project."

"The man—"

"Uncle Sam."

"Ah!" Cromwell relaxed: a pleased smile eased the pressure of his lips. "Tell me why you think the United States could succeed where France has failed."

"There are several reasons. We could profit by French mistakes, we could carry on from where France stopped, and so have the advantage of the work already done—valuable work, if I may say so, sir, in spite of mistakes they have made a fine beginning. If I were a Frenchman I should sincerely regret the reasons that brought French building to an end."

"Why?"

"Because the building of the canal will be an achievement of which any nation should be proud to the end of time."

"Proud to the end of time! Good! Good! A line to appeal to doubting congressmen. Any other points?"

"Yes, Mr. Cromwell. We have the money—"

"France is not a poor country."

"I know, but we have two things that no other nation in the world has. A determination to finish anything once begun—"

Cromwell nodded his satisfaction. "Go on."

"And a constructional potential second to none. The French machinery was never capable of finishing the canal. A boy sent to do a man's work."

The attorney inspected Wesley's earnest face, and was satisfied. "That's the spirit, Mr. Adam." He rose to end the interview. "We have booked rooms for you both at the Waldorf for a week. I shall let you know when I want to see you again."

He shook hands with them, and having rung for his secretary to show his visitors out he sat down at his desk again, and turned over some papers. It was obvious that his thoughts were already occupied with other business—

The desk clerk nodded when the two men gave their names to him.

"Yes, sir, Sullivan and Cromwell have booked two rooms for one week, four-fifteen and sixteen, Mr. Adam—" He looked inquiringly at each in turn.

Wesley nodded. "Yes."

"We have a letter for you that arrived this morning." He passed it over. It was from Dulcie, and quite short.

Wesley, darling,

So sorry not to welcome you on your return. Cannot be in New York until late afternoon. Will explain when we meet.

All my love,
Dulcie.

Wesley and Ericson lunched together; but the meal was dismal, and in no way a celebration. Neither man was in any mood for lighthearted conversation, and as the subject of the canal was, by mutual consent, taboo, they ate in silence and did not speak until the coffee stage was reached, when they exchanged only a few commonplace remarks. As soon as the meal was over they parted company, Ericson having previously announced that he intended to stroll along to Times Square. He had invited Wesley to accompany him, but the offer was not sincere and Wesley had no hesitation in refusing it. He watched the blond giant stroll out of the hotel, looking smart in a morning suit of pin-stripe gray, which he wore over a shirt of heliotrope linen, and blue necktie. Kid shoes, a straw boater with a band to match his shirt, and a pink camellia in his lapel completed his outfit which was quite obviously intended to dazzle any female eyes which should chance to glance in his direction.

As soon as Ericson had disappeared Wesley retired to a quiet corner of the entrance lobby and there selected an armchair from which he would be able to see Dulcie as she entered the hotel. The lobby was filled with smartly dressed men and women, and the sound of their voices was like the loud hum of an electric dynamo, revolving at varying speeds; for sometimes the hum swelled to a higher pitch of interest or excitement, and sometimes to a lower confidential note. At any other time he would have enjoyed idling away half an hour, watching passers-by and trying to guess who and what they were, but today his only conscious thought was one of bitter disappointment that Dulcie was not with him. For so many weeks and with such intense longing had he looked forward to the moment when he could take her into his arms and kiss her cool lips into responsive warmth that the additional few hours' delay brought about in him a mood that was almost one of sullen anger, and a sadistic desire to hurt her. He reflected with cynical bitterness that he had partly himself to blame for the intensity of his feelings, for had he not time and time again resisted the urge to seek consolation and relief in Panama's restricted district he would not now be experiencing that emotional crisis which so often had produced those distorted desires that shocked him later in his calmer moments.

There were increasingly fewer calmer moments as time passed and still Dulcie had not appeared. His face unconsciously assumed a glowering expression as he sat forward in his chair and stared at the door through which Dulcie must come. His reflections grew more bitter and turbulent.

59

Always in the past he had cheerfully forgiven her casual disregard for appointments, and her habitual unpunctuality; mainly because he was wax in her hands whenever she wheedled and coaxed him with her pretty ways and her thistledown kisses. But this time would be different, he decided: he would greet her with a frigid anger that would make her recognize once and for all that he was the lord and master of the household; that he would no longer consent to be kept at arm's length; nor kept waiting. And if she were slow in learning he would use force to see that his wishes were respected—just once, as a warning, and a lesson to her that her slim, tiny body would be powerless in the grasp of his arms. He had not Ericson's strength, which was massive; but in comparison with hers—

Then he became conscience stricken. In God's name, what had the tropics done to him? Never before had he ever contemplated striking her. A brutal, disgusting idea, merely thinking of it degraded him. Of course, he had never been quite so impatient, so desperate—but to use force—

It was unfortunate that a nearby couple chose that moment to kiss each other good-by. The kiss was correctly chaste for so public a spot, but he was sure that he detected a lingering wistfulness on the part of them both—

Damn all women! he explosively reflected. Damn, and damn, and damn—

An hour or so later she entered the hotel. At the first glimpse of her tiny oval face, and serene eyes of cerulean blue, his anger with her vanished completely. He leaped to his feet, hurried forward, and reached her as she moved toward the reception desk. Gathering her into his arms he kissed her cool lips.

Her small hands pushed him away. "Wesley! Not here," she whispered. As he stepped back to look upon and enjoy her loveliness, he saw that her forehead was puckered in displeasure.

He forgave her embarrassment, and reproached himself for not remembering that she was particularly self-conscious. He turned to the bellboy who was staggering beneath a load of baggage. "Room four-fifteen."

As he walked beside her, on the way to the elevator, he realized that he was trembling with happiness. He gave a quick glance toward the lobby, challenging any man there to produce a wife half as dainty, half as slim, half as pretty. He felt immensely proud; and grateful for his good fortune. It was almost worth many weeks' absence, he thought, to experience this moment.

At last they reached the bedroom. In his anxiety to be alone with her he overtipped the bellboy, who grinned broadly with understanding sympathy. As the door shut behind the red-cheeked cherubic face Wesley lifted his wife into the air and fervently covered her mouth and cheeks with kisses.

As soon as she could free her mouth she did so. "Put me down! Wesley, you're crushing my dress."

He put her down. "Then take it off, sweetheart."

"Take it off—now—"

"Because I'm going to kiss you for the next half-hour, darling—longer, maybe—"

She glanced into his unsteady eyes, and shrank away with a gesture of disgust. "At this time of day! What has come over you?"

He was scarcely conscious of her words. He sat down on the bed. "God! You're wonderful, honey; a sight for sore eyes. There isn't a woman in the lobby downstairs to compare with you." He held out a hand. "Come and sit beside me so that I can touch you and know that I'm not dreaming."

"There's unpacking to be done—"

"Hang the unpacking! I've waited too many weeks for this moment. Sometimes I haven't been able to sleep for wanting to hold you in my arms."

"Have you been drinking?" she asked coldly.

"Drinking!" He laughed unsteadily. "Don't you understand what it means for a healthy man to be parted from his wife for so many weeks, my sweet? He grows desperate for her company—especially in the tropics. Now that we're together are you surprised I'm impatient?"

"How disgusting!" Her cheeks crimsoned. "You make me feel like a—like an animal. One would think you only married me to—to—"

He felt limp. "You're right, honey," he muttered. "I guess it was just the effect of the tropics." He gave a sour laugh. "There's a time and place for everything, as Dad used to love saying." He lit a cigarette. "Why weren't you in New York to meet me?"

"Mother went back home this morning, so I just had to wait until I had seen her off, Wesley dear. I couldn't leave her alone on her last morning in Providence, could I?"

"Of course not." He yawned, and laid back on the pillow. "Guess I'll have a nap while you're unpacking." He looked at the mound of valises. "And that will take time, too."

For two days Wesley had no word from Cromwell, but on the morning of the fourth day of his stay in New York he received a letter from the attorney asking him to call at the Wall Street office at 11 A.M. He hurried off to the next room, to warn Ericson. To his astonishment the bedroom was open; and the room occupied by three women who were stripping the linen from the bed, and sweeping the carpet. None of Ericson's belongings was to be seen.

"Where's Mr. Ericson?"

One of the women looked up. "Who, sir?"

"Mr. Ericson—the occupier of this room—"

"The gentleman checked out early this morning, sir."

"Impossible—there's some mistake—"

"Best take it up with the office, sir." There was a shrug in the woman's voice though outwardly she remained respectful. "We had orders to prepare the room for a new visitor."

Wesley hurried downstairs to the office, but there was no mistake. Ericson had checked out before 7 A.M. that morning.

"But he said nothing to me last night about leaving. Did he say why? Do you know where he went? Did he leave any message for me?"

"Your name, sir?"

"Adam. Wesley Adam."

"Ah, yes! Room four-fifteen. No, sir, Mr. Ericson left no message. Apart from that I'm afraid we cannot help you. We do not interrogate our visitors—"

The mystery of Ericson's abrupt and secretive departure haunted Wesley. He would have liked to discuss it with Dulcie; but she was still fast asleep, curled into a little ball that made her outline beneath the sheets look no larger than a child's. In fact, her face, too, looked absurdly childish; for her complexion was flawless, and as yet was untouched by any visible evidence that she was much older than sixteen or seventeen.

His expression softened as he looked down upon her. Emotionally, she was little more than a child, though in other respects she was as self-possessed as a woman twice her age. To think of her as his wife seemed to put him on a level with Ericson, which was a revolting thought: he had to comfort himself with the knowledge that, whatever age she might look, she was in fact approaching her twenty-second birthday.

Though he could not discuss Ericson's disappearance, he was not able to banish it from his mind; the more thought he gave to it the less he could think of any reason for it. The sudden departure from the hotel seemed so senseless, for even assuming that some young girl had caught his fancy, that was no reason for secrecy from Wesley, or for prejudicing his future career: being unattached, there was no one in New York to criticize or deter him.

What Cromwell would have to say alarmed Wesley. With reason, too, for Cromwell was still Ericson's taskmaster, as it were. Besides, it was unlike Ericson. One of his better traits was, or had seemed to be, a readiness to finish a job once started—and his present job, as such, lasted until the end of the week. Why, then, had he anticipated its finish by three days only? Especially as there was still a balance of pay and expenses due to him.

Wesley arrived at the offices of Sullivan and Cromwell two minutes before time, but was immediately shown into Cromwell's office. The attorney received him with a genial welcome.

"I have finished reading your report, Mr. Adam. It is a fine businesslike job of work, on which I congratulate you."

"Thank you, sir."

"What is more important, it is precisely the type of report I hoped you would draw up—and was led, by Mr. Ackermann, to anticipate. That is why I selected you, a young man, from so many older, more experienced men whom I could have sent instead. You have courage and daring of youth, which is reflected in your report. An older man might have been appalled by the difficulties, and have seen the prospect through a glass darkly, as it were. Would you consider me impertinent if I asked what your future plans are?"

"As soon as you have finished with me I am returning to Providence, sir."

"To Mr. Ackermann's employ?"

"I think so. I have hopes that Mr. Ackermann will make me a junior partner in his firm. He always promised to do so as soon as I had proved myself."

"Which you have certainly done. Good luck to you, Mr. Adam. I hope you achieve a big success. If you care to, keep in touch with me. I could make use of a man of your ability in one of the firms with which I am connected." He laughed dryly. "Perhaps building the Panama Canal if all our plans go through."

Wesley was puzzled why Cromwell had not missed Ericson.

"Excuse me, Mr. Cromwell, but regarding Mr. Ericson—"

"Well?"

"When I went to inform him of this appointment this morning I learned that he had checked out of the hotel without a word to me."

Cromwell nodded. "I know. On my advice. I sent for him yesterday."

"But—but—"

The attorney smiled thinly. "Are you surprised, Mr. Adam? And a little hurt? Let me warn you never to be surprised or hurt at anything that happens when political issues are involved, as they are at the moment.

"You may have some idea of the various efforts to build a canal across Panama, so I shall only mention one or two salient points. The suggestion that the United States should build a canal to connect the Atlantic and Pacific oceans was first mooted as long ago as eighteen twenty-five, and was several times renewed during the next half century, but the French were the first to begin building operations, in eighteen eighty-one, after Colombia had granted to Lieutenant Lucien Napoleon-Bonaparte Wyse in eighteen seventy-eight, a concession which De Lesseps purchased the following year.

"You are not old enough to remember the feelings of the people of this country when they realized that French enterprise had invaded the new world—they had managed to defy the Monroe Doctrine by establishing

63

a legal foothold, to which the United States could have no moral objection. This foothold became a handhold when the Canal Company purchased the American-owned railroad.

"As soon as it was realized a few years ago, that the French company could not complete the canal, and that the task was beyond the private enterprise of any country, the directors of the new company here came to the conclusion that the only chance of cutting their losses would be to sell the concession to the government of the United States. Ours was the firm honored with the delicate task of carrying through the complicated negotiations. To confirm my belief that a canal could be built was the purpose of your visit to Panama." Cromwell coughed dryly. "You have satisfied me that I can continue to act in this matter with the sincere conviction that it will be for the benefit of our great country to carry negotiations through to a successful conclusion. You follow me, Mr. Adam?"

"Thoroughly."

"Unfortunately, there are circumstances which make this deal less simple than it sounds. The people of this country are rightly determined that we shall, and that any other European nation shall not, build a canal. But where shall that canal be built? Across the Isthmus of Panama? Or—the more favored of several routes—in Nicaragua. Suppose the Nicaragua plan is chosen! What then would be the worth of the Panama concession?"

"A nickel," Wesley murmured.

"Precisely. A nickel would be a generous offer. Meanwhile, I am sure you are aware, Mr. Adam, that public opinion is strongly in favor of the Nicaragua Canal. The Panama Canal is looked upon as a vanished dream. Boards of trade, state legislatures, and party conventions all over the United States are passing resolutions in favor of a canal at Nicaragua. Last year the Republican party formally endorsed its construction. Bills have been constantly introduced into both Houses to ensure the adoption of the Nicaragua route. At the head of the Nicaragua group are Senator Morgan, who is Chairman of the Nicaragua Canal Committee of the Senate, and Representative Hepburn, who is Chairman of the Committee on Interstate Commerce. Together with their numerous followers, and, generally speaking, the Republican party, they are determined to see that the transocean canal shall be built at Nicaragua, and not at Panama. Can you imagine, therefore, what a weapon I should be putting into the hands of the Nicaragua group by allowing them to get hold of Mr. Ericson?"

Wesley laughed grimly. "There wouldn't be a chance in hell of selling the Panama concession."

"Quite so. Therefore—" Cromwell smiled. "I made arrangements for Mr. Ericson to leave the country at the earliest possible moment. I gave him the choice of sailing to any country of the world, and there having three years' leave on full pay. Do you know which country he chose?"

64

"One of the Scandinavian countries," Wesley replied with confidence. "It is his life's ambition to see the land of his forefathers."

Cromwell smiled. "You are wrong, Mr. Adam. He has gone to— Panama!"

10

PANAMA! Of all places in the world—

During the rest of that day Wesley's thoughts frequently turned upon the puzzle of Ericson's return to the Isthmus. Up to the moment when the ship carrying them back to New York had steamed toward the horizon and they had watched the line of land slowly dissolve, the blond giant had never once expressed any liking for the country, or any wish to return there. True his demeanor, in contrast to that on the outward journey, had been mopish and reserved toward the other passengers, but this, Wesley had assumed, was because this time women passengers were not young girls.

Once or twice he wondered whether the magnet that had drawn his companion back to the tropics lived at the far end of Coco-nut Grove in Panama City, where the street became merged with the fringes of the jungle. For Ericson had not returned to the carriage—much to Eugenio's mischievous delight—nor to the hotel until the early hours of the morning; and the last night of their stay there Wesley had had to spend by himself. On the other hand the girl had never been mentioned; and Ericson had never let fall the least hint that the girl meant any more to him than an amusing few hours' diversion. In fact, he had never even mentioned her name.

But Ericson was soon crowded out of his thoughts by his newly aroused interest in the subject of an interocean canal. Until the moment when Ackermann had said to him, "I've heard from an old friend of mine in New York that he's looking for a young, enthusiastic surveyor to do a job in Panama. Care to go? It will be fine experience for you, and I'll give you leave of absence—" he had never concerned himself with the question of where the canal should be constructed; or even whether there should be a canal at all. But Cromwell's brief explanation of the events leading up to a new survey of the Panama Isthmus route absorbed him, and inspired him to delve more deeply into its history. He began to question some of the people he knew in New York.

Bill Godwin, for instance. Uncle Bill was a newspaperman who had grown gray haired and weary spirited trying to reach the city editor's desk. He had once wooed Wesley's mother, but had borne no malice toward John Adam for stealing her from him. Instead, he had turned for solace to a ginger-haired wench who sold watches at Wanamaker's. He should have known better, for he always had loathed ginger from childhood. Still, the marriage was not completely disastrous, for she still kept house for him, and was happy in her memories of the five love affairs she had had under her husband's nose, without his ever suspecting the fact.

Being simple of heart, in spite of being a newspaperman, Bill continued to appreciate Elizabeth Adam's serene, domestic nature. During the few hours between assignments which never seemed to hit the headlines, he was more often at the Adam home—then in New York—than he was in his own apartment in Long Acre. Thus it was almost inevitable that he should become Uncle Bill to the boy who was born to Elizabeth and John Adam just twenty months after marriage. And Uncle Bill he remained; for even after the Adams' had moved to Providence, he visited them whenever he could snatch an odd night off; and he contacted him whenever they went to New York, which they did, several times a year, when John Adam was summoned there for a managers' conference. But in all those years he never allowed them to meet his ginger-haired wife.

"I know plenty about the Panama Canal scheme, my boy," he asserted in answer to Wesley's question. "Wrote an article on it, some years ago, but nobody wanted it." Bill had more unpublished articles to his debit than any other writer in New York. "What do you want to know?"

"Any chance of the government taking over the concession?"

"The French government?"

"Ours."

Bill Godwin laughed. He was at his saddest, weariest when he laughed. "You're crazy, son. Don't take notice of Cromwell's talk. That's his job, to try and make Uncle Sam buy the concession lock, stock, and barrel."

"But why not, Uncle Bill? A canal can be built at Panama. I've been there—"

"Yeah, I know! You've surveyed the Isthmus, and you can't see any reason why Uncle Sam shouldn't finish what the French began? Well, I'm neither surveyor nor engineer. I don't know one end of a shovel from the other. And for me, water's something you wash in—hot! But I do know that Cromwell hasn't a dog's chance of getting a canal in Panama finished by Uncle Sam or anyone else."

"Why not?" Wesley persisted.

"Look, son, what do you know about the background of this canal business?"

"Almost nothing, Uncle Bill. That's why I'm asking you."

"Want me to go back to the beginning?"

"Almost, except that bit about the king of Spain and his spiritual advisers, both for and against."

66

"Right! Then we'll skip the first two hundred years, and pass on to the middle of the eighteenth century. But not before we've ordered a couple more highballs. Talking history makes me that thirsty—"

The highballs were ordered, delivered, and sipped. Then Uncle Bill lit a cigar.

"You know that the Isthmus of Panama was made part of New Granada at the beginning of the eighteenth century—Well, perhaps you don't. I didn't till I looked up its history for the article that nobody wanted. In seventeen seventy-one the Spanish decided that maybe after all God wouldn't object to a canal, and ordered surveys to be made. So Spanish *caballeros* went to Tehuantepec to see what could be done. Tehuantepec not pleasing them any they moved south to Nicaragua. This was liked better, so a company was formed in Spain to do something about it.

"This company took a siesta one day, and never troubled to wake up again. Meanwhile, some of those god-damned limeys, who don't like to be left out of anything worth while, had accompanied the Spaniards on the survey route. Upon their return to Belize they wrote to old Farmer George at Windsor Castle, and told him that a canal at Nicaragua was feasible, so what about seizing the country and building one. Of course, it's only coincidence that war between England and Spain broke out the following year, but the limeys are never slow to seize an opportunity. Horatio Nelson was given command of a naval contingent and a hint to look over Lake Nicaragua. He wrote in his dispatches: 'As it commands the only water pass between the oceans, its situation must ever render it a principal post to insure passage to the Southern Ocean.' Not boring you, am I, son? Any time I start talking—well, you know me."

"Go on."

"Nelson didn't have much trouble dealing with the Spaniards; but when he landed an expedition to seize the lake, nature took a hand. Only ten out of two hundred survived to return to Jamaica.

"Soon after this the world began to interest itself in an interocean canal, so Spain thought she had better get busy first. She was too late. New Granada, Ecuador, and Venezuela united to break away from Europe, and formed the Republic of Colombia, under old Bolivar. Panama soon followed suit. It wasn't long before Colombia was receiving offers for a concession from people in Great Britain and over here. In eighteen twenty-five Colombia advised the United States that she would welcome co-operation in building an interocean canal. So Secertary Henry Clay ordered a survey of the Nicaragua route, while Bolivar had the Panama route surveyed by an Englishman. Soon after that Ecuador and Venezuela withdrew from the Republic, which then went back to its original name of New Granada.

"When nothing worth while developed from these surveys a concession was granted to a Dutch corporation to build a canal through Nicaragua, but just about then revolution broke out in the Netherlands, so that scheme fell through.

"By now Uncle Sam was really beginning to see the advantages to the canal. In 'thirty-five Charles Biddle investigated possible water or railroad routes across the Isthmus. Apparently he preferred the idea of a railroad, for he obtained a railroad concession from New Granada. I give you three guesses what somebody did with it. Yeah! Just like what the editor of the *Saturday Evening Post* did to my article. Threw it in the wastepaper basket.

"The next people to become interested were the French. They obtained a similar concession in 'thirty-eight, but that, too, fell through. I should think hell must be paved with Panama and Nicaragua concessions. But at last something happened that was to bring the business to a head. That was in California—"

"Gold!"

"Right the first time. The California gold rush started, and believe it or not, the best route from the Eastern Seaboard was by way of ship to Aspinwall as Colón was then called, a trek across the Isthmus, and by ship again up to California. A group of smart Yankees decided that the time had come to build a railroad across the Isthmus, so a railroad was built. Of course you know the old story that every tie cost a life. That just isn't true, but mortality was high enough. More than twelve hundred men died in building forty-eight miles of track, or twenty-five to every mile if my mathematics aren't wrong. Panama Isthmus sure is a killer, son.

"We were still dickering with the idea of a canal someplace in the Caribbean region, so when some smart guys started thinking of all the money the Panama railroad would make once it got going they were smart enough to revive the Nicaragua Canal idea; and the result was the Atlantic and Pacific Canal Company, which held the concession for that route, ordered another survey to be made. A plan was prepared, submitted to the President, and approved by a commission of Army engineers. Maybe, if the Civil War hadn't happened, the Nicaragua Canal would have been built, and there never would have been a canal begun at Panama.

"As soon as we had stopped licking our wounds after the war the subject of an interoceanic canal was reopened with both the United States of Colombia, as New Granada had renamed herself in the meantime, and with Nicaragua. From which you will understand, son, that we sure meant to build that canal. But did we do more than talk about it, and sign concessions? While we were still yammering the French jumped in ahead of us. Before we properly realized what was happening the dirt was beginning to fly.

"Let me tell you, we were pretty sore at the thought of a European nation doing what we should have been doing. So sore that, three years after work had begun on the Canal in Panama we negotiated a fresh treaty with

68

Nicaragua, which gave the United States the right to build a Nicaragua Canal. A fresh survey was made by a civil engineer in the naval service, by the name of Menocal."

"But the world isn't big enough for two canals," Wesley protested.

"Sure it isn't. P'raps that's why President Cleveland withdrew the treaty from the consideration of the Senate. But maybe Menocal didn't think so; or maybe a gypsy had told him the French were going to bankrupt themselves; or maybe he had a look at the Panama works, and decided it never would be dug. Anyway, he obtained another concession from Nicaragua in favor of the Nicaragua Canal syndicate, and the next year he wheedled Costa Rica into giving him a similar concession. A bright boy, that Menocal.

"On February fourth, eighteen eighty-nine, the old Panama Canal Company was declared bankrupt and dissolved by the *Tribunal Civil de la Seine*. Sixteen days later Congress approved an act granting a charter to the Maritime Canal Company for the construction of a Nicaragua Canal."

Wesley whistled, and Bill Godwin grinned with sardonic amusement. "You can't say Uncle Sam doesn't work fast on occasions. Congress did the Maritime Canal Company proud: I guess you studied enough political history at Brown to know that Congress doesn't often grant charters. The people weren't slow to realize the significance of that charter. It kind of gave the scheme an official backing, and it wasn't long before people were calling it the American Canal."

Wesley nodded. "I remember Dad and you discussing the American Canal all of one evening."

"I always was interested in canals. If I had been a canal builder instead of a newspaperman maybe I'd have gone places. But to get back to the Maritime Canal Company. It soon grew in importance when it was known who its backers were, and that an ex-senator was its president.

"Preliminary work on the Nicaragua Canal started in June of the same year, so no time was wasted. And from that day to this the American public has continued to look upon the Nicaragua Canal as the future and only possible interoceanic canal. But I don't need to tell you that; you read the newspapers—"

"I usually turned to the sports columns," Wesley apologized.

Uncle Bill sighed. "P'raps you were right. Being a newspaperman I never had the chance. No, my boy, Cromwell won't ever sell the Panama Canal either to Uncle Sam or the American public. He's up against something too big: vested interests in the Nicaragua Canal, and popular opinion. The Panama Canal smells bad in the noses of the American people. Too many travelers have publicized their observations and opinions about the ruin and decay which you can't miss seeing—"

"It's not so bad. I believe a lot of it might be repaired and restored."

"So it could! A drop in the bucket! The point is, that whatever the truth may be, the majority of the people—and count me among them—are convinced that it is folly to try and build a canal at Panama; and Cromwell's not going to alter that idea in a hurry." He beckoned to the waiter. "I told you history made me thirsty. Another highball, son."

Uncle Bill's frank opinion that an interoceanic canal would never be built at Panama, was Wesley's cue to take over the conversation. He halted Bill's volubility—not easily, for he was wound up—then gave his reasons why it should be possible to take over and complete the original French project.

Presently, as he talked, something of his enthusiasm at his first sight of Culebra Cut—which time had deepened rather than diminished—transformed his voice. It grew warm and full and commanding; and reflected his confidence in the certain success of any American attempt to construct a lock canal. There was pride, too, in his voice; pride of nationality. The inference that American drive, American inventiveness, and American grit could be relied upon to master all obstacles.

Bill Godwin was too amazed at the change in his "adopted" nephew to interrupt. He could not follow all Wesley's arguments, for they were largely technical, and engineering as a subject was Greek to him. But he could and did recognize that he was seeing a new and different Wesley—an aspect of his nephew's character which he had never suspected. For the first time he appreciated that the ingenuous Brown graduate with whom he had so often discussed the merits of the Boston Beaneaters, and in particular their recent spectacular success in defeating the Baltimore Orioles in a close finish for the National League Championship; and the dismal failure of the New York Giants to finish higher than third. Wesley, he saw, had bolted away from those carefree happy days and had developed into manhood.

In response, his own weary face stiffened with pride. The boy—no! this glowing-eyed, confident man—could so easily have been *his* son, had John Adam not crossed the path of Elizabeth Fuller, that he, in his childlessness, looked upon Wesley as his spiritual son, while conceding that he was John's by natural, physical descent. So it didn't matter a tinker's cuss whether the boy was right or wrong in his incomprehensible arguments, the only thing that really mattered was that he was a man with spunk in him; a man who wasn't going to let the world knock any chip off his shoulder; a man who was going places. If Wesley had been a newspaperman, Uncle Bill wistfully reflected, he wouldn't wait all his life to sit at the city editor's desk. He would pass it by, on his way up—

"All right, son," he interrupted. "Save it for others. I don't understand a word you say, but I'll back you, by God! You watch the headlines."

Poor old Bill Godwin! He wasn't too old to dream sometimes.

Schwartz wasn't so easily swayed, but then one couldn't expect a five foot seven inch man weighing two hundred pounds to be easily swayed. Especially one who had voted Republican all his votable life. He had listened with amused tolerance to Wesley and had not remained altogether unimpressed with Wesley's enthusiasm. But facts were facts to Schwartz.

"Listen to me," he began, mopping his bald head, which was divided from a cherubic face by the thickest, heaviest eyebrows in Manhattan. "This is year eighteen ninety-seven, ain't it; with not many more months to run?"

"What difference—"

"Does the date make? A hell of a lot, let me tell you. You know the terms of the concession that there Napoleon Wyse obtained from the Colombian government?"

"No, but—"

"You see! You're looking at the Panama Canal from only one point of view. Can it be dug?"

"I say it can."

"In how long?"

"A few years, of course. Ten or so, I'd say."

"You'd say ten! Don't you know that Wyse's concession, dated eighteen seventy-eight, called for the canal to be completed within seventeen years of that date? That is, five years for organization and survey, and twelve for construction. That concession was due to expire two years ago."

"I thought the new company obtained an extension."

"Yes, for ten years from October, eighteen ninety-four. That leaves seven years to run. How's about your ten years?"

"I'm sure the Colombian government would grant a further extension."

"You think so!" Schwartz beamed, and patted Wesley's shoulder. "Look, mister, I'm just a plain hard-boiled businessman, so I don't believe in fairy tales. Do you know what will happen in seven years' time if the concession isn't renewed? The concession, the half-dug canal, all the equipment—the whole shebang will fall into Colombia's lap for nothing. Do you think she is going to hand all that over to the U.S. government with a smile and a friendly, 'Help yourself, Uncle Sam. We aren't interested in money—' "

"Well, for a price—"

This time Schwartz bored Wesley's shoulder with a rigid forefinger. "And what's the Panama Company willing to sell out for? More than one hundred million dollars. Are we suckers to pay out money all over the world when we could build one much more cheaply in Nicaragua?"

"But could we, Mr. Schwartz? The Nicaragua route's longer."

The businessman winked a fat-lidded eye. "But it's a talking point, ain't it, mister?"

11

AS THE HACKNEY cab ambled across Market Place, Wesley looked at St. James's Church, in its isolated dignity, and saw the mellowed timber structure in a new light. Compared with the florid Spanish architecture of the Panama cathedrals, and more especially with the aggressive modernity of New York's churches, it had the simplicity and integrity of the sturdy faith to which it had been dedicated; the charm of centuries; and, above all, a homeliness which reflected the serenity of its cultural background. Comforted by its quiet welcome he slipped his arm about Dulcie's slim waist.

"Feeling good, honey?"

"Why?"

"See St. James's—that means we're home. Home! Sounds wonderful, doesn't it?"

"*I* haven't been away for months," she reminded him.

He nodded. "You know it's quite true about appreciating home best when one's been away from it for a long time. Especially if one's been to foreign places. It makes me feel good, just to look about me. Good—and safe—and thankful to return."

"You seemed happy enough in New York," she pouted.

"So I was, darling. We've had a wonderful week together. But now— well, it seems even more wonderful to be back in the old home town."

"It isn't your home town. You were born in New York."

"I know, but Father's family have lived here for several generations. Besides, Mother was born in Boston, and lived there until Grandfather moved his home to New York when she was eight years old. Father came back to Providence when I was six. Don't you feel glad to be back, too?"

She was so long in replying that he had to repeat the question, this time with anxiety. "Aren't you, darling?"

"Of course, but—"

"But!" he repeated.

"Well, dear, a house doesn't always mean to a woman what it does to a man. A man leaves it six days out of seven, so of course he's glad to get back to it. A woman is glad to get away from it sometimes—for a change." She sighed. "It was so lovely to be in New York."

Although he could appreciate her reasoning it pained him to think that she was as reluctant to return to Providence as her attitude suggested.

She went on hesitatingly, "Wes, darling—" She paused, to nibble the lobe of his ear with her lovely teeth.

72

He grinned, for he recognized the opening gambit; she was about to wheedle him.

"Well, sweetheart?"

The cab had crossed the bridge over the river, passed across Main Street, climbed up College Street, and turned left into Benefit Street North before she spoke again.

"Isn't it about time we thought of moving?"

"Moving!" The question startled him, for this was the first time Dulcie had ever spoken of moving; and certainly he had never given the matter thought. Why should they move? he reflected. Did they not live in Benefit Street North, one of Providence's nicest, most gracious neighborhoods? He gazed about him as they jogged along the elm-lined street; at the Beckwith House, and the adjoining stables; at the First Baptist Meeting House opposite; then at the Golden Ball Inn, at the Old Arsenal, at Hogg's private garden and greenhouse.

Still he did not speak, for as they approached the Samuel Chace House, and all about him, and ahead, he saw lovely houses, spic and span, and set, many of them, amid lawns that were smoother than a billiard table, and shaded by lovely trees, he reflected upon how fortunate they were to be living in this street, even though their home was one of the smallest and most inconspicuous, situated at the far end, almost opposite Olney Street. Why, as often as not, whenever he walked home after a day's work, he reveled in its subdued silence; in the loveliness of its gardens; in the sight of the children who roller-skated down Jenckes hill, so skillful in their balance, so merry with infectious laughter, and yet so naturally dignified in their respect for neighbors and elders.

They passed George Washington John Adams Lafayette, who was sweeping the sidewalk and garden of the Murphy home—for the Murphys, with eight children to care for, could not afford a permanent gardener. Old Lafayette recognized Dulcie and Wesley. His dark face beamed at them as he swept an old hat off his gray head; and he called out in his friendly voice, "Welcome back to Providence, Mr. Adam. Ah hope you had a good trip." There was not one resident along the length of Benefit Street whom old Layfayette did not know, and greet as they passed him by.

"Fine, thank you," Wesley called back. "But it's nice to be back."

Lafayette grinned, then off came his hat again, for the Hon. Charles Warren Lippitt was going south in his victoria.

"You haven't answered, Wes darling," Dulcie prompted.

"I've never thought of moving, honey. I shouldn't care to leave Benefit Street."

She nibbled his ear. "Silly!" she reproved. "Nor should I. But our house is almost the smallest in the street."

"Well, it's only thanks to Great-aunt Bessie leaving it to me in her will

73

that we are able to live in Benefit Street at all. I couldn't have afforded to buy a home here otherwise."

"Not in the past, but now that you are going to become Mr. Ackermann's partner it would not be right for such an important man to live in such a poky little house."

He laughed. "Perhaps you would like me to try and buy the Doir Mansion." He pointed to a large house that fronted on Bowen Street. "Or perhaps the Crocker house." This time he indicated the stately red-brick house with lawns and terraces which stood next to the Doir Mansion.

She pouted. "Now you are being a meany, laughing at me just because I want to live in a bigger house, and have nice pictures and nice furniture and a garden with a lawn—"

"And a gardener or two to look after it; and three servants to look after the house; and maybe one of those newfangled electric broughams, with a chauffeur to drive it."

"Mr. Ackermann has a gardener and two servants."

"After all, he is the boss," Wesley dryly remarked.

"So will you be, one day."

"*One* day I might, if I do well during the next ten years. Until then, honey, you'll have to put up with our present home." They passed by the old gardens attached to the home of Mrs. George Owen, and terraced uphill a full block. The Seckel pears had ripened, and in the speckled sunlight the sheen of their glossy skins looked too waxlike to be real. God! It *was* good to be in Benefit Street again, even if one did live at the less-fashionable end, in a small, aging six-room house.

The absence which makes the heart grow fonder found a confirmed victim in Wesley. With the memory still fresh of the lonely months he had spent in Panama, his love for Dulcie perceptibly deepened. For the first time in his life he appreciated the spiritual significance of marriage. Because her presence gave unsuspected depths to life—an intensity, a reponsibility, an emotional richness—he realized how utterly dual nature was, and how unnatural was the solitary.

He realized, too, that the months in Panama had bridged the gap between the inconsequence of youth, and the responsibility of manhood. Life—love—home—marriage—all these words had a different, richer meaning for him. No longer was the house in Benefit Street just a shelter in which to eat and sleep. It was a home, he found, whose architecture was steeped in the tradition of Colonial days; whose rooms were reminiscent of generations of Adams who had lived and loved and died there; whose whispering murmurs were inspired by the inexorable cycle of life—birth, marriage, death. He ceased to regard Dulcie, with the possessive pride of honeymoon days, as a beautiful decoration, as someone to have fun with, or someone to welcome one home after a busy day. Now she was his mate, sanctified by solemn vows to be the repository of his seed. When he took her into his arms on the night of their return, and softly kissed her lips into warmth, he did so with the reverence of dedication.

That week end was the most contented of his life, but it passed all too quickly. On Monday morning he returned to the offices of H. C. Ackermann Company.

Ackermann received him with a boisterous welcome, and a moist handshake.

"Welcome back to Providence, Adam. Sit down and have a cigar. I don't need to ask you whether you've been successful. I've heard from Cromwell. He is more than satisfied with your reports."

The sleek, dark eyebrows twitched. "You've changed. I don't mean that your cheeks are leaner or browner than they were, or that you're looking extremely well. Of course you are. That was to be expected. I mean, you're older."

"I feel older, Mr. Ackermann. I don't mean physically. Mentally."

"How come?"

"Through meeting nature at close quarters, I suppose. Sounds trite, but—"

"I know what you mean. I felt like that when I saw Niagara Falls for the first time. And the Grand Canyon. Yosemite, too."

Wesley nodded. "Something along those lines. It's her vastness, her ruthlessness, her challenge to mankind. She seems to mock one, make one feel puny—but determined to get the better of her if its humanly possible."

"That's how you feel about the canal, Cromwell tells me."

"Yes, Mr. Ackermann. It can be done—if terms can be agreed with Colombia."

"Whether it will ever be finished or not, the trip should have been a wonderful experience for you, Adam, and of inestimable value. And now—" Ackermann leaned back in his chair, and slipped his thumbs under his armpits. "I don't know whether you want your old job back or not, but of course it's still open if you do."

"My old job— But, Mr. Ackermann, sometime back you led me to believe—"

"Well, speak up."

"You promised me a partnership once I had had experience. I've had that—"

"*Promised,* Adam?" Ackermann sharply questioned.

"Well, half-promised. At least, that's what I understood."

"Do you remember my words?"

"Yes. You said that after I had had sufficient practical experience you would favorably consider making me a junior partner."

"I said that, did I?" Ackermann nodded his bullet-shaped head, then began to clean his glasses. His voice became more genial. "A promise is a

75

promise, Adam, and now is as good a moment as any other to discuss the matter."

Wesley sighed with relief. For one horrible moment he had believed that the other man had intended to go back on his word. But he had merely been indulging his ponderous humor, it seemed.

"Yes, Mr. Ackermann," he agreed with eagerness.

"The first point to be settled is, how much capital are you prepared to put up?"

An agonizing silence. "Capital, Mr. Ackermann!" Wesley began. "I didn't think—"

"Think what?"

"That—that the question of capital was involved."

"You mean, you thought I would give you a junior partnership for nothing?"

"I have no capital—"

"Come, come, Adam. You certainly did not think enough. My father set up here in Providence fifty years ago, when he was about twenty-five years of age. By the time he retired in my favor, eighteen years ago, he had established a reputation second to none in New England. I flatter myself, not only that I have just as good a reputation but also on being twice as successful, financially, as he was. Do you seriously look upon me as a philanthropist willing to *give away* a substantial part of the good will my father and I between us have built up? Have you no capital at all?"

"Only the money saved from the Panama trip, and my house in Benefit Street. I might raise a mortgage—"

Ackermann made a discouraging gesture. "Chicken feed, Adam. Besides, I am not in need of a partner. I am neither in need of capital nor additional business. With the help of a paid staff I can handle all the business that comes my way. Of course, if ever you are prepared to invest capital, say fifty thousand dollars or more, I'll keep my word. A promise is a promise—"

Wesley swallowed. "How can I ever hope to raise that much on my present salary?"

"That is your affair, of course, Adam. Meanwhile, your old position remains open, as I've already said. But if you prefer to try elsewhere for a partnership, I should understand." He held out a moist hand. "No hard feelings I hope, Adam. Take today off to think matters over, and let me know your decision tomorrow."

There could be only one decision, of course. Wesley knew that even before he left the office. But the walk home was nonetheless an unhappy experience. After his high hopes of the past week, and particularly his mood of exaltation during the week end, this blow was all the more bitter.

Aside from the rebuff to his pride, he was more concerned on Dulcie's account than on his own. He had been happy enough in the past, living in the small house Great-aunt Bessie had left him, and had found his salary, if not generous enough to keep him in luxury, at least adequate. But the week end, blissful and happy though it had been, would always remain a barrier to prevent their looking back over their shoulders and remaining satisfied with that standard. Dulcie had made it plain to him that she had been in no petulant mood when speaking to him of her wish to move into a larger house. It seemed that she had been mulling the matter over ever since his departure for Panama. For about that time Elizabeth van Thal had moved into one of the larger houses on the west side of Benefit Street, not a stone's throw from the Chapin House—and not many years previously Elizabeth had had to be content with living on the west bank of Providence River. And what Dulcie wanted she should have, if it were possible for him to give it. What was the worth of love if it didn't inspire a man to give his mate everything she wanted?

His steps grew slower as he neared home. He dreaded having to tell Dulcie his news. In his imagination he saw a pained look spread across her face, and tears gather in the corners of her eyes. Twice during their marriage he had seen her cry, and was not able to forget. He had once looked into a dog's eyes as the animal's owner raised a gun to shoot it. He hadn't been able to forget that sight, either. Sometimes it still haunted him, though it had happened nearly twelve years ago. Dulcie's eyes, when she cried, always reminded him of the dog's; they were so reproachful, so hurt—

He found her in bed, still asleep, but as his shadow passed across her eyes she opened them.

"Wes darling!" The eyes widened with astonishment. "What are you doing here? I thought you were going to the office today?"

He sat down heavily on the rocker. "So did I. Ackermann told me to have the day off."

"You've seen him?" Her expression reflected her excitement as she sat up in bed, pulling the bedclothes well round her as she did so. "What did he say about the partnership? Please tell me quickly, Wes darling. Don't tease me. I'm too anxious."

"He said plenty. And wants plenty. Fifty thousand dollars."

"What's he want all that money for?"

"A junior partnership."

She looked puzzled. "I don't understand what you mean, Wes dear. You know what a silly I am about such things."

"If I want a partnership I have to invest fifty thousand dollars in the firm."

"Oh!" Her lips quivered; her eyes grew moist. "But you haven't all that money." she added naïvely, "Have you?"

"Of course I haven't. Not even five thousand."

77

"Then—then aren't you to be a partner?"

"Just that!" he exclaimed bitterly. "I'm not."

"Oh, Wes!" The tears gathered, and began to overflow. "You must have made a mistake. Mr. Ackermann has been so kind to me all the time you were away."

"There's no mistake, darling. But Ackermann has offered me my old job back."

"But that means—we won't be able to move—and I won't have help—" Her tear-stained face pleaded with him to contradict her.

"I'm afraid so, honey," he answered gently.

"Oh!" She turned away from him and faced the wall. He saw her shoulders shake.

So Wesley went back to H. C. Ackermann Company, and after a time settled down to the ordinary routine. With one exception. When he read the newspapers he no longer restricted his interest to the sports pages. He searched the columns for news of any developments in government plans for an interoceanic canal, and read every word he found with an avidity which exasperated Dulcie who could not understand his interest in a silly canal. He could not entirely understand it himself. He was not likely to share in its construction, whether in Nicaragua or in Panama. But he did know that he wanted to see the canal built. He wanted, as a citizen of the United States, to have a share, even at second-hand, in the thrill and excitement of challenging nature, and eventually, in the proud satisfaction of success. For he did not doubt that, once started, the canal would eventually be built. There would be too much at stake for the project not to succeed. It would *have* to succeed. The world could not be allowed to scoff at Uncle Sam, and call him a quitter— And of the two localities he desperately wanted Panama to be chosen.

12

WITHIN A FEW months of his return to Providence the question of an interoceanic canal assumed a new and terrible importance for the American people. On February 24, 1898, Spain declared war on the United States at a moment when the battleship *Oregon* was in the Pacific, sixteen thousand miles from the place where it was most wanted— in the North Atlantic!

Interest in the *Oregon*'s dash for the most likely scene of action was intensified when it was learned that the Spanish fleet, consisting of four armored cruisers and some torpedo-boat destroyers, had sailed from Cape Verde Islands to challenge the American fleet. Although the Americans had more capital ships available, some of these had to be used for blockading Cuba, and the *Oregon* was sorely needed to deter the Spaniards from pouncing on a depleted American fleet.

Next to the war as a whole, the progress of the *Oregon* became the most popular item of news, both in conversation and in newspaper columns. Daily bulletins appeared in the press, together with maps and charts of its journey. When it was realized that it would have to travel south the length of the South American continent, and then north, an even greater distance up the east coast—besides possibly running the gauntlet en route of the Spanish fleet—before she could join Rear-Admiral Sampson's squadron at Key West, public opinion was alarmed.

Simultaneous with this concern for the *Oregon*'s progress, interest in the question of an oceanic canal became widespread when it was appreciated that, had such a canal existed, the battleship would have been saved some nine thousand miles, and what was even more important, more than two weeks steaming time—time which could make all the difference between winning and losing a war. Before long, articles began to appear in the newspapers demanding not only that an interoceanic canal be constructed as a vital measure of self-defense, but also that such a canal must be owned, operated, and fortified by the United States government. These articles created a wave of patriotic emotion which swept the country from coast to coast. The time for procrastination was past. A canal there must be at the earliest possible moment.

At first Wesley was delighted, and frequently wondered whether Cromwell was quietly congratulating Fate for the hand she had taken in his schemes. But later Wesley realized that the intervention of the war was not altogether an unmixed blessing so far as Panama was concerned. When cables from Europe reported a marked French sympathy with the Spanish cause, an indignation at France and everything French flared up in the States. More and more the words "interoceanic canal" became synonymous with the Nicaragua Canal. Not one newspaper article in a hundred had envisaged the canal anywhere else; and the public adopted a similar outlook.

In Providence, Wesley was laughed at when he tried to argue in favor of Panama.

"You're prejudiced because you had a fine holiday there at somebody else's expense," Matthew Bartholdt stated with an amiable grin, thereby summarizing in a few words the opinion generally held by Wesley's friends. "Good luck to you. Wish I could do the same. Then you'd find me on your side. But don't think we're going to pull French chestnuts out of the fire, because we're not."

79

"But the French have sunk more than three hundred million dollars in the canal—"

"That sum includes seventy-eight millions spent in Paris," Bartholdt pointed out.

"All right, but that still leaves two hundred million spent in Panama. Work and equipment worth that much must be of some use to anyone who carries on."

"Not for us, I hope. We couldn't trust any French workmanship we took over—"

Apart from an interest in the war that was inspired more by excitement than by anxiety as to its eventual result, life in Benefit Street flowed on its normal unruffled course. Its residents lived the serene but full life of the leisured and professional classes. Winter and summer evenings alike there was usually some social function to draw them together: by jingling sleighs to the ice-bound ponds at Roger Williams Park to watch the skaters; to one of Professor Crosby's Shakespeare readings; or on a summer's eve, in an open victoria to Pawtucket, on the Seekonk River; to vespers at the University; to the sidewalk outside Judge Durfee's lawn, to listen to the itinerant German Band playing selections from Wagner's operas; or to the chrysanthemum show at Infantry Hall; or to amateur theatricals at Mr. Angell's auditorium; or to private views at the School of Design; or—joyful and rare occasions—to Boston, on a clothes-buying expedition, or even to New York. And when there was no public function to attend, there were always the more intimate, less formal affairs; Mrs. Brett's At Home, or a musical evening at Professor Braunsweiger's house, or a concert at the Arion Club....

After the first pangs of acute disappointment had dulled, Wesley became resigned and only reflected upon the long-cherished but vanished partnership when he surprised Dulcie in a pensive mood. At such times she would rest her embroidery on her lap, and gaze moist eyed out of the window at one of the larger houses farther down the street; soon her tiny mouth would pout, and then quiver. Whenever that happened he knew her thoughts were on the larger home and the hired help that she so passionately coveted; and he would chide himself for having failed her, and resolve to grasp success that he might give her her heart's desire.

He adored her; most of all on Sundays, when they walked along Benefit Street to St. John's Church. Then he felt at his proudest when he saw tall silk hats dipping to her with a flourish that was inspired by more than formal greeting. There was homage to her beauty in the graceful gesture, a masculine interest, and, where the younger men were concerned, frank admiration and envy. The stiffer, half-bows of the women were equally pleasing to him, for he knew that the younger beauties of the neighborhood were resentful of the fact that she was their queen.

Not even her unwilling "subjects" could deny her flawless beauty, her

80

exquisite perfection. As she walked beside him, the top of her flowered hat barely reaching to his shoulder, she resembled a dainty doll into whom some kindly genie had blown the breath of life. And if sometimes a sympathetic feminine gaze rested on her escort longer than was polite or discreet, the fault was indirectly Dulcie's. Wesley's glowing possessive pride in her loveliness reflected itself in his eyes and in the poise of his head, and gave a suggestion of arrogance to his long, lean face.

As summer progressed these Sundays mornings came to represent highlights of happiness. Dulcie's sad periods grew more frequent, and less silent.

"Wesley, dearest," she would whisper in his ear after nibbling the lobe, "the Rimington house is still empty." The Rimington house was far down Benefit Street, almost at the bend near the Angell residence. It had five bedrooms, a large attic; three reception rooms; and stood in a garden famed for its roses.

"I know. I pass it every day."

"Maud Matilda told me they are willing to sell it cheap."

He laughed. "Something cheap in Rimington eyes could represent a small fortune to many people."

"Really cheap," she insisted.

He tried to remain patient with her; she never had had any idea of figures. "Darling, we haven't the capital to buy it however little it costs— and it would cost plenty!"

"Couldn't you sell this house?"

"I could, but it wouldn't buy a third of the Rimington house."

"Couldn't you raise a mortgage on the balance?"

"Probably—if I were willing to pay a thousand dollars a year interest."

"You could manage that, Wes dear."

"Suppose I could, honey, that's just about all."

"Well, then!" she exclaimed in triumph. "Wouldn't it be worth having the Rimington house for a thousand dollars a year?"

"And where would the money come from to repay the capital?"

"What capital?"

"The capital, the money advanced to buy the house."

"You said it would cost only a thousand dollars a year."

He kissed her. "We'll have to wish harder—" he temporized.

She returned to the attack one week later. "We've an invitation to a garden party," she told him. Her eyes shone brightly. "Guess who?"

"Ackermann."

"Oh! He told you."

"This morning. Wanted to know if we could come. I told him yes."

"Wes darling, do you think it means he is going to offer you a partnership after all?"

81

"It might have meant it if we were the only people from the office to be asked."

"Some of the others, too—"

"All of 'em. It's a staff party, plus some lesser clients."

She pouted as the tears gathered. "And I thought—"

"Ackermann doesn't change that easily. He's not the type."

"Why don't you ask him again about a partnership—quickly, while the Rimington house is still for sale?"

"I just told you. He doesn't change that easily."

"He must have been in a bad temper the morning you asked him. I'm sure he thinks well of you. He was *so* nice to me while you were in Panama, taking me out to keep me from becoming moody in your absence."

"Sounds more like he thinks well of *you*, honey." He frowned. "Was he often solicitous of your loneliness?"

She pouted. "Not often enough. You know how I *love* going places."

"But how often?"

"Never more than once a week."

He stiffened. "You never told me, Dulcie."

She looked at him, wide eyed. "I did, too. I wrote you about the Dionne garden fete, and the special Paderewski concert at Boston."

It was true. He had forgotten. "But you never said anything about his taking you out once a week, regularly."

"I didn't think you would be interested. Besides, I knew you wouldn't mind, so long as I was happy for a few hours."

Her naïve explanation, and above all the frank innocence of her china-blue eyes, reassured him and allayed his suddenly aroused suspicions. He felt contemptibly mean for even the fleeting thought.

He slipped an arm about her waist. "Of course I didn't mind, honey. All I want in life is for you to be happy."

She untidied his hair, and brushed the tip of his nose with her lips. "Then you will speak to him again? Promise?"

Because he loved her so he promised, though unwillingly. "But I insist upon waiting for the right moment," he added.

That meant waiting another two weeks, and then the moment proved not to be the right one.

"No, Adam," Ackermann curtly replied. "I cannot reconsider my decision. You must know that business has been slack of late. I cannot afford the luxury of a junior partner to share what profits there are, and it is useless for you to continue hoping that I will."

August brought news of the end of the war with Spain; but the agitation continued for an interoceanic canal at Nicaragua. So far as the people were concerned there was to be no repetition of the *Oregon* affair. In the

82

unhappy event of another war, the U.S. fleet must be able to move freely between ocean and ocean.

One day Uncle Bill visited Providence, and stayed the night. They were sitting round the fire, for the first sign of the coming winter had made the night chilly.

During a lull in the conversation a crooked grin passed across the tired face.

"By the way, your friend Cromwell is recently back from France. Did you know he had been over there for more than six weeks?"

"No. I've had nothing more to do with him since the trip to Panama."

"I suppose not. The people in Paris have raised their limit to the sky, so he's preparing to bring his artillery into action. Now ask me how I know all this." There was a twinkle in Uncle Bill's weary eyes, and an air of suppressed excitement about him, that was at variance with his normally dry, disillusioned manner.

"All right. Give."

"He's approached me. He liked some of the articles I've been writing in favor of Panama for the canal."

"To write for him?"

"Right you are, and then some! He wants me to organize a press bureau for the preparation, publication, and distribution of articles throughout the country. And a compilation of the diplomatic history of the canal scheme, which he reckons will run at least to a thousand pages."

"You're going to?"

"I'd like to see anything stop me. Son, this is my chance. If the name of William Godwin isn't known from New Orleans to Seattle before I'm through it won't be my fault. And it'll be thanks to you—"

"To Wes! Why?" Dulcie asked, wonderingly.

"It was he who put me wise about the advantages of the Panama over the Nicaragua route, my dear." He turned back to Wesley. "And that's where you come in, son, if you're interested."

"Me?"

"Sure. I'm a writer, not a surveyor or engineer. The articles must be written under expert supervision if they are to be of any use. Cromwell has already commissioned General Abbot, and Mr. Corthell—the engineer—"

Wesley nodded his familiarity with the name.

"Now he wants you, to deal with the surveying. What do you say—" As if Uncle Bill need have asked!

From that time forward Wesley saw far more of Uncle Bill. Inspired by long-thwarted ambition, Bill Godwin worked like a maniac. During the months he built up a nationwide organization to feed the press of every State. Meanwhile, the New York office turned out an enormous number of both technical and popular articles which sought to emphasize the advantages of the Panama, and the disadvantages of the Nicaragua route; dealt with correspondence, held interviews, conducted research work, both in New York and in Washington. There, too, in the Capitol, Cromwell began the work of lobbying.

But progress was slow. Public opinion remained solidly in favor of the Nicaragua route. All through the country, shipping interests, boards of trade, and commercial organizations continued to pass resolutions calling upon Congress to build the Nicaragua Canal as a matter of public safety. Always Nicaragua. Petitions to the same effect poured into Washington. And this opinion was shared by members of both parties. As one newspaper writer said, never had such unanimity been so forcibly expressed.

In political circles activity was even more marked. When the pro-Nicaragua group made preparations to force a bill through the coming session, Cromwell countered by drawing up a memorial in favor of Panama, and arranged with Secretary Hay officially to present the memorial, together with a technical report, to President McKinley before Congress reassembled.

Copies of these important documents Uncle Bill released simultaneously to the press over the entire country. But the Nicaragua group were too well intrenched. Not one leading newspaper agreed to publish either the documents in their entirety, or extracts from them. Uncle Bill was in despair, and began to wonder whether he had not jumped from the frying pan into the fire of adversity. How long, he asked Wesley, would Cromwell remain tolerant of failure? Urged by this fear, he tried new tactics, and persuaded General Abbot to write an article suitable for the popular magazines. This important contribution he offered in turn to magazines of good standing, but also without success.

On the other hand, articles on the Nicaragua route were welcomed by the press, as was also any material which might help to defeat the tiny pro-Panama group. When the news reached the States that the Colombian Congress had refused to grant the New Panama Company any extension of existing concessions the press pounced upon this item with the avidity of a terrier worrying a rat, and headlined the news. The result was most unfortunate. The few well-wishers that Cromwell and Uncle Bill had between them managed to win for the cause were speedily lost again.

Wesley happened to be in New York that day, and was with Uncle Bill at the press bureau. The newspaperman was glum, but not more so than Cromwell, who arrived five minutes after Wesley. He recognized Wesley at once.

"Good morning, Mr. Adam. Thanks for your continued support and help. I appreciate your good will." All this at rapid speed. He turned to the newspaperman.

"Well?"

"It's not true, I take it, Mr. Cromwell?"

"Of course not. What do you suggest?"

"Send a cable to your man at Bogotá to send an official correction which I can circulate. I'll do my best to see that it is published."

"Your best—"

"You don't know newspapermen if you think they'll publish the corrective without pressure."

"You're not losing heart—"

"Look, mister—" Uncle Bill eyed his employer with a cold stare. "You got me out of the rut I've been wanting to get out of all my life. Since I've been here I've found things out about myself that I never suspected. That I enjoy a fight, f'rinstance. We've got a hell of a job ahead of us, selling the Panama route to Uncle Sam, but, by God! I'll enjoy every moment of it, and if we don't win through in the end, it won't be my fault."

"We've got to win. There's a hundred million dollars at stake."

Uncle Bill whistled. "That makes it more exciting than penny ante. See here, mister, I don't guarantee to get that correction in—we haven't had time yet to establish our contacts—but give me time—"

"All right. I trust you." Cromwell rose and shot out a slender white hand. Then he turned to Wesley. "How is the partnership working out, Mr. Adam?"

"It isn't, sir. When it came to the point—"

"Ah!" Cromwell nodded his understanding. "Keep in touch with me. Through Mr. Godwin here, if you like. Good day to you both." He walked quickly out of the room.

Uncle Bill looked at Wesley, jerked his thumb toward the door, and grinned. "That man's dynamite. I wouldn't take a bet on the Nicaragua route—"

But Uncle Bill didn't know then what he was to know some days later. On December 5, when Congress reassembled, President McKinley officially recommended the building of the Nicaragua Canal under American control.

13

TWO DAYS AFTER Congress had reassembled Ackermann sent for Wesley.

"Morning, Adam. Sit down. How is progress on the Tauber factory project?"

"Still having trouble working out how to dispose of the water which

drains on to the site, Mr. Ackermann. Mr. Williams won't co-operate—
he's the dominant landowner."

"And the Martingale Corporation building?"

"Well in hand; everything straightforward so far."

"There's nothing that couldn't safely be left to Macdonald?"

"No, sir, but—"

"Well?"

"Don't you want—am I not to see the two projects through?"

"That's up to you." Ackermann tapped the desk in front of him. "I've
had a letter this morning from Sullivan and Cromwell, asking me whether
I would be willing to grant you leave of absence."

"I know nothing of any such suggestion—"

"I know. Mr. Cromwell has made that clear in his letter. Are you interested in working for him again on the Panama project?"

"Well, sir, I want to see the Panama route chosen. I'm convinced it's a
better route than Nicaragua, but—"

"And I'm sure it isn't; however that's your affair."

"And your two projects?"

"For the sake of having a canal built somewhere I'm willing to put up
with temporary inconvenience. Particularly with work slacking off. Anyway, there's no need to make a decision until you've talked the matter over
with Mr. Cromwell. He would like to see you at Mr. Godwin's office
tomorrow afternoon at three."

"It's very generous of you, Mr. Ackermann—"

Ackermann waved him away. "That's all now, Adam." He added,
ungraciously, "I'm not being entirely generous. I shall be saved your
salary as long as Mr. Cromwell is paying it."

Fifteen minutes before the appointment with Cromwell, Wesley went
to see Uncle Bill. The newspaperman's face was glummer than ever; his
sparse gray hair was ruffled. He chewed the end of a half-smoked cigar
which looked as if it had been out for a long time.

"Hullo, son. So your boss let you come? No trouble?"

"None. He seemed glad to see the back of me."

"Poppycock; You're a darned good surveyor, my boy. Up and coming.
Ackermann's no fool. He wouldn't let go of you without good reason."

Wesley's face crinkled in a broad grin. "Thanks for the few kind
words—"

"Kind words nothing, my boy! Cromwell has had reports on your work
in New England, believe me, and reckons you're pretty good at your job."

"Then what's Ackermann's reason for letting me go?"

Uncle Bill shrugged. "I wouldn't be knowing, but no doubt there's a
tie-up somewhere between him and Cromwell. Cromwell has a finger in
many pies."

86

"What am I wanted for, Uncle Bill?"

"Can't say. Hell's broken loose—"

"The President's message?"

"Sure! But let's leave that for Cromwell. How's Dulcie? Still hankering after a larger house?

"Yes," Wesley admitted hesitatingly, for he felt it to be disloyal to Dulcie to say that much to a third party—or even to himself! Though Uncle Bill was one of the family in a sense.

Uncle Bill shook his head. "Women!" he muttered with scorn. "Never satisfied."

As usual the dynamic Cromwell was punctual. He bustled in and wasted as little time as possible on formalities. He soon asked, "Well, Mr. Adam, what do you think of the President's message to Congress?"

"It wasn't very—helpful, sir."

"Helpful!" The thin lips were pressed together in grim tightness. "There's worse to follow. I've just had news that Senator Morgan is making a speech in the Senate announcing his determination to force the passage of the Nicaragua Canal Bill—"

"Old stuff!" Uncle Bill muttered.

"Wait! He's gone on to accuse the representatives of the Panama Canal of being in league with the transcontinental railroads to prevent the American people having an American canal through Nicaragua."

"Ha! Ha! Ha!" Uncle Bill exclaimed heavily.

Again the thin lips tightened. "Some of the mud will stick, Mr. Godwin. The public will believe that story, because they would like to believe it. They are sheep, and because the best-known men in Congress support Nicaragua they do the same. They haven't the intelligence to think for themselves. Morgan's speech will do us incalculable harm."

Uncle Bill was anxious. "You'll fight back, make those congressmen eat their words?"

Cromwell was long in replying. At last he turned to Wesley.

"That partly depends upon you, Mr. Adam. Do you still remain of the same opinion, that given sufficient time and capital the canal could be built at Panama?" He raised a warning finger. "Wait! Before you answer reflect carefully upon the immense importance of the project. It is not something to be entered into lightheartedly If the United States should start to build a canal and fail it would be one of the blackest episodes in our history. Our prestige, and our national economy would suffer alike. Once started we could not afford to stop halfway, as a private company could do—and has done—both in Panama and in Nicaragua. On the other hand, do not hesitate to answer frankly. I am not paying you the compliment of relying solely upon your judgment. But you are a young man with courage and high hopes, qualities which may well be needed before the canal is finished."

Silence followed this long speech. Wesley swallowed with embarrassment, and almost regretted having accepted Cromwell's invitation to
the meeting. It was ridiculous to place so much responsibility on his
shoulders—

Cromwell's dark eyes were keenly watching the changing expression on
Wesley's face. His tight lips loosened in a sardonic smile.

"The future of the United States will not depend upon your conclusions, Mr. Adam, so do not look quite so worried. I have another, less
complimentary reason for seeking your opinion."

The acid comment restored Wesley's mental equilibrium. Instead of
reflecting upon the consequences of his decision, he concentrated upon the
task itself. His thoughts traveled back to the months he had spent in
Panama. Item by item he considered the obstacles and one by one he
thought of means of overcoming them. All but two.

"I'm nervous of two great difficulties, sir—"

"And those?"

"The first, disease."

A gesture of impatience. "That does not concern you, Mr. Adam. So
far as the mechanics of building a canal are concerned disease does not
enter into the question."

"But it does, sir. An army of laborers will be needed to build the canal.
Without sufficient labor to work it, machinery is useless."

"Your second objection—"

"Is essentially an engineering problem. Frankly, sir, I am afraid of
slides at Culebra Cut. I talked with French engineers on the spot, and
they told me that slides had entirely upset their calculations. Of course
they might decrease if we got down to rock strata. On the other hand,
they could get worse."

"I don't quite understand what happens."

"As a boy did you ever try to dig a channel in sand so as to let the sea
flow along it?"

"Ah! The deeper one digs the more the sides fall in and fill up the
bottom?"

"Yes, sir."

"Even if our calculations include the risk of having to excavate the entire
mountain, you would still advise the attempt?"

Wesley breathed deeply, then swallowed. "Yes, sir, where national security is concerned no cost is too great."

Cromwell nodded, satisfied. "We shall have no difficulty in persuading
the American people to agree with that sentiment, Mr. Adam, but unfortunately it applies equally to the Nicaragua route. Have you studied the
survey reports on the Nicaragua route which you took back to Providence
with you last week?"

"Yes, sir."

88

"Then tell me, in words the public could understand, the advantages of the Panama route over Nicaragua."

"The proposed route by way of Nicaragua is from Greytown on the Caribbean to Lake Nicaragua by way of the San Juan River, a distance of about one hundred miles; seventy miles across the lake to the mouth of the Las Lajac River; along the Las Lajac valley, and then fifteen to seventeen miles through the valley of the Rio Grande to the Pacific town of Brito.

"The reports suggest utilizing the whole length of the San Juan River, by blasting the rapids that obstruct it; and at approximately the halfway point along the San Juan, to deepen it by diverting the San Carlos into it. Above this point a dam would maintain the river water on a level with the lake. The summit level would be, according to season, from one hundred and four feet to one hundred and ten feet above sea level, reached by five locks on the Caribbean side, and four on the Pacific.

"The total length of the transisthmian journey would be about one hundred and eighty-six miles, of which forty-seven would be deep water in Lake Nicaragua. Of the remainder, seventeen miles of river water could be used without alteration; this would leave more than one hundred and twenty miles of canal construction.

"The distance from ocean to ocean by way of Nicaragua would therefore be some hundred and thirty miles more than by way of Panama—"

"One hundred and thirty! A day's journey! Nearly twenty-four hours' steaming time! The saving of a day's time and a day's fuel is a point to appeal to every shipowner throughout the world—"

"Throughout the world—except the United States, sir."

"Why should we prove the exception?"

"Because a journey from New York to San Francisco would be more than three hundred and seventy miles longer by way of Panama than by Nicaragua—nearly three times the distance that would be saved by the shorter canal route."

The attorney angrily thumped Uncle Bill's desk with his flat hand. "Tell me the disadvantages of the Nicaragua route—there must be some—"

"Several, sir. The first is the lack of railroad facilities. At Panama a railroad is at hand for the disposal of excavated material, and other purposes. At Nicaragua many miles of railroad would have to be built, an unnecessary waste of time and expense, in comparison—"

"With the Panama route? Undoubtedly. Go on, Mr. Adam. This is the information I want."

"Above all, sir, a Nicaragua canal would be subject to the constant risk of damage, even of being totally wrecked by volcanic eruption."

Cromwell's eyes glowed. "You have satisfied me, Mr. Adam." He chuckled. "Totally wrecked by volcanic eruption! That shall be the pivot

89

on which to base the campaign ahead of us." His manner became brusque and formal.

"These are my plans for fighting the Nicaragua interests, gentlemen. First of all we must attack it on political grounds. I and my colleagues in the Wall Street office by lobbying; you, Mr. Godwin, through the press. In eighteen fifty a treaty was signed between our country and Great Britain, known as the Clayton-Bulwer Treaty, by which neither party should obtain and maintain for itself any exclusive control of any waterway across the isthmus between North and South America. We must bring to the attention of the people, as well as the administration, the fact that the Nicaragua scheme, provided for by bills under consideration, will be contrary to the Clayton-Bulwer Treaty, and bound to result in difficulties with Great Britain. I shall follow this up"—Cromwell smiled dryly—"by making sure that the attention of Lord Pauncefote, the British Ambassador, is drawn to the contemplated infringement of the Treaty. I have no doubt that a formal protest will follow, which the administration is bound to consider."

Uncle Bill's eyes filled with admiration for his employer's strategy. Wesley however was puzzled.

"Surely, sir, the treaty would be equally violated if the United States Government were to take over the Panama Canal and maintain it?"

"Never cross your bridges until you come to them, Mr. Adam. What we need right now is time. We must prevent, at all costs, Senator Morgan from forcing one of the Nicaragua bills through Congress. Speaking confidentially, I have reason to believe that the British Government would be agreeable to a new treaty, on terms which would permit the U.S. Government to own a canal at Panama as long as it was kept strictly neutral, and available to ships of all other nations."

Wesley nodded. No wonder, he reflected, that Cromwell had the reputation of being one of the astutest attorneys of the day, that he was a determined and crafty fighter, and would play every trick in the pack.

But what role was his, Wesley's, to be? Surveying and politics did not, on the surface, appear to mix.

"In short, Mr. Godwin," the attorney briskly continued, "it is your job to frighten the people into withdrawing their moral support from the Nicaragua bills."

Uncle Bill chuckled. "'Will the Nicaragua Canal be finished in time for the next war? No! For the first excavation blast of a U.S. government-owned Nicaragua Canal may be answered by a British naval shell on Boston harbor.'"

"Splendid! But that will not be enough." He turned to Wesley. "I am sure you are wondering why I have sent for you, Mr. Adam. Frankly, I like the way you wrote your surveying reports, also your drafts of articles, which Mr. Godwin showed me, and which we have used from time to time. You write with sincerity, yet with a punch. Are you prepared to come to New York for a time, and work at the Press Bureau here? I want articles written which will make the people, and congressmen, realize the difficulties and expense of constructing a canal at Nicaragua. It will be arduous work, I assure you, and at times unpleasant, I don't doubt—" He smiled dryly. "That is, until you can develop the tough hide of a news-paperman! I will pay you whatever salary you are drawing from the H. C. Ackermann Company, together with a bonus to cover the cost of having to live away from home, and an additional bonus when the New Panama Company's concession is sold to the U.S. government." He ges-tured a warning. "Give me your answer tonight. That will allow you time to think the matter over. And if you agree, Mr. Godwin will appreciate your help in another matter of extreme urgency."

He faced the newspaperman again. "To counter the activities of the Nicaragua group we must prepare and print a descriptive pamphlet ex-plaining in detail the aims of the New Panama Canal Company, the amount of work so far accomplished toward a completed canal, the terms and conditions of the concessions, a summary of the report of the technical committee, a plan of the canal itself, photographs of work in progress. Finally, an authoritative statement that the company intends to complete the undertaking. This pamphlet must have sufficient punch to force a public hearing before the committee in the House. Finally, it must be ready for circulation before the end of the year. Can you do that?"

There was no hesitation in Uncle Bill's reply. "Sure," he drawled. "Especially with Wesley's help. What about it, son?"

"Give him time to think," Cromwell ordered.

Uncle Bill shook his head, and showed his tobacco-stained teeth in a crooked grin. "The boy doesn't need time to think, Mr. Cromwell. He's young enough to enjoy a good fight, isn't he? 'Sides, what's he got to lose?"

Wesley's eyes glowed. What had he to lose? Nothing, as Uncle Bill had said. But even suppose he had something to lose? Suppose that to throw in his lot with Cromwell and Uncle Bill would be a gamble, wouldn't the risk be worthwhile? After so many years with Ackermann, who was con-servative by nature, and a stickler for etiquette and formality, who wouldn't take a risk? It would be joy to work with two such men as Cromwell and Uncle Bill. Uncle Bill, of course, he had always liked; but never more than since he had undertaken the job of running Cromwell's bureau. He had come alive, had Uncle Bill. He had changed from a weary, hopeless au-tomaton to a square-shouldered thrusting personality, with a cock-eyed sense of humor, and a crooked grin.

As for Cromwell, it might be possible not to like him, but one had to admire and respect his dynamic qualities. And that made one proud to follow where he led.

Yes, it would be fun to work with these two men, fighters both. With them to control one's waking hours life would never become static, would never fall into the kind of groove one fell into, working for Ackermann.

And Dulcie—what wouldn't she give for the chance to live in New York for a time? She loved New York; liked going places—

Good God! Nothing to lose! Of course not. Just everything to gain.

"Count me in," he replied, feeling gloriously, recklessly happy.

14

WESLEY HAD MISJUDGED Dulcie. "Which hotel shall we stay in? The Waldorf—"

"Land sake, Dulcie! The monthly salary Cromwell is to pay me wouldn't keep us at the Waldorf for a week. Or any hotel for a month. We shall have to look for a furnished apartment. A small one at that."

"You know I hate apartments. Especially small ones. They are worse than small houses. It makes a person feel"—she shuddered—"like being in prison."

He frowned in perplexity. There were times when he did not know his wife. "But, honey, it won't be for long. Perhaps for less than six months. You could stand an apartment for that long, couldn't you?"

"Will it lead anywhere, if I do? Will it mean a partnership with Mr. Ackermann, this time?"

"Well—no—not that I know of. But it won't do me any harm. I'm more likely to meet someone in New York who would offer me a partnership. Cromwell is sure to have contacts—"

"Then you must go, darling."

"*You!*" he repeated slowly. "Why did you say *you* instead of *us?*"

She kissed the tip of his nose. "Now don't be cross, Wes dear."

"I'm not cross. I just want to know what's going on behind that pretty little face of yours."

"I was just thinking—you know I always help Mrs. Thomas with her Christmas party for poor children—and I've promised to go to Mr. Savi's concert next Tuesday week—and Mother's coming here for Christmas—"

"All of which adds up to what?"

"Wouldn't it be a good idea for you to go to New York by yourself—" She glanced at his face and added quickly, "At least, until after Christmas, when Mother has gone back?"

He became angry. "You're my wife, Dulcie. Your place is by my side. What sort of a man would I be, leaving you behind? Don't you understand, darling, that it isn't natural for a man to live without his wife?"

"You didn't think of that when you chose to go to Panama."

Her remark silenced his protests.

"Besides," she went on poutingly, "you know how cross Mrs. Thomas would be if I wasn't able to help with the party, as I have for the past few years. She might not speak to us again." Her eyes filled with tears. "And that would be awful, Wes dear. Lots of people wouldn't receive us any more—"

"Would that be such a great loss?"

Her eyes opened wide with astonishment. "Don't you want friends?"

"Not if the friendship depends on whether or not Mrs. Thomas happens to be friendly with us."

"Wesley! Mrs. Thomas is one of the most important women in Providence. It's only natural for people to respect her friends. Besides, you know Mother wouldn't want to be in New York at Christmas, of all times."

"She wouldn't have to come to us. There's Jane, or Emily—"

"Mother would sooner die than spend Christmas without me." She sat on the arm of his chair, and ruffled his hair. "Please be reasonable about this, darling. Don't insist upon my going to New York with you."

"You've always said you loved New York. You've been glad to go with me before."

"Yes, for a short time—in a hotel—"

"You want me to give up the idea of going."

"No, darling. I want you to go, and leave me behind. At any rate, until the New Year. Four weeks is so little in a lifetime—"

He would have insisted upon her accompanying him, but the fact that he had been willing to leave her for almost as many months, in order to visit Panama, made the exercise of his prerogative seem unreasonable and cruel. So he went alone, and was lucky enough to rent a two-room furnished apartment in the same block as Uncle Bill's.

Within a matter of hours of reporting to the press bureau for work he had no more time to brood upon Dulcie's capriciousness. He discovered a new side to Uncle Bill's character, for William Godwin the friend, and William Godwin the editor were two different people. A lifetime's work as a newspaperman had destroyed his perception of time. When there was a rush job on hand food and sleep became secondary considerations, and there was no such word as recreation in his dictionary. He was a slave driver to himself, and to all who worked with him. He had promised Cromwell that the pamphlet on the New Panama Canal Company would be ready for circulation before the end of the year, and nothing this side of hell was going to stop him from fulfilling that promise.

Wesley worked as he had never worked before. His waking hours became a nightmare of research at the New York offices of the Panama Railroad Company and the New Panama Canal Company; of numerous consultations with Cromwell, General Abbot, and Corthell; of journeys to

Washington to consult State documents; of writing against time; of passing proofs—

He was too busy to dwell upon the fact that all about him New York was gaily prepared for Christmas. The shop windows were transformed into Aladdin's caves filled with lovely and expensive gifts that attracted all too many wistful glances of young emigrants whose parents had worked a lifetime for a fraction of the cost of any one of the articles. The wind blew with searching persistence down Fifth Avenue, and one morning, after a hard, lasting frost, the surface of the roads had to be sanded to prevent the horses from slipping. A flurry of snow whitened the red capes of the Santa Clauses who stood outside so many stores: Christmas trees appeared behind lace curtains, and garlands of leaves, and colored streamers.

About once a week Dulcie wrote to him, but there was little in her letters to make his blood race with impatience to return to her side. They were long letters, full of news about the doings of the people of Benefit Street, or of her particular friends all of whom lived elsewhere. They were friendly letters—and that was the trouble. They were *too* friendly. She called him dearest, sweet husband, and used other endearments; but had the letters been addressed to an old school friend they would scarcely have read differently. Behind the lighthearted, friendly chatter he was unable to detect any note of regret that they were living apart, or sincere longing for his return. He contrasted them with his own letters, written in moments snatched from the sleep which threatened to engulf him, and yet every word, he knew, underlined his deep, deep longing for her.

These letters from Providence hurt him more than he dared admit. He could forgive her not saying in as many words that she was impatient for their next meeting, for he recognized the existence of her deep-seated distaste for any outward manifestation of emotion. But a love such as he felt for her could not, he believed, be entirely concealed among trivialities. A word here and there could not fail to betray that love. But he searched in vain for "I'm counting the days until your return," or "I miss you so," or "I dream of you every night, my darling." Once, it was true, she had written, "The house seems empty without you, Wes darling." Unhappily she had added, "I had to prepare an evening meal for Mrs. Brewster, when she came round last Tuesday to discuss the church bazaar: the effort quite tired me out."

Christmas Day was the strangest he had ever celebrated. It was spent at the office with Uncle Bill and Cromwell. The pamphlet was due to be published the following day, and the attorney had called for a conference to decide among whom it should be circulated. While the rest of New York was feasting, and sleeping off the effects of one meal before romping with the children, and working up an appetite for another meal; while carefree laughter, and music, and games were Santa's Order of the Day, the three men in the press bureau pored over lists of congressmen, governors, officials, newspaper editors, commercial undertakings, libraries, presidents, and heads of educational and influential institutions.

Several times during the day Wesley thought wistfully of his home in Benefit Street. But not for long. Cromwell saw to that. Or if not Cromwell, then Uncle Bill did so. One must not dream of wife and home in the midst of battle—

The following day the pamphlet went out to the many hundreds of people whose names the three men had considered and selected.

Even its most venomous critics had to acknowledge the authenticity of the pamphlet. And its success. With reluctance the Committee on Interstate Commerce gave permission for a public hearing of the Panama group's demand that the French concession should be taken over. This hearing was fixed for January 17, 18, and 19.

More work for Wesley. "In less than two weeks' time, Mr. Adam, we have to present our case before a Committee of the House. Our brief must be ready without fail. Is that understood, without fail. I need your help."

"Mine, Mr. Cromwell? But—I know nothing of procedure—"

"Naturally. That is my affair. But the brief must be technically foolproof. It will be shot at by everyone of our opponents, not least of all by the Chairman of the Committee, Mr. Hepburn, who is one of the foremost champions of the Nicaragua group. If he or anyone else finds a single flaw in our technical arguments we shall have done more harm than good. You understand?"

"Perfectly, sir."

"Then prepare a survey report that will make those fool committeemen appear traitors to their country if they fail to prefer the Panama to any other known or unknown route. It must be ready by the seventeenth."

No time now to write letters to Dulcie; or to read hers to him with anything but eyes and a brain too bleary for want of sleep to be critical. For ten days Wesley worked on the preparation of the brief; for ten weary, brain-destroying days, from 8 A.M. through midnight or later. No set time for meals. No set place. No set meals, in fact; just a sandwich here, or there. And cups of coffee in relays to keep one awake. And only the driving force of William Nelson Cromwell to keep one's flagging brain at work. Only ten days—for the preparation of a detailed study of all technical aspects. Only seven more days. Five days for the prepa—prepa—his drowsy thoughts groped in a fog of sleep—for profound study of technical as—as—aspects. Four days more. Three days only for profound technical brief. Two days only for—for—tech—tech—nical brief. One—one more days for—for—

As Wesley's head dropped onto his manuscript, the scratching nib scored the sheet and splattered it with ink. He didn't care. Just one hour's sleep, for the love of God! Just one hour—but Cromwell arrived, dynamic, alert, vigorous.

"One more thing you might add, Mr. Adam. Be sure to emphasize—"

One more thing—one more day—

At 1 A.M. of January 17 Wesley's eyes closed again; but this time there was no Cromwell, no Uncle Bill, to prod him into wakefulness. Cromwell was on his way to the Capitol—

On January 21 Senator Morgan forced his bill through the Senate, by 48 to 6, whereupon it was sent to the House. There, in spite of the hearing of the Committee, a large and enthusiastic majority was pledged to Nicaragua. Once the vote was taken the Panama route would be doomed.

"Looks like you can write your Dulcie that you'll soon be home," said Uncle Bill, looking mournful. "We're on the run. No propaganda is going to help any, now. Well—" he grinned crookedly. "It was fun while it lasted. S'pose the Irish in me likes a good clean fight."

Wesley scowled at the wastepaper basket which, for once, was indecently empty. "To hell with politics. Just because the Republicans—"

"And many Democrats, Wesley."

"Whichever they are, facts are facts, aren't they? Our pamphlet proved that the Panama route is a far better proposition than Nicaragua, but just because they once voted for Nicaragua—a lot of old women!"

Uncle Bill grinned. "Oh! I don't know! If they were women they might find it easier to change their minds."

"I wonder what Mr. Cromwell's next move will be, if any."

Swinging his swivel chair around so that he could see himself in a mirror which hung on the wall behind him, Uncle Bill smoothed some loose gray hairs into position.

"He won't take a licking easy. If there's anything to be done he'll do it. I have faith in that man."

"I'd work for my share of a hundred million dollars, Uncle Bill."

"Yah! Cynic!" Godwin scoffed.

"But I still respect him."

Within the hour they learned from Cromwell's own lips that he was not yet licked.

"Yes, of course, carry on, Mr. Godwin," he brusquely ordered. "It will be time for us to admit we're beaten when the House has voted for Nicaragua."

"But isn't the vote due—"

"A great deal can happen in a few days."

Uncle Bill looked up. "You have a plan, Mr. Cromwell?"

"A desperate one. If we could establish a new canal commission, for the examination of all possible routes, the House would postpone a vote until the commission had reported back to Congress."

96

"Any hope of that?"

Cromwell smiled slyly. "My partner, Mr. Curtis, comes from the same State as the Speaker. At least, he'll listen—"

The Speaker did listen, and was impressed by the arguments of Curtis. The attorneys also gained the ear of Mr. Cannon, leader of the Republican party and Chairman of the Committee on Ways and Means; and the Chairman of the Committee on Rivers and Harbors, Mr. Burton. These three members, together with a handful of others who had been impressed by the arguments in favor of Panama, became convinced that it might not be in the best interests of the nation to rush through the Morgan bill. In consequence, the bill failed to reach a vote.

Cromwell was pleased with himself, as he had every reason to be. He was more genial than Wesley had ever known him; even his eyes smiled, which was unusual.

"We've won that round, gentlemen," he told Wesley and Uncle Bill, on his return from Washington. "It was hard work, but thanks in part to your excellent survey report, Mr. Adam, Mr. Curtis persuaded the Speaker into giving us his support.

"I've won time for us. The new commission will probably take years to reach a decision. That will give you every opportunity to flood the country with propaganda, Mr. Godwin."

"It'll cost money, Mr. Cromwell. It's already cost plenty—that pamphlet didn't cost a dime—"

The attorney waved an elegant hand. "I confirm that we cannot afford to stint expense. Too much is at stake."

Uncle Bill nodded, then chuckled. "I'd have liked to see some of the faces of the Nicaragua party when the news got round about their bill."

"They were not unamusing," Cromwell admitted with a fleeting smile of self-satisfaction.

"Have they any move they can make in their turn, Mr. Cromwell?" Wesley asked.

"If they have you can be sure they will make it. They will not readily admit defeat. But for the moment—" He was interrupted by a tap on the door.

"Come in," Godwin called out.

The young man who entered was a stranger to Uncle Bill. "What the heck—" he began.

The newcomer addressed himself to Cromwell. "A telegram from Washington arrived just after you had left the office. Mr. Cohen thought you should see it at once."

Cromwell took it. "Excuse me," he muttered, unfolding it.

His chagrined expression informed the others present that the telegram was not only unexpected, but unfavorable as well. He dismissed the messenger, then held up the telegram.

97

"I'll read it out, gentlemen; it's from a friend in the House:

SENATOR MORGAN INTRODUCING AMENDMENT TO RIVER AND HARBORS BILL
STOP AMENDMENT ALMOST WORD FOR WORD PENDING NICARAGUA BILL
WITH APPROPRIATION OF TEN MILLION DOLLARS BEGIN BUILDING OF NICA-
RAGUA STOP ADVISE RAPID ACTION."

Uncle Bill shook his head. "What's that in English?"

"You know that the Rivers and Harbor bill appropriates funds for the improvement of rivers and harbors throughout the country?"

"Yes."

"The current bill has already been passed by the House, so Senator Morgan has taken advantage of its being a bill in which every State in the country has an interest, and more particularly, of its being before the Senate Committee on Commerce at the present time, to reintroduce the Nicaragua bill in a new and novel form."

"The cunning coot!"

"It's a clever move. If the Senate passes the bill, as it is almost certain to, it will only need the concurrence of the House to make the bill law, and irrevocably pledge the country to the building of the Nicaragua Canal."

"Damn him!" Uncle Bill exploded.

"Amen to that!" Cromwell softly muttered.

The Senate was only too happy to support Senator Morgan. On February 25 the amendment was passed by 50 to 3. With only a few days left before the end of the session, Cromwell had to work quickly. What could possibly be done, in a matter of days, to prevent the House from giving its assent to the fatal amendment which would, in effect, make the choice of the Nicaragua canal a binding duty? As he frankly admitted, an irresistable current was carrying Nicaragua to victory.

Once more Wesley and Uncle Bill foresaw an abrupt winding-up of the Press Bureau, to which personal interest in the battle had made them become extraordinarily attached. Perhaps, too, this time Cromwell shared their pessimistic outlook. But he fought on, wracking his brains to invent some way of preventing the impending catastrophe, and the consequent failure of his mission to sell the French concession to the United States.

Within forty-eight hours he had conceived a desperate plan; that of reincorporating the Panama Canal Company in one of the States, thus leaving the United States free to invest in the company only if she chose so to do.

Together with his partner, Curtis, he interviewed the Chairman of the Committee on Rivers and Harbors, who granted a public hearing before the Committee. The House reacted quickly to the new proposal, by insisting upon an investigation of the two projects by a new commission.

98

At the subsequent conference committee—composed of three members from each House, whose duty it was to confirm or reject the proposed amendment—the fate of the Panama route was finally put to the test, for it was traditionally customary for both Houses to adopt the report of a conference committee. Thanks to Cromwell's influence, the House conferees stood firm on their demand that a clause appointing a new commission to report on all routes should be substituted for the Nicaragua amendment. The Senate conferees were equally resolute. But they were defeated by the impending closure of Congress. Unless the bill were passed by Congress during the present session, it would fail; and the many millions of dollars which it normally appropriated would not be immediately available for the upkeep of the rivers and harbors of America. Faced with this dilemma the Senate conferees yielded. To the consternation of the Nicaragua party who were preparing to celebrate their victory, the substituted amendment became law during the last hours of Congress.

The Panama route was saved—for the time being!

15

TO CELEBRATE CROMWELL'S success, Wesley returned to Providence for a long week end; the first real break since he had joined the Press Bureau. He had spent an occasional night at home and Dulcie had traveled to New York as many times. On her first visit, he had urged her to stay longer, but she had taken one horrified look round the tiny apartment and had asked ingenuously, what would be the use? Considering that he would be at the office from 8 A.M. until after midnight, he couldn't *really* want her to spend all that time alone in an empty apartment?

There was just enough justification for her argument to decide him not to press his demands—for the moment had been one of the busiest at the Bureau. Nevertheless, her words had perplexed him. There were times when he wondered whether she would ever grow up. Didn't she realize that, for a man at any rate, marriage comprised more than companionship, however delightful? She went back the next day, and he never reopened the subject.

She greeted him with a quick, cool kiss. "Your telegram came just too late, darling. Couldn't you have sent it earlier?"

"Too late for what?"

"Mother had just gone home. If she had known you were coming back she would have stayed a few days longer."

He was careful to turn away, for he was afraid his expression might betray his hopelessness. He liked his mother-in-law well enough. The two of them were friendly in a guarded manner. But what made Dulcie believe that in the circumstances he would welcome a third person. Couldn't she understand the meaning of the oneness of marriage? He would not allow himself to dwell on that subject, for he had been thinking along those lines too much of late.

Later that day he told Dulcie of Cromwell's fight to save the Panama Canal from extinction. She listened without being able to understand until she gathered that Cromwell had won a victory.

"Does that mean you'll soon be coming back to Providence?" she interrupted.

"That depends."

"On what?"

"You, darling."

"Why me?"

"Mr. Cromwell wants me to stay on, because the battle isn't over yet. We shall have to present our case to the new commission I was telling you about, and I can be useful in preparing the papers."

"Do you want to do that?"

"Yes—" he hesitatingly admitted. "In many ways. I never thought I should be interested in the kind of work I've been doing, but I am. Terrifically."

"Then why does it depend on me?" She seemed to be on the defensive.

"Are you content to go on living apart, which we shall have to do?"

"Now you're asking me to join you in New York, if you stay on," she said petulantly.

"No, honey, I don't want to ask you to do anything you don't want to do. The point is, if you want me to come back, I'll come."

She was so long in replying that he grew impatient. "I did ask you a question, darling."

"Yes, I know—"

"Well, then?"

"I don't know what to say, Wes dearest."

Her answer was a blow to his pride. "If that's all I mean to you!" he began angrily. "So it doesn't matter to you whether I'm here or in New York."

She looked at him with the pained expression of a dog unjustly punished. Tears gathered in the corners of her eyes. "It isn't that. You know I miss you all the time you're away. You might give me time to explain—"

"I'm sorry," he muttered.

"I was thinking of the money you're earning. You've already saved some, haven't you, sweet?"

He had. Cromwell was a generous paymaster. He had already given both Uncle Bill and Wesley a substantial bonus for their hard work. He nodded.

"Well, then, if you continue to work for Mr. Cromwell in New York you might make enough to help buy a larger house, mightn't you?" She hurried on. "It would be worth a year or two's unhappiness now to be able to buy a nicer house when you come back to Providence."

"If you think I'm going to put up with living apart from you for years—"

"I'll write you more often," she promised with eagerness. "And go to New York once a fortnight. After all, that wouldn't be so bad as your being a sailor, or something like that."

"You really want me to go on there, Dulcie, don't you?"

"If—if—it means our having a larger house—and help—"

Feeling cold he leaned forward, and stirred the fire.

He often thought of Anne Perrigot, wondering what had happened to her since his journey to Panama. She would be, how old now? About nineteen, or thereabouts. Humph! Of marriageable age. Anne Perrigot married! A lucky man, her husband. For if any girl ever showed promise of growing up into lovely womanhood, Anne had done so. Unless, of course, the climate was already beginning to spoil her beauty. The tropics had the reputation of bringing beauty to early bloom, and then destroying it.

He remembered how he had dreamed of Anne, and how ashamed he had been of his erotic imaginings. He chuckled now, at his ingenuous scruples. He wouldn't have them now—or, to be more realistic, he hadn't got them now. For there were times when he dreamed— If Anne were in New York—

He did not want deliberately to be unfaithful to Dulcie. God knows, he still loved her too much for that. But at least he could have fun with Anne, take her places, show her the sights, take her to the theaters, perhaps to Coney Island once in a while. He was sure she would enjoy herself there. He could almost hear the sound of her laughter, and see her excited face crinkling with excitement. Unlike Dulcie, who disliked such places and would be miserable there.

Dancing, too. Sure, Anne and he would go dancing. Did she dance? He didn't know—but he was certain that she would love it. Equally as certain that she would be a superb dancer. She had the slim figure for dancing, and the lightness, and a sense of rhythm. Graceful, too, he felt sure. She had shown signs of a developing, exquisite gracefulness.

One morning, upon reaching the Bureau, Wesley was told by the office boy that a young lady was waiting to see him.

"Who is she?"

The lad grinned cheekily. "She wouldn't give her name, boss. Said she wanted to speak to you private."

Wesley's spirits soared. Surely not Anne— By some miracle— But of course not. It wasn't likely that Anne would come to New York. And if she did it wasn't likely that she would know how to trace him.

"All right, kid. Show her in."

The girl was not Anne, although her face was strangely familiar. He studied the tall girl. Her complexion was as fresh as buttermilk and ripe cherries. Her hair was the warm color of corn, and piled high on her head in a squat bun. Her clothes were ill fitting, and outmoded, and looked as if they had come from some upstate store.

The more he looked at her the more it seemed to him that he must know her: everything about her, in a vague way, was so familiar.

"Mr. Wesley Adam?" she asked.

"Yes."

"My name is Ingrid Ericson."

Ericson! That was the explanation. Allowing for the difference in age and sex she and Olaf Ericson were as alike as two peas.

"Olaf's sister?"

At the mention of Olaf's name, her face lit up. "Yes," she confirmed eagerly. She moved nearer to him, tense with excitement. "Please, please, Mr. Adam, do you know where he is? We haven't heard from him—" She gulped. "Ever since he went to Panama. Mom is—is ill with worry—" Tears filled her eyes; big genuine tears which rolled down her buttermilk and cherry cheeks and splashed on her white shirtwaist.

Poor kid! was his first thought. His next was of self-pity, for having to increase rather than relieve her misery.

To delay that moment, "How did you find me?"

"I went to Sullivan and Cromwell's office. Mr. Cromwell wasn't there, but when I said I had come specially from Jamestown—that's in North Dakota—just to find out what had happened to Olaf, a nice gentleman said to come and see you."

"Why did you come? You're only a kid. Your father—"

She swallowed. "He couldn't afford to give up a day's work, Mr. Adam, nor my older brothers. I was the only one left who was old enough. But won't you please tell me where he is? Oh! please, sir, tell me."

"I—I can't, Ingrid. I don't know."

She stared at him, unbelievingly. Her eyes were ice blue, just like Olaf's. "But at the office, they said—"

"I'll tell you all I know, Ingrid. You know he went with me to Panama—"

She nodded her flaxen head. "Yes, sir. He wrote and told Mom and Pop how lucky he was."

"Do you know he came back with me?"

102

"Yes, sir." She smiled, and the effect was that of the sunshine breaking through a bank of rain clouds. "He sent Mom some money. We had such a lovely meal that day, and Pop bought some new clothes, 'cause his own weren't fit to work in, they were—" She paused abruptly, as if realizing that her chatter was delaying his reply. "But Olaf—"

He realized that he was keeping the girl on tenterhooks. "Went back to Panama a week later."

"Went back—" She shook her head. "You're teasing me, sir."

"No, Ingrid. Mr. Cromwell gave him a sum of money to—as a reward for his good work in Panama, so Olaf went back there. Haven't you heard from him?"

"Not since he came back to New York, sir."

He looked with commiseration at the distressed face of his young visitor, still pretty in spite of her tears. He wished he could help her in some way.

She continued, "Why did he go back there? He said he hated the climate because it was too hot."

"I don't know, Ingrid. I don't know anyone who does."

Her despair made him feel a brute. He tried to add some words of sympathy but could think of nothing to say.

"What am I to tell Mom and Pop?" she whispered. "I must tell them something." Her ice-blue eyes, frightened and grief-stricken, pleaded for help.

He made a gesture of helplessness. Her lips quivered. Before he could prevent her she had turned and hurried out of the room. Too late, he realized that he had neglected to obtain her address.

The days extended into weeks, the weeks into months, as the battle raged between the Panama and Nicaragua parties. In spite of the extensive propaganda put out by Cromwell's Press Bureau, the country remained solidly pro-Nicaragua. And when the names on the Senate committee, were announced Cromwell knew that three of the seven men were notoriously in favor of the Nicaragua route, and had even sat on the Nicaragua Commission of two years previously—not least of the three was Professor Lewis R. Haupt, who had publicly declared that nothing would ever affect his preference for Nicaragua.

Toward late summer Cromwell sailed for Paris, to brief the directors of the company there for a visit by the commission. He left Curtis and other partners of his firm the uphill task of converting congressmen; and Uncle Bill and Wesley, the equally thankless job of doing the same to the people.

Now that time was no longer against them Wesley found that the work encroached less on his leisure hours. As soon as he was leading a more normal life, he felt increasingly lonely. Pride restrained him from directly reopening the subject of Dulcie's joining him in New York, but indirectly he did his best to wear down her determination not to share his small apartment in Long Acre. He failed. Whether she was willfully resolved not to understand his hints, or whether she was blissfully unaware of the meaning behind his words he could not be sure; but not once did she suggest that she was willing to take her share of the sacrifice which he made for the sake of his growing deposit balance at the Mercantile National Bank.

Nor did she keep strictly to her promise of regular visits to New York. There always seemed—to her—some good and valid reason why she should have to postpone the trip. A visit to Newport—a charity garden party at John Brown's House—a charity concert at the Opera House—

At last he reached the state when he felt that he could bear the separation no longer. Their occasional meetings were sufficient to keep his physical desires in a state of constant provocation, but were too infrequent thoroughly to satisfy them. He found increasingly difficult the effort of keeping his thoughts from dwelling on their next meeting—a state of mind which disgusted him, for his upbringing had taught him to believe that it was neither decent nor manly to allow the sexual side of marriage to assume such importance.

Besides, he missed the companionship of their evenings together, in the parlor of their home in Benefit Street. He had reveled in the quiet contentment of relaxing in the rocker, while she worked at her embroidery and chattered to him about what she had done that day, or retold local gossip, or discussed their friends with him. Nothing of consequence; but it pleased him to be allowed to listen with only half an ear, as it were; for this allowed him the chance of reflecting on how pretty she was, what an attractive talking voice she had, how lucky he was to be her husband.

These things he missed, too. So much so that, when the ache became too intolerable, he would wander aimlessly down Broadway, or along Forty-second Street, or Fifth Avenue; or waste many twilight hours in Central Park, trying to make up his mind to try his luck with some of the willing-eyed girls there.

So, one day, in late fall, he resolved to return to H. C. Ackermann Company. He decided to say nothing to Uncle Bill until the date was settled, for he knew the move would not be welcomed. The two men had worked too happily together. He dropped in on Ackermann.

The surveyor was affable. "Well, Adam, still enjoying your leave of absence? Doing well in New York, I hear. Good, good! Like to hear of young men forging ahead. Shows aptitude and determination."

"I'm doing well enough, Mr. Ackermann, but I'd like to come back."

Ackermann's expression turned stony. "I thought you were happy in your work there."

"More than happy, but—"

104

"Well, then, if you're doing well financially, and are happy enough...."

Wesley did not intend to discuss his domestic life with the other man. Ackermann's square face, with its shaved hair and thick-lensed spectacles, was not one to encourage confidences.

"My old position is open, isn't it?" he challenged. "I have your promise."

Ackermann pursed his thick lips. "Yes and no. A promise is a promise. You can have your position back, Adam, but you will have to accept a reduction in salary."

"A reduction!" Wesley stared at the expressionless face. "But it would be less than I was worth, then."

"Maybe. But we are doing badly. So is every surveyor in New England, in the U.S.A. New business is drying up. Our country is heading for a slump; and we, in company with other surveyors, are the first sufferers. I don't mind admitting to you, in confidence, that we have lost money this past nine months."

Wesley wondered whether the story would have been quite the same if he had come to put up fifty thousand dollars for a partnership.

"My advice to you," Ackermann continued, "is to stay where you are for the time being, and consider yourself a lucky man to be doing so well when others are wondering what their future will be. In a year's time business may be booming again. When it is, come and see me again if you want to. A promise is a promise."

So Wesley returned to New York glad that he had said nothing to Uncle Bill.

Cromwell returned to New York soon afterward, and set into operation his plan for Americanizing the Panama Canal Company, believing that as long as the company was wholly a French concern it would have no success against the Nicaragua project, which was American from its inception.

Fresh propaganda had to be devised in order to attract American capital; a herculean task, for toward the end of the year Ackermann's prophecy came true. A financial panic swept through Wall Street, and capitalists, being in no mood for a gamble, shied away from the Panama Canal Company.

This setback might have upset the plans for someone less influential than Cromwell, but he had his finger in many a financial pie, and was able to obtain enough promises for his purpose.

In Congress the fight between the rival parties continued unchecked. Led by Senator Morgan, the Nicaragua party used every trick of parliamentary procedure to commit the Government in support of the Nicaragua project. But the watchful, wily Cromwell was equally a master of legislative chess. Each rival move was checked.

But in the summer of 1901, the attorney suffered defeat. Not at the hands of the Nicaragua party, but at the hands of none other than the New

Panama Canal Company itself. Back in Paris the directors decided to dispense with his services as counsel.

16

"GOOD MORNING, GENTLEMEN." Cromwell waved a hand towards two vacent chairs close to his desk.

Wesley tried to deduce from the attorney's face the reason for the urgent summons to Wall Street, but it was more than usually expressionless.

"I have bad news for you both, so I will deal with it at once. The New Panama Canal Company has relieved Sullivan and Cromwell of the responsibility of conducting their affairs in the United States. Henceforward they will undertake the management of their own affairs over here."

"That's plumb crazy!" Uncle Bill exploded. "You've done a hell of a fine job for them over here. What in Pete's name do they think they know of our politics?"

Cromwell's lips parted in a thin smile. "It will not be long before they find out. It is a case of the old English proverb: 'Penny wise, pound foolish.' They object to the size of the expense account they have been called upon to pay."

"What do they want for a dime. A champagne supper?"

"More or less. They could scarcely have chosen a more unfortunate moment. Eight days ago Admiral Walker, chairman of the Isthmian Canal Commission, was kind enough to call at this office to ask me to quote a price the company would accept for the concession."

"Then the Commission favors Panama?" Uncle Bill asked eagerly.

"Ah! I cannot categorically state that that is so; but I would infer, from Admiral Walker's attitude, and his questions, that in the event of the price for the Panama concession being an acceptable one the Commission would probably reverse their preliminary report in favor of Nicaragua."

Uncle Bill was delighted. "That's dandy! We pulled it off." He paused abruptly. "Do you mean that, now that you've practically got the concession in a bag, they're trying to ditch you?"

"We must be just, Mr. Godwin. That is not quite an exact representation of their attitude. The difficulty is that the company is unwilling to quote a price. They want to fix the sum by arbitration, and resent my urgent demands for a definite and final amount."

"Scared of quoting a thousand dollars too low."

"Probably. But that is the position. Instead of quoting me a price to put before the Commission they have decided to dispense with our services, no doubt with a view to further haggling."

Because of the setback, both Wesley and Uncle Bill expected dismissal, but when Uncle Bill referred wryly to having to find a new situation Cromwell brushed the suggestion aside.

"Not yet, gentlemen, if you are satisfied to stay on awhile. Of course, the Press Bureau will cease all official functions, but there is still work behind the scenes which you can do."

"But, sir, if you are no longer representing the New Panama Canal Company—"

The attorney's quick brain easily completed the sentence which the embarrassed Wesley left unfinished.

"Why should I accept the financial responsibility for your salaries? Because, gentlemen, I am not satisfied that the directors of the company have the acumen to succeed against the tricks of our politicians. To begin with, I prophesy that the Commission will now vote in favor of a Nicaragua canal."

"And after that, sir?"

"I think that the company will be forced to the conclusion that if they wish to sell their assets to the United States they must reappoint Sullivan and Cromwell as their attorneys."

Events soon proved Cromwell a shrewd prophet. In spite of the assassination of President McKinley in September, and the inauguration of Theodore Roosevelt, a declared advocate of the Nicaragua route, the president of the canal company continued to maintain his irritating procrastination by refusing to quote a definite and binding sum for the sale of the concession. In the face of this uncompromising attitude, the Commission voted unanimously in favor of a Nicaragua canal.

"So that's that!" gloomily declared Uncle Bill, following the announcement of the Commission's vote. "What hope have I of finding work easily? Ex-newspapermen of my age are a dime a dozen."

"You're not out of your present job yet, so why start looking for the next? If Mr. Cromwell's second prophesy's as true as the first, you won't have to."

"I wish I could think you were right, Wesley. But—" Uncle Bill shook his head.

In spite of Godwin's pessimism, work at the ex-Press Bureau went on as though Sullivan and Cromwell were still acting for the Canal Company. With one difference: they were not working against the clock. Wesley had even more time for reflection. In consequence, before long he became aware of a growing restlessness. Life—at least life as it affected him—seemed to be strangely meaningless and dull. It was fun to create, to produce dream towns from nowhere, as it were, or a block of apartments, or modern skyscraper office buildings, with all the latest improvements and amenities. But as he walked along Broadway of an evening, on his way home from the office, he began to look about him with prejudiced eyes. The long, straight street with its tall buildings, its theaters and shops, and its teeming thousands was an awe-inspiring sight, and so was Times Square. It was a tribute to the genius and ability of mankind. And to the skill of mankind, too. As a surveyor he could give ungrudging admiration to the bold inventiveness of the city's builders as they faced the approach of the new century in the certain knowledge that it was to bring them pre-eminence in every form of world leadership.

From his personal point of view it was too orderly, too civilized. From a long line of Scottish forebears, who had farmed the lush soil of Devil's Glen from time beyond record, he had inherited a nature that looked for and throve on opposition; one that took pleasure in overcoming difficulties and surmounting obstacles; one that was as inherently adventurous as it was ruggedly independent and individualistic. He was immensely proud of those dour ancestors from across the ocean, and occasionally regretted that he was descended from them on the distaff side and thus deprived of their name.

There were few details of his grandfather's and his great-grandfather's history unknown to him. The story of Duncan Stewart's flight from Devil's Glen to escape from a hated and hating father; of the years he had spent in London as the adopted son of Doctor Anderson; of a second flight, this time from the country, to avoid the consequences of killing a French emigré; of his arrival in the French colony of Santo Domingo, and of the tremendous events there in which he had shared.

An ancestor to be proud of indeed. One who had had the courage to accept the enmity of men of his own color in order to give medical help and friendship to stricken Negro slaves. Yet in these days Wesley's thoughts dwelled more often on Henry Stewart, Duncan's only son. For now that he had seen, and used, the Panama Railroad which Henry had helped to construct, Henry seemed so much closer to him than Duncan. Besides, it was from Henry he had inherited his aptitude for survey work, for Henry had become a successful surveyor following his return to the United States.

No wonder, he reflected, that any man with Stewart blood running in his veins should ultimately become dissatisfied with the smug routine of a civilized community. It was no life for one bred to high adventure. And by degrees, his restless thoughts crystallized into resolution, which one day he revealed to Uncle Bill, when Godwin asked casually, "What news of Dulcie, Wesley? You haven't seen her for some weeks now."

"It's my fault. I've put off going up."

Godwin's eyes crinkled with unease. "You've had the time." Still casual, but now questioning. "Of late, especially."

"I know I have, but I'm a coward."

"You!" Godwin's scorn rejected the possibility.

"I'm dreading a discussion that's certain to be unpleasant."

This explanation Godwin could appreciate. He hadn't been married to a sharp-tongued redhead for nothing.

"It's this way, Uncle Bill," Wesley continued. "I've found out that my place isn't here any more."

"I see." A bleak voice, for Godwin was selfish in his affection for the younger man. "Hankering after Providence? Well, I can't blame you. You've all your friends there."

"That's the rub. I'm not hankering after Providence, or any place north of parallel nine. Since my visit to Panama I've found out that I'm a Stewart."

"Ah! And Dulcie isn't?"

"That's it!" Wesley continued. "I'm still in love with Dulcie. Don't think I'm not. But that doesn't prevent my realizing that she's—she's essentially urban, Uncle Bill. She's not going to understand what's got into me, so she'll do her damnedest to persuade me it's just a passing fancy."

"Are you sure it isn't?"

"Haven't I just said I'm a Stewart? You know about Grandfather Henry and Great-grandfather Duncan."

"Maybe you are a Stewart, lad, but you're also an Adam. Your father didn't have any leanings to leave Providence that he ever told me about. Or he ever told your mother, either, or else I think she'd have told me. They were both satisfied, the pair of 'em, to stay put someplace in either New York or New England. So—"

"Are *you* trying to persuade me it's a passing fancy?"

Godwin chuckled. "I wasn't meaning to. But what you going to tell Dulcie? That you're suffering from tropical fever, so she's to pack up and be ready to accompany you to some godforsaken hole on the Equator? Or maybe you've Haiti in mind?"

"Haiti didn't do my great-grandfather any harm, as a matter of fact, but the fever isn't that bad, Uncle Bill! Besides, I'm not deserting you or Mr. Cromwell until our work here is finished, one way or the other. I'm enjoying our fight too much. What I had in mind was, when it is, to volunteer for work in Panama if the Government should buy the concession."

"*If!* Me, I put the odds on Nicaragua right now."

"Then I'll volunteer for Nicaragua. So long as it's some place where I can do a man's job of work, and help in building something really big, something of benefit to the world."

Godwin's gaze sharpened. "You've really got it bad."

Wesley nodded. "It's writing about the canal, talking about it, dreaming of it. It's becoming more real to me now than it was when I was there."

109

"That's because you were in a hurry to get back to Dulcie."

Was there a note of reproof in Uncle Bill's voice? Wesley couldn't be sure. "So I am still," he maintained agressively. "That's why I'm dreading the moment when I tell her that I'm not going to be satisfied living the rest of my life in the States. Time enough for that when we're older."

Godwin nodded understandingly. "Care to take the advice of an older man?"

"I'd appreciate it, Uncle Bill, so long as it's not giving me a hundred reasons why I shouldn't."

"On the contrary, lad. If I were younger, maybe I'd go with you. All I wanted to say is, don't say anything to Dulcie until you're practically ready to go. Don't give her a chance to brood."

Wesley nodded. Perhaps Uncle Bill was right. Back in that empty house in Providence Dulcie had too much time to brood.

The news reached Paris that the Commission had voted unanimously in favor of a canal through Nicaragua, and the unhappy shareholders of the New Panama Canal Company became desperate. When they heard that the United States had opened negotiations with that country for a treaty, and that January 7 had been set aside for a debate in the House on the Nicaragua bill, they despaired of saving anything from the financial wreck that loomed ahead. An extraordinary meeting was at once called, which authorized the directors to cable the Canal Commission offering to sell the concession and all the company's property in Panama for the sum of $40,000,000. This cable was dispatched on January 4, 1902. In spite of the fact that the Commission had already conceded that the sum of forty million dollars was reasonable, the House refused to consider it, and by 309 votes to 2 passed the Nicaragua bill.

In a triumphant mood Senator Morgan made plans to push the bill through the Senate, but President Roosevelt was wiser. On January 16 he called a meeting of the Canal Commission, and instructed the members to consider the new offer, which by then had been ratified by letter. Two days later the Commission reported in favor of the Panama route. One week afterward the second part of Cromwell's prophecy was fulfilled.

It seemed like old times, to be in conference again with Cromwell and Uncle Bill. Wesley felt warm with contentment, and listened to Cromwell's crisp voice with a feeling that the past few months had been no more than a bad dream.

"The New Panama Company has agreed to sell for forty million dollars, as you know, gentlemen. The offer is a reasonable one which would, I am sure, have been acceptable to the Commission had it been made last June. But by now negotiations for the building of a canal at Nicaragua have so far progressed that only a miracle will help Panama.

"To begin with, Nicaragua and Costa Rica have made most liberal proposals to our Government, which have been found satisfactory and endorsed—in fact a protocol with Nicaragua has already been signed, in furtherance of the Hepburn bill.

"On the other hand, Colombia is being most difficult, and is inclined to refuse her consent to the transfer of the French concession to our country. In Bogotá they make no secret of the fact that they look forward to acquiring everything, lock, stock, and barrel, in nineteen ten, when the concession will lapse by reason of nonfulfillment. Even the more scrupulous oppose any suggestion of transferring the concession to a government, as opposed to a private concern, since this would mean, it is argued, a loss of sovereignty. A third group in that country wants to hold us up for ransom: a tribute of fifty million francs from the Canal Company, and a hundred-year concession at an enormous rental from our Government."

"And you're supposed to try and make Congress accept the Commission's report?" Uncle Bill laughed cynically. "Colombia wants more than a pound of flesh. She wants the whole carcass."

"The trouble is," Cromwell continued, "we've lost seven months' time. All the good will toward the Panama route that we won over the past year is lost to us. The Nicaragua party is stronger than ever. It has always been my habit to finish whatever I start, otherwise I shouldn't have agreed to attempt such a hopeless task."

Uncle Bill's expression was gloomy. "Then you think it is hopeless, too?"

"Hopeless!" Cromwell shook his head. "My apologies, gentlemen. I should have said 'seemingly hopeless.' "

"Then there is still a chance?"

"There will remain a chance until the moment President Roosevelt signs the Nicaragua bill." He smiled dryly. "An outside chance. Certainly, an outside chance."

So the fight was on again! A harder fight than ever. No time for reflection, for recreation, for anything save work, and work and work inspired and encouraged by the indomitable will and the crafty ingenuity of William Nelson Cromwell. He didn't miss a trick. By a mixture of blarney, sincerity, and determination he first won the wholehearted support of Senator Spooner, who agreed to sponsor and introduce in the Senate a bill for the adoption of the Panama route and the acquisition of the French company's properties—the Spooner bill; and next, the support of the influential Ohio industrialist, Senator Hanna, whose conversion to the Panama route had begun in Paris the previous year as a result of a meeting there with Bunau-Varilla, formerly chief engineer of the Old Panama Company, and a large stockholder in the new.

While the Spooner-Hanna combination was contesting every move of Senator Morgan's to force the Hepburn bill through Congress, Cromwell

III

and his helpers were equally busy in the background. Chief among their activities was to rush the preparation and publication of a book intended to prove the validity of the French title. Senator Morgan countered this move by causing officials of the Panama Railroad Company to give testimony before the Senate Committee that if the U.S. Government were to acquire the Railroad Company's stock it would find itself committed to honoring an extraordinary number of transportation contracts as well as embarrassing engagements with the Government of Colombia and the State of New York.

Move and countermove. Check and countercheck. Cromwell's reaction was sharp and swift.

"We've been on the defensive too long. We're going to attack for a change. Mr. Godwin, do you know what it will cost the U.S. Government if the Nicaragua route is finally chosen? Thirteen million dollars, which the Nicaragua Company claims to have spent for concessions, construction material, and work."

Godwin whistled. "And that before the first American pick is lifted?"

"Exactly. See that the information is publicized. Also another fact—that the Nicaragua Company has already acquired an essential section of the route in anticipation of selling it to the U.S. Government at an enormous profit—"

"Just wait till I get my pen."

"And lastly, that the company will present to the Government a heavy claim for damages, on the ground of the alleged irregular declaration by Nicaragua of the forfeiture of its concession."

"I don't know what that means, sir, but just you leave it to me; I'll make the public rub their eyes, and think again."

The battle of the routes continued at an ever-increasing tempo; and on March 7 nature took a hand in it. The volcano Momotombo, a few miles north of the proposed Nicaraguan route, erupted. The Panama supporters gleefully made the most of this. Nevertheless four days later the Committee presented a majority report to the Senate in favor of the Hepburn bill, and against the Spooner bill.

Cromwell heard of this setback with a wry expression. Once again Godwin, who seemed to have the unhappy faculty of always looking on the darker side of events in which he was personally interested, prepared for the worst. The attorney, on the other hand, was spurred on to new efforts.

"We'll publish a minority report," he threatened.

"When are the two bills to be debated?" Godwin asked.

"June."

"Less than two more months to go—" was Godwin's gloomy and only comment. "Jumping catfish!"

With the approach of its climax the struggle between the rival factions grew more bitter. Convinced that the Senate committee had not given the

Momotombo eruption sufficient consideration, Cromwell decided to concentrate on this aspect of the battle. He ordered Godwin to obtain the advice of a distinguished scientist, an acknowledged expert on volcanic eruptions, and to have him write a series of articles which would force both congressmen and public alike to realize the danger of relying upon a canal driven through country subject to volcanic eruption. At the same time Godwin was to prepare a questionnaire, designed to ascertain the relative advantages of the two canals for practical navigation. These were sent to a number of shipowners, ships' officers, and other officials.

More work for the small staff at the Press Bureau, but the questionnaire went out on time, and authoritative articles on the dangers of volcanic activity in Nicaragua duly appeared in the pro-Panama press. As if pleased with this tribute to her awful power, nature once more came to the aid of Panama. On May 8, Martinique's Mont Pelé erupted, destroying the town of Saint-Pierre.

Cromwell's Press Bureau acted swiftly, by publishing maps reproducing all the known volcanoes in Central America. Copies of these were distributed to every senator, who was thus able to see for himself that no volcano existed within two hundred miles of the projected route through Panama.

More than eighty replies to the questionnaire were returned. These confirmed all the arguments in favor of the Panama route, and were extensively quoted by Senator Hanna during the course of the subsequent debate.

With the critical days of debate only a week ahead, both sides stepped up their activities. Scarcely a daylight hour passed that did not see fresh publicity material flowing from the indefatigable Press Bureau. Cromwell and his partners maintained a shuttle service between Washington and New York, so that at least two of them could be on hand for consultation; or to assist senators in replying to arguments directed against the Panama route; to supply vital information; to lobby senators in their own homes; and generally, to frustrate the hostile maneuvers of the Hepburn bill supporters.

Public interest was whipped up by such unprecedented rivalry, and like the Senators, divided into opposing camps. The Press likewise. Day after day the battle of the routes was headlined, and partisan moves fully reported. As soon as the debates began, a capacity audience thronged the Senate Chamber. From coast to coast the public eagerly awaited the answer to the great problem that had tantalized them for so long: which bill would win the day? The Hepburn bill with its majority report, or the Spooner bill which only a minority had favored?

The question was answered on June 20. By 42 votes to 34 the Senate voted to substitute the Spooner bill for the Hepburn bill.

17

NOBODY WAS MORE pleased with the latest development than Dulcie. Wesley went back to Providence for the week end. On the Friday, as they sat on the porch in the cool of the evening and watched the residents of Benefit Street taking the air, he told her of all that had happened since his previous visit, three weeks back. He was agreeably surprised by her interest, which was in sharp contrast with her usual attitude of barely concealed boredom. She left her own chair, and sitting on the arm of his played with his hair.

"Wes darling," she whispered. "I'm so happy."

Her delight made him aware how much he had missed her during the past months. This was the old Dulcie, the winsome, starry-eyed Dulcie of honeymoon days. Impulsively, he slipped an arm round her waist, and kissed her neck just below her ear.

"Extra happy, honey?"

"Extra," she confirmed.

"Why?"

"For your sake. And—"

"Well?"

"It means that your work in New York is finished."

The significance behind her words was not immediately apparent to him. He realized only their literal meaning, and chuckled.

"Finished! Not while Senator Morgan and his cronies have any fight left. Mr. Cromwell has won the latest round, honey, but there will be others."

"But I thought the bill settled the fight in favor of the Panama route."

"The Spooner bill? All the Spooner bill does is to leave the choice of routes in the hands of the President, and at the same time authorize him to pay forty million dollars for the concession and all property in Panama belonging to the French company."

"But isn't that the same thing? Isn't it certain that the President will choose the Panama route?"

"No, darling, it isn't. Before the President will agree to pay forty million dollars of public money for the Panama concession, we've got to prove to him that the Panama route *is* the best route. We shall also have to prove the legality of the French title to sell. The President will also have to come to terms with the Colombian Government over the transfer of the concession—"

"Wes! Please!"

114

The strained expresison in her voice caused him to twist his neck so that he could look up at her face. What he saw there startled him.

"Honey! What is it?"

"Don't tell me any more. I don't want to hear."

"But you asked—"

"I thought your work in New York was finished; that you would be coming home." Her expression hardened. "Aren't you, Wesley?"

"But—but—Dulcie, my sweet—" The unexpected attack left him helpless. "I—I could, I suppose, but—"

She took her hand away from his hair. "But what? You're a surveyor, not a—a clerk. Couldn't someone else do the work as well as you? Uncle Bill doesn't have to have a surveyor as his office boy."

He ignored the spite in her last remark, and answered her question. "Perhaps, at this stage, Uncle Bill doesn't need a surveyor permanently by his side. I think he knows almost as much about that aspect of the two canals as I do."

"Well then?" And still more sharply, "You haven't lost interest in your surveying work, have you? The only work you've been trained for."

Her malice hurt, but he determined not to lose patience with her. "No, my sweet, I haven't. I'm eager to get back to it—but not until the question of which canal has been settled once and for all."

She rose and returned to her own chair, where she regarded him with moist, mutinous eyes.

"You don't understand," he continued evenly. "When I start something I like to finish it."

"Don't flatter yourself, Wesley. *You* didn't start it. Mr. Cromwell did."

He shrugged. "Well, I was in it from the beginning, which is much the same thing. Besides, I have faith in the canal. I believe the United States needs one. The world too."

"What difference does it make either to our country or the world which route is used?"

Not much hope of making her understand the answer to that question, he wryly reflected. If the House couldn't!

"What's all this leading to?"

The question wrought another chameleonlike change in her. Again she rose from her chair, but this time she sat down on the porch floor so that she could rest her cheek on his knees and take his hands within her own.

"It's you who won't understand, my darling. Our married life isn't natural this way; you in New York, me in Providence."

"That's what I've been saying ever since I went there," he dryly interrupted. "And don't forget what you said at the same time; that a nice house would be worth a year or two's unhappiness."

Too intent upon pleading her own cause she ignored his comment. "You don't know what it means, to be left alone night after night; not to have anyone kiss me good night and good morning." She gulped. "I've been so lonely without you, Wes darling."

With bleak eyes he stared at a passing victoria. Would she never grow up, mentally? he wondered. Surely she was capable of realizing that if she had been as lonely as she maintained she had only herself to blame. Trains between Providence and New York were quick, and frequent. How many times had he pleaded with her to join him in New York? How many excuses had she found not to do so? Those hours of pleading and argument might never have been, for all the lasting effect they had upon her memory. By a feat of subconscious mental alchemy she had transferred the blame, and believed, in all sincerity, that he alone was responsible for the present duality of their marriage.

It would be easier to deal with her, he went on to think, if only her thought processes were less ingenuous. Temper he would know how to handle; or slyness or ingenuity. But to make her realize the truth would be as difficult and as cruel as depriving a child of his most cherished illusions.

On the other hand he felt warmed by the knowledge that she had missed him so much. Of late there had been too many occasions when he had surprised a distrait expression in her eyes, and noticed her irritating delay in answering unexpected questions. He had begun to feel that his married happiness was gradually slipping away.

He leaned over and kissed her cheek. "Let's not be parted any more."

She lifted her head, all smiles. "You *will* come back? Dear, dear Wesley. Oh, I do love you so. You must telephone Mr. Ackermann tomorrow first thing. No, tonight. He's sure to be home for dinner. He always is, Friday nights. And there's a lovely house coming on the market next month, Wes darling, just past the Phillipsons'—"

"Wait a minute, honey. You do rush ahead. I wasn't meaning that I should come back to Providence."

"But you said we wouldn't be parted any more."

"Of course I did. If you come to New York we won't be." He kissed her hands, and gazed at her with tender eyes. "If you come, we'll be rash, and rent a larger apartment. Mr. Cromwell's being very generous. Twice he's given Uncle Bill and me a raise."

"No!" As she drew back from him he saw that her mouth was mutinous. "I won't go to New York, Wesley. You know how much I'd hate to live there. I won't go."

"Then you didn't mean what you said about being lonely?"

"I did! I did! I did! But I want you to come back here, not for me to go to New York. Please, Wesley, come back. And please don't ever think of leaving Providence again."

He frowned. He had believed that he knew Dulcie in all her moods, but

116

there was a strange element in her present attitude which eluded him. Fear? Frenzy? Hysteria?

"Look, honey," he explained with all the patience he could muster, "I'm being paid enough to make it worth while for me to work for Mr. Cromwell for as long as he wants me. Besides, I'm interested in what I'm doing. I love it. I want to see a canal across Panama almost more than I want anything else in the world."

"More than my love?" she exclaimed.

He grimaced his irritation. "Of course not. That's different. I'm talking about my job now, not my private life. There are a dozen reasons why I should continue to work for Mr. Cromwell; not least of which is that I would be a fool to desert him at this stage. Right now I can see a better future with him than I'm ever likely to have with Mr. Ackermann."

"What future?" she asked with contempt. "As soon as he gets his stupid canal—*if* he does—your work with him will be finished, and you'll have to find another job. It might be too late then for Mr. Ackermann to want you back."

He was tempted to tell her of his wish to help build the canal, but he remembered Godwin's warning and resisted the impulse. Believing his silence to be the first sign of acquiescence she stood up, then curled up on his lap. When he wrapped his arms round her tiny body he felt it tremble.

"Come back to Providence, darling. Say you will. Please, please say you will. For my sake."

There was a note of urgency in her voice, and a queer tenseness in the way she was holding herself, that puzzled him. He had never known her so emotional.

"Honey, listen to me—"

She went on, as if unaware that he had tried to speak. "It's the first time I've ever asked you to do something specially for me. It's so important, darling, for you to come back here, soon—"

"But why soon, my pet? After all this time, I don't understand."

"Don't ask me questions. You'll make me cry." As if she wasn't crying already! "Besides, I—I couldn't answer. I don't know. All I do know is, that I want you to come back soon, next week, and never leave me again. Please don't leave me. Even this week. Stay here now. Don't go back."

"I couldn't stay here, just like that, Dulcie. It wouldn't be fair to Mr. Cromwell. I should have to give him proper notice."

She squirmed with delight at having gained her point. "Will you do that? Next week?"

"I'll think about it," he promised.

The promise to think about her demand was an easy one to keep. His trouble was, to forget it. The more he thought of the strange scene the more inexplicable it became. He could not rid himself of the feeling that she was afraid: yet he could think of no likely reason for fear. Over the

117

week end he discreetly questioned her on this point, but she derided the mere suggestion.

"Nervous to sleep alone in the house? Of course not, darling. Why should I be? Just because I'm lonely without you?"

He knew her too well not to believe her. She was essentially a truthful person; chiefly because she was too naïve and could not lie without patently betraying the fact.

On another occasion he slipped in a question, was anyone troubling her about anything? Mrs. Schultz wasn't being scandalous about his absence in New York, for instance?

Mrs. Schultz wasn't being unduly scandalous. She certainly wasn't worrying Dulcie. Nor was anyone else.

Was she worrying because Ackermann might not take him back if he were too long absent from Providence? If so, there were other firms who employed surveyors. New England Engineering, for instance; Biddle and Krautz, of Boston; Lavery Realty Company, of New London....

But she wasn't worrying about Ackermann. Ackermann was to be trusted. He wasn't the kind of man to break a promise. Wesley forbore to point out that she had, only two days previously, tried to gain her ends by pointing out that Ackermann might *not* want to take him back if he were away too long.

No matter how deeply he thought about it he could not find a satisfactory explanation to account for her fear. He could only conclude that she was not consciously aware of such fear. So he returned to New York on Monday morning none the wiser; but nevertheless committed to reach a decision that week as to his immediate future.

The detachment he had hoped to find in New York, in order to solve his own problem, was not to be found in the Press Bureau. The struggle between the two routes was still on. True, the Senate had passed the Spooner bill; but the House—which five months previously had voted for the Nicaragua bill by the overwhelming majority of 309 to 2—proved less malleable to Cromwell's advocacy. When the Spooner bill was sent to the House it was firmly rejected; and the Hepburn bill confirmed.

"What happens now, Uncle Bill?" Wesley asked.

"The bill will be sent into conference, to be considered by delegates from both Houses." Godwin chuckled. "Whichever House outtalks the other, wins."

So Wesley found himself with less opportunity than ever for sustained reflection. Cromwell sent him to Washington so that he might be on hand to give information to the conferees. There he met Senator Mark Hanna, who was the leading supporter of the Panama route. A shrewd observer, with the businessman's keen appreciation for a man who knows his job, Hanna soon came to rely not only upon Wesley's knowledge of the Panama route, but even more so upon his sincerity and enthusiasm for it.

118

In consequence Wesley was compelled to spend considerable time in the company of the redoubtable old senator, and for his part came to respect Hanna for his courage and tenacity. But for a long time no arguments of his sufficed to convince the senator that a lock canal could be preferable to a sea-level canal. As they traveled back and forth by carriage, between the Capitol and Hanna's hotel, or walked the journey as they sometimes did, according to the weather and the senator's mood, they frequently debated the point.

"Look here, young man, once we have forced the country to accept the Panama route, the question of what kind of a canal we shall build won't interest me. I'm a businessman, not an engineer, so I look for the shortest and the most convenient route between point to point. Between you and Mr. Cromwell, and Monsieur Bunau-Varilla, whom I met in Paris, I'm convinced that the Panama route is the best. That's why I'm fighting for it. But you won't make me believe that it's easier to raise the sea to the level of mountaintops than to blast the mountaintops away until sea level is reached."

But, one day, as they walked along Pennsylvania Avenue, Wesley placed a hand on Hanna's arm.

"Excuse me, senator."

"Well?"

"Look, sir. At that chip of wood in the gutter."

They had stopped opposite a subsidence in the gutter. Higher up the road men were at work on another, larger subsidence, close to which a load of sand had been dumped, ready for the making of concrete. A water carrier, parked nearby, was leaking. The water was trickling downhill in a narrow stream, carrying with it the chip of wood. A small pile of sand, dropped in the vicinity of the subsidence in the gutter, had formed a barrier, which prevented the flow of the water, to which Wesley pointed with his cane.

"Suppose we call the water the Pacific Ocean, senator, and the chip of wood, an ocean-going liner." He pointed to the subsidence. "The Isthmus of Panama, that sand on the right, the Continental Divide."

The senator's eyes sharpened. "Go on, young man."

Wesley fetched more sand from the load with which he built a slight wall round about the subsidence. "Mountains surrounding the valley of the Chagres," he went on to explain. "And on the far side of it, the Atlantic Ocean. What would you estimate the length of the subsidence?"

"About three and a half feet."

"Very well, senator, if we want to take that chip of wood to the far side of the subsidence, we should, theoretically, have to dig a channel three and a half feet long. But watch."

With the ferrule of his cane he channeled the wall of sand which obstructed the flow. The water trickled along it and into the subsidence which began slowly to fill. Soon the subsidence was no longer a hole but a pool. When its surface reached the height of the road Wesley channeled the wall of sand on the left. The water ran through the new gap into the gutter, and carried on downhill, so creating a slight stream which carried the chip of wood into the pool, across it, through the second channel and so into the "Atlantic Ocean."

"There is your lock canal, senator. Except that the lake at Chagres would be created by an internal rising of dammed water, the principle is the same. To take that chip of wood from one side of the 'Isthmus' to the other I made less than an inch of channeling instead of three and a half feet.

Hanna clapped Wesley on the shoulder. "You've converted me, Mr. Adam, and I thank you." He observed his companion's face, unexpectedly gloom. "Well, sir, aren't you satisfied?"

Wesley pointed to the channel he had made with his cane. Both sides of it were slowly subsiding into the water. "That's the second greatest enemy the canal builders will have to face, senator, when they cut through the mountains—slides."

"Humph!" After a pause, "And the first?"

"Disease, sir."

"Yet you still believe in the Panama route, young man. Why?"

"Because I believe in American courage and inventiveness."

"That's good enough for me, Mr. Adam." Hanna thumped the sidewalk with his cane. "I'll make those mule-headed conferees of mine see reason if it's the last thing I do in this world," he promised explosively.

In spite of Hanna's optimism about converting the conference as a body to his way of thinking, it became evident that neither side intended to yield. The factions on both sides were kept busy. Wesley was rarely out of the company of either Cromwell or Hanna.

Nevertheless, there were odd half-hours now and again when he found himself free to consider the future, but the resulting conflict of loyalties conspired to prevent his reaching any decision. He likened his own problem to the one being thrashed out in the conference room—except that in his own case it was Panama versus Providence instead of Panama versus Nicaragua.

The recollection of Dulcie's tears for her loneliness, and her impassioned plea for his return home, disturbed him. Worse, it made him feel conscience stricken, for he had inherited from two generations of New England ancestors something of their rigid morality. Believing that it was his moral duty to sacrifice his own desires to his love for Dulcie, he was aghast that he could even contemplate an action which was likely to cause her unhappiness. On the other hand, it was impossible to ignore that other characteristic, that inflexible obstinacy which was part of the Stewart heritage—the Stewart obstinacy which had made Great-grandfather Duncan accept the risk of ostracism in Haiti in order to practice medicine on Negro slaves; the same obstinacy which had kept Grandfather Henry in voluntary exile in Panama for five years in the hope of proving his innocence.

Duty versus obstinacy. Conscience versus desire. Which?

Panama versus Nicaragua. Which?

Day after day the conference remained in session, obstinate, unyielding.

Day after day Wesley tried to write out his letter of resignation from the Press Bureau, but he never reached the point of stretching out his hand for paper and pen. Likening himself to a theatergoer who has been asked to leave an exciting melodrama during the intermission before the last act, he loathed the idea of being away from the Bureau at the moment of victory. He wanted to see Cromwell's round, florid face light up, and see the triumphant toss of his arrogant head.

Above all, he wanted to ask for a job with the canal builders. More than anything else he wanted that. What if he had spent so much time writing propaganda that he had injected himself with the virus? It would be a magnificent achievement, and he wanted a part in it, however insignificant. He wanted to go back to the tropics, and help tame nature when she was most untameable. He wanted once more to experience the thrill of wandering along the narrow, crooked streets of the City of Panama, and to sample all the elusive charms of a town that had not stepped out of the sixteenth century. In fact, he even wanted to drive through Coco-nut Grove once more, and steal an embarrassed glimpse of the blatantly nude, bold-eyed, ample-breasted women who inhabited it. Damn it! He was a Stewart! All the Stewarts had been strong men, men of restrained but fierce passions.

A week wasn't long enough to reach a decision. He didn't want to surrender all his dreams and ambitions to what was probably no more than a passing whim, he sullenly reflected. He would be a fool to sacrifice the opportunity of a glorious future because of Dulcie's black week-end mood. He had been married to her long enough to know that all her moods were mercurial. It was possible that she had already forgotten her demands; and that were he able to speak to her at that moment, she might have completely different ideas, and might even beg him to try and get work on the canal project, for the sake of their future.

His conscience refused to allow him to believe wholeheartedly in this easy theory, but it suggested a compromise. Let Fate be the arbiter of his future. If the conference chose the Hepburn bill he would do as Dulcie wished, and resign. After all, he reflected rather more cheerfully, if Nicaragua were to be selected as the route for a canal, it was probable that Cromwell would disband the Press Bureau, and give up further hope of selling the French concession to the U.S. Government. If, on the other hand, the Senate should gain the victory in the conference room—well, he would give the proposition further thought, and make certain that Dulcie really did want him to return to Providence before he reached a final decision.

Fate, in the guise of six delegates, three from the Senate and three from the House, seemed in no hurry to decide Wesley's future. The irresistible appeared to have met the immovable. But the conference could not last forever, and it was a fact that the nearest volcano was more than two hundred miles distant from Panama! At last the delegates from the House gracefully yielded to the senior statesmen, and the Spooner bill was resubmitted to the House. After further discussion and die-hard opposition the House approved the decision of its delegates, and the Spooner bill was passed. Two days later, it received the President's signature.

"What's the matter, lad? What's worrying you?"

Wesley hesitated to burden Uncle Bill will his troubles, but he welcomed the opportunity of airing his worries and perhaps having the benefit of the older man's advice.

"Dulcie wants me to go back to Providence. She's lonely, and developing nerves about sleeping alone in the house."

"Oh!" Godwin took a long time in lighting a cigar. "So you'll be leaving us?"

"I don't know. I ought to."

Unconsciously he injected a question mark into the simple statement. Godwin sensed this, but willfully refused to answer. He knew better than to interfere in the domestic life of another man, however much he might sympathize with one or the other of the partners.

"You still don't want to?"

"You know I don't, Uncle Bill. I've enjoyed the fight. Every moment of it. As you have."

Godwin grinned. "Sure I have. I wouldn't have missed it for all the tea in China. Not that it's finished."

"Not finished? But the Panama bill is law."

"Yes, subject to conditions. I was talking to Mr. Cromwell last night. The Panama route will be used *if*, first, the title of the company is approved; and secondly, if a satisfactory treaty can be concluded. Unless both these conditions are fulfilled the Nicaragua route will be adopted by default."

"The title is clear, according to Mr. Cromwell."

"It isn't the title that's worrying him. He's investigated that. But the treaty—" Godwin gestured his private opinion of the prospect of an early treaty with Colombia. It was not a polite gesture. "In which case we haven't finished with those Nicaraguan fanatics yet. But this problem of yours, lad?"

"What would you do, Uncle Bill?"

"I'm not answering that question," he retorted sharply. "Every man

122

must solve his own domestic problems. But if Dulcie is missing you, and that's as it should be, bring her to New York."

"She won't come. She hates to be in New York for more than two or three days at a time. She says the noise makes her head ache."

He sighed. "Women are difficult, sometimes. Tell you what! Why not compromise? Rent a house some quiet place in the country, where the noise won't make her head ache. Someplace from which you could come into the city easily. She would soon make new friends to keep her happy during the day. Go back to Providence next week end, and talk it over with her."

After reflection Wesley nodded. Uncle Bill's suggestion was worth trying. If only Dulcie would leave Providence for more than a few days at a time she might grow accustomed to the change, and like it. She might even agree to accompany him to Panama—

18

BUT DULCIE DID NOT approve of Uncle Bill's compromise, although Wesley showed her photographs and descriptions of seven houses, all within easy reach of New York. Not only did she refuse to consider any suggestion of moving to New York, but now seemed indifferent about his returning to Providence. When he apologized for not having reached a decision about the future, she replied coldly.

"You must please yourself, Wesley. If you are content to live away from me then I must accept the situation with the best grace I can. Of course, it is not pleasant for a woman to learn that she has lost her husband's love."

"Honey," he protested. "It's ridiculous to talk like that. If I were content to live away from you I shouldn't have bothered to spend two weeks looking at houses. If only you will come to New York everything will be dandy. Just the way it used to be."

"If you will come back to Providence it can be that way again."

"It isn't fair to our future to ask that, Dulcie. Not now."

"Why not now?"

"I wrote to Mr. Ackermann about the partnership. I heard from him two days ago. He says there's no hope of one, not even if I put money into the firm. He's thinking of retiring, and going to Europe to live. Italy. maybe."

"Oh!" she exclaimed flatly.

"You can see for yourself that I must stay on in New York if I want to make a career. Mr. Cromwell has promised both Uncle Bill and me that he'll look after us once the Press Bureau closes. Come along, honey," he coaxed. "Be reasonable. Have another look at these houses, especially this one at White Plains—"

"No."

"But, darling—"

"No, Wesley. It's no use your persisting. If you want our marriage to be all it should be you must come back to Providence. Otherwise you will have to put up with the consequences—"

"Consequences!" he interrupted sharply. "What consequences?"

She swallowed. "I don't really mean consequences. You're flustering me." Her lips began to tremble. "What I mean is, just being married to me one week end in every three or four."

He began to feel angry and obstinate. "It's your duty as my wife to go with me wherever I choose to go. I'm beginning to think I've been too damned considerate—"

"There's no occasion to swear."

"I'm sorry. But I'm serious, Dulcie. I've the right to insist upon your coming to New York—"

He stopped abruptly, startled by her expression. He had never seen her normally placid features so passionate.

"If you did I should leave you."

"Dulcie!"

"I mean that."

His angry retort was checked by the knowledge that, if he failed to keep his temper in check, they would become involved in a passionate scene of mutual recrimination. He answered with studied patience:

"You wouldn't really do that, honey. We love each other too much." He held out an inviting hand, and smiled at her. "Come, my dear, we mustn't lose our tempers."

She ignored his peace overture. "I'm not angry. And don't think I'm saying things I don't mean. I'll do almost anything you want me to do, except leave Providence. But if you start claiming possession of me, body *and* soul—"

"That's stupid and farfetched." Despite himself his sharp voice had an undertone of exasperation. "To say I'm claiming possession of your soul just because I want you to live with me in New York! Grow up, Dulcie. You're a married woman, not a romantic young thing."

"I am not leaving Providence." He realized that in spite of his good intention they had reversed roles. It was he who was becoming hot with fury, and she whose deliberate manner offered convincing evidence of her dispassionate calm.

She went on. "You haven't objected overmuch to our having been parted all this time, Wesley. Now that I'm getting used to seeing you only occasionally why are you so anxious to change an arrangement that suits both of us?"

"It was you who wanted to change. Last time I came home, you said I didn't know what it meant, to be left alone night after night, asked me to come back to Providence for your sake."

She nodded. "And you refused. That horrible canal meant more to you than my loneliness. Well?"

"I didn't refuse—not as you make out—"

"No, you didn't refuse. That's true. You just went around the country-side looking for a nice house that you hoped would make me change my mind about going to New York. I suppose that isn't refusing, really."

"Dammit! Dulcie—" He stopped, shrugged. "God! What's the use of talking? We just go round and round the same old argument."

She smiled sweetly. "So let's not, shall we?"

"But what's Providence got? I like the old place more than well enough. Don't know of a better city to live in, all things being equal. But they're not. At the moment my future's in New York—and God knows where else—"

"So you must stay in New York, my dear, and come back to Providence when Mr. Cromwell permits. As for what Providence possesses for me—" She glanced wistfully out of the window. "Mother. My family. Friends. Benefit Street—especially if we can ever buy a bigger house—"

Her mention of mother, family, and friends pricked his conscience. He leaned forward, remorseful but eager to prove his case.

"That's the point, honey. I'm making money in New York. In a few years' time we shall be able to afford your dream house."

"A few years' time!" she repeated. "A few *years'* time! By then it will be too late."

"Too late for what? We're both still young, aren't we?"

"Yes," she agreed with indifference. "Don't forget that the Wilsons are coming tonight. Go tidy yourself. Your hair's awfully mussed-up. For Heaven's sake! And put on another shirt—"

Wesley realized that his relations with Dulcie had reached a state of crisis. As long as the Wilsons remained in the house she kept up a pre-tense of affection for him. She smiled at him, called him Wes, rubbed her fingers through his hair and kissed his cheek. Then, as the final shouted good nights were drowned by the clop-clop of hoofs and the rumble of iron-bound wheels, a change came over her. Her shoulders wilted, her voice turned morose.

"How that woman can talk! I thought they were never going."

"So did I, honey." He felt gay and forgiving. Slipping an arm about her he pulled her close to him. "Give me a kiss, darling. A long one." His lips sought hers, but they eluded him. She squeezed her small hands between their two bodies and pushed him away.

"With all the clearing and washing-up to be done!"

"Come along then." Determined to break down her frigid attitude before they went to sleep that night he went to work with a good will. Soon the parlor and the dining room were tidy, again, and the dirty china stacked ready for washing.

"You're looking tired. Like to leave it till the morning?"

"You know how I hate having to do the dishes before church," she snapped.

"Suits me," he agreed cheerfully. He slipped on an apron and began washing. Presently, "Do you think Nellie Wilson's having another?"

"Yes."

"The fourth in seven years. Tsk! Tsk!" After a pause, "Don't you sometimes wish, honey, that we—you—"

"No."

He grimaced. It wasn't being easy to thaw her out. Yet it used not to be so difficult. What had come over her?

"Darling."

"What is it?"

"Is it only New York you'd hate to live in, or wouldn't you leave Providence for any place?"

"Such as?" There was a flat note in her voice as if she spoke without conscious reflection.

"Oh! No place in particular," he prevaricated. "Some place in the British West Indies, maybe. Or Cuba. Once you learned Spanish you would love the way of life there. The food, the color, their markets and narrow streets." He laughed reminiscently. "Even the smells sometimes. A mixture of garlic, coffee, and perfume. Funny how one comes to appreciate it. What do you say? Do you think you'd like to try sometime?"

She did not reply. He turned and saw that her expression was blank. She was drying the same plate over and over.

"Well?"

She started. "What?"

"Never mind."

He made the next overture in bed. As she turned out the small oil-lamp which stood on the night table beside her he took her in his arms, fondling one of her little breasts.

"Honey! Honey darling!" he whispered, seeking and capturing her mouth. Her lips were cold, her body limp and trembling. Slowly her unwillingness communicated itself to him. He lifted his head, feeling bitter and frustrated.

"Please, Wesley, not tonight," she pleaded.

"Tonight should be a night of nights," he urged. "Lord! I haven't kissed

126

you properly for three weeks, and you don't know what that means—at least, I suppose you do." But even as he spoke the question passed through his thoughts, Does she? Perhaps it doesn't mean so much to a woman—

The same old nagging thought that had frequently plagued him since his return from Panama. In the past, trust, love, understanding had helped him resolutely to ignore the suggestion, but tonight it was less easy to overlook that unhappy, soul-chastening possibility. Tonight of all nights he could think of no reasonable excuse why she should try to avoid the sweet and natural communion of mutual love. She was in good health. She was young.

Perhaps she was in a mood to be wooed. So he kissed her again, not with passion but with affection; kissed her again and again, never in the same spot twice: on her forehead, on each eyelid, on the tip of her nose, on her chin and underneath. Then lower until his lips caressed the first swell of her breast. But there he stopped short, as always, not daring to explore further for fear of shocking her sensitive modesty. Besides, he was chilled by her lack of response and sensed that although physically she remained dutifully passive, mentally she was repelling his advances.

"Dulcie—"

"I've told you no," she whimpered. "I've an awful headache, listening to Nellie's chatter. Please, Wesley."

As far as he was concerned any charm the moment had possessed evaporated. With an irritable jerk he turned over and settled himself for sleep.

It was inevitable that his subsequent restlessness would fend off sleep, and just as inevitable that his thoughts should dwell upon Dulcie's present mood. The indifference with which she had greeted his apology early in the evening, followed by her present attitude worried him exceedingly. During their marriage he had seen her in many humors, for she had a childish habit of expressing her feelings by simulating whatever mood she calculated would attract and hold his affection. At first he had suspected their insincerity, but he had accepted the fact as being part of the give and take of married life.

Dulcie's present mood was different. For once it lacked the urge for exhibitionism. It seemed unhappily genuine. The thought that she could possibly regard him with genuine indifference made him feel sick with apprehension. Oh, God! he thought. Suppose she no longer loves me! Oh, God!

Soon he heard her breathing softly in sleep; and the sound, by proving that his wooing had had no effect whatever on her emotions, increased his misery and his fear. Perhaps he had lost her. The phrase repeated itself in his thoughts with sadistic monotony. He had lost her! He had lost her! He had lost her!

In spite of his agony, he did not entirely blame her. Remembering how passionately she had begged him to return to Providence, he realized now that he had had warning of what might happen if he continued to live away from her. The probability that she had realized the meaning of what was happening no more than he, only added to his bitterness. Three weeks ago he might have avoided wrecking their marriage; three weeks ago she had not been indifferent to him. On the contrary, she had clung to him in complete trust, loyally convinced that in the last resort he would give her desires preference over his career. And he, poor fool, had betrayed her trust. He had sacrificed her love to personal ambition.

Now he had lost her! But had he? Common sense reassured him it was unlikely that such irreparable harm could be done in three weeks. Perhaps there was still time to salvage their marriage. Damn Panama and its canal! On Monday morning he would hand in his resignation to Cromwell. Dulcie, and their mutual happiness, were more important. No more vacillating—

Uncle Bill was quick to see that the week end had not been a happy one for Wesley. Perhaps he had anticipated trouble.

"So this time you really mean to resign?"

Wesley started. "How do you know that? I haven't mentioned it—"

"It's written all over your face. You look as if you'd lost your last friend."

"I'll have to go back to Providence, Uncle Bill. If I don't I may lose Dulcie."

"*Lose* her?"

"Her love, I mean. All this week and she's been acting like a stranger. Formal and indifferent except when we've had visitors."

The older man nodded gravely. "You know how much I'll hate to see you go, but you're right." His eyes turned wistful. "Happiness in marriage is the most important thing in life."

Wesley kicked a wastepaper basket out of his way. "I'll have to write Mr. Cromwell right away—"

"You won't have to. He sent a message to say that he'll be in this morning." He watched Wesley slump moodily into his chair. "Wouldn't she consider a house someplace in the country?"

"No. I tried to show her the pictures I took up with me, but she wouldn't even look."

"Why wouldn't she, lad? After all, you are her husband."

"So I tried to point out to her. She won't leave Providence because of Mother, and the rest of her family, and friends. She said she'd leave me rather than live anywhere else."

Godwin looked startled. "As bad as that? Does she mean what she says? After all—" He stopped short in embarrassment.

"You can say what's in your mind, Uncle Bill. Dulcie's always acting some sort of a dramatic role. Isn't that it?"

"Well—"

"I've always realized that, but it hasn't mattered much. I've had fun, coaxing her back on an even keel. This time she isn't acting. She's in deadly earnest." Wesley was bitter. "It's not so funny, suddenly finding out that your wife doesn't care a damn for you."

"Not so funny," Godwin agreed. Presently, "So long as you're here, will you help me with an article for the London *Times?* Something technical. The problem of keeping up the canal level—"

Cromwell arrived as the first draft of the article was nearing completion.

"Sorry to interrupt, gentlemen, but I'm accompanying the Attorney-General to Paris in a few days' time to help him investigate the New Panama Canal Company's titles, and obtain the stockholders' approval of the transfer."

"Won't be long now," Godwin commented with satisfaction.

The lawyer's lips registered disagreement. "I wish I could agree with you, Mr. Godwin. But the Colombian Minister, Concha, is proving even more intractable than I had anticipated. One of his demands is an annual sum, in perpetuity, of six hundred thousand dollars."

Godwin whistled. "That's a lot of money."

"Of course," Cromwell snapped. "And it is only one among other equally outrageous conditions. Senator Morgan is openly jubilant, and boasting that we shall eventually fall back on the Nicaragua route."

"I guess he's not one to leave it at mere boasting?"

"Naturally not. He and his friends are constantly scheming to bring pressure on President Roosevelt. But the matter which has brought me here today concerns you, Mr. Adam. Do you know that, besides acting as attorney for the New Panama Canal Company, I act for the Panama Railroad Company in a similar capacity?"

"Yes, sir."

"I received a letter from Colón this morning to say that one of the railroad's permanent survey staff has resigned as of the end of this month, and they are asking for a man to be sent down to replace him. The pay is excellent, as you know. Would you care to accept the post?"

Wesley's expression made the attorney frown. "I understood from you that you were hoping to be offered a job in Panama as soon as digging operations begin?"

"Yes, sir, that's right, but—"

"I'm sure it will be possible to effect a transfer from the railroad to the canal when the time comes. Meanwhile, you could be familiarizing yourself with the terrain."

Wesley glanced hopelessly at Uncle Bill, which annoyed the attorney. "If you don't want the job, Mr. Adam, say so at once."

"He'd like the job well enough, Mr. Cromwell," Godwin interrupted. "Mrs. Adam's the trouble. Wesley reckons she may leave him if he doesn't soon return to Providence for keeps."

"That's right," Wesley confirmed miserably. "I was going to write you a lettter of resignation today."

"I'm sorry. In that case—" he rose.

Godwin looked at Wesley's forlorn face. "Look, sir, Wesley would give his eyeteeth to take that job. Isn't that so, Wesley?"

"Yes."

"Well?" Cromwell asked with an impatient gesture.

"Could you give him the day off, sir, to go back to Providence and talk the matter over with his missus? If she knows he's got a definite offer maybe she'll look at things differently."

"Would you like to do that, Mr. Adam?"

Hope warmed Wesley through. "Yes, sir."

"Very well. Be at my office not later than nine fifteen tomorrow morning, to give me your decision." Cromwell held out his hand. He could be very gracious when he wished. "Good luck! Remind Mrs. Adam what Panama meant to your grandfather. If you do half as well as he did there—"

The house in Benefit Street was empty. There were dirty dishes in the kitchen. The bed had been slept in, but was unmade. The room was untidy. An envelope lay on the floor near the door, flap side uppermost: it looked as if it might have dropped from Dulcie's pocketbook. Wesley picked it up, and turned it. It was stamped, and addressed to him in New York.

He chilled with apprehension as he slit open the envelope with trembling fingers. The letter inside was not long, but his eyes were drawn to the only words that mattered:.... *gone away with Mr. Ackermann* ....*Paris and afterward Florence and Venice*....*the blame is all yours. If you had come back to Providence in time....*

19

WESLEY SNUGGLED into the hay. He was cold, and painfully tired. His feet ached abominably; so did every bone in his body. His contentment in feeling the yielding softness was sensual; which was grimly ironic. For, an hour or so ago, he wouldn't have given a dime for his chances of coming out alive. The battle between common sense and heartbreak had been long and painful, but it was over. He knew, by now, that the crazy impulse to commit suicide no longer existed. His manhood had saved him from the extreme act of cowardice.

Now that he could look objectively at the events of the past hours it gave him some sense of relief to reflect that if one was determined to die, one might as well die easily. The barn was as good as any other place in which to expedite one's departure for the next world, for the smell of the new-mown hay was as sweet as its bulk was warming, and both were incredibly soothing.

Suppose that his decision had been different what would his reflections be right now, he wondered. He would have been thinking that, as soon as his nerves were steady, he would put the automatic to his forehead, and pouf! that would be the end of Wesley Adam; and the end of a career that twelve hours earlier had offered a lot of promise. The end, too, of all worries and troubles. No more heartburning; no more treachery.

No more heartburning! He pulled the weapon from his hip pocket, and rubbed his fingers up and down the barrel. Here was his ticket and passport to the next world, with no limit to the period of availability. Inexpensive, too, for such a long journey. It took courage *not* to use it, and so bring eternal peace to a nature that he was sure would not easily recover from the blow it had received that afternoon. In fact—perhaps—

His mouth hardened with the knowledge that his resolve to live was weakening. Perhaps it would be better to unload the gun and throw the slugs away while he still had the spunk to do so. Which thought suggested another, absurdly ridiculous: he could not be certain that it was loaded. It was the one he had taken to Panama. Afterward, when he had first gone to New York, he had loaded it and left it handy for Dulcie's protection, in the drawer of her night table. He had not looked at it since, until this afternoon. Even then, in the moments of frenzy following the reading of Dulcie's letter he had been too wrought-up to check up on whether it was still loaded.

He fumbled for his matches, and struck one. The small flame was reflected on the smooth barrel.

"Murder, robbery, or suicide? If it's the middle one, brother, count me in."

Already that day shock had unsteadied his nerves. The weapon fell from his hand as he impulsively leaned forward with the intention of moving on. Solitude was what he wanted. Not company. A hand caught hold of his jacket and pulled him back into the hay.

"Don't go, bud. It's more comfortable here."

"Let go of my coat."

"All right! All right! If I've made a mistake I'm sorry. If you'd tramped the roads as long as I have you'd know that men don't flourish guns in the middle of the night for no reason at all."

"Well?"

"I guess you're no exception."

In spite of his annoyance Wesley was interested.

"Is it any affair of yours?"

The other man laughed. "From your voice I can tell you ain't no hobo. That means robbery is out." He sighed. "Pity! I could've done with a few bucks. Haven't seen any real dough for years. Hell! If it ain't robbery it must be murder or suicide, in which case I can tell you something better than both of 'em."

The more Wesley listened the more his curiosity was aroused. There was something extraordinary about the voice that came from his left. It was coarse and husky, but sometimes an odd inflection betrayed itself, a hint that its owner had been an educated man.

"Who are you?"

"That's my business," the voice replied cheerfully. But I'm known to me pals, a number of sheriffs, and some New York cops as Larry. Anything more you'd like to know?"

"Yes. Where am I?"

"Somewhere near Cranston."

"I must have walked all of twenty miles," Wesley bitterly commented.

"Practicing for a marathon?"

Already tiring of company, Wesley was in no mood for levity. He rose to his knees, but only to be pulled back again into the hay.

"Don't go, friend. I haven't talked to a—a guy like you for years. It's quite a change." There was a wistful note in the voice which made Wesley reluctant to leave.

"What are you? A farm hand?"

Larry chuckled. "Nothing so high up in the scale of civilized society. Just a bum, me."

"A bum. A man like you should be something better than a bum."

"What do you mean, a man like me?"

"You sound as if you had a good education."

"Never mind. The past is *past,* see! Now, what are you doing with that gun? Suicide?"

On second thought, perhaps it was less painful to talk, even to a bum, than mull over Dulcie's treachery. Wesley decided to prevaricate.

"That's what I had in mind."

"Money trouble?"

"No."

Larry laughed. He had a curious way of laughing, by expelling the air through his teeth in a series of short blasts that sounded like air being pressed out of a rubber container.

"Then it's a woman. For the love of God! Fancy a grown man shooting himself on account of some girl won't have him. As if there weren't millions of others to pick from."

"This one was my wife. She ran away this morning."

The other man was silent for a second or so. "I'm sorry, brother. That's different."

"Of course it is. It's like having someone cut three quarters of your heart out of you. What's left doesn't seem worth having." Wesley laughed unhumorously. "I don't know why the hell I'm telling you all this. Why should I?"

"Because it's a relief to tell someone, even a bum. It's better out than in, ain't it?"

"Probably."

"Well, then! Besides, I can tell you a better idea than scattering your brains to the four winds."

"I doubt it. When you love someone the way I loved my wife, would you want to go on living?"

"Of course."

"I suppose you think you're the only man who's ever loved a woman so much, and that a bum like me doesn't know what real love is, anyway?"

Wesley reflected. The bum was right. All evening he had been wallowing in self-misery, telling himself he was a fool for having allowed himself to fall so desperately in love with anyone, and thinking that his great love was exceptional. Maybe other men could love, too. Maybe some woman was the cause of Larry's being a bum.

"Sorry!" he curtly apologized.

Larry's laughter sissed between his teeth. "I got more sense than to fall for a woman. But I seen enough of life, while I've been bumming my way from coast to coast, to know a damn sight about human nature."

"Go on."

"You think love's the most powerful emotion there is, don't you, and that without love life's not worth living?"

"I don't know. I'm past thinking."

"Let me tell you that it ain't. There's a stronger, much more powerful feeling in most of us. D'you know what that is?"

"No, what?"

"God! Hate!" There was a sudden change in Larry's voice. The light-hearted flippancy, the casual levity which had previously underlined every word, was discarded, and the savage intensity with which he uttered the last word startled Wesley. He did not have an opportunity to speak, however, for Larry went on. "I've hated once in my life; the kind of hate that tortures and half kills you, until you're crazy to revenge yourself on the other man. And see here, brother, the worse your hatred, the greater your satisfaction when you finally get your revenge. God! There's no happiness in this world or the next to equal that."

Wesley stirred uneasily. Deep, abiding love he could comprehend and sympathize with; but the hatred that the man beside him was trying to describe wasn't natural or human. There was an unbridled, satanic quality about it that shocked his New England conscience.

133

"Nonsense!" he muttered. "A normal man doesn't obtain satisfaction from hurting someone, just because that someone hurt him first."

"Is that so? Suppose a dog bit your hand through to the bone! You'd shoot the animal dead, wouldn't you, if you had the chance? What's that but revenge? Suppose a man deliberately drove his carriage over your child. Suppose there wasn't proof to convict him of murder or manslaughter. Wouldn't you crave to grind his face in the mud with your heel until the brains spurted out? That's revenge, ain't it? That's hate, ain't it? Justice, too, but it would be hate, not a sense of justice, that would make you smash his brains in."

Wesley hesitated to contradict. Fond as he was of dogs, some years ago he had whipped one for snarling at him. Of course, his object had been to teach the animal a lesson, but he had applied the whip hard enough to make the dog howl, and afterward had felt ashamed of himself for losing his temper. But suppose the dog had bitten his hand, to the bone, as Larry said. Would the punishment have rested at a whipping?

Suppose someone should deliberately drive a carriage over a child of his? Good God! Larry was right. Hate, and a determination to avenge the child's injuries would be a natural sequel. Especially if the murderer were someone like Ackermann. Ackermann! Wesley became aware that his fingers were crooked and stiff. He realized, to his dismay, that he would give much to have Ackermann's thickset throat within reach of those crooked fingers. The pig! The god-damned dirty pig!

He straightened his hands. "What of it?" he asked harshly, resenting the effect Larry's words were having upon him. He was capable of working out his own problems, wasn't he? Without having to listen to melodramatic advice from a strange bum. "What's all this leading up to?"

"Well, I nearly committed suicide once, only I was too damned weakminded. Afterward I was glad I hadn't. Instead of killing myself I settled for revenge. After that I didn't rest until I had gotten it, and, by God, was I happy then? Have been ever since. I'm known as the happiest bum north of the Mason-Dixon line. It doesn't matter to me whether it rains or snows, whether I have any money in my pocket or not, whether I'm in jail or out of it."

"Why don't you work? You sound healthy enough to."

"Work! I'd as soon—well, do what you're thinking of doing. Why work when I can beg or steal?"

Wesley experienced a revulsion of feeling. Up to that moment he had felt vaguely sympathetic toward Larry, though the casual words had made it obvious that he had only himself to blame.

Wondering whether the bum had any pride left, he decided that a quick inspection would help him more easily to judge the man's character. A method of doing this occurred to him.

"Smoke?"

134

"Butts—when I can find 'em."

"How about a cigarette now? A whole one?"

The hissing laugh was answer enough. "Can a duck swim, brother?" Wesley took a cigarette from his case. "Where's your hand?"

"Here, waiting."

The cigarette changed hands.

"That's funny!" Wesley murmured.

"What is?"

"I can't find my matches. I had them—"

"Don't fret, brother," Larry sissed. "I took them from you ten minutes ago. Your tobacco pouch as well. That was all I could reach."

Wesley knew it was ridiculous to be angry with the man. Larry struck a match to light his cigarette, which gave Wesley the chance he had maneuvered for to inspect the man.

Only his head and arms were exposed. The rest of him was hidden by the hay. His clothes, as much of them as could be seen, were torn and dilapidated. A hat, which he wore at a jaunty angle at the back of his head, was more than adequately ventilated.

It was the face, however, upon which Wesley concentrated. The weakness which he had already sensed, and which Larry had frankly admitted, was unmistakably revealed; especially by his mouth. But for this the man might be considered almost handsome.

His features revealed good breeding, and looked finely sensitive; his dark eyes were filled with puckish humor; his complexion was tanned and flushed with health—but even its healthy color did not disguise the layer of dirt, nor hide the scrubby chin which obviously had not been touched by brush or razor for more than a week.

Although it was the kind of face Wesley had anticipated, it saddened him to see such a wreck of a man; a fine nature coarsened by environment.

For nearly a minute Larry pulled at his cigarette; inhaling deeply, and then exhaling with a sigh of contentment. Then, "Were you satisfied?"

"What do you mean?"

"Well, you offered me a cigarette, didn't you, to give yourself the chance of studying me while I lit it?"

Wesley felt deeply chagrined. "Yes."

"Were you—disgusted?"

"Yes and no. After all, you had more or less warned me."

"What I mean is, what were your thoughts concerning a man you probably consider as having sunk pretty low?"

"You want the truth?"

"It won't hurt me. I'm tough."

"I'm just—disappointed."

Larry laughed. Wesley began to think that the one hateful thing about the bum was that laugh. It was scornful and derisive. It mocked one.

135

"Just what I expected you to say, although you couldn't have been more cutting. Still, it leaves me unrepentant. Like to hear my story? Might do you good. If you commit suicide afterward it will be your own blamed fault, and you'll get no sympathy from me."

He did not trouble to wait for a reply. "I did have a college education. And paid for too. None of your working your way through for me." He chuckled. "I shouldn't have graduated that way. You can guess my parents were rich. If I were to tell you my name you would know how rich."

Wesley noticed that Larry's accent and intonation unwittingly improved as he went on to speak of the past.

"A week after I graduated from college my father died. His will left everything to Mother. Unfortunately for me, a year later she married again. It's not easy to describe the sort of man her second husband was, but he was a devil, and after her money. Naturally, he loathed me, and persuaded Mother to make me enter a god-damned office; next he forced her to alter her will, leaving all Dad's money to him instead of to me— and this after Mother had promised Father that I should never be in want. Lastly, he murdered her."

This Wesley could not accept. "Oh, come—" he began.

"Oh! quite legally. You can't execute a man for badgering a woman to death. He took care to stab her with a weapon that was invisible, intangible by falsely proving to her that Father had made his money by fraudulent means. After months of mental torture Mother died of a broken heart, and he collared the cash. Then he turned me out.

"It was then I went down to the river. On the point of throwing myself in, the thought of floating about as a corpse sapped my resolution. I couldn't face death. But I began to hate my stepfather. Worse than— than—the river.

"I had cause to hate, brother, and God! how I hated, because he had turned me out of what ought to have been my own home. Day and night I dreamed of nothing else but revenge; I knew I would never be happy till I got it. I didn't intend actually to kill him. I saw no sense in risking my life *swinging* for him. But I thought if I could see him in prison, well, I wouldn't mind going there as well.

"In the end I did it. By means of forgery and trickery I got him into the pen beside me. The more he raved at me the more I became an innocent cat's-paw in the eyes of the jury. He protested his innocence, but it wasn't much good. I had worked the scheme out too thoroughly. He got seven years, and I got two.

"I tell you, brother, that day was the happiest of my life. When I thought of his spending seven whole blasted years in prison I laughed for sheer joy. Much better than being a corpse, I thought, while he spent my money.

136

"Now go to sleep, and tomorrow you think over what I've said. Revenge is sweeter than death. Go after that couple and pay them back in their own coin! It won't matter much what happens afterward, you will have paid your debts. Good night, bud."

Wesley heard a rustling of straw. He settled himself down to think, but just as he was comfortably stretched out he heard Larry speaking again.

"Oh, by the way, friend! If you still insist upon shooting yourself, you might go somewhere else to do the dirty work so as not to wake me up. You will, won't you?"

"I promise," Wesley agreed.

20

WITHIN A MINUTE Wesley knew Larry was asleep. Quick work, he reflected with envy. It wasn't likely he would drop off with the same facility. Not tonight. He'd be lucky to sleep at all. In spite of the interruption brought about by his encounter with Larry, already his mind was being flooded by the bitter thoughts which had tortured him ever since he had read Dulcie's cold note of good-by.

In the light of subsequent happenings it was easy now to follow the sequence of events. It must have begun during his stay in Panama—and, to make matters even more painful, had probably sprung from his own hint to Ackermann that he would earn the thanks of an absent husband if he were to keep in touch with Dulcie. "If you could drop in to see her now and again, Mr. Ackermann, I would be more than grateful. She'll be lonely without me. And if you're not taking anyone else to a concert, well, you know how fond she is of music. Especially the Boston Symphony—"

That would have been how it had started; and Ackermann, damn his hide! must have fallen for her like a ton of bricks. Simple, now, to understand why his promise of a partnership had never been fulfilled. He must have discovered quite soon that Dulcie had extravagant tastes; and no doubt he had planned his campaign by deliberately pandering to them. With Machiavellian cunning he had probably emphasized the difference between his own standard of living and that of his employee. He had subtly encouraged Dulcie to prefer and desire luxury, and the companionship of the elite of Providence. He had played upon her shallow nature, and unsettled her.

To be just to Dulcie, Wesley did not believe that she had been a conscious party to Ackermann's unscrupulous scheme. For a long time she had been a victim rather than an accomplice. Then, when at last she had realized the abyss toward which she was drifting, conscience had influenced her. "Come back to Providence," she had pleaded. "Please, please, Wesley, come back and never leave me again. Please—"

And he, comprehending nothing, had done nothing. Convinced that only in the weeks following her plea had she capitulated for the first time to Ackermann's advances, Wesley stirred restlessly in the agony of remorse. If only he had regarded her wishes, on that occasion, instead of his own.

He did not absolve her from all blame. When she had persistently refused to live with him in New York, her dislike of that city had not been her only reason for refusing. Even then she must have been so fascinated with Ackermann's company that she was not willing to forgo it, however innocent she may then have regarded it. She had neglected her duty to her husband for a selfishly personal reason.

His imagination pictured the guilty couple in some distant hotel. He tortured himself by seeing them in the most compromising circumstances, and in doing so comprehended more vividly than hitherto the feelings of hate about which Larry had talked so glibly. God! There was something satisfying about hating somebody, for other emotions were consumed in the fire of hatred.

His vision of Dulcie in Ackermann's short fat arms, for instance—already its effect on him was less poignant than had been the case an hour ago, as he had walked blindly on along unknown roads. In fact—and his lips parted in a smile of grim satisfaction—almost as clearly as though the scene were being enacted before his eyes, he saw Dulcie shrinking away from her lover. It was certain that Ackermann wouldn't have suspected that he had seduced a woman in whom the flame of sexual passion flickered only feebly. H.C. was a man whose interest in women was solely physical. Affection was a word not in his dictionary of human relationship.

Wesley was loath to admit that injured pride was fast taking the place of heartbreak in the confused tangle of emotions which were shocking his normally placid nature, yet already a new aspect of Dulcie's elopement had occurred to him. Her going had freed him of the one tie which prevented his accepting Cromwell's offer to join the staff of the Panama Railroad Company. He could return to Panama with a clear conscience! Now that it was no longer disloyal to her to do so, he remembered those occasions when he had doubted whether she was capable either of accepting or returning the passionate love which the average man hopes to find in his marriage.

The gentle breathing next to him reminded him of Larry. He was grateful for their chance encounter. It was as if the weakness of Larry's

138

character had, by contrast, developed the strength of his own, and had enabled him to evaluate the situation in its true light. Perhaps, in the morning, he could do something to express his thanks in concrete form—

The day was bright with sunshine when Wesley awoke from a sound, dreamless slumber. He felt rested, his brain clear. Remembering the events of the previous night, he rose to his feet and looked about him. Everywhere his glance ranged the scene was cheerful. The day, the countryside, everything was in the nature of a good omen for the new chapter in his life that was just beginning.

His bedroom, he saw, was a Dutch barn, half filled with freshly gathered hay. It stood near a road bordered by pasture on either side. Half a mile to the east were two farmhouses and several field hands were at work, pitching hay on to a wagon. It was fortunate that he had awakened before the men drove the wagon into the barn to be unloaded. He was not anxious to be taken for, and perhaps treated as, a bum.

Thinking of bums, he remembered Larry. It might be as well to wake the other man up, and warn him to move on while there was time. He stepped back into the shelter of the barn to do this, and at the same time demand the return of his tobacco pouch. Larry was not there. Evidently his day began early. Wesley returned to the road, and turned to the east, where he hoped Providence lay. Somehow he was sorry not to have said good-by to Larry.

There was a bite still in the wind—or maybe it felt that way in comparison with the warmth of the hay—which made him glad of the protection of his clothes, but he soon became warm. Almost too warm for comfort. The day gave promise of considerable heat, and the prospect reminded him that he was on the first stage of his journey back to Panama. Now that his decision was made he was impatient to be there. The sooner the better. Different surroundings and hard work would help to dull the echo in his heart and he was anxious to see the country again, for it had become steadily more fascinating in retrospect.

In his impatience to reach the nearest Western Union office so that he could send a telegram to Cromwell, his pace quickened. He passed a field where a farmer and his help were gathering hay, and was amused to see the men stop work in order to stare curiously at a stranger from nowhere. He passed the two farmhouses, and began to breast a hill. Upon reaching the summit he saw, some distance ahead of him, a figure which moved grotesquely along the road, slowly and limpingly—up and down, shuffling and slouching forward for all the world like a bundle of rags being dragged along at the end of a rope, and bumping awkwardly over every rut in the world. Larry!

It did not take him long to catch up with the other man.

"You're in an almightly hurry, Larry."

Larry grinned. "Of course I am. I wasn't waiting about for any of those farmhands to give me a boot in my behind. I've had too many."

"Why didn't you wake me up? I suppose it didn't matter to you if it was my behind that got kicked?"

"Not much. You were so sound asleep, I hadn't the heart to disturb you. Besides, I didn't want to rush you out of this world, even if it is a god-damn awful one."

Wesley reflected. Why not give the poor devil the satisfaction of believing that it was solely due to his efforts that there would be no suicide? No harm in that. Perhaps good.

"You don't have to worry. I'm doing what you advised."

"Oh! What was that?"

"I'm going after my man, Larry. I'll not rest until I've had my revenge like you."

"I?" The other man sounded surprised.

"Yes. On your stepfather."

Larry's laughter for once developed into a genuine guffaw, so loud it startled some lambs into antics.

Wesley felt nettled. "What's so funny?"

Larry turned a dirty, grinning face toward his companion. "I never thought you'd believe such a fairy story. Remind me sometime to tell you about Goldilocks and the Three Bears."

Wesley caught hold of Larry's arm—it felt as thin as a skeleton arm— and swung him round. "Just what do you mean?"

"For God's sake! You sure are a mother's boy, brother. I was spinning that yarn to keep your mind off suicide."

"There wasn't a word of truth in it?"

Larry's eyelids flickered. His mouth turned sullen.

"Wasn't there?" Wesley's grip on the skeletonlike arm tightened, until its owner winced.

"In parts, maybe."

"The way in which your stepfather killed your mother?"

"Yes, god-damn him!" The weak face turned savage.

"And the story of how he turned you out of a home that was rightfully yours?"

"That was true, too."

"Your hatred?"

The pale eyes blazed. "God Almighty! Can you doubt that? I'm human, aren't I?"

Wesley did not doubt. One couldn't, looking into those eyes.

"Then it was the story of your revenge you invented? You didn't try to avenge your mother? You didn't sacrifice yourself for the sake of sending him to prison?"

The flabby mouth twitched, and pouted sullenly. "No."

"Didn't you think two years in jail would be worth while if your stepfather was there for seven?"

Larry winced at the contempt in Wesley's voice. "Yes, but there was never a chance."

"Another invention?"

Larry shrugged.

"And the story of the river?"

The man straightened up. "That was true. I went to the river to throw myself in, but when I got there I couldn't. The water looked too cold. I was afraid of—of—drowning."

"Wasn't that the idea?"

Larry shivered. "I just couldn't."

"You thought bumming was easier?"

"Rub it in. I know I haven't any guts. I was born a weakling. Look at my foot! Crooked as sin. It's all the fault of my foot. I've never been able to stand up for myself. Other boys could always bully me because they could run circles round me. All my life I've been dictated to, trodden on, pee'd on. Now I don't care a damn. I'm happy as I am. A haystack to sleep in, a crust of bread and a glass of beer to live on, a cigarette once in a while, and the world can go drown itself for all I care."

Wesley inspected the tramp. Seen in daylight he looked even worse than he had the night before. His face was soft, effeminate in its weakness.

Nevertheless, Wesley could not wholly despise the little man. Larry's clear, truthful eyes, his wry humor and his philosophical, happy-go-lucky nature somehow helped to redeem him. Besides, there was this to be said in his favor; that he had sincerely tried to save the life of a fellow sufferer. Not by heroic means, perhaps; but still, he could have shrugged and turned the other way. He could, in fact, have lived up to his custom of letting the world (in this case, Wesley) go drown himself for all he cared!

"Look, Larry, I haven't thanked you for what you did last night."

"Shucks! You would probably have gotten cold feet at the last minute, as I did."

"That's not the point. I might not have. Now I'd like to do something for you."

"Mean that, brother?"

"If it's in my power."

"Give me what's left of your cigarette pack."

Wesley had to chuckle. "That's no compliment to the value of my life."

"Don't forget I have your tobacco pouch as well. When I've finished the tobacco I'll be able to sell the pouch and buy some more. Besides, I'll get a couple of dollars for your gun."

"My gun!" Wesley automatically felt his pocket, but it was flat.

141

"Yeah! I took it from your pocket while I was keeping you interested with my life story."

He glanced searchingly at Larry. "Why did you take that gun? For the sake of the money you'd get selling it, or to make sure I wouldn't use it the moment you turned your back?"

Larry's eyes twinkled. "Do you want the truth?"

"Yes."

"Both."

"Ah!" But Wesley did not believe that reply. No doubt Larry would ultimately have sold the revolver, but Wesley was convinced that his only object in taking the weapon was to prevent its being used.

"So I've even more reason to be grateful than I believed. Listen, Larry. I meant what I said about wanting to do something for you if I can. Isn't there something I can do for you?"

Larry stared up into his companion's more serious, darker eyes. "I believe you mean that," he said presently.

"Well?"

"Are you a rich man?"

Wesley grinned. "Like any other worker."

Larry sighed. "Pity! I could've sponged on you for the rest of your natural life. Ah well! Just my luck to save a poor man's life."

"You wouldn't like a job some place?"

"I thought you wanted to reward me, not punish me."

"I don't believe you're that work-shy."

"Don't you? But then you believe in fairy stories."

"How about a new suit?"

"I don't accept charity, brother. Unless you got an old suit you don't want. I'll call in sometimes when I'm your way."

"You'll be lucky! I'm leaving for Panama any day now. Got a job there."

"Panama!"

Wesley stared at his companion. Larry's face blazed with excitement. "What's the matter, man? You look as if you'd just seen Santa Claus."

"Brother, if you mean all you said about doing something for me—" The stuttering words overlapped one another. Wesley could barely make out what was being said. "You can stake me to a passage there." His thin fingers clawed hold of Wesley's coat. "I'm not asking for a first-class passage. Steerage will do me. Only so long as I get there."

"Why the sudden excitement? If you're so crazy to get to Panama why didn't you go there years ago? You are free, aren't you? Nothing to stop you."

"Money."

"What's wrong with working a passage? My grandfather did."

Larry ignored the question. "Will you?" he went on hoarsely. "It's not much in exchange for your life. Just a few greenbacks—"

His hysteria aroused Wesley's excitement. "What's your interest in Panama?" he demanded.

The other man sucked at his lips, then pressed them together with decision as his expression turned sullenly obstinate. Convinced that the reason would not readily be revealed Wesley half turned. The move deceived Larry. He began clawing at Wesley's jacket again, and after he had looked about him with frightened eyes, he began to speak; frantically, indistinctly.

"Don't go, brother. I'll tell. I'll tell. So long as you promise to pay my passage. I'll give you a cut, too, by God! if you'll help me—"

"What the devil are you jabbering about?"

"Promise? Promise?"

Wesley hesitated. He disliked being forced into making a hurried decision which he might later regret. Then he remembered that he had said that he would do anything that was in his power to do. He could afford the passage—

"It's yours, as soon as I get back to New York to book it."

Larry's relief was ludicrous. He gulped several times before he could speak. Then he gasped, "Gold!"

"You, too!" A recollection of Ingrid Ericson's pathetic face flashed before him. "You poor fool! There's no gold there. The Spaniards got it all, centuries ago. If there is any left, only the Indians know where it's to be found, and they're not talking."

Larry's smile was more guileful than humorous. "I mean Californian gold, brother. A quarter of a million dollars' worth. Ever heard tell of a man named Jim Holmes?"

The name had a vaguely familiar ring to it, but no more than that. After a few seconds' thought he shook his head.

"Holmes lived way back in the middle eighties, about the time of the Californian gold rush," Larry explained. "One day he found himself in San Quentin prison, serving a stretch for robbery. Not liking the place any he sent a message to the Hon. John Bigler. Know him?"

Wesley had heard of Bigler, one-time Governor of California. "Yes."

"Holmes told Bigler that he knew of the whereabouts of a quarter of a million dollars' worth of Californian gold, cached in Panama, and offered to guide the governor's agent to it in exchange for a free pardon."

"A trick!"

"Sure it was a trick. As soon as Holmes and the deputy lands at Panama, Holmes tells the other man go chase himself. The deputy couldn't do a darn thing about it, because his writ didn't run on Panamanian soil. So he goes to the U. S. consul, who refers him to a man named Ran Runnels."

"Ran Runnels!"

Larry peered up at Wesley. "Heard of *him?*"

"I sure have! Go on."

"So this Runnels, who was law and order in Panama at that time, takes a couple of his ten-cent cops, arrests Holmes, and sends him to the mines of Veraguas for the rest of his life."

"Well?"

"The gold's still there, isn't it, brother? And when I get to Panama, that's what I'm looking for, see!"

"Why not go back to that barn where we slept last night, and search for a needle?"

"Because, brother, I've more than a hint where that gold's hidden. Before Holmes died in the mines he told a fellow prisoner, who told my father, and he told me, two years before he died."

"But, Larry, the odds are a thousand to one that this Jim Holmes was lying about the gold. Isn't it obvious that he invented its existence as a trick to get out of San Quentin?"

"Yeah, obvious to anyone who didn't know who his pal was."

"Well?"

"You don't know his name, brother, but the people of Panama do. When you get back there just ask anyone about El Jaguar, who robbed the gold trains of upward of half a million dollars' worth of gold—"

But Wesley knew the name of El Jaguar better than Larry did, for the bullet which had killed the bandit had been fired by Henry Stewart, Wesley's grandfather.

21

WESLEY LEANED, cross armed, on the wooden hand-rail of the *S. S. Yucatan,* and gazed at the thin line of misted brown which smudged the horizon. Within a matter of hours the ship would be berthing at Colón. The prospect excited him. However hot, stinking and pestilential the place might be, its strangeness fascinated him, and would help him to forget Dulcie. Although anger and wounded pride had hardened his heart, and made it easier for him to look upon his marriage as a closed chapter, there were occasions when he missed her terribly, and would gladly have forgiven her for the sake of having her back. Nevertheless, with each fresh day these painful periods became fewer until he was convinced that the exotic life of Colón would complete the cure.

From Colón and the future his thoughts turned to the present, Larry in particular—Mr. Larrabee, as he was called on the ship's passenger list. For nothing could tempt him to reveal his family name. When asked for it he had grinned his slyly working smile and answered, "As my surname begins with a B that makes me Larry B. Call me Mr. Larrabee." So Larry Larrabee he had become.

An hour previously Wesley had passed by the smoking room, and overheard Larry talking Spanish with two of the stewards. Even to Wesley's ear it had sounded fluent enough to make him wonder whether Larry was of Spanish ancestry. Or more likely, of Panamanian. The knowledge interested him. Not once in the past few days had Larry once revealed this.

It had not been Wesley's intention to have Larry in the same cabin, or even aboard the same ship, but as it happened, the *Yucatan* had been fully booked; and only through a married couple's last minute cancellation had he been able to sail on the ship at all. Preferring Larry's company to that of a total stranger, he had taken the cabin. Afterward he had given Larry money to outfit himself for the voyage.

This Larry had done, thoroughly and conscientiously, even down to a rubber-ferruled walking stick for use aboard. "I'll need it if the trip is rough," he had blandly explained. With that he had presented a sheaf of receipted bills, together with three dollars and fifteen cents balance from the money he had been given. Wesley had winced, but had said nothing—and knew Larry had known from the first that he would say nothing. Proof that the bum was a shrewd judge of character. After all, Larry had done no more than carry out instructions.

Later he was glad that he had kept quiet, for when Larry came aboard wearing the new clothes he might have been any normal traveler. He looked so clean. With the dust of the roads had gone the coarse slang of the roads. He was a credit to his new clothes. Within a matter of hours he had endeared himself to a number of fellow travelers. Women grew soft eyed and maternal when they looked at him; being sorry, on the one hand, for his slight deformity, but reveling, on the other, in his courteous attentions. Especially some of the older women. Their softness took the form of wistful regret for the old courtesies that were fast disappearing. But men liked him, too. They were sorry for the poor little guy, and appreciated the fact that he never used his deformity to try and win their sympathy.

Within twenty-four hours of sailing Wesley had reproached himself for having feared that Larry might disgrace him. He half convinced himself that Larry's story of being well-born had some grain of truth. The trouble was, one could never be quite sure when the other man was telling the truth, or when he was lying. After another twenty-four hours, during which time Larry and he had spent several hours discussing a variety of subjects from cabbages to kings, he was ninety-nine one-hundredths convinced that Larry really had had the college education he claimed to have had. But the odd hundredth part of a doubt remained. Although Larry spoke casually of "college," he never mentioned which college. Although he told several glib stories of his fraternity he never mentioned whether it was Alpha Delta Phi or Delta Kappa Epsilon. He even spoke of a game when "Lew" had run the length of the field to the Harvard goal line from his own twenty-five yard line. But he forgot to say for which college "Lew" had played, or in which year. Nor did he let slip "Lew's" surname, or the surname of "Hook" or "Hans" or "Bob" or "Cy" or any of the other undergraduates or people he spoke about with such familiarity. Again, there was the matter of which subject he had majored in. Wesley had tried to find out, but without success. Larry always managed to avoid a direct, compromising answer.

All this sly, and seemingly deliberate evasion sometimes exasperated and sometimes amused Wesley. Which was Larry? he found himself wondering far too frequently for his own peace of mind. One of the world's cleverest charlatans, or one of the most misused? Of course, it really didn't matter a damn, he still remained good company, but it annoyed Wesley not being able to decide.

He was still thinking along these lines when the subject of his deliberations limped up, and stood beside him.

"They tell me land's in sight, Mr. Adam."

Ever since Wesley had agreed to pay Larry's passage to Panama he had been Mr. Adam. No longer was he brother or bud or friend. He accepted this as a graceful expression of Larry's thanks.

"Yes. See that smudge just above the horizon? Ahead of the bow?"

"Ah! Think we'll be there before dark?"

"Easily."

"Not too soon for me."

"I thought you had enjoyed the trip."

"I have. Immensely. I've had more fun these few days than I've had in years. But—"

But! Wesley shrugged. "I still think you're crazy, if you're thinking of that gold. Even if you're not, what difference will a few hours make after fifty years?"

"Enough, when you've dreamed of this day as often as I have."

"You've always wanted to look for El Jaguar's gold?"

"Ever since I first heard about it."

"Why didn't you look for it at that time?"

Larry chuckled. "At that age? Besides—"

"Besides what? You left the country to go north?"

A sharp hiss of surprise. "Who told you?" Larry fiercely demanded.

"Keep cool. Nobody told me. I heard you talking Spanish to some of the Panamanian stewards. I just wondered."

146

"I was born in Panama City. My mother was Panamanian. But you won't take advantage of knowing? Please, Mr. Adam. Promise."

Larry's voice trembled with apprehension. That, and his uncalled-for suspicions nettled Wesley. "Take advantage! Doing what?"

"Making inquiries about my family. It would be easy—"

"As if *I* care a damn who or what you are. Don't be a fool."

"I am a fool about my family. I can't help it, Mr. Adam. I suppose it's because I haven't any moral courage." As usual when Larry grew excited he talked at top speed, and so jumbled his words together that it was not easy to understand what he was saying. He went on, "Mother's family is one of the oldest in Panama. Goes back to the first Spanish settlers. They're proud of their history. If they knew what had happened to me!" His shrug was eloquent.

Poor devil! Wesley reflected with compassion. He believed the main features of the story because its apparent truth made plain at least one characteristic of Larry's which had puzzled him from their first meeting: the violent, savage hatred which the other man had revealed, then and subsequently. Until now he had hesitated to accept it as genuine.

In one possessing Spanish blood the existence of such violent emotions was more understandable. So, too, was the conflict between cowardice and the fierce inherited pride of the conquistadores. To some extent, also, the rule of *dolce far niente* which dominated Larry's life. Yes, even if one discounted that part about the family's assassinating him because of his failure to avenge his mother's death, and the flamboyant claim that he wanted the gold chiefly for the purpose of hiring a professional killer; the rest of the story was credible enough to make Wesley feel intensely sorry for the other man.

His voice reflected his sympathy when he spoke. "Thanks for your confidence, Larry. You have my word that it will be respected."

He paused in the hope that Larry might feel tempted to add further details, but the other man remained silent, staring with moist eyes at the line of land ahead. Seen in profile the face looked weaker than ever.

"Your father was American?"

Larry nodded. "Yes. He was in banking. He lived in Panama two years before he met Mother. Eight years afterward when I was seven we all went to the U.S. to live."

"And never returned?"

"Mother and he did, on vacation. Not I."

"When did you hear about the gold?"

"On my twelfth birthday. Father told me about it, pretending that he was giving me a birthday present of quarter of a million dollars."

"Did you believe the story?"

"Of course. But something seemed to tell me it was true. Intuition, perhaps. I made up my mind I would search for it as soon as I had

graduated, just for the adventure." He grew bitter. "At that time I anticipated having the money to organize an expedition."

"Your father believed it?"

"No more than you do."

"But I do believe."

Larry's laugh was scornful. "As you do in Santa Claus! You laughed
at me—"

"I believe it *was* there; but not that it still is after all this time. I've heard
about El Jaguar's gold before."

Larry turned so swiftly that he nearly lost his balance: Wesley caught
him just in time. "You're joking," he accused in a high pitched, sobbing
voice. "It was Father's secret. He never told anyone else. You couldn't have
known—"

"Fifty years ago quite a number of people believed that most of the
gold stolen by El Jaguar from the gold trains was hidden in the mountains. Ran Runnels, for one. My grandfather, for another. He told me
about it quite often." He saw Larry's face register scornful disbelief. "You
see, Larry, it was my grandfather who shot Jim Holmes's partner, El
Jaguar."

Larry's expression turned crafty. "But he didn't give you a clue to where
it was hidden?"

"He didn't know. Nobody knew."

"Except Jim Holmes."

Wesley nodded. "Except Jim Holmes."

A gentle breeze wafted the smell of Colón over the bow of the ship
long before she tied up alongside one of the covered piers, which the
French Canal Company had built twenty years earlier. The foetid, unpleasant smell was redolent of the decayed vegetation forming the
scummy surface of the Black Swamp, a mile or more behind the town. As
Wesley wrinkled his nose his memory went back to the days when he
had sat on his grandfather's knees and listened, open eared and goggle
eyed, to Henry Stewart's description of the smell.

"Like a witch's brew of cabbage water an' putrid flesh an' rotten onions,
m'boy. An' mark you, I said witch's brew, for there's death in that smell,
Wesley. A vile, horrible death for hundreds of white men every year.
From malaria, and yellow fever, or yellow jack as they call it, grandson.
Did I tell you that more than ten thousand builders of the Panama Rail-
road died from sniffing that brew—"

Of course he had told the story before, a score of times. Even as he told
and retold the story to his grandchildren hundreds more died the same
vile, horrible death while trying to dig a canal alongside the railroad.
That dreaded, miasmic stink—but although Wesley's nose wrinkled, it
was with distaste, not fear. Thanks to a band of gallant workers in Cuba
148

under the inspired leadership of Walter Reed, he now knew what Grandfather hadn't lived quite long enough to know, that the mass murderer of white workers in Panama was not the pestilential odor of the Black and other swamps, but the female *stegomyia* mosquito.

Wesley's grimace changed to eagerness as the *Yucatan* nosed gently toward the pier. The scene before him scarcely differed from that which had thrilled him some years ago, but now it had the added allure of familiarity. He savored again the picture before him, a restless tableau of exotic brilliance: colorful flags of different countries flying from the sterns of the ships already berthed alongside other piers; the white toothed gangling Negro carriers who disdained the heat of the dying afternoon by running up and down the pier, waving their long arms to attract attention while bawling competitively in Spanish and broken English for custom; the picturesque uniforms of port officials, customs officers, and a few lazy-eyed Colombian soldiers; the dark green background of rising mountains silhouetted by a molten sky; and not least of all, Colón itself, set on the fringe of white coral reef; an ugly town of two-storied frame buildings, overflowing with a population of all the dusky hues, from the sickly yellow of malaria-ridden whites to the coal-black of the African Negro; from the purer yellows of the ubiquitous Chinese, to the bronze of the indigenous Indians.

Wesley paid less attention to the town than to the water front. Time enough for further inspection during the months ahead. Meanwhile he concentrated on the docks and the piers, and the ships warped alongside. Seven in all; three British, one Norwegian, one French, and two American. A trifling number, he reflected, compared with the ships which would pass by Colón one future day, when the completed canal became one of the main transport arteries of the world.

The faintest of shuddering impacts as the ship gently slid against the bamboo fenders—hullabaloo as colored workers maneuvered gangways into position—a hiatus for port officials to step aboard with the slow deliberation of conscious authority—formalities—and at last the signal for general landing.

Wesley descended the gangplank with a feeling of barely suppressed agitation. His emotions were contradictory. He was glad, he was sorry; he was terribly excited, he was philosophically calm; he was apprehensive of fever, he was healthily contemptuous of it and confident of his own good health to keep it at bay.

Of one emotion alone was he intently aware. He was proud to be among the first of the canal builders to arrive at the Isthmus.

22

BY THE TIME Wesley had settled in the hotel, unpacked, and eaten a meal the hour was close to nine o'clock. He felt more contented and at ease than at any time since Dulcie had left him. He had been up early but was not tired. It seemed silly to go out and explore the town so soon, considering the hundreds of nights that lay ahead of him but he was very much tempted.

At this point Larry called at the hotel—they had parted outside the docks, Larry to find his own accommodation elsewhere, for Wesley had considered that his obligation to the other man ceased at that stage.

"Hello, Mr. Adam." Larry's grin was mischievous. "You see, still the bad penny. Care to go out and see the town?"

"Is there so much to see?"

"Well, this *is* the Isthmus of Panama, isn't it?"

"Meaning what?"

"That it's one of the world's hot spots, like Buenos Aires, Marseilles, Alexandria. And I don't mean sun hot, either."

"You forget I stayed here a night or two on my last trip."

Larry's expression became eager. "What did you see?"

"Nothing to get excited about."

"Then you didn't visit the right spots. Bottle Alley, for instance."

Bottle Alley! The name leaped at him from the past. He recollected an occasion when his grandfather had been entertaining some old school friends of his mother's with stories of Panama. The words Bottle Alley had cropped up in a tale of the early days of Colón, when it was called Manzanilla. No sooner were they muttered than his mother had interrupted with a shocked, "Father! Please! Remember." and Wesley suddenly had noticed that every eye was upon him. He wondered what he had done wrong, for he had been as quiet as a mouse listening to Grandfather, waiting with glee to see the shocked faces of the ladies when Grandfather reached that gruesome part where he had assisted in the hanging of thirty-seven brigands.

Larry misinterpreted Wesley's expression. "At any rate, you went *there*," he accused with a salacious chuckle.

"I did not. I was remembering that Grandfather once spoke of a Bottle Alley."

"Your grandfather must have been quite a sport, Mr. Adam. What did he say about it?"

"Nothing. Mother stopped him. I was a boy of nine at the time. What is it? A street of saloons?"

150

Larry grinned. "You'll see. If you feel like coming out."

"I was thinking of doing just that when you showed up. How about a drink first? I'm dry."

"Suits me." Larry pulled impatiently at Wesley's sleeve.

They had a couple of drinks at a near saloon before moving on deeper into the town. The streets were crowded, for there was no place for the inhabitants of Colón to exercise themselves save up and down the narrow concrete sidewalks. There were no paved or surfaced roads, but only stinking byways which were ankle deep—and during the rainy season, waist deep—in oozing slime. Not even the household slops and garbage of fifty years had sufficed to establish a dry, reliable surface, for the morass on which the town had been erected had a voracious appetite and greedily absorbed anything less substantial than concrete.

Lighted windows, a few street-lamps, and moonlight together created a weird light that was sufficient to reveal the main features of the town while concealing some of its squalor.

In the wide residential street along which they first passed, the doors and windows of most of the houses were thrown open to reveal, unashamed and unembarrassed, family life in all its domestic intimacy; a colorful, exotic and noisy intimacy uninhibited by race and color bars. There to be seen were the Chinese husband at table with his French wife, the Hindu man grumbling at his Negro woman, the Spanish-American mother holding her bronze-skinned child over a tin chamber pot; the full-blooded American Negro singing lullabies to his red-haired baby daughter.

Presently the two men passed into a street that was lined on either side by two-storied frame buildings roofed with corrugated iron, each with a covered balcony projecting over the sidewalk. There they passed by shops of variegated nationalities, where Chinese and Panamanian mestizos and Hindus and Jamaican Negroes and outcast Americans lived and worked cheek by jowl, noisy and quarrelsome and excessively prolific.

They passed into still another section of the street. This one even less prepossessing than the last, where the stench from the open sewer made Wesley understand why so many native inhabitants were rarely seen without small cigars in their mouths. So into the sorriest and noisiest section of all.

"That's it!" Larry announced, waving his hand. "Bottle Alley, I guess."

At first glance Wesley failed to see anything that could possibly make the street a center of attraction, for the two lines of wooden buildings which bordered the mud strip resembled small railed storehouses. In fact, one would have expected to find them closed at that time of night, and the street deserted. Far from this being the case though, the street was a blaze of light, partly from naphthalene lamps spaced along it at irregular intervals, partly from light reflected through the open doors of the buildings.

Moreover, the narrow sidewalks were crowded with men of all colors, and the street resounded with music, laughter, and shouting.

Bottle Alley, apparently, was a street of saloons and Wesley turned to his companion to point out that he had been right when he noticed the expression on Larry's face. The pale-blue eyes were leering and salacious.

"Interested in women?" Larry inquired. "Take your pick, Mr. Adam. Fat ones. Thin ones. Dark ones, yellow ones—"

Colón's Bottle Alley! Panama City's Coco-nut Grove! The buildings were different, but the trade was the same.

The idea of joining the men who thronged the sidewalks was distasteful to Wesley. He slowed down to a halt, the memory of Dulcie's desertion still fresh in his mind. All women were treacherous and self seeking. He wanted nothing more of them. He would content himself with the company of other men.

Larry plucked at his arm. "Come on, Mr. Adam," he urged, sensing his companion's reluctance, and also what he believed to be the reason for it. "What's the harm? You're not properly married any more, so what have you to worry about?"

What, Wesley reflected. On previous occasions when a hungry gnawing had tempted him to seek the company of women, a conscientious desire to be loyal to Dulcie had made resistance comparatively easy. That particular barrier no longer existed, and he was free to indulge himself as he wished, but he no longer had the appetite to do so. Nowadays he felt contemptuous of human frailties.

He shook himself free from Larry's grasp. "If I want amusement, I have books to read, back at the hotel. They last longer," Wesley pointed out with irony, "by several hours."

Larry sissed. "So does a woman if you pick the right one. Come on, Mr. Adam. It's fun just looking. You don't have to do more, if you don't want to."

"You can go on your own. You don't need me."

"I don't want to walk down there on my own."

The toneless voice, and the quick downward glance at the crippled foot, told Wesley the real reason for Larry's desire for company. Evidently the little man shrank from walking alone down the crowded sidewalk, fearing ridicule and even an intolerant push that might precipitate him shoulder-first into the garbage-strewn mire.

Feeling sorry for the poor devil Wesley relented. "Come along then." He moved on down the sidewalk, thrusting men aside with his burly shoulders. Larry, limping fast, followed in his wake.

Fat women. Thin women. Dark women. Yellow women. White women. As Larry had said, every imaginable kind of woman was to be seen inside the dreary buildings. Dusky-eyed belles from the South American countries competed with tiny-limbed yellow-skinned Orientals. The dregs of

European brothels rubbed shoulders with grinning Negresses, and the chocolate mestizo women of the country. Some wore gaudy kimonos which did no more than cover their shoulders, arms, and backs. Others, more subtle in their approach, wore flimsy draperies, while some flaunted their doubtful charms in complete nudity. There were Eastern girls who danced to the exotic strains of music played on pipes or reeds by expressionless men with smouldering eyes who squatted, cross legged, in one corner.

Earlier Wesley had likened Bottle Alley to Coco-nut Grove, but further inspection of Colón's street made the comparison unfair to Panama City's restricted area, where at least the surroundings were mellowed by antiquity, and the ghosts of conquistadores and Spanish grandees and foreign pirates mingled with the living descendants, and watched proceedings with benevolent and probably wistful eyes.

But Colón was new and blatant and vulgar, and had no grace; and the seamen who bought thirty minutes of recreation with a week's wage, were often alcoholically obstreperous, and bestial. At Panama, Wesley reflected, he might have felt tempted—and perhaps, as soon as his blood had reacted to the tropical heat, he would be tempted—but the sordid atmosphere of the Colón district revolted him.

To his surprise Larry seemed equally unimpressed. He sissed at this, chuckled at that. Otherwise he expressed no inclination to play a more active part. Only once did he betray any excitement. Following an involuntary exclamation from his companion Wesley turned and saw that Larry was staring across the mire at a shack on the other side of the road. Like many of its neighbors, its door was wide open to permit a view of the room behind, a plainly furnished bedroom. Standing in the middle of the room was a woman of more than generous proportions. Because she was tall her fatness was less repulsive than would have been the case with a shorter woman; but her naked breasts were immense and heavy.

Wesley thought he had never seen a less attractive figure. Certainly he could see nothing about her to arouse desire. Yet Larry was undoubtedly attracted, and with encouragement would, Wesley believed, have joined her.

He was reminded of the comments of one of the *Yucatan*'s passengers, who had first spoken of Larry's veneration for size and strength, and had then gone on to embarrass Wesley by insisting that he was a hero in the eyes of Larry. Wesley had considered the remark about Larry's veneration for physical size as a conversational exaggeration, but he was less sure now of his own judgment. Two of him could have hidden behind the woman; yet she, apparently, would have been Larry's choice; not some of the smaller, frailer women they had passed by.

Wesley freed his arm. "Come along, Larry," he urged gently, for the pathos of Larry's weakness embarrassed him.

153

Larry allowed himself to be led away. "She wouldn't look at a runt like me," he muttered bitterly. But he soon recovered his usual joyous spirits. "Guess she'd be too expensive for me, anyway, if the women here charge by weight!"

They had almost reached the end of that part of Bottle Alley where the prostitutes congregated when Wesley saw, on the other side, the tall figure of a fair-haired man whose shadowed face was familiar. The man was drawing abreast of them and would soon pass on.

Tantalized by some elusive memory, Wesley halted, and impulsively called across the mire, "Hey, there!"

The other man halted uncertainly, and turned, so that his full face was yellowly illuminated.

"Ericson! You old son of a gun—"

But Ericson turned on his heel, and quickly merged with the comparative darkness of a nearby cross road.

The next few days passed quickly for Wesley: they were full of incident. On the second morning after his arrival, a letter was brought up to his bedroom.

Wesley inspected the envelope, wondering why the people at the Panama Railroad Office had troubled to write to him. He was due there within the hour.

The letter was not from the P.R.R., but from Larry.

> So long, Mr. Adam. Am starting off on my travels about the time you read this. A thousand thanks for all you've done for me. Maybe it will pay you a dividend.
>
> Be seeing you sometime.
>
> LARRY.

> P.S. Thanks for the clothes, too. As I need money to go on with, I've pawned them for a tenth of their value with one of the original usurers driven out of the Temple. Am enclosing receipt in case you'd like to redeem them.

The contents of the letter were so characteristic of Larry that, in reading it, Wesley could almost imagine the sheet of cheap notepaper was watermarked with Larry's mocking smile. Poor Larry! Incapable of being wholly honest, or wholly dishonest. Wesley resolved to redeem the pledge at the first opportunity. The bad penny might yet find the clothes useful.

Shortly afterward he entered his new office for the first time. There he spent an hour or more meeting the people with whom he would work. At first glance they appeared to be amiable and pleasant enough; but the sight of their pallid and wasted faces gave him an unpleasant shock, forcibly reminding him of the ever-present danger of fever. He could not think why he had overlooked such obvious evidence during his previous visit, and concluded that he had been too preoccupied to pay attention to anything outside the scope of his work or his eagerness to return to Dulcie.

In a short time he had fallen into the swing of his new work, and the hours passed pleasantly enough as long as he was at the office; but the evenings he found lengthy and tedious. He liked reading, but only for a while. He did not care overmuch for drinking, and had no desire to spend his evenings at any of the numerous saloons.

Thus he found himself thrown more and more on his own resources. The projected canal featured largely in his thoughts. Now that he was living in Panama, with time to see, digest, and discuss, he saw clearly the heartbreaking problems which would confront the builders of a canal—which had already confronted and defeated the French engineers. Engineering problems, that was to say, with which a field surveyor was not necessarily concerned. From a strictly personal point of view his conscience was clear. His own survey had merely confirmed the previous surveys and showed that a canal could be built. But blueprints were one thing; reality was another; as the French builders had found to their costs. He hated to contemplate the possibility of a second, calamitous failure—an American one this time.

American engineers were human, after all, not miracle men. . . .

He thought about the canal so often that sometimes his brain grew weary, from grappling with the problem; and it turned, almost subconsciously, to the Perrigots. Now that he had returned to the surroundings in which he had met them, all three seemed to take on a quality of vividness in his memory. They were as clear in his imagination as though he had met them only a few hours ago. Anne, particularly, with her raven-black curls, her dark eyes, her warm, olive skin, and her attractive figure. Maybe she was married by now; might even be a mother—but the idea was somehow distasteful to him. And plump little Marie, with her swelling breasts and thighs! Had she fined down since his visit to the Perrigot home? Surely she must have, and now would be rivaling Anne for beauty. In fact, she might well surpass Anne, he reflected, for a certain mystery had slumbered in Marie's eyes. Mystery and passion. Whereas Anne's eyes had had a spiritual quality in them. Ericson had been interested in Marie, hadn't he? Had he seen anything of the Perrigots since his return to Panama? The possibility made him frown. The blond giant wasn't to be trusted with young girls.

It did not take him long to reach what he tried to reassure himself was only a casual decision to visit the Perrigots at the first convenient opportunity. In his more honest moments he realized that the decision was not as casual as he tried to think!

Then came a letter from New York, two weeks after his arrival at

Colón. Not a long letter, but full of news. There wasn't much doing at the Press Bureau, Uncle Bill wrote. No fireworks worth mentioning, though one or another of the Sullivan and Cromwell partners was living in Secretary Hay's pocket, trying to amend the proposed treaty with Colombia so as to make it acceptable both to that country and Senator Morgan and his friends. No easy matter, it seemed, for Minister Concha wasn't playing.

"So long, son," Godwin finished up. "One of these days I'll surprise you by turning up in Panama on vacation."

Wesley chuckled. As if Uncle Bill was ever likely to desert his beloved Times Square in favor of Panama.

23

FREDERICK JOHN SANDERSON of Atlanta, was the first resident to invite Wesley to his home. Sanderson was Assistant Freight Agent to the P.R.R. and lived in a neat little frame house standing on the coral beach close to the Railroad club buildings.

Wesley was leaning against the office wall one morning, in the only shadow available, trying to mop his forehead, face, and neck with a handkerchief already soaked with perspiration. All that morning the rain had teemed down; but the clouds had finally moved on, and left the sun sizzling in a molten sky. He felt dizzy with the moist heat.

Sanderson saw him. "Killing, isn't it, when you first arrive. You'll get used to it." He added, with a wry smile, "More or less."

"It's not my first visit. I was here some years ago for a few weeks."

"Then you came here with your eyes open, so you haven't my sympathy! Settling down?"

"Yes, thanks."

"Good!" He paused. "Doing anything special tonight?"

"No."

"Care to have dinner with us? Mrs. Sanderson has invited a friend of hers, so you'll make a fourth. I'll need someone to keep me company while the two ladies gabble." His grin was friendly, inviting.

"I'd love to. What time shall I come?"

"Come back with me when we leave the office. I'll send a message to let Mrs. Sanderson know that you'll be coming. I suggest we stop off at the club for a drink."

From the window of his room, which overlooked P.R.R. Pier 1, Wesley later saw Sanderson approaching from the freight house, which was situated between P.R.R. Pier 2 and the Royal Mail Company pier. By the time the Assistant Freight Agent had reached the main offices, Wesley was downstairs waiting for him.

As the earlier heat had been tempered by the trade wind blowing off the Caribbean, they decided to walk the comparatively short distance.

The club was beginning to fill up by the time they arrived there, and Wesley recognized several faces. He was received with heart-warming friendliness, for the staff at the P.R.R. office had already spread the news that the newcomer was a nice guy. Sanderson introduced him to half a dozen more Americans, five of whom had nothing to do with the P.R.R.; three were shipping agents; the remaining two, bankers.

It was comparatively cool in the club; the drinks were chilled, and potent. His recent misgivings engendered by loneliness were quickly dispersed by the cheery atmosphere. He was satisfied that the impulse to seek a career in Panama had not played him false. Relations between the members of the small American colony were more cordial than would have been probable anywhere in the States: as fellow exiles they were bound together within an intangible framework of mutual tolerance and pride in their nationality.

"Hullo, there, Jimmy! Thought you were going back to Panama to-night."

The man whom Sanderson had hailed joined them. "So did I, Frederick, but Chabert, of the Canal Company, isn't satisfied with our adjusting. He wants me to go over it with him again tomorrow morning."

"That fellow is a nuisance."

"Sure he is, but since he's by way of being our boss—"

"Have you met our latest newcomer, Jimmy?"

"Not yet."

"Meet my immediate boss, Adam, Captain James Beers. Jimmy is the Freight Agent and Port Captain at the Panama terminus. Jimmy, this is Wesley Adam, taking Travers' place in the Survey Department."

Wesley and Beers shook hands. A shrewd face, Wesley reflected. Shouldn't think Chabert will find it very useful to argue with him.

Sanderson went on, "This is Adam's second trip here. He helped to make a survey for Mr. Cromwell."

"For the canal?" Beers was immediately interested. "I hear there's still a lot of lobbying going on in Washington. You can't lick that Senator Morgan easily."

"No," Wesley agreed. "His deck of cards seems to have twenty-six trumps in it."

Beers chuckled. "I'm still backing Mr. Cromwell to hold the ace. Hope to see you again, Mr. Adam. Look me up if you come to Panama. There are two or three questions I'd like to put to you about rerouting the railroad."

With a quick, friendly nod Captain Beers moved away. The two men soon followed his example, and walked back along the pleasant palm-bordered beach road toward the small group of frame houses which had been reserved for the principal executives of the P.R.R.

Mrs. Sanderson greeted Wesley with a smile. She was a pleasant little body with round cheeks, twinkling eyes, and charming dimples. She was small, barely reaching her husband's shoulder, but shapely in a plump sort of way.

"How nice of you to come along with Frederick tonight," she said, with genuine warmth. "You don't know how grumpy he is when I have a friend in and he doesn't have another man to talk to. He's such a woman-hater that I can't think how ever he came to marry me."

Sanderson winked at Wesley before giving his wife a hearty hug. "Because I'm psychic, and can recognize an angel when I meet one, even if she is too solidly made to fly."

"You see!" she appealed to Wesley. "He says the nastiest things, just because I'm not as thin as a scarecrow. Frederick dear, go clean yourself up while I blackmail Mr. Adam into giving me all the latest news of home."

"Yeah! And what threat are you going to blackmail him with?"

"Not to serve him any of my turtle soup."

"Turtle soup! You win, Madge, my dear. Adam, if my wife is an angel, her turtle soup is something straight from Heaven, believe me! Tell her everything she wants to know. Invent, if necessary. But see that you get us that soup."

"Frederick! You say the stupidest things!" she dimpled.

"Where's Nan?"

"Just beautifying. Now, Frederick Sanderson, will you go clean yourself up this instant?"

"Going, my love."

As soon as her husband had vanished Madge Sanderson turned eagerly to her guest. "Did you see any National League games this year—"

For ten minutes she plied him with questions. He had to speak quickly in order to answer one question before she interrupted with the next.

Presently the door opened. Mrs. Sanderson looked up, dimpling. "There you are, Nan. We have a new man in Colón! Nan, my dear, this is—"

"Mr. Wesley Adam," the girl concluded. "So you did come back?"

Wesley recognized Anne Perrigot.

That is to say, he recognized from her words that she couldn't be anyone else. But the visionary Anne Perrigot who had so often obtruded on his thoughts bore very little resemblance to the real Anne. She was so many times more beautiful than he had imagined. She swayed from her hips as she walked, slender and graceful as a willow twig in a summer breeze.

158

Her eyes were large and lustrous, like two dark, mysterious pools. Her lips were sensitive, her complexion warm and unblemished.

He bowed, the ostensible formality a secret dedication to the perfection of her beauty.

"I have been here less than two weeks, Mademoiselle Perrigot. I have not forgotten my promise. I am only waiting for an opportunity to call on your father."

Her smile was politely grateful. "Thank you."

Mrs. Sanderson looked with bewilderment at each in turn. "You know each other?"

"A few years ago I stayed one night at Monsieur Perrigot's home. Mademoiselle Perrigot and her sister were extremely kind to us."

Their hostess dimpled with pleasure. "How nice! What a lovely party we'll have tonight. I simply must tell Frederick. He will be thrilled." She bustled excitedly out of the room.

The two left behind studied each other with cool detachment. "You've changed, Mr. Adam. Your hair isn't so red, and your face is—"

"Older?"

"No, not older. Not older, I mean, than it should be. But it has more character. It's more resolute." She frowned in perplexity. "And is more *triste.*"

"Domestic trouble," he explained harshly. "My wife left me."

"Oh! I am so sorry."

"I'm getting over it. Fast."

"No. Not too fast."

"Why not?"

"That wouldn't be true to character. I guess that you are not a man of slight emotions. Whatever you feel, you feel deeply. Probably more deeply than you realize."

"Perhaps that explains—" He stopped.

"What, Mr. Adam?"

"It's not anything to be proud of."

"I'd like to hear."

"For a while I thought of suicide. But I got over that."

"Of course," she exclaimed with quiet confidence. "Only weak men commit suicide."

Her naïve statement embarrassed him. "The fault was partly mine."

"Why?"

"You see, I left her alone too much. I was too eager to see the canal completed. Our home was in Providence—that's about a hundred and eighty miles from New York—and I worked all the time in New York."

She nodded. "Marriage should not be separation. But surely she lived with you in New York?"

"Well—she hated New York. So!"

Her serene eyes speckled with flashes of reflected sunshine. "Then it was not your fault, after all, Mr. Adam. It is a wife's duty to accompany her husband wherever he goes, if that's possible. Is that why you've returned to Panama, because your wife left you?"

"I told you I was coming back."

"Yes, and Father said you wouldn't."

"Does he still hate the idea of an American canal?"

"More and more and more. Will you be working on it?"

"That's the idea. So your father won't welcome me?"

The pools of her eyes darkened.

"He would not welcome you, Mr. Adam."

He grimaced. It did not make pleasant hearing. Noticing his expression she added quickly. "Marie and I would be happy to, if we could. But while Father is at home, as he always is—"

"Do you often come to Colón?"

Her sad mouth looked sadder. "Only twice a year. When Father brings us."

"You mean, he's in Colón?"

"For one night."

"And your sister?"

"She, too. Tonight she's visiting friends."

The two Sandersons entered, Frederick's voice loud with amazement. "Well, well, well! So you two know each other!" Like his wife he seemed genuinely pleased. Wesley warmed to them both. "Think she's changed much?"

Wesley grinned. "As much as a promise when it's fulfilled."

Madge Sanderson dimpled. "You dear man! Of all the nice things to say!"

The conversation switched to more general matters, but an evening that had begun so well could scarcely go wrong. In any event, Sanderson was a born host. And his wife a born cook. The turtle soup proved as exquisite as her husband had promised. So did the course that followed, a Panama variation of *paella,* a delicious chicken dish.

They were drinking coffee, when Anne turned to Wesley. "Is it true that after leaving us you were lost in the jungle, and nearly killed by the Indians?"

"A matter of seconds saved us, plus the happy chance that one of the railroad workers saw Olaf and me go along a trail where we shouldn't have been."

"How could you have lost yourselves? It is such an easy trail from our home to Alhajuela."

"That's what we thought. When we left your home we continued on the main trail as far as the first cross trail, where we turned left at the shrine—"

160

"The first cross trail? But the shrine is at the junction of the second cross trail."

"It wasn't that day," Wesley assured her.

"It must have been. It couldn't be anywhere else. Besides, it was certainly there a few days later when Marie and I and Father went to Cruces." The deep pools clouded. "You couldn't have turned left at the shrine."

Sanderson quizzically inspected his two guests. "Do I understand that you were lost in the jungle and nearly killed by Indians?" he asked Wesley.

"Yes."

"For Heaven's sake!" Madge Sanderson exclaimed. "You must tell us all about it. Is the jungle really so dangerous? Of course, I've heard people talk—"

So Wesley repeated the story of all that happened to him and Olaf following their departure from Perrigot's home.

At its conclusion Sanderson shook his head. "As Madge says, we've lived here more than long enough to hear about the wildness of the interior away from the Chagres valley, but you're the first person I've met who's actually been in contact with it. I'm afraid we had come to believe that it was mostly poppycock."

Wesley grinned. "You can take my word for it that it isn't. But I want to ask you, don't you ever hear the drums?"

His host looked blank. "What drums?"

"The drums of the Cimarrones. When my grandfather was here they were often heard. In fact, one night he and some friends witnessed a voodoo dance, and saw a Zombi killed for sacrifice."

Mrs. Sanderson giggled. "Now you all are teasing us, Mr. Adam."

Sanderson answered for Wesley. "I don't think he is, my dear. There used to be quite a number of wild Negroes living away in the mountains; and I've heard that they used to have witch doctors and hold sacrificial dances to African gods, and live much as they still do in Haiti. In fact, even as late as eighteen sixty-eight the Governor of Panama, Vicente Olarte, died from poisoning, reputedly administered by a witch doctor. But the P.R.R. has had a civilizing effect on the country. In my opinion the only Negroes left in Panama today live in the Chagres valley, and are no wilder than they are back in the U. S., or in Jamaica, say."

"Even in Jamaica they still practice obeah."

"Maybe, but I doubt whether they do here. What do you say, Nan?"

"I think you are only half right, Mr. Sanderson. Negroes don't lose their superstitions easily. I don't think it is nearly so bad as it was before the railroad was built—I've heard Father speak about the drumming one used to hear in those days, and of their dances—but in the valley it hasn't altogether disappeared. They still hold rather wild *danzons* in Panama City and in Colón."

Mrs. Sanderson looked horrified. "Nan, dear! You don't mean that such horrible things happen here, right under our noses?"

"They are very mild now, Mrs. Sanderson. You can still buy their potions and charms, if you know where to go, and sometimes they kill and eat a monkey."

Their hostess shuddered, to her husband's amusement. "We've lived here ten years and never had trouble with the colored population so why begin to worry now. Besides, monkey may be quite nice to eat for all we know." He turned to Wesley. "The effects of civilization are contagious, Adam. They are spreading all the time. Only the Indians are obstinate enough to resist them."

As Wesley walked back to the hotel he was happier than he had been for a long time. He had made several new friends that day, not least of all the Sandersons; the evening had gone with a swing from first to last; he had met Anne Perrigot again.

He smiled as he realized how, during his stay in New York, he had been keeping mental company with the wrong girl. The visionary Anne whom he had taken with him to the theater, to Delmonico's or the Café Martin, to the beach at Long Branch; the Anne with whom he had danced, picnicked, who had accompanied him on Hudson River steamers to Poughkeepsie and Albany; that merry, roguish-eyed, slightly plump little minx just didn't exist. She no more resembled the slender Anne with her deep, dark eyes and sad mouth than he resembled Larry.

He did not regret the change. It was not only her physical beauty that excited him, but also the serenity of her character, and her intelligence, so faithfully mirrored in the dark depths of her eyes. Moreover, in spite of the wistful droop of her mouth, she quickly reacted to cheerful surroundings; and during this merry evening she had bubbled with high spirits. Only when her home was mentioned did sadness shadow her lovely face. Why, Wesley found himself wondering.

24

TIME NOW MOVED more quickly for Wesley. During working hours there was more than enough to keep him fully occupied. His growing circle of friends rarely allowed him a free evening. As a single man he was in constant demand to squire the handful of unmarried daughters who lived in Colón.

Meanwhile, regular letters kept him in touch with events in New York and Washington. Negotiations with Colombia were, wrote Uncle Bill, far from satisfactory. Minister Concha openly expressed hostility to the U. S. Government and refused either to meet or communicate with Secretary Hay. Colombia demanded extortionate terms for her consent to the transfer of the canal concession from the New Panama Canal Company to the U. S. Government.

Early November brought further bad news. Without official notice to the U. S. Government, Minister Concha had suddenly sailed for home, leaving the Colombian Legation in a state of demoralization, and Mr. Herran, Secretary of the Legation, without instructions or authority.

Wesley was not surprised when later letters detailed the complications following Concha's return to his own country.

Washington was in ferment, Uncle Bill wrote. The Nicaragua group was trying every possible means to influence the President to desert Panama, by intensifying their press campaign, besieging the White House, pressing for a resumption of negotiations with Nicaragua.

Not without success, he went on to write. Secretary Hay had agreed to this last course. Which meant, of course, that the Press Bureau had to take countermeasures—"churning out propaganda every hour of the day and night. Lucky you, to be someplace where you don't have to eat, drink, and breathe politics."

The last paragraph of Uncle Bill Godwin's letter was written under a misapprehension about Panama. Where political chicanery and intrigue were concerned, Washington was a mere tyro in comparison with Central American towns. In spite of the defeats the Colombian forces had inflicted upon Panamanian rebels, and the enforced treaty of peace which had come into force within the past twelve months, Panama was still restive.

As Wesley's knowledge of Spanish improved, he became increasingly aware, from snatches of overheard conversation, of the hatred in which the Colombian overlord was held by subject Panamanians. During a long series of uprisings too much Panamanian blood had soaked into the rich soil of the Isthmus for that hot-tempered people to forgive and forget. Colombia's refusal to enter into a treaty with the United States was, in the majority Panamanian opinion, just one more reason for detesting Colombia, added to an already long list. For Panamanians, remembering the millions of French francs that had lined their pockets during the heyday of French digging days, were vitally interested in having the United States take over the French concession. They had dreams of those glorious days returning.

Meanwhile, no news of Larry; no news of Ericson. One day it occurred to him that both men had disappeared into the jungle with the same object in view—gold! He went on to wonder, not without misgiving, what would happen if the two men should run across each other's trail—there were more unlikely contingencies. What chance would the crippled weakling stand against the young giant? At first thought the obvious answer was—none. But after further reflection he was less sure: Larry's craftiness might well prove a match for the other man's brute force. Wesley hoped so. He still felt a tolerant liking for little Larry.

In spite of so many other distractions, Wesley found that Anne Perrigot was occupying an increasing share of his thoughts. He could not forget her slim loveliness, or the serenity of her dark eyes; and somehow he was convinced that one's troubles, if shared with her, would sink into the deep waters of her understanding, and despair would thaw in the warmth of her sympathy.

Soon he grew impatient to see her again, and considered a visit to her father. He realized that Perrigot might refuse to let him enter the house, for a would-be murderer was not likely to balk at a mere discourtesy. On the other hand, the knowledge that he would probably have to wait several months for an opportunity to see her again made him obstinately determined not to wait.

When ingenuity failed to suggest a solution he turned to Madge Sanderson for advice. He called there one night when he knew Frederick would not be home for a few hours.

"Why, hello, Wesley!" Her dimples were more than usually evident, for she liked Wesley and saw no reason for concealing the fact. "Frederick's out tonight, playing billiards at the club," she said, regretfully.

"I know. It's you I came to see, Mrs. Sanderson."

"Me!" Her eyes turned wary. "But, Wesley—"

Quick to interpret her expression, he realized that she had mistaken his meaning, and out of love and loyalty to her husband she did not intend to allow him even to enter the house.

"I want to talk to you about Anne Perrigot," he explained quickly.

"Oh!" she said in relief. "Come in." She showed him into the parlor and offered him the rocker. She always occupied a small straight-backed wooden chair which she claimed enabled her to do her needlework more easily. "I'll make some coffee."

"Let me help."

She nodded, and led the way into the kitchen. "You fill the kettle and put it on while I put out the cups and saucers."

He filled the kettle from the water cistern, which was replenished daily from the water carts which brought drinking water from the mainland into the town. Then he put it on the oil stove.

"Well, what about Nan?" she asked.

"I should like to meet her again."

"Why not? She's a nice girl. I'm very fond of her."

"But I don't know how to, Mrs. Sanderson. I don't think it would be any use my calling at the house. Probably her father wouldn't let me inside. He hates me, though for no good reason that I know of except that I am concerned with building a canal here."

"He hates you and won't let you into his home, because you're a young man, Wesley."

"Why—"

"Because he's an unnatural, selfish father who wants to prevent his daughter's marrying so they can continue to keep house and care for him."

"The scoundrel!"

Her voice grew indignant. "I've begged Nan to leave him. Frederick has offered to let her stay here with us for as long as she likes, but she's too proud to accept charity—"

"Charity!"

"Of course. She hasn't a cent of her own, Wesley. Even if she had she's too dutiful to leave him."

"What about the sister, Marie?"

"He is just as strict with her. One sacrificial daughter in the family isn't enough for him. He wants two. Oh! The beast! I can scarcely keep my temper when I think of him." As if she were capable of losing it! "The hours I've wasted, arguing with that dear child. I could cry every time I think of what her life is. And worse still, what her future will be."

He gazed out of the window at the gently undulating carpet which the moon had unrolled across the Caribbean; but was conscious neither of its scintillating, glacial beauty, nor of the star-studded velvet infinity beyond. He was equally unaware of the fact that Madge had stopped rattling crockery and was studying him with speculative eyes.

"Wesley!"

He looked up.

"Are you entitled to want to see her again? I mean, except by chance, or in company?"

"Why shouldn't I see her?"

"Because you are a married man."

"That depends on what you mean by marriage," he answered bitterly. "My wife left me last June."

"You are still married."

"But I like Anne. Surely my marriage doesn't prevent my wanting to meet her again?"

"Doesn't it? Suppose she should fall in love with you."

"Holy smoke!" he exclaimed reproachfully. "Surely two people can be friendly without falling in love with each other. I've been friendly with dozens of girls, played tennis with them, taken them to picnics, danced with them, had fun with them, and there hasn't been any suggestion of love on either side."

165

"Panama isn't the United States," she sighed. "If only you weren't married."

"But I'm not really. Not any longer."

"You're not unmarried, Wesley, which is the important thing to consider. A friendship between you two might easily compromise Nan."

"In that case, may I write to her? Surely there can't be harm in that?"

"I don't know what to say."

"Say you'll help us to correspond. It might cheer her to receive an occasional letter."

At last she relented, dimpling. "I'll see what can be done."

Two weeks later Madge Sanderson told Wesley that if he wrote to Señorita Espinosa, care of Señor San Chu Sing of Bohio, the letter would be kept and handed to Anne when next she visited the town to buy provisions. San Chu Sing, it seemed, was the owner of the local store, and devoted to the two Perrigot girls.

So began a correspondence which brought pleasure to both. At first, Anne's letters were formal. He gained the impression that she had done very little letter writing, and was self-conscious about expressing herself freely, which was strange, he thought, for ordinarily she had poise and assurance. But after a time her letters grew more friendly and intimate, as if the joy of finding a friend had released her from shyness.

Naturally, it did not take long for Madge's admonition to wear off. He was young, and hungry for companionship. Anne's letters kept her constantly in his thoughts. So at last he yielded to temptation. He wrote and asked if there was not some means by which they might meet—surreptitiously, if necessary.

She answered his letter, but ignored the suggestion of a meeting. So he asked her again. Again she deliberately avoided making any reference to his pleas. This disgruntled him so much that he sulked, and did not reply.

Later, when he had recovered his good humor, he wrote again, and scrupulously avoided any mention of a meeting. But his impatience was stronger than his conscience; and his determination to see her soon took command. Once more he wrote, pleading for a meeting.

This time he received a brief note in reply. "Come next Sunday," she wrote. "Papa will be in Panama," and signed it simply "Anne."

Early on Sunday morning he caught a train for Panama, and alighted at Bohio. There he hired a pinto for the day, and set off for the Perrigot home. Soon he had left the small town behind him, and was heading for the fringe of the jungle.

It was the first time he had penetrated into the interior since his return to the Isthmus. He was conscious of a stirring, pleasurable excitement not wholly accounted for by the fact that he was on his way to see Anne. In spite of having nearly lost his life in the jungle, he had responded to its

166

primeval savagery with all the turbulence of his Stewart blood, not yet subdued by a century of American civilization. His great-grandfather had killed his man; his grandfather had killed his man. Perhaps, who knows, he might one day kill his man.

Wesley chuckled self consciously. Duncan Stewart had loved, turbulently, passionately; Henry Stewart likewise. But nobody could accuse Wesley Adam of having loved Dulcie with turbulent passion. Maybe that was her fault. On the other hand it could be his; maybe the gentle Adam blood had watered down the rude virility of the Stewarts. At any rate, he could not imagine himself indulging in the ardent love affairs which he knew had characterized the two former Stewarts.

But the jungle now!—so his reflections completed their full circle. Its green, boundless depths, its black shadows, its splashes of crimson so suggestive of the blood mingled with its lush fertility, its remorseless savagery, its hushed mystery. The jungle excited him in its challenge, and made him resent the weeks and months spent in the imprisoning walls of the railroad office, or out on the orderly right of way. He smiled happily as the first dark shadow of an espevé tree threw a cooling veil across his face; and he whistled back at the parakeets who angrily scolded him for his intrusion. When his pinto shied away from the rustle of an alarmed snake he laughed aloud, convinced that he felt at home in the jungle.

So, after a joyous, uphill ride he reached the point from which he could catch his first glimpse of the Perrigot house. He lightly spurred his animal, and feeling exhilarated called himself a damned fool for not having come before. To hell with old Perrigot! As for Madge Sanderson—well, Madge was a product of the Old South and the nineteenth century which was past and done with.

He entered the clearing, and anxiously surveyed the veranda. It was empty. In spite of his contempt for Perrigot, and Anne's assurance that her father was to be in Panama, he was relieved not to see the old man seated in his rocking chair. On the other hand, he had hoped to see Anne there instead.

As he leaped off his horse and made it fast to a hitching post, the door connecting the porch with the interior of the house opened; and a girl stepped out of the dark shadows. He waved a greeting, then the shock of surprise made his arm limp. The girl was not Anne.

She was shorter than Anne, and slightly plumper. She had the blackest hair he had ever seen. Its sheen captured the light and transformed it into a blue flame. Her lips were broad and vivid, arched downward in sultry insolence. Her eyes were as dark as Anne's, but unlike shadowed pools speckled with glinting light, they glowed with the fierce heat of a noonday sun. Her limbs were softly rounded; but her waist was over slim

167

in proportion, and had the effect of exaggerating the swell of her breasts, which were firm and pointed.

She was Anne without being Anne; a voluptuous replica in many respects. Remembering the young girl Marie, with her puppy-fat and prominent breasts, who had sat and embroidered on the veranda some years back he had no need to be told her identity.

"Mademoiselle Marie!"

Her smile warmed him; her whole being seemed to envelop and caress him.

"Monsieur Adam! So you really have come back?" She took both his hands and held them, as her lips drew back to expose teeth even more perfect than Anne's.

"I always knew you would," she went on. "I bet Anne one peso you would." Her laughter echoed round the porch disturbingly.

"Didn't she think I would be back?"

"Probably she did, deep down; but Anne is so easily disheartened. Not like me, now!" She walked backward, pulling him after her along the porch. "Now just you sit down there," she ordered, pointing to the rocker. "When the cat's away—" Again that disturbing laugh of hers as she drew a stool close to him, and sat down upon it. He thought she looked like a sleek, black cat curling itself up in the sun.

"Tell me all about yourself. Is the canal going to be built? How long will it take? Will you stay here long? I mean in Panama?"

He looked about him, "Where's your sister?"

"Anne! Poor Anne! At the very last moment Papa insisted upon her accompanying him."

He was angry and disappointed. Of all the cursed luck! His one chance—

"And not you?" he rasped, remembering how careful Perrigot had always been never to leave the two girls in the house, much less one of them alone.

"I wasn't feeling well—" She added quickly, "I'm better now. Besides, there is Dolores to take care of me. You remember. The cook." She was laughing at him, mocking him. "Disappointed?"

"It would have been nice to see her again. Meanwhile—"

"You have me to keep you company?"

"Yes," he said shortly.

"I'll try very hard to make up for Anne's absence," she continued.

He realized that she had become serious. He turned to smile his thanks, found himself looking directly into her eyes, and in their sooty depths surprised a sensual expression.

"Tell me of yourself," she commanded, and again she drew back her lips in a slow, tight smile. "Is it true that your wife ran away?"

168

"Yes," he answered brusquely. "But I did not come here to talk of her. I prefer not to be reminded of her."

She seemed not to have understood. "Why did she leave you? I'm sure you were a good husband to her; did you love her?"

"Of course." His voice was rasping. Damn the little fool! he thought.

"Then what was her lover able to give her that you couldn't? Money?"

"Yes." He answered automatically; and was annoyed with himself for doing so.

She nodded understandingly. "The dream of all cold-blooded women. Are you not happier without her?"

"Why the devil should I be?"

"Because you are free." She sighed. "It must be fun to be free. If you're a man."

"And if you're a woman?"

Her eyes mocked him. "A woman is never free, so how could she know what it's like?" There was no doubt of the mockery in her voice, and in her words, too, which only added to his uneasiness. Why the devil had Perrigot taken Anne to Panama? Why the devil had he come to the house at all? Why—why—why? Lord, it wasn't easy to think coherently confronted with those burning, mocking eyes.

"What made you come back to Panama?" she continued without pause. "To help build the canal, or because?"

"Because what?"

"You like the tropics? Or our way of life? Or us?"

"Everything. Because I wanted to. I don't know." Nor did he, at that moment. Those damned eyes of hers! They seemed to scorch one!

She smiled, showing her teeth. Vicious little teeth they could be, he reflected wildly.

"I'm glad. I would like to think you came back because you liked life in Panama." She paused, meaningfully. He waited.

"Didn't you have a companion with you when you came here before?" she asked coolly. "A big blond man. Has he ever come back here?"

Why, he wondered, should mockery accompany such a natural question? Watching her closely, he guessed that Ericson had returned to the Perrigot household as he had promised himself he would.

He ignored the question, and rose abruptly.

"I must be going."

She caught hold of his hand. "Not yet. Not before you've had a drink. Your train won't be in for hours yet." She rose and stood before him, her dark eyes mocking. "Don't you want to hear about Anne?"

He felt uneasy. There was something about Marie's behavior which worried him. On the other hand, her offer was tempting. He was damnably thirsty—and so long as she would talk about Anne—

As soon as he had sat down again she disappeared into the house. He heard her call "Dolores," and then, after a momentary pause, a few curt words in Spanish. Almost immediately she rejoined him.

"Dolores is just coming." She chattered on, telling him how lonely her life was, until the big-bosomed cook entered. She carried a tray with glasses on it, and three bottles. As she set them all down on a rattan table he saw her glance first at himself and then at Marie. Her lips parted in a broad smile as her eyes filled with pride. Pride? Or mischief, maybe? Or what? He could not decide, but whatever the expression was, it did nothing to lessen his feeling of uneasiness. Had she been a party to Marie's ruse? he wondered. She had a lecherous mouth.

Wesley did not find it easy to forget Marie. Her liaison with Ericson assumed the shape of something unclean. He was convinced that it had done the girl irreparable harm, had awakened in her an incipient nymphomania which, like a noxious drug, demanded an ever-increasing satisfaction.

With the arrival of subsequent letters from Anne, none of which expressed regret at having missed him that day or indeed made any mention of his visit, he became convinced his visit had been planned by her sister; and further, that Marie had forged her sister's handwriting.

More for Anne's sake than Marie's, he, too, never referred in his letters to his call at the Perrigot home. Nor did he again ask Anne to meet him. He had no wish to afford further scope for Marie's distorted sense of mischief. All he allowed himself to do was to send her Christmas good wishes.

The New Year brought no better news from Uncle Bill. Bogotá had given Dr. Herran, now the Colombian minister, instructions to continue negotiations with the U. S. Government—on a basis of a cash payment of $10,000,000, and a perpetual annuity of $600,000! This the Government refused to pay; but thanks to the intervention of the persistent Mr. Cromwell, Secretary Hay at last agreed to offer an annuity of $100,000. This compromise did not satisfy the Colombian Government, so Secretary Hay authorized the attorney to inform Señor Herran that, unless the U. S. terms were immediately accepted, the President would approve the Nicaragua and Costa Rica treaties, as he was authorized to do under the terms of the Spooner Act.

The Colombian Government remained adamant, but although Senator Morgan and his coterie took advantage of the delay to increase their pressure on the President, Uncle Bill's next letter was jubilant.

Cromwell had badgered the two parties into agreeing to a compromise annuity figure of $250,000. A treaty known as the Hay-Herran treaty had been signed. "Digging won't be long now," he finished off.

Uncle Bill hadn't reckoned with Senator Morgan, no less doughty a fighter than William Nelson Cromwell. In spite of the Hay-Herran treaty, which only required ratification to make it effective, Senator Morgan continued to fight in an effort to prevent that ratification. His first act was to move that the treaty be referred to the Canal Committee, of which he was chairman. This failed, but the treaty was referred to the Committee on Foreign Relations, of which he was likewise a member.

To prevent ratification being voted by the necessary two-thirds majority in the Senate he next introduced a resolution calling for proof that Herran was authorized to sign the treaty. Other Nicaraguan adherents brought in more than sixty amendments to the treaty, the addition of any one of which would have made the revised treaty unacceptable to Colombia.

Sullivan and Cromwell fought back. A number of Senators were impressed by their arguments, appreciating the fact that it was in the national interest to reject all amendments and adhere to the treaty. The battle in favor of ratification proved to be a vigorous and hard-hitting affair. The heated debates extended beyond reasonable limits. An extra session had to be summoned. As Uncle Bill wrote, on March 2, "The damn option expires in two days' time."

News from New York no longer depressed Wesley. Uncle Bill had cried "Wolf! Wolf!" too often. That wily old fox, Cromwell, would find some way of having the option renewed, he thought. His confidence was justified. The attorney maneuvered his government into giving a conditional undertaking to buy all properties and rights of the New Panama Canal Company; at last they were too deeply involved to retreat. The Nicaragua group recognized their final defeat, and the treaty was ratified.

The dry season passed all too soon, and the rains started. Immersed in his work, always in demand at other times, Wesley was scarcely aware of the passage of time. The United States was faraway, both in time and distance.

His awakening came during the first week in June. Prescott, Assistant Superintendent of the Panama Railroad Company, sent for him.

"Good morning, Adam. I've had a telegram this morning from Mr. Cromwell. He wants you to return to New York, by the next available ship, on a short leave of absence."

Wesley was astonished. "Do you know why, sir?"

"Haven't the faintest notion. Have you?"

"No, sir."

"Ah well! I suppose you have no objection?"

"Can I be spared, sir?"

"You must be spared. Mr. Cromwell's word is law in this company."

"Did he say how long he wants me for?"

"A week or less were his words."

Wesley nodded. "I'll make arrangements at once, sir."

"Right! Have the cashier send me a slip for your expenses so that I can countersign it."

"Yes, sir."

He sailed exactly one week later. The first person he met aboard was Captain Beers.

Beers greeted him with a friendly slap on the shoulder.

"Hallo, Adam! Off on leave?"

"No, sir. Short leave of absence. Mr. Cromwell sent for me."

"Did he!" Beers looked surprised. "He sent for me, too. Has he sent for any more of the P.R.R. men, do you know?"

"No, sir."

"Don't answer if the reason's private, but do you know why he's sent for you?"

"Haven't a notion. Must be something to do with the canal."

"H'm! That wouldn't apply to me. I don't know, either, what he wants with me. Unless it's to alter the freight rates. Which isn't the business of the company's attorney. H'm!" he repeated, frowning.

The journey to New York was uneventful, apart from the opportunity it gave Wesley to get to know Captain Beers better. He found the freight agent an extremely good businessman, and pleasant shipboard company.

Uncle Bill was at the dock. Wesley introduced him to Captain Beers, explaining that Beers also had been summoned to New York.

Uncle Bill nodded pleasantly to Beers. "I know. Mr. Cromwell told me you'd be aboard, and asked me to meet you as well. He'd like to see you both at my office. At once, if it's convenient. I have a carriage waiting."

"It's like that?" Beers queried.

"It's like that," Uncle Bill answered. "But don't ask me what it's all about. I just don't know."

They were not long finding out. Ten minutes after their arrival at the Press Bureau Cromwell bustled in.

"Good morning, gentlemen." He wasted no time in polite formalities. Following his nod of greeting he hung his hat on the clothes stand, and with quick incisive movements went over to the chair he usually occupied and sat down. Wesley thought that he had never seen the attorney looking more preoccupied.

"To get to the point at once, gentlemen," Cromwell began as soon as the other three men were seated. "I want your co-operation."

Beers answered for them all. "Of course, Mr. Cromwell. Anything—"

"Then start a revolution in Panama," the attorney stated with a dry smile.

25

"CHRIST!" exclaimed Uncle Bill.

Wesley whistled softly.

Captain Beers stiffened. "A *what,* sir?"

"A revolution, Captain Beers, against Colombia."

"Good God!"

"You all look startled."

"Well, sir—"

"Of course! It's natural you should be. I expected you to be. Revolution isn't the institution in our country that it is in Central and South America. But I'm perfectly serious. Three months ago the Hay-Herran treaty was ratified by our government, in the expectation that Colombia would do the same and that work could begin forthwith. But listen to this extract from an article published in Colombia a few weeks back: 'The Herran treaty will be rejected, and rejected by a unanimous vote, in both chambers. The insult which Señor Herran has cast upon the Colombian name will never be wiped out. The gallows would be a small punishment for a criminal of this class.' In short, gentlemen, instead of ratifying the treaty, Colombia is demanding an indemnity from the New Panama Canal Company of fifty million francs as the price for her consent to the transfer of the company's concession to our government."

"The bastards! Of course you won't pay."

Cromwell did not directly answer the question. He continued, "In case you do not know the background of the concession, these are the facts, gentlemen. The original concession, granted in eighteen seventy-eight for twelve years, was extended for another ten years as from eighteen ninety. Three years later it was again extended on the understanding that the canal would be completed in nineteen hundred and four. At the turn of the century it was further extended to nineteen hundred and ten. But mark this well, gentlemen. The last extension was granted by the President of Colombia, not by the Colombian Congress.

"The President's act is now being used by a powerful faction in the Colombia Senate, as an excuse to declare the extension *ultra vires,* that is, illegal, and the concession liable to forfeiture."

"Why do they want it forfeited?" Beers asked. "It will pay them handsome dividends to have the canal completed."

"Of course, but if the concession is forfeited the money which our government will pay to the New Panama Canal Company will go to Colombia instead."

173

"Those Colombians don't miss a trick!" Uncle Bill drawled. "So the choice is ransom or deadlock?"

"That, roughly, is the position."

"But, Mr. Cromwell—"

"Well, Captain Beers?"

"This revolution in Panama?"

The attorney stared at the questioner. "I'll ask you this: are the Panamanian people anxious to have the canal built?"

"They like butter on their bread, the same as other people, Mr. Cromwell."

"If Panama seceded from Colombia, there would be no trouble in persuading a Panamanian government to grant a concession to the United States?"

"Try to stop them." A doubting expression chased away his smile. "But, sir, there wouldn't be a chance of such a revolution succeeding. Panama has tried often enough without success. She is still suffering from the last attempt. Colombia would crush it as she's crushed every revolution since Christopher Columbus."

"Are you sure, Captain Beers? Could Colombian troops hope to crush a rebellion unless they have the use of the railroad?"

"I shouldn't think so."

"Upon the first intimation that Colombian troops are threatening to use the railroad,—which is the property of an American company, gentlemen—Sullivan and Cromwell would, as general counsel for that company, call upon the United States Government to take all necessary precautions to protect the property of the canal and railroad and, under the treaty of eighteen forty-eight, to guarantee free and uninterrupted transit across the Isthmus."

The cunning of this plan staggered the attorney's small audience even more than his first words had done.

"My God!" Beers breathed. "One move on Colombia's part would make the U. S. a virtual ally of Panama." He shook his head. "The President wouldn't dare."

"No!" Cromwell's thin-lipped smile was significant. "I'll come back to that point later, Captain Beers." He turned to Uncle Bill. "Mr. Godwin, I've work for you. I want a draft of an article for the *World*."

Uncle Bill recognized his employer's mood. He snatched up a pen and poised it over his scribbling pad.

"Begin along these lines: head it, Washington, June thirteen, nineteen hundred and three. Quote: President Roosevelt is determined to have the Panama Canal route. He has no intention of negotiating with Nicaragua for an alternative route."

Godwin glanced at Wesley, and his mouth parted in a questioning smile. Rumors had already reached New York that Cromwell had been summoned to the White House the previous day, to discuss the Panama Canal with President Roosevelt. Could the secession plot be the outcome of that interview?

"The view of the President is known to be—etc. etc.—and finish off that it would be unfair to the United States not to obtain and use the best route. Paragraph. Advices received here indicate great opposition at Bogotá to the canal treaty. Its defeat seems certain for two reasons: one, the greed of the Colombian Government—elaborate that point—and two, the alleged relinquishment of the sovereignty of lands essential for building the canal. Paragraph. Information has reached this city that the state of Panama stands ready to secede from Colombia and enter into a canal treaty with the United States."

Godwin stiffened. "That's dynamite, sir. The *World* won't publish that."

The attorney ignored the interruption. His crisp words flowed on. "Elaborate on the wishes of the people of Panama to have their own republican form of government. Continue: After secession that government will make a treaty with the United States, giving this country the equivalent of absolute sovereignty over the Canal Zone, the city of Panama alone being excepted. There will be no increase in price or yearly rental. Got that, Mr. Godwin?"

"I got it, Mr. Cromwell, but—"

"But?" The tight-lipped word challenged.

"You saw the President?"

"Yesterday."

"Is this his plan or yours?"

"Never mind whose. The President knows of it, and approves."

Godwin's pen moved swiftly. "What about the treaty of eighteen forty-six?" he muttered as he wrote.

"I'm coming to that. Quote: The treaty of eighteen forty-six, by which the United States guarantees the sovereignty of Colombia over the Isthmus of Panama, is construed as applicable only to foreign interference." Observing Godwin's expression he paused. "Well?"

The newspaperman chuckled. "Sometimes I wonder why countries bother to make treaties."

Cromwell shrugged, then relaxed. A dry smile parted his thin lips. "Necessity is the mother of invention," he conceded. Then, crisply, "Add: The formal abrogation of the treaty of eighteen forty-six is under consideration."

"Heads you win, tails I lose." Wesley muttered.

"What's that! Heads—ah yes! But one must fight with every legal weapon at one's disposal, Mr. Adam. Quote: It is known that the Cabinet favors the President's idea of recognizing the republic of Panama if this step is necessary to secure the canal territory. The President has been in consultation with leading senators and has received overwhelming encouragement."

"Senator Morgan!" Godwin muttered as his pen traveled.

"A die-hard!" Cromwell scornfully derided. "He *and* his friends. Their obstinacy makes them blind to realities. Quote: The President, Secretary Hay, and other officials maintain that no foreign government must be permitted to construct a canal along the Panama route. Ad lib about no danger of a competing canal's being built over the Nicaragua route because of cost."

"Fair enough!" was Godwin's comment. He added, "On the contrary, if we finally build on the Nicaragua route the Panama route could be taken over by a foreign government and still be beyond the zone of our country."

"Excellent!" Cromwell approved. "Please add that, Mr. Godwin. Follow up with mention of allowing reasonable time for the Colombian Congress to act."

"Or else?"

"Exactly! If nothing is done, the above plan will become operative. Add that a bitter fight is being waged against the treaty by representatives of foreign governments at Bogotá and by transcontinental railroad interests opposed to the canal. Lobbyists from the United States have gone to Colombia and are prepared to spend unlimited money to defeat the treaty. Finish on that note." As soon as Godwin had finished writing, "Well?"

"Like I said, it's dynamite, sir."

"It's meant to be. Colombia's hand must be forced."

"But it won't look too good abroad, Mr. Cromwell. It'll almost look like the U. S. annexing a slice of Panama as a price for helping the Panamanians to obtain their independence."

"You have scruples, Mr. Godwin?"

"Me!" Godwin's chuckle was sufficient denial. "So long as we build the canal! But the President's reputation—when the opposition press reads this article!" He whistled.

"His shoulders are broad. And he will be able to justify any action the U. S. Government may take. How many times already in their history have the Panamanians fought for their independence? Fifty-three revolutions in fifty-seven years, and two attempted secessions. On six different occasions marines and sailors from United States warships have landed on the Isthmus to protect property, and maintain transoceanic transit—the last time, less than three years ago, in company with British and French forces."

"A knight-errant's one thing, sir; a highwayman another."

"I ask again, are you criticizing this plan, Mr. Godwin?"

"Hell! A newspaperman with morals! I'm just looking into the future, and I don't see it all milk and honey for you and the President if your

176

plan does go through. But that's none of my business. Good luck to the plan so long as we build the god-damned canal. But will the Panamanians rise?"

"That is where I look to you three gentlemen for co-operation. Mr. Adam, how is your knowledge of Spanish? Fluent?"

"It may not be Castilian, but it's fluent, Mr. Cromwell."

"Good. Are you still as enthusiastic as you were about a Panama Canal?"

"More so."

"Do you know that I have—er—intelligence agents in Bogotá?"

"I didn't, sir. "

"Well, I have. So let us come to the point at once. Are you willing to combine your work as surveyor to the P.R.R. with intelligence work on behalf of the—" he coughed. "On behalf, indirectly, of the U. S. Government, work intended to prove our sympathy with the people of Panama in their revolt against their Colombian taskmasters?" He raised a hand to prevent a quick answer from Wesley. "I must point out that the work will possibly be dangerous. The Colombian Government have spies even in Washington and New York. They are sure to have them in Panama."

"Especially after they've read this article," Uncle Bill remarked dryly.

Wesley's reply was prompt. "Yes, sir. But I'll need instructing."

"Naturally." Cromwell turned to Beers. "What about you, Captain Beers?"

Beers' reply was no less prompt than Wesley's. "Sure."

"And you, Mr. Godwin?"

Uncle Bill looked bewildered. "Where do I come in? What can I do here in New York?"

"Nothing, here. But Señor Gabriel Duque, owner of the *Panama Star and Herald* needs an associate editor—"

"Not now, he doesn't," Godwin interrupted. "When do we sail?"

Such scruples as Wesley had about deliberately fomenting rebellion among the people of Panama, were largely dispelled by the first Panamanian to whom he spoke on his return to Colón.

"What news from New York?" politely inquired Señor Mendez, when they met in the hotel lobby. Mendez owned a huge plantation in the San Pablo region to the northeast of the Cierro Gigante. He was a frequent visitor to Colón, ostensibly to arrange transport for his produce; but Wesley suspected that a certain Iñez was the more likely reason for his journeys to the Caribbean port. Mendez always engaged a bedroom at the old Washington, but it was rumored that the chambermaid responsible for his room was seldom called upon to make his bed. "Is the canal still one of the chief topics of conversation?"

"More so than ever."

The Panamanian shrugged. "It will never be built."

"The railroad was."

"Colombia was not so greedy then. The *Star and Herald* writes that she is still holding out for an annuity of six hundred thousand dollars. Is that so?"

"Yes, and in addition an outright sum of ten million dollars."

"Your government will never agree."

"Of course not. The canal isn't that valuable. We offered a compromise of a quarter of a million annually, but that's not good enough." Wesley continued casually, "Pity the Isthmus should be deprived of such urgently needed funds. A lot of good could be done to improve conditions here. New roads, for one thing."

The Panamanian laughed. "You cannot know Colombia, señor. Even if that sum were agreed, and paid, most of it would remain in Bogotá. For generations the capital has lived in luxury at our expense."

"There seems only one way out of the deadlock."

"And that, señor?" Mendez asked. His tone was more polite than interested.

"For Panama to keep the whole of the ten million dollars outright, and also the annuity of a quarter of a million. Our government wouldn't mind who the money was paid to so long as she would be given the concession for a canal."

The Panamanian brightened, but immediately succumbed to despondency.

"There's no hope of our seceding, señor. Panama has often tried to break away, and failed—bloodily!"

"Next time could be different."

"How so?"

"I cannot speak officially, you understand, but only on behalf of Mr. Cromwell, who is attorney for the railroad of which I am an employee, as you know."

"Quite! Quite! But it is said that Señor Cromwell has the ear of President Roosevelt." Mendez's formal manner gave way to one of alert eagerness.

"In the event of an attempted secession it is certain that Mr. Cromwell would ask the President to land U. S. forces for the purpose of protecting the railroad, and keep it running free from—er—outside interference."

"Ah!" The exclamation was long, satisfying, significant.

"It is also said, in authoritative circles, that he favors immediate recognition of an independent Panamanian government with whom we could sign a treaty guaranteeing sovereignty of the Isthmus."

Mendez stood so stiffly upright that his mustachios appeared to bristle. "Señor Adam, you have made me a happy man." He rightly interpreted Wesley's expression. "You want to know why? Two years ago, when Colón was besieged by the Colombians, after they had taken my only son prisoner they shot him because he had killed one of their captains in fair fight. Since then I have prayed for the opportunity of avenging his death. When and if a signal is given to rise against the Colombians I shall be the first to offer my services."

The response to Wesley's sly probings was always the same. Given a little help and encouragement, the people of Panama were eager to rise and this in spite of their losses during the recent insurrection which only American intervention had brought to an end. In fact, several Panamanians assured him that fighting between Colombian troops and Panamanian civilians was still going on in the interior. Without doubt the inflammable material existed; only a tiny flame was needed once more to involve the small country in the conflagration of civil war.

These facts he reported not only to Cromwell in New York but also to Captain Beers, who was concentrating on the citizens of Panama City; and to the *Star and Herald* office, where Godwin was quickly digging in. Articles, inspired by his wily, practiced suggestions, though not actually written by him, appeared in the newspaper at frequent intervals. Clever articles that, by inference, pointed out how much more easily a canal treaty with the United States could be negotiated if Panamanians instead of Colombians were in charge, and what improvements two hundred fifty thousand dollars could achieve if paid direct to Panama.

Exactly four weeks after his return to Colón Wesley encountered Larry outside of the offices of the P.R.R.

26

"HELLO, BROTHER!" Larry's amiable smile had not changed. It still reminded Wesley of the disarming grin one sees on the face of a boy discovered in an act of mischief. "Still alive, and still here, I see."

"As if you hadn't taken the trouble to find out so that you could lie in wait for me! Besides, any reason why I shouldn't be alive?"

"Sure." After a short pause, "Malaria, for one. You haven't had it yet?"

"Only a mild attack." Wesley inspected Larry's face. It was much browner than on the last occasion he had seen it; but it was drawn and looked thinner. "You look as if you have."

"Yeah," Larry did not appear anxious to discuss his illness. "Mind if I walk a ways with you?"

"Glad to have you. How about something to eat?"

"If *you're* ready to pay for me."

"Meaning you're not?"

"Meaning I can't. Do I look as if I can?"

He didn't. His tropical clothes were threadbare. His limp was more noticeable. He looked intensely weary.

"Would you rather eat Chinese, Indian or Italian?"

"Brother, so long as it's food the choice doesn't mean a thing to me. I could eat a house."

"Let's make it Italian—Luigi's." They moved off, and walked nearly a hundred yards before either spoke. In the meantime Wesley became aware that his companion seemed uncommonly disturbed: he seemed unable to keep his head still, and walked more quickly than usual. Several times he nearly tripped. Then Larry said, "All right. Ask."

"Ask what?"

"You want to know what's happened to El Jaguar's gold, don't you?"

"Of course. But there's time."

"You're an understanding pal. But you don't need to be told I haven't found it."

"Don't I?"

"Do I look like I have?" Larry sounded scornful.

"I wouldn't know, Larry. I think you might still be wearing those clothes even if you had."

"That's where you're wrong. I like food and clothes same as you. The only difference is, I'm not anxious to work for them. But come a fortune falling into my lap, as it were—" He turned bitter. "Not a damned centavo have I found, brother. Not a smell of the gold."

"I didn't think you would. Fifty years is a long time."

"I don't see how anyone could have found it. It was well hidden."

"Accident! Coincidence!"

Larry shrugged. "I haven't given up hope. I'll try again, as soon as I can buy a mule. This damned leg of mine—"

Nothing more was said. They reached the restaurant, and were lucky enough to get a table. Wesley ordered a substantial dish for his companion, a lighter one for himself. Larry finished his plate and was obviously still unsatisfied. He looked apologetic when Wesley ordered another portion.

"A little wild fruit doesn't go far."

"Is that all you've had?"

"Almost all, for the past week. The woman who was looking after me hadn't much herself."

"Woman—"

Larry smiled. *"Caramba!* You're jumping at conclusions, brother. She's old enough to be my mother, and as black as soot. She found me in the jungle and nursed me back to life."

"Fever?"

Larry nodded. "Strange part of it all is, I was on my way to see you."

180

"Why?"

"To ask for work."

"You!" Wesley laughed. "I thought you and work weren't on speaking terms."

"I am with the kind of work you can offer me." Larry's smirk was sly. "If you want to raise a revolution in Panama, I'm your man. Give me back those clothes—did you get them out of pawn? And some dollars to jingle in my pocket, and you'll have hired yourself as capable an *agent provocateur* as Mr. Cromwell could wish for."

Wesley thought the boast justified. He had seen for himself, aboard the *Yucatan,* that Larry's physical disability allied to his casual geniality, and unfailing courtesy toward those whom he wished to impress, quickly won sympathetic regard. As he was partly Panamanian himself, he stood a better chance than an interested American of pleading the cause of secession. Nevertheless, Wesley was puzzled.

"How did you find out what I'm doing?" he asked sharply.

Larry's hissing laughter had a scornful undertone. "You've been in Panama long enough to know of its bush telegraph. I knew two weeks ago that you and Captain Beers were trying to incite the Panamanians to secede from the United States of Colombia."

Wesley frowned. "If you could hear that so could the Colombians. Which means they will take precautions."

"Of course they could. And probably will."

"I still don't get your reason for wanting work."

"Money, brother, money. To keep me going while I continue the search." Larry tried to repress a hiccup, and failed. "Sorry about that, but it couldn't be helped. Bellies do queer things after a bout of starvation. Shall we get going?"

"Going where?"

"Back to the hotel, of course. We've got things to talk about."

"Such as?"

"Giving me back my clothes, to begin with. Don't forget you've hired yourself a man."

Larry suggested a comparatively high wage to which Wesley agreed, certain that Cromwell would approve. The little man then took back his clothes, changed, and wished Wesley—now Mr. Adam once more!—a blithe farewell before disappearing into the dark night, bound for a destination he refused to divulge but which Wesley had a shrewd idea would be somewhere near Bottle Alley. He was beginning to identify that particular light in the eye. He had seen it so often on the faces of newcomers to Panama. He had been tempted, too, just lately. In fact, only that morning, having heard from Anne that the family's long-overdue visit to Colón would have to be further postponed, he had decided to wait no longer before satisfying his growing hunger. Companionship with her, however limited, would have helped him to keep control of himself, by reminding him at first hand of the decencies of life. But with little hope of seeing her in the near future—

Larry's visit had driven Bottle Alley from his thoughts; but only temporarily. There was still time if he really wanted to go. Yes, no? Yes, no? Just this once, he argued weakly. He longed just for once to feel the yielding softness of a woman's body within his arms; to fill his nostrils with her scent; to experience the ecstasy of an uninhibited kiss and the excitement of stroking the soft sheen of her flesh with his finger tips— He snatched at a coat, and left the hotel. By this time he was sweating from the humidity of the night. Now that he had brushed aside his scruples and taken the first step, his need was all the greater for having been repressed for so long. Not even the sordidness of the scene had the power, at that moment, to chill his passion—neither the grinning, glistening faces of Negroes, dressed in dirty white suits of coarse denim, and battered straw hats; nor the more furtive-looking chocolate faces of the mestizo population; nor the group of half-tipsy white seamen in nondescript clothes whose cap badges indicated that one of the Royal Mail liners was in port; nor the greedy-eyed but self-conscious party of Americans. Nothing in fact mattered to Wesley just then but the need to assuage an insistent, urgent want.

Heedless of the men who milled about him, he moved along the sidewalk, searching for a woman who would gratify not only his sexual desires, but who, with good luck, might go some way toward satisfying what little was left just then of his aesthetic taste. Not that one! Nor that one! Certainly not that one! That one, perhaps, for want of a better! Not that one—

He halted abruptly, as both his progress and attention were arrested by a fight between two Negroes for the right of entry into the stall of a young girl with timid eyes, a slender body, and hair the warm shade of ripened corn.

The sound of his horror-bred oath was drowned by the encouraging cheers of onlookers who were enjoying the fracas. The object of the bloody fight was Ingrid Ericson.

27

IT WAS NONE of his business, he told himself again and again. It was none of his business. The girl was a common prostitute. If she chose to expose her body for public hire in a notorious district such as Bottle Alley, then she must endure the consequences: accept what offered whether it was white, yellow, chocolate, or black.

He tried to turn away from the scene, but without success. Bad enough to think of any woman having to offer herself as the prize in a vicious contest between snarling, wolfish men; worse if the victor would inevitably be colored; worst of all when the woman concerned was an acquaintance; young, fresh looking, clean eyed.

Wesley's fight with his conscience was more swiftly settled than that between the Negroes. He could not stand by without trying to save Ingrid. Yet what could he do? Strong as he was, big as he was, he was no match for either man. Both were thick shouldered and well muscled—dock workers, in all probability. Besides, the chances were that, if he interfered, both men would turn on him, smash him down, kick in his ribs, stamp his face into the stinking mire.

He was still desperately striving to think of some stratagem to rescue the girl when the sound of noisy singing from the party of seamen suggested a possibility. He shouldered his way back and found them clustered round the stall of a Spanish woman who was dancing a fandango for their benefit.

"Hey!" he gasped. He had to repeat his call to claim their attention. "Hey, men!" he shouted, clutching one by his thick arm. "Give me a hand, some of you—"

"Shure I'll be giving you a hand, and here it is," the seaman retorted drunkenly as he gave Wesley's chest a powerful thrust which sent him reeling against the wall.

Thank God for the Irish! Wesley recovered his balance.

"Do you want a fight—"

"So it's a fight you'll be wanting, is it? Thin it's meself will oblige." The man put up hamlike fists, and began weaving to and fro.

"No. Not me. Down the street. Two Negroes. Fighting for my girl. A white girl—"

The information penetrated the alcoholic fog. "A white girl, begod! A couple of dirty niggers!" He turned to his companions. "Come on, me boys. Who's for saving a white mavourneen from a couple of dirty niggers?"

The seed fell upon fertile ground. The seamen were ripe for battle. A shout went up.

"Which way, Paddy, old cock? We'll show the bastards—"

"This way. Quick, for God's sake!" Judging from the roar of the crowd ahead, Wesley feared that one of the Negroes had gone down, in which case the fight was not likely to last much longer.

Side by side he and Paddy cleaved a pathway along the crowded sidewalk; a path widened by the seamen behind, shoulder to shoulder. A howl of rage rose from men who, by sheer pressure, were forced painfully against the walls of the buildings, a howl splutteringly echoed by others less fortunate, who were shoved off into the mud. Blows were exchanged, bottles and brass knuckles began to draw first blood, but the advantage of surprise made their advance irresistible. An angry crowd closed in behind them, comprising not only native Panamanians but also men of other nationalities, who hated the Anglo-Saxons.

"Sales Anglais! God-damned limeys! *Verdammte Engländers!*"

Empty bottles by the hundreds lay to hand in the fetid mud—not for nothing was the road named Bottle Alley! A foul assortment was hurled at the charging seamen, who grunted with pain or swore and blasphemed whenever a hit was scored. As the sullen roar grew louder, there spread up and down the street a frantic anxiety to close and bolt all windows and doors. So it was in every street within earshot of the alarming noise, for residents of Colón knew from past history that they had reason to dread the baying signal of a race riot.

By the time Wesley and Paddy had reached the scene of the original fight Bottle Alley was exploding into a general melee but neither they nor the seamen behind were conscious of the commotion. By the uncertain light of a flickering oil lamp which hung from the roof of a nearby shack they saw the motionless bloody body of one Negro lying half on the sidewalk, half in the mud. His chest looked motionless, but when they glanced at the man's head they saw that, although his eyes were closed, his mouth which was partly submerged in a pool of black water, bubbled and frothed as it alternately sucked in and ejected a small amount of the filthy liquid.

The victor, scarcely less bloody than his beaten opponent, had shambled into the stall and was already wrapping his apelike arms round the shrinking clawing girl.

The sight enraged the Irishman. With a furious shout he pulled a bottle of whisky from his pocket, and with his full strength smashed it down on the Negro's skull. The man gave a sobbing gasp of pain as blood spurted from the wound and, mingling with the whisky, flowed down his face and neck. Then his legs gave way, and he subsided to the ground, unconscious.

A gaudy kimono, lying on the iron bedstead, attracted Wesley's atten-

184

tion. He snatched it up and wrapped it about the girl, who was sobbing with the exertion of fighting off the Negro.

"Come," he ordered brusquely, and pushed her toward the door.

Outside the shack the situation was worsening. Among the witnesses who had watched the Irish seaman attack the Negro were several colored men who yelled their fury at the sight of spurting blood. One of them pulled a machete from his belt, and slashed at the head of the nearest seaman. At the last moment his arm was jogged and the steel missed its main objective, but sliced the man's left ear in half.

"White pig!" the colored man mouthed.

A white fist smashed into the Negro's mouth. "God-damn, nigger," shouted a sailor off a United Fruit Company ship. A moment before he had been exchanging blows with one of the Royal Mail men. But all that changed. "Sick 'em, you limeys. Show them black bastards what!"

The roar took on a deeper note as passions flared. The milling crowd divided into white against colored. Fists, feet, heads; fair blows, foul; nothing mattered so long as you could wipe that snarling, ferocious grin off the face of the other fellow. Weapons appeared: knives, blackjacks, even a marlinspike; and all the empty bottles that were to be had for the picking up. Men went down, a white man here, a colored man there, and many did not rise again, for as the fight surged to and fro they were trampled beneath the feet of ally and enemy alike. This time the luckier ones were those who went down into the road, for the mud made a cushion for them to sink into and saved their chests and ribs from being crushed.

The scene was ugly and bestial; a sad commentary on civilization, Wesley thought, as he bent his broad shoulders protectingly over Ingrid's slighter back, and tried to edge away from the vortex of the savage fight. The dirty-yellow lighting made everything even more macabre, for the women along the street had hastily dowsed all lamps and candles in the stalls and only a mere four overhead lamps in double that number of blocks were left to high light the horror below.

Foot by foot Wesley edged toward the comparative safety of a crossroad, but he did not escape scot free. The Irishman was no longer with him, nor the other seamen. As he aproached the radius of the only lamp on that block a colored man noticed him. The man carried a short length of two by two, which he cracked down on Wesley's shoulders. The blow made him stagger, and he nearly tripped, but before the Panamanian could aim a second blow a seaman stabbed the man in the arm and gave Wesley and Ingrid time to squeeze past a pair who fought only with their fists.

So, at last, he came to a corner, and a clear space. He forced her forward at a stumbling trot.

"Run, girl."

They ran on. Others were running too; a handful away from the commotion, but more toward it, drawn thither by the echo of ferocious shouting. At last they reached Front Street, which, athough people stood about in apprehensive groups, was otherwise normal. When Wesley slowed down, Ingrid began to struggle.

"Let me go. Let me go. Where are you taking me?" she gasped.

"Friends," he told her shortly. "At any rate, for tonight."

"Men—no more men—"

"A married couple."

She had no more fight left in her. She walked beside him with lifeless, dragging steps. Neither spoke again before reaching the Sanderson home. Frederick opened the door. His eyes opened wide with amazement.

"In Heaven's name, Wesley!"

"I'll tell you in a minute. Is Madge here?"

Madge supplied the answer by joining them. There was no vestige of her usual laughter as she glanced at Ingrid. "What is it, Wesley?"

"Could you give this girl shelter for an hour or so? Some English seamen and I have just rescued her from a Negro—"

"You poor dear! Do come in." She held out a hand to Ingrid, who hesitated before moving on into the house with dragging feet.

"This gentleman didn't tell you—" she began.

"I'll not listen to a word until you're rested," Madge said firmly.

"Wait, Madge. I think you should know. She was in Bottle Alley."

"Oh!" Madge Sanderson's mouth closed with a snap, and her soft eyes hardened as they inspected the disheveled girl beside her. But she quickly gave way to compassion. "She shall tell me about it herself, later. Is she the cause of all that noise?"

He nodded. "All hell's broken loose there. A race riot."

"Those awful riots. How I wish—" Eyes betrayed her anxiety. "You're not hurt?"

"Only a few bruises. If I may wash up?"

"Of course. Frederick, go give Wesley a hand, while I attend to this girl. Afterward we'll have coffee."

The two men had been sitting in the parlor for quite some time before Madge joined them with the coffee.

"She's resting," she explained as she poured out three cups. "She won't tell me her name—"

Wesley grinned. "I will. It's Ingrid Ericson."

The Sandersons did not hide their astonishment—and Madge, her disapproval.

"You know her?"

"I met her once, in New York. She came to Mr. Cromwell's Press Bureau, and asked me if I knew why her brother had come back to Panama, and where he was."

186

"So she *was* telling the truth," Madge looked sad. "And I didn't believe her. We're not very Christian, are we, when we don't want to be."

"You wouldn't think there was any such thing as Christianity if you had been at Bottle Alley tonight. What did she tell you?"

"That her brother had disappeared in Panama; that she had saved for years to buy a passage here so that she could search for him; and that after she had spent all her money, without success, she looked about for work. While doing so she was helped by a kind woman from Buenos Aires—well, you can guess the rest for yourself. It's a horrible story, but with a bright lining. Tonight was her first night, she says. She swears that no man has—has touched her." Madge's earnest eyes pleaded with each man in turn. "Do you think she is being truthful?"

"It won't be hard to prove, my dear," Frederick pointed out.

"I hated to disbelieve her," she went on apologetically. "She has such pretty eyes, so sincere and so truthful. But her story was—well, just the sort of story a girl of that type, I mean a girl of the type we thought she was, would have made up to gain our sympathy."

"I wonder where the brother is," Frederick said. "Dead, probably."

"He's not. I saw him not long ago. That is, he saw me."

"Then you know him, too. I'll be damned!"

"He helped me survey the Isthmus for Mr. Cromwell."

Madge looked relieved. "You must try to find him, Wesley. Oh dear! This will be a happy night for that poor girl. God must be watching over her to guide your footsteps to her rescue just in time."

Wesley flushed. "I'm afraid it wasn't God."

Madge's eyes twinkled. She was broadminded. One had to be, to live in Panama. "What's to happen to Ingrid Ericson?"

"I'll send her back to the States," Wesley suggested.

Madge shook her head in doubt. "I have a feeling she won't go without news of her brother."

"What of it? If somebody doesn't see that she returns home she'll drift back to Bottle Alley, as sure as God made little apples." Frederick stared at his wife. "What's brewing?" he demanded. "See that tiny frown, Wesley? She's hatching up one of her plots. Watch out for yourself if she looks in your direction. That'll mean you'll be involved."

She smiled. "Don't be ridiculous, Frederick. But I was thinking—"

"Here it comes!"

"You know that Carmen isn't going to work for me any more after her marriage next week. If Ingrid is willing to help me run the house and become my companion until her brother turns up again, I'm sure she would be more useful than any of the Panamanian women I could get. She could sleep in the spare bedroom."

"If you are quite sure you can trust her!"

"I am certain we can," she asserted with conviction.

He nodded. "Very well, honey. The house is your department."

Their conversation was interrupted by an echo of distant shouting which grew louder with every second. Soon they were able to distinguish an odd word or so. "—kill the bastard!—black scum!—look out he don't—" Then they heard above the shouts the rapid pounding of feet on the shell road, a gasping scream of fear.

Madge turned pale. "Dear God!"

Outside: "Damn, he got away. Look out he don't double back." The noises grew less, as pursued and pursuers passed out of hearing. Frederick mopped his forehead.

"What was that you were saying about Christianity, Wesley?"

The riots continued well into the night, and when the new day dawned many men, white and colored, wore bandages, or showed other evidence of having taken part. For an hour or so the events of the previous night formed the principle topic of conversation in Colón. After that it was scarcely mentioned. What was one melee more or less in Colón?

That same day also brought a message to Wesley from Colonel Shaler, Superintendent of the P.R.R. Would Mr. Adam please report as soon as possible? Wesley did so.

"Ha! There you are, Adam. Sit down, sit down. Cigar?"

"Thank you, sir."

Shaler seemed embarrassed. He took time to light his own cigar, and walked to and fro across the floor before finally settling in his own chair.

"About this business of encouraging the Panamanians to revolt! You've done good work, I understand."

"I hope so, sir."

"Yes, quite! You have faith that the canal can be built. It's more than I have, sometimes. What I had you here for is to tell you to drop all further—er—propaganda among the Panamanians. No more, do you understand? No more."

"But, Colonel Shaler—"

"Well? Well?"

"It was Mr. Cromwell's suggestion—"

"Nonsense. Mr. Cromwell is counsel to the Panama Railroad, not an *agent provocateur*. No legal man would commit himself to such a plot. The Panamanians must be allowed to work out their own salvation, do you understand? Without any assistance from members of the P.R.R. I have a letter from Mr. Cromwell to this effect, arrived this morning. Listen, I will read you an extract.

While there may be no real foundation for newspaper statements of possible revolutions at Panama, I advise and request that you take extra and every precaution to strictly perform our obligations to

188

Colombia under concession, and instruct officials and employees to be careful as heretofore not to participate in any movements or hostilities whatever, and that you make at once your attitude known to government officials there, and make careful record of your acts in this regard in order to prevent even a pretext for complaint or claims by Bogotá or Panama Governments; also take every precaution to protect the property in your care from possible damage or interruption of service.

(Signed) W. N. CROMWELL

"I repeat, do you understand?"

"Not absolutely, sir, I thought that you, too—I mean, that the reason for your recent visit to New York—"

Colonel Shaler winked.

Wesley understood.

28

DAY BY DAY the atmosphere in Colón and the neighboring district grew more tense. The well-informed no longer doubted the probability of another revolution. The only doubt in their minds was —when? and would Colombia forestall it by sending extra troops to Panama while there was still time.

Bogotá knew that a plot was being hatched in three cities—Panama City, New York, and Washington. To begin with, the article which Cromwell had inspired had duly been published in the *World*. Possibly Bogotá had accepted the publication of the article as flying a kite, as diplomatic circles would say; a stratagem to force Colombia into making a countermove. The Colombian government, however, decided that the whole maneuver was a bluff to be treated with contempt, so they rejected the treaty, and adjourned Congress until October.

Since then there had been ample evidence that neither the Panamanians, nor President Roosevelt and his colleagues intended to treat with Bogotá on Colombian terms. Certainly the Colombian minister in Washington, Dr. Herran, realized this when a number of prominent Panamanian citizens and residents landed in the States, and shuttled between New York and Washington: among them Gabriel Duque, editor and proprietor of the *Star and Herald,* Dr. Manuel Amador, chief of the P.R.R.'s medical service, Pablo Arosemena, ex-deputy for Panama in the Colombian legislature, and Tracy Robinson. Herran was sufficiently concerned to hire

189

private detectives to trail the new arrivals so that he might send an account of their movements to Bogotá.

Nor was this all. A more definite pointer appeared in the editorial columns of the *New York Herald:* "Public sentiment may yet be called on to determine whether the United States shall take action which would lead to war with a sister republic over the right to complete the Panama Canal."

Early in October, when copies of the *New York Herald* reached Panama, the startled residents read that their Washington correspondent had telegraphed to the effect that William Nelson Cromwell, after calling that day on President Roosevelt, had declared: "The Panama Canal will be built, and by the United States Government."

But the Colombians remained defiant, or perhaps wishfully blind. A cable to the State Department from the American Minister in Bogotá forecast that when the Senate Committee met to consider the Hay-Herran treaty, their recommendation would again be: rejection. So the people of Panama went ahead with their plans to secede from the United States of Colombia, and under cover of night began the distribution of arms that had been recently and secretly landed.

Some days later Uncle Bill showed up at Colón. He was a changed man. His face was brown and less sepulchral; it had filled out. His shoulders no longer drooped with the cares of the world. The biggest change of all, however, was in his eyes. These were tremendously, excitingly alive.

He laughed when Wesley asked him how he liked living in Panama. "My boy, do I like the life here? Sure, I like it. I like it lots. It's exciting. Exhilarates me. I feel a new man."

"You look it! What's brought you to Colón?"

"Plenty. To see Shaler, for one thing. Beers didn't dare come himself in view of Mr. Cromwell's letter. Wily old fox."

"Cromwell?"

"Sure. You know why he sent that letter to Shaler? Having promised Amador to finance a revolution in Panama, he heard from Dr. Herran that if the P.R.R. or the New Panama Canal Company take any part in a revolutionary movement both concessions would be cancelled. So Beers keeps undercover, leaving me, as an independent agent, to run errands for him."

"This visit to Colón being one of them?"

Uncle Bill nodded. "To warn Shaler to be ready if matters come to a head on the third of November."

"Any particular reason for that date?"

Godwin's long face twisted into a mischievous grin. "A very good reason, Wesley. November third is election day in the States."

"I don't see—"

"You would if you were a newspaperman—or a politician. The newspapers will be too busy with election news to give prominence to late cables from Panama. I can just see night editors pulling their hair out trying to tear down and make up fresh front pages."

"Maybe I'm dull, Uncle Bill. Will that be an advantage?"

"The President thinks it will be. The less publicity about the role America is going to play in the revolution, the better pleased he'll be. Listen, my boy. Strictly between you and me, I'm to tell Shaler that the revolutionaries will be sitting pretty. The Navy is on the job."

"Already?"

"Sure. A week ago the Navy Department ordered Admiral Glass, in command of the Pacific Squadron, to proceed on an exercise cruise to Acapulco."

"But that's in Mexico."

"It's also on the way to Panama, isn't it? Listen, what do you think of this?" He pulled a small bundle of telegraph forms from his pocket, and began to read aloud. " 'Following message sent out by Navy Department on nineteenth instant to Glass, *Marblehead,* San Francisco, California. Message begins, Send *Boston* or other vessel ahead of squadron to Acapulco. Message continues, in official cipher. Send the *Boston* with all possible dispatch to San Juan del Sur Nicaragua stop She must arrive by November one with coal sufficient for returning to Acapulco stop Secret and confidential stop Her ostensible destination Acapulco only stop signed Moody.' "

"How in Heaven's name did you get hold of that information, Uncle Bill?"

He chuckled. "Trade secret. It's a newspaperman's business to obtain private information. That's not all, for that wasn't the only telegram the Navy Department sent off that day. One went to the Navy Yard, Brooklyn, ordering the *Dixie* to be ready for sea by the twenty-third; and to sail from League Island the same day, with a contingent of four hundred marines aboard. The U.S.S. *Atlanta* has also been given sealed orders. She's proceeding to Guantanamo meanwhile."

"Four hundred marines!" Wesley shook his head. "Not enough, I'd say. What about the regular garrison of Colombian troops here?"

Godwin chuckled and winked. "Good American dollars will keep them out of the way. The garrison commander, General Esteban Huertas, is with us fifty thousand dollars' worth, so there won't be any trouble from him."

"And the police?"

"They're controlled by Governor Obaldia, who's a Panamanian born, and has business interests here, so he—and the police—are safe. Captain Tascón's not so safe. Huertas thought he might have double-crossed us, so he and Obaldia hatched us a forged dispatch from Chiriquí, to say that Costa Rican troops have invaded the country. So Tascón's pinned on his medals, and ordered the brass band to play a farewell march as he and his gallant company of infantry march off to Penonome, death, and glory." Uncle Bill roared with good humor.

It was not only a shrewd piece of thinking to dispose of Tascón and his company of Colombian infantry, it was also a first class jest: one so good that it had to be elaborated for the benefit of posterity. Governor Obaldia and General Huertas formally notified the President of Colombia of the steps which had been taken to repel and avenge the invasion of Chiriquí province by Costa Rican troops.

It is amazing that the obvious sequel had not been foreseen by the good-humored jesters. The President of Colombia took all those steps which one normally would take when national dignity and national safety are involved. He cabled back to Governor Obaldia to have no fear and to stand firm: reinforcements, in the shape of Colombia's crack battalion of Tiradores, or Sharpshooters, under the command of Generals Juan Tovar and Ramon Amaya, had been ordered to sail immediately for Colón aboard the transport *Cartagena;* and as a further measure of safety, would the Governor please be kind enough to order the warships *Padilla* and *Bogotá,* then in Panama Bay, to proceed at once to Buenaventura to pick up additional reinforcements?

President Marroquin was not averse to a jest on his own account. He considered that it would be a capital joke to relieve Obaldia of his gubernatorial duties, so he ordered one General Gutíerrez to proceed secretly to Panama to supplant the governor.

Wesley was just leaving his office for the midday meal when Assistant Supervisor Prescott entered.

"Good evening, Adam. How is the work? Anything urgent on hand?"

"No, sir.

"What about social engagements? Could you spare two or three days to come with me to Panama?"

"I am due at the Sandersons' tonight, sir, but they won't object to my postponing the visit."

"Good. Did you know that Dr. Amador arrived in Colón this morning?"

"I've heard rumors."

"I met him to see whether he had brought anything which might have been safer with me. He hadn't. All he brought back with him was the complete plan of revolution in his head, the newly designed flag of the new Republic-to-be wrapped round his waist, the good wishes of the American Government in his heart, and a promise of one hundred thousand dollars from Monsieur Bunau-Varilla in his pocket."

"Bunau-Varilla?"

"You know he was chief engineer of the canal under the French regime, and is at the moment a large shareholder in the New Panama Canal Company—large enough to make him more than a little interested in having someone else buy the company so that he can get his money back. In fact, as far as I can make out, the plan which Amador has brought back with him is largely of Bunau-Varilla's making.

"Amador is continuing his journey to Panama tonight, where he is to meet members of the junta. Afterward he wants to go over the plans with Colonel Shaler and myself. Shaler can't spare the time, and in any case it would be wiser if he didn't see too much of Amador or any other member of the junta at this stage. He has suggested your going in his place if it's agreeable to you."

"Of course, sir."

"Good. Meet us at the station."

It was nearly seven by the time the small party reached the capital. They hired a carriage to take them to the house of Federico Boyd on the Cathedral Plaza. There they found several members of the junta anxiously awaiting their arrival: among them Arosemena, Arango, who was attorney and land agent for the P.R.R., the two Arias, Tomas and Ricardo, who had big business interests in Panama, and Duque.

Scarcely giving Amador and his companions time to recover from their journey, the conspirators began questioning the doctor.

"Were you successful?"

"Have you brought a treaty with you?"

"Are funds forthcoming?"

The old man smiled. "One at a time, my friends, if you please. Permit me to give you a brief account first. You can question me afterward. You sent me to the United States, as a representative of this committee, to obtain confirmation of the promise of assistance from Mr. Cromwell, to obtain the aid of any other interested parties; to secure assurances that a revolution would have the support of the armed forces of the United States; and lastly, to obtain the money and arms necessary for the revolt.

"I went to the Hotel Endicott in New York. At first, as I cabled you my visit proved disappointing." He glanced apologetically at Prescott and Wesley who sat at the far end of the table. "Mr. Cromwell was unwilling or unable to promise us the help we asked for. Indeed, a member of his firm told me, all too frankly, that the Panamanians must be fools if we expected the United States to give any guarantee of armed assistance before the revolution; and that we must make the movement ourselves; but that, once we had established our independence, the United States would never permit Colombian troops to land for the purpose of attack."

An angry buzz broke out, but Amador raised a hand. Wesley noted that the noise quickly subsided.

"Peace, my friends, let me finish. Toward the end of September Monsieur Bunau-Varilla arrived from Paris. I called upon him at the Waldorf on the night of his arrival. He not only promised us much-needed financial support, but also undertook to arrange with the United States Government to send warships into Panamanian waters, to protect us against any Colombian attempt to suppress our revolution."

"Which promise he has carried out, señores, as you know," Arango smoothly interrupted. "Thanks to Duque here we know that the American Navy Department has ordered units of their navy to make for neighboring waters."

"Exactly!" Amador nodded his head. "It is certain that the U.S. Government will recognize the Republic of the Isthmus immediately it is established, and will thereafter protect us in perpetuity from outside attack." He smiled. "There are many countries in the world who would be glad to be thus comprehensively assured without payment of premium." He stood up. "Now for a pleasant surprise, my friends. Permit me to show you the flag of the Republic of the Isthmus, designed by the wife of our good friend, Monsieur Bunau-Varilla." With a dramatic gesture he unbuttoned his coat, unwrapped the flag from around his waist, and held it up for all to see.

Wesley was startled. For a moment he thought that he was looking at the Stars and Stripes, but then he saw that the jack containing the stars had been substituted by a piece of pale blue silk on which had been superimposed two white stars connected by a narrow strip of white ribbon.

"See," Amador continued with enthusiasm. "Two stars to represent the two oceans, the Atlantic and the Pacific, soon to be connected"—he indicated the strip of ribbon—"by the Panama Canal. *Our* canal—" He paused as if to give his friends the chance to applaud. When they did not do so, when, on the contrary, he saw their frank expression of hostility, he looked bewildered.

"Well, my friends?"

"I do not like it."

"Nor I."

"Nor I."

"But why not? I do not understand—"

"It is too much like the American flag," Boyd brusquely asserted. "We are seceding from Colombia to become a free, independent and sovereign country, not to become another state in the American Union."

"Agreed!" Arias seconded. "And how much of independent Panama is to be incorporated in the Republic of the Isthmus?"

"Approximately a fifty-mile strip north of a line from Cape Tiburon to Point Garachine—"

Wesley did not hear the end of the sentence for the storm of protest which interrupted it. Not until Arias made a gesture of annoyance did the noise slowly die away into an uncomfortable silence.

"I think I speak for several of us here, Amador, in protesting against

194

such a proposal." "Hear! Hear!" from two of the other conspirators confirmed his statement. "In fact, I go further. I am not interested in risking my life at the worst, ruination at the best, to free a fifty-mile strip of Panama for the sole benefit of French shareholders and American commerce."

"Ruination—death—" Amador shook his head in bewilderment.

"If the U.S.A. does not guarantee to protect the whole of Panama from Colombia, what hope will there be for me and many other men of substance, whose estates and interests are outside the fifty-mile strip?"

"Arias is right, Amador," Boyd added.

"As far as I am concerned it must be the whole of Panama or nothing," Arias angrily continued. "What do you say, friends? Am I right?"

Wesley was not surprised when the other members of the junta left Amador in no doubt about where their sympathies lay. His own feelings were not dissimilar: he felt that the junta's resistance was justified. At last the doctor shrugged his shoulders.

"Very well, señores, we will declare the whole of Panama independent when the day of liberation arrives, but the provinces must be warned: they must be prepared to support us."

"Personally," broke in Boyd, "I expected you to bring back a signed treaty with the United States. What guarantee have we that President Roosevelt will keep his promises? You know what an impetuous man he is."

"Frankly, Amador, you have made me nervous," Arias continued angrily. "As one who would suffer more than any of you if our plans should miscarry, I am not prepared to take undue risks. I withdraw my support from the revolution."

Amador looked at him with reproach. "Are all of us here risking our lives for the selfish cause of self-interest, my dear Arias? Not so. We are patriots, ready to die, if need be, to set our country free. Surely, if Arango and I—"

Arias laughed scornfully. "You are old men, you and Arango. Maybe you don't care if you are hanged. I do care. I do not like the idea of being hanged."

"Do nothing rash tonight, dear friend," Amador pleaded. "At least wait awhile before making your final decision. Anything may happen tomorrow."

"What did you think of the meeting last night, Adam?" Prescott asked the following morning as the two men walked through the narrow streets on their way to the home of Dr. Amador.

"Not too good, sir. It seemed to me that the majority of the revolutionary junta will drop out of the conspiracy if given half a chance. Especially the

Arias family. The only two who seem ready to take any real risks are Amador and Arango."

"I agree." The Assistant Superintendent shook his head in doubt. "I sincerely hope Mr. Cromwell isn't too deeply involved, for I wouldn't risk a dollar on the success of the revolt as matters stand at the moment. However, as the doctor said last night, anything may happen."

Something did happen, less than ten minutes later, As the two Americans entered Dr. Amador's parlor they saw that his lined face was drawn, his eyes apprehensive. He waved a piece of paper at them, and spoke in a husky voice.

"The revolution is doomed, Mr. Prescott. Colombian troops are on their way here. Read—" His hand shook as he passed over the telegram addressed to Governor Obaldia from the President of Colombia.

29

"THE DEVIL!" Prescott thrust out a disturbed lip. "Are you sure?"

"Ask Obaldia himself."

Turning, the Americans realized for the first time that a fourth person was present. "Good morning, Excellency," Prescott greeted him formally.

"Good morning, señores." His manner was flustered. "There is no doubt. The telegram arrived just now, from President Marroquin. It says that a battalion of the Tiradores are sailing immediately from Barranquila, under the command of Generals Tovar and Amaya."

"Hum! Not so good—"

"Wait, señor. There is worse to come. I have been ordered to give the two warships *Padilla* and *Bogotá* orders to sail for Buenaventura at once to fetch other troops to help in repelling the invasion."

"What invasion? What's happening?" Prescott was startled.

The Governor wrung his hands with Latin emotionalism. "It was a stupid idea of Huerta's and mine, to get rid of Captain Tascón, and some of the garrison. We pretended that Costa Ricans had invaded Chiriquí province, and sent him to drive the Costa Ricans back. The plan would have been a good one had I not, fool that I am, tried to embellish it by advising the President."

"So now Colombian troops are on the way here! I dare not contemplate what will happen when the other members of the committee hear what is happening," Dr. Amador added.

"You think they will want to withdraw their support?"

196

"I am certain they will. You saw how lukewarm they were last night."
Prescott chewed at his cigar. "Don't tell them yet, Dr. Amador. Let's
bluff it out. I'm not so sure the news might not be a blessing in disguise."
"How so?"
"Send a cablegram to Bunau-Varilla. If he advises the State Department
what is happening it might force the Government's hand."
Amador looked more hopeful. "Do you think it might?"
"It's worth trying."
"Then we'll try. I'll get pen and ink and paper." These were quickly
produced. "Now, señor. What shall I say?"
Prescott pulled thoughtfully at his whiskers, and rolled the cigar round
in his lips. "We must be careful. We don't want anyone in the cable office
to start rumors."
"That's easily prevented," the doctor pointed out. "Before I left America
Bunau-Varilla and I worked out a code. I have it in my pocket." He pulled
a paper from his pocket, and studied it. Then he looked at Wesley. "Would
you write it out for me, if you please, Señor Adam?"
"Glad to." Wesley took charge of the pen, ink, and paper.
"Send it to *Tower,* New York." He turned to Prescott. "The telegraphic
address, señor, of Joshua Lindo, of Piza, Nepheys & Company, who has
agreed to accept all messages for Bunau-Varilla. First word, *Fate,* which
means, 'Cables with this word are for Bunau-Varilla: transmit to him.'
Now, *news,* which means, 'We have news of the arrival of Colombian
forces.' Third word, *bad,* which stands for 'Atlantic.' Fourth word, *powerful,* for 'five days,' and now *tiger,* which means 'more than two hundred'—
that is, more than two hundred troops disembarked or disembarking. Now
urge, which is not code but plain; *vapor,* 'warships' you understand, and
lastly *Colón.* Sign it Smith. You have that, señor?"
Wesley passed it over. Amador read it aloud, nodding his head. " 'Fate
news bad powerful tiger urge vapor Colón.' This shall go off immediately." He hurried from the room, to return in a matter of seconds. He
was clutched by the agitated Governor.
"It's all very well to appeal to the United States for future help against
the Colombians, but what is to be done about the two warships already
here?"
The other men had overlooked the warships. "Holy Mother!" Amador
exclaimed. "Must you do anything at all in the matter, Obaldia, before we
get a reply from Bunau-Varilla? If the reply is satisfactory you could forget
to pass on the message."
But the Governor turned obstinate. "I'll risk my neck so far, but no
further. If I 'forget' to pass on the message, as you suggest, what will
happen to me if the revolution fails? Marroquin is no fool. He'll put two
and two together."
"*Caramba!* If the warships bring reinforcements to Panama City we

shall be just as badly off as if they are brought to Colón. We must send a second telegram to Bunau-Varilla at once."

A long embarrassed silence followed, which Wesley ended.

"Excuse me, sir."

"Well?" Prescott stubbed out his cigar.

"I was wondering whether the Colombian warships have enough coal to fetch reinforcements. If they haven't—"

The pleased Prescott glanced inquiringly at the Governor. Obaldia waved his hand in a gesture of uncertainty.

"I doubt if the bunkers are full enough to take them on to Buenaventura. Why?"

The superintendent nodded his satisfaction. "I can guess what Adam has in mind. Suppose I instruct Beers not to sell any coal?"

The Governor shrugged, and looked unhappy. "My instructions are to requisition in accordance with the terms of the concession to your railroad."

The American chuckled. "Captain Beers will shortly be informing you officially, Excellency, that all available coal stocks are at Colón, and that same have already been contracted for by the steamship companies. He will also suggest that you approach the Pacific Mail, who would no doubt be glad to sell you some of their existing stocks."

"How should we be any better off?"

"Don't worry, Excellency. The Pacific Mail will do nothing contrary to Mr. Cromwell's wishes," Prescott dryly indicated. "You won't get the coal."

On receipt of Amador's cablegram, Bunau-Varilla caught the next train for Washington, where he called on Secretaary Hay to ask for American warships to be sent at once to Colón, to forestall the landing of Colombian troops. Faced with the possible failure of the Panama revolt, the Navy Department telegraphed in cipher to Commander Hubbard, of U.S.S. *Nashville,* at Kingston, Jamaica, instructing him to proceed at full speed to Colón. The race between the Americans and the Colombians for the strategic port of Colón was on.

Upon their return to Colón, Prescott and Wesley found that the approach of Colombian troops, which had been such a carefully guarded secret in Panama City, was no secret in Colón. Everybody there knew that a contingent of Sharpshooters was on its way.

Sanderson told them this news, in Colonel Shaler's office.

"How the devil could they know?" Prescott demanded. "Only four of us have been told about the cable: the Governor himself, Dr. Amador, Adam here, and I."

"It's leaked out of the cable office, thanks to Samuel Boyd, the Panama correspondent of the *New York Herald*. He sent a cable to New York to report the coming of the troops."

"Hell!" Shaler frowned. "Looks like the end of another comic-opera revolution—and possibly the end of the canal proposition, too, until Colombia comes down in price or our government goes up."

"The trouble is, sir," Sanderson pointed out, "the last revolt wasn't a comic opera. The townspeople can still remember the siege, and aren't willing to see another."

"They won't, if we send warships here," Prescott said. "Colombia won't risk a war with us."

"But will they be sent? And if they are—"

"They've been sent in the past, to maintain order and protect American property."

"All right, I'll give you that. The question still remains, if they are sent, will they reach here in time to prevent a landing? If not, the boot will be on the other foot. We should have to make an aggressive move, which would mean open war."

"According to Cromwell, President Roosevelt is ready to declare war, if necessary."

"Do we need the canal that bad?"

Shaler shrugged. "Glad I'm no politician. The best thing we can do is to prepare for all eventualities. What plans are being made in Panama to start the revolution?"

"I can give you that information. Plans have been prepared, and when Adam and I left Amador's house the place was already humming like a beehive. To begin with, the junta didn't much care for the flag Amador brought back with him from the States, so his son Manuel has designed a new one which my future sister-in-law, María Amelia, sewed. At this moment enough new flags are being made to supply an army."

"But what about an army to wave 'em?" the superintendent queried in a dry voice.

"Duque's private army, the *bomberos,* his privately subsidized volunteer fire brigade, would act as shock troops."

"The fire brigade! What are they going to fight with? Water pistols?"

Prescott chuckled. "Don't worry, J.R. They're hand-picked, and were recruited specially for an emergency of this sort. Nearly every member of the brigade is a young son or relative of a family favoring independence. They'll be armed with small caliber revolvers to begin with, and as there are nearly three hundred of them they'll give a good account of themselves. It has been arranged for them to begin operations the moment a sky rocket is shot off."

"Humph!" Shaler looked more cheerful. "Then they should make a good core around which to mass the rest of the population. And Huertas has been bought?"

"Yes."

"What about the Governor, and other high Colombian officials?"

"They are to be arrested at five o'clock—the Governor with them, for the sake of appearances."

"And the Colombian troops?"

"Have offered to accept fifty dollars silver each; which Ehrman's Bank will supply against the draft Amador brought back with him. The joke is, the Colombian Government owes their troops almost fifty dollars per man from two years back, when they suppressed the revolution of nineteen one."

"So everything would be in the bag if it weren't for the Sharpshooters who are on their way here?"

Prescott nodded. "Likely enough—and Señora Amador has a plan for dealing with them, J.R."

"The deuce she has! I thought revolutions were usually a man's job of work. Not this one, it seems. Well?"

"Her idea is that we should try to stall off transporting the regiment, by offering to take the generals and their aides to Panama in a special train to see for themselves that all is quiet at Panama."

"Will it be?"

Prescott laughed. "They won't have a chance of finding out. They'll be arrested, and given the chance of accepting a fat bribe to take themselves and their men back to Colombia."

"If they refuse?"

"Then they'll be given free board and lodgings in a nice damp cell under the sea wall, and somebody else will negotiate a bribe with the soldiers."

"Suppose they won't play, and seize the rolling stock by force?"

"I'm coming to that. I'll be waiting at Miraflores with a powder gang, dynamite, and a detachment of Huertas' soldiers. When the train comes along they will blow the damn thing up, and take the Colombians prisoners, or shoot them."

Shaler gave thought to this scheme, and nodded approval. "It's good, but can be improved upon, and might save the lives of some poor devils. Make arrangements tomorrow, Prescott, to move all rolling stock to Panama. The Colombians can neither use nor seize by force what isn't here. Keep back one engine and my private coach, which I can offer to their generals.

"You return to Panama with the stock, contact the junta, and keep in touch with me by telegraph." He chuckled. "If you are questioned about what you are doing you can reply that, as assistant superintendent of the P.R.R. it is your duty to guard the property of the company against seizure by a hostile force for purposes which might disturb the free and uninterrupted transit across the Isthmus which the United States is pledged to maintain."

Having already interrupted that transit by withdrawing the rolling stock! Wesley dryly reflected. But as a minor employee of the railroad he thought it wiser to maintain a discreet silence.

In Washington the first two days of November saw considerable activity in the Navy Department. The cable company was scarcely less busy. To U.S.S. *Dixie,* at Kingston, Jamaica, went out the message in cipher:

Secret and confidential. Proceed with all possible dispatch to Colón. Maintain free and uninterrupted transit. If interruption threatened by armed force, occupy the line of railroad. Prevent landing of any armed force with hostile intent, either government or insurgent, either at Colón, Porto Bello, or other port. Send copy of instructions to the senior officer present at Panama upon arrival of *Boston.* Government force reported approaching the Isthmus in vessels. Prevent their landing if in your judgment this would precipitate a conflict. Acknowledgment is required.

A message, couched in similar terms, was sent, care of the American Consul at Colón, to the *Nashville,* already speeding from Jamaica as quickly as its engines could turn. A third was sent to Admiral Glass, on the *Marblehead,* at Acapulco; but the message to Admiral Glass was supplemented by instructions: *If doubtful of the intention of any armed force, occupy Ancon Hill strongly with artillery.* A fourth cable, also including instructions to occupy Ancon Hill if necessary, was sent to San Juan del Sur, Nicaragua, where U.S.S. *Boston* was waiting.

Unaware of the strong naval forces that were converging on the Isthmus of Panama, the people of Colón awaited with apprehension the arrival of the Colombian troops. Their uneasiness increased when the railroad rolling stock steadily disappeared as one long line of cars after another pulled out of the assembly yards. Knowing nothing of the reasons prompting this move, they could only conclude that the railroad officials were preparing for the worst.

The faces of the Panamanians grew gloomier as the hours passed. The Colombians, however, officials and garrison personnel alike, were jubilant and aggressive. On his way to the Sandersons for the evening Wesley was almost shouldered out of the way by a truculent Colombian. Only at the last moment, as Wesley deliberately faced him did the Colombian realize he had accosted a North American. He called out a hasty apology and hurried off as quickly as he could.

The encounter angered Wesley. His face was still clouded when Madge Sanderson opened the door. With the maternal regard of an older woman she was immediately solicitous.

"Why, Wesley Adam! You're looking like a thundercloud."

201

"I'm feeling like one, Madge," he explained as he stepped into the house. "I've just been pushed aside by a Colombian who mistook me for a Panamanian."

She knew her Wesley. "You made him apologize," she stated in the positive conviction that neither Wesley's sensitive pride nor his Stewart temper would submit to treatment of that nature.

"I didn't have to: he apologized quickly enough when he saw what I was. But it wasn't altogether what happened to me that's making me feel bad. Now I understand why there have been so many revolutions in Panama. I'm beginning to realize how unpleasant it must be to know that one's country isn't absolutely one's own; and to have to bow and scrape all the time to high officials who are really foreigners."

She patted his cheeks. "But then, you're a born rebel, aren't you, Wesley?"

"Suppose so," he admitted, relaxing in the serene atmosphere of the Sanderson home. "Suppose I should think myself lucky that I was born in a country that suits me fine."

"Yes." She glanced at the window. "Any further news of the Colombians?"

"No, but it can't be long now before they're sighted." He realized that she was looking worried. "Nervous?"

"Not really, but I hate the thought of war. It may mean glory for a chosen few, but for the majority it means misery and sorrow." She shuddered. "Frederick and I had been here only two months when the Liberals organized a revolution in Colombia. The fighting spread to the Isthmus. Just two years ago this month the rebels captured Colón. There was some terrible fighting in and about the town before they were forced to surrender. The next day—" Tears filled her eyes. "It was horrible, Wesley. We heard shooting from behind the church, and were told that rebels were being executed there in batches of six."

Sanderson entered abruptly. "Sorry I'm late, Wesley. You, too, honey." He gave his wife a quick, affectionate kiss. "The town's in a ferment. A vessel's just been sighted off the Point."

"The Colombians?"

"Could be; they're due any time now. Let's have a drink, then go see."

They sipped their drinks out on the porch from which they could see the line of palms ghostly in the light of the town; and beyond, the coral beach, white bordered by the thin line of opalescent spume left by the wavelets as they rippled inshore and lazily turned over; and beyond that, into the depths of the darkness which cloaked the horizon in the mystery of night; and four stars approaching—a red and a green below two white masthead lights—

For the most part they sat in silence for they were conscious of the fact that the hour might well be a critical one, not alone in the histories of

202

Colombia, Panama, and the United States, but equally so in the history of the world.

"I was telling Wes about the last revolution in Panama," Madge said presently.

Sanderson's expression turned gloomy. "With the prospect of more bloody carnage ahead of them one can't feel surprised at the people of Panama looking like death just now."

"You know," Madge continued flatly, "if there are any more deaths here I'm not sure that we Americans will be held blameless."

"For God's sake!" Wesley protested, ignoring his personal feelings in his anxiety to defend the canal. "Because we want to build a canal here? What about the French? Did anyone accuse them of starting a war?"

Sanderson grinned. "They didn't plan to annex the country first," he pointed out.

"We're not—"

"Not in so many words, maybe. But if the revolution is successful it will mean that complete sovereignty will be given in perpetuity to the U.S.A. over a part of the Isthmus."

"That's different."

"Of course. Everything is different if you view it from a different angle. You know that better than I do. You're a surveyor. What's the difference between a Colombian overlord and an American overlord?"

"It will benefit the world for the canal to be built," Wesley argued. "Not excluding Colombia herself. Merchandise will be landed more cheaply in Bogotá."

"American merchandise!" The P.R.R. man laughed at Wesley's reproachful expression. "Don't let's deceive ourselves, even if we do try to pull the wool over the eyes of the rest of the world. For security reasons America wants a canal, and means to have one by fair means or—er—Machiavellian."

"Well—"

"We don't have to be ashamed of the truth. All I pray is, that she may have it without the shedding of innocent blood."

"Amen to that!" Madge whispered.

The ship's lights had grown appreciably larger. Wesley stirred restlessly. "Shall we go?"

Frederick nodded. Madge said. "You two go. I'll help Ingrid get the meal ready. Don't be too late."

As the two men neared the P.R.R. piers they saw that many other people shared their anxieties. From all directions small groups were making their way toward the piers. People of all colors and shades of colors. Like themselves many walked in silence. The few who talked did so in low, anxious voices. Before they had proceeded far Wesley and Frederick found themselves hemmed in.

The four stars of light grew larger. The pause was dramatically interrupted by the notes of a bugle from the approaching ship. The crowd surged to and fro restlessly. Somebody shouted, "The Colombians!" and the cry was taken up and repeated as it traveled away from the dockside. Some nervous watchers started to run.

Sanderson said, "Could be an American warship sounding to quarters."

Although he had spoken in a low voice, ears, sharpened perhaps by anxiety, overheard. An excited voice called in Spanish, "Might be an American warship, *amigos.*"

The message of hope traveled in the wake of the cry of despair. "The Americans! The Americans are coming to our help! Maybe it's the Americans!"

Hope battled with fear. The Colombians? The Americans? Which? The crowd shuffled in restless anxiety until they were silenced by hearing the rattle of winches, the clanking of chain jumping the hawse-pipe, the splash of water as the anchor plunged into the water.

Tension grew as the minutes passed. Sharp ears heard the splashing of oars. A shout went up. "They're coming."

But who?

A cutter nosed slowly into the radius of the pier lights, and a mighty cheer of relief rang out. The oarsmen were in American naval uniform.

U.S.S. *Nashville* had arrived.

30

"THAT'S THAT!" Sanderson exclaimed. "Now we'll be able to enjoy the meal."

Wesley agreed. It gave one confidence to know that the Navy was anchored a stone's throw away, in all probability with Leathernecks aboard. If the Colombians were looking for trouble—

"How is Ingrid getting on, by the way?" Funny how quickly one's thoughts, freed from tension, could revert to the routine of everyday life, he reflected.

"Couldn't be better. You did both my wife and her a good turn when you brought her along. She's a fine cook." Sanderson's voice reflected his satisfaction. "In fact, she's a nice child. It's a pity she makes herself unhappy worrying about that brother of hers."

"I've been thinking about that lately, Frederick. Do you think I ought to find some way of letting her know her brother's alive?"

"I'm not sure she'd be satisfied with that much information. Probably she'd plague you for further particulars. Where? When? How is he? Can you take her to him? While we're on the subject is there any news of him?"

"I haven't thought about him in weeks," Wesley admitted with an embarrassed grin.

"What sort of a man was he, before he came to Panama? Ingrid thinks the world of him."

"Can't say much from personal knowledge. I hadn't met him before we sailed from New York."

"You found him normal?"

"Perfectly, until the day he found an old Indian gold ornament in the jungle, and I told him about the gold mined here by the Indians before the Spaniards arrived. He was never the same from that moment."

"The fool!" Sanderson growled.

Some minutes later Wesley was able covertly to watch Ingrid as she waited at table. She was a different girl from the one he had rescued from Bottle Alley. Regular food had rounded her cheeks, and given a luster to her lovely yellow hair. Her flesh, in spite of the tropical sun, mysteriously retained its Scandinavian fairness and rivaled her Arctic eyes in purity.

When she smiled a welcome, he wondered how long she would remain in the Sanderson household. It was unlikely that so lovely a young woman would be overlooked by the restless young men who nightly promenaded Front Street and the coral road, to many of whom her blonde coloring would be an added attraction. Poor Madge! he thought. She will miss the girl—

After the meal they returned to the porch where they sat and gossiped and waited for Ingrid to bring the coffee. Out in the harbor the *Nashville's* riding lights rose and fell on a sleepy swell.

"I can't help wondering what would have happened if that had been the Colombian ship instead of our own," Madge said. "By now, I suppose, the town would be filled with troops."

"Sure," her husband agreed. "And that would be the end of a beautiful dream. I don't think even our Teddy would have dared to land troops if the Colombians were already entrenched here in force."

"You're not suggesting that our boys would have been afraid—"

"Of course not, honey. I mean from the point of view of diplomacy. To land forces in the face of active opposition by the Colombians would lay the States open to a charge of forcibly annexing the country."

"Won't the effect be the same if our navy prevents Colombian forces from landing? After all, this is legally their country."

"Of course it's Colombian territory—unless the Panamanians declare it independent."

"Who landed? The Captain?"

Sanderson shook his head. "Looked more like the doctor as far as I could see. He probably came ashore to obtain pratique."

"What's that mean?"

"Permission for people from the ship to come and go."

Following a brief silence Madge said, "You're very quiet, Wesley. Sleepy?"

"No. Can you see the lights of another ship, between the fifth and sixth palm from the left?"

Both Madge and her husband stared out to sea. At last Frederick exclaimed, "By Heaven! you're right."

"That's about nor'-nor'-east, wouldn't you say?"

"I would too. Coming round from the south, eh? From Colombia perhaps."

"The Sharpshooters?" Madge's voice was anxious. "If they are—"

"Most likely are, honey. We know they're due."

"What will happen?"

Sanderson shrugged. "God knows! Perhaps nothing. Perhaps war. Between Colombia and us."

Ingrid arrived with the coffee. There was enough light coming from the parlor behind for Wesley to observe the warm confiding smile she gave him. He thought she looked like a goddess at that moment. He was not the only one to think this.

"Brunhild herself!" exclaimed a voice from the shadows of the coco-nut palms. A figure materialized from the darkness and with dragging steps approached the porch.

"Larry! What the devil—"

In the faint luminous glow reflected from the parlor light Wesley could see that the dark eyes were filled with mischief. He wondered how long Larry had been hiding, how long he had been eavesdropping on their conversation. Quite some time, hinted the mischievous eyes.

"A friend of yours, Wesley?" Madge asked. "Would he care to have coffee with us?"

Wesley tightened his mouth, but he saw no way of avoiding an introduction.

"Larry Larrabee," he announced stiffly. "Larry, meet Mr. and Mrs. Sanderson."

Madge smiled graciously. "Coffee, Mr. Larrabee?"

"Please, no. It's an imposition," he protested insincerely.

"It's fresh this minute, and there's more than enough."

He smiled winningly at her. "In that case, ma'am, I'd love some."

"Another cup and saucer, Ingrid."

As Ingrid turned to re-enter the house the blue eyes glanced quickly down at Larry's dragging foot, and Wesley was sure they were compassionate.

206

"What are you doing here?" he demanded, thin lipped.

"Looking for you. The receptionist at the hotel said you were visiting friends, so I wandered about in the hope of finding you. I was lucky." He smiled at Madge again. "Very lucky," he added with pointed gallantry.

How much of this explanation was truth and how much a lie Wesley was unable to decide; but it did not matter. Larry had forced his company on them, so would have to be accepted with as much grace as possible. Meanwhile, he noted with wry amusement that Madge Sanderson was already a victim to Larry's charm.

"I am so pleased that you didn't allow formality to stand in the way of your calling here tonight, Mr. Larrabee. Any friend of Mr. Adam's is always welcome."

"I know that, Mrs. Sanderson. Otherwise I should not have dared to trespass on your kindness." There was an inflection in his voice which intimated quite plainly that she was the only woman in Colón on whom he would have risked dropping in so informally.

She dimpled her appreciation. "Have you been long in Panama?"

"As long as Mr. Adam," Larry glanced mischievously in Wesley's direction. "We were cabinmates."

"You were! And he has never even mentioned your name." She turned on Wesley. "Shame on you, Wesley. You've been neglecting your duty. You know how much we love to welcome people from home."

Larry glanced toward the harbor. "Especially naval friends, eh?"

"Yes indeed." Madge's reply was heartfelt.

"It's lucky for the canal that the *Nashville* arrived before the one transporting the Colombian troops. You can take my word for it, Mr. Adam, that if the Sharpshooters had arrived first there would be no revolution the day after tomorrow."

"What's this nonsense you're talking about—revolution—" Frederick growled.

Larry smiled. "You don't need to worry, sir. I'm on your side. Ask Mr. Adam."

"That's so, Frederick. He talks Spanish well enough to be a Panamanian, so Mr. Cromwell confirmed that he could be useful in—er—influencing people."

"We agreed that agent provocateur is the word, didn't we, Mr. Adam?" Larry's chuckle was full of mischief; rarely had it been more so. He seemed in very high spirits.

"I came back tonight," he went on, "to let you know that the majority of the influential people this side of Bohio will support the revolution." He added dryly, "If the Americans guarantee their safety."

"Otherwise?"

"They've had their bellyful of civil war—if you will excuse the language, ma'am. Their words, not mine."

"There's another ship heading this way, Larry. We suspect it's the Colombian transport."

Larry turned sharply. "Where?" he snapped.

"There, by the fifth palm."

"I see it!" His voice filled with anxiety. "Will the American ship prevent the Colombian troops from landing?"

"That's what we were discussing when you arrived."

"If the troops do land you can kiss your revolution good-by. All the Panamanians I've talked to want the canal because they know that it will fill their pockets, so they'll give a revolution moral support. But, in the event of trouble, don't look for active support, because you won't get it."

Ingrid arrived with the extra cup and saucer, gave them to Madge, and retired again. Larry's gaze never shifted from her until she left the room.

"I meant to ask you, Mr. Larrabee—"

He started. "Yes, ma'am?" he answered in a flustered manner.

"Didn't I hear you mention Brunhild at one moment?"

"You did, ma'am. Your maid looked exactly the way I've always imagined Brunhild."

Madge smiled. "Why, yes, now that you mention it, she does have a classical beauty, doesn't she?"

Just before dawn the following morning Colonel Shaler called at the hotel, where he found Wesley awaiting him.

"Morning, Adam." Shaler's manner was curt, and preoccupied. "Sorry to have you up so early after last night. Suppose you waited up to see what would happen?"

"Yes, colonel."

"Most of us did, no doubt. I was keeping my fingers crossed for a full hour after midnight." He started off at a sharp pace for Pier 1. "I telephoned Prescott to inform him of the *Cartagena's* arrival."

"Did he have anything to say, sir?"

"Not then, but he telephoned me back an hour later. The junta took the news badly, and were for calling off the revolution then and there. They would have done so, too, if it hadn't been for Señora Amador. She told the men it was too late to recant, and that, if necessary, they must put up a fight. Splendid woman. Splendid."

"They're going ahead with their plan?"

"Yes, and we're to do the same at this end. If we can get the generals aboard a train I'd like you to accompany them to Panama City on my behalf."

"Of course, colonel."

By the time they reached the waterside dawn was lightening the eastern sky. They could clearly see the two ships at anchor, a stone's throw from

208

one another; and in the distance, the sharp hull of an incoming vessel, streaking the blue sky with its smoke.

"The *City of Washington*," Shaler announced.

A boat waited to take the two Americans out to the warships. Within a matter of minutes they were being received by Commander Hubbard.

"Glad to meet you, gentlemen," Hubbard welcomed them with a handshake, after Shaler had introduced himself and Wesley. "What can I do for you?"

"First of all, accept the grateful thanks of all concerned for your prompt arrival."

"It was my duty to do so, sir, but why does it earn thanks? Is there trouble here?"

Shaler looked surprised. "You do not know the position here, commander?"

"No, sir. While we were at Kingston, I received orders from the Navy Department to proceed here at full speed. That is all I know, but I shall shortly be reporting to the Consul, who will doubtless be holding further orders for me."

"Then it is not my place to speak, commander, until you have seen him. I really came aboard to ascertain what measures you propose taking with regard to that." Shaler nodded his head at the Colombian vessel.

"The *Cartagena!*" It was Hubbard's turn to look surprised. "Is there reason for me to do anything about her?"

"She is acting as a troopship at this moment, with five hundred Sharpshooters aboard."

The Commander whistled. "Another revolution?"

"Not yet. It is due to break this time tomorrow."

"Indeed!" He laughed dryly. "I didn't know rebellions were usually announced beforehand."

"This is a particularly important one for our country, commander. Panama is planning to secede from the United States of Colombia."

"Ah!"

"So you can understand how vital it is that those troops should not land."

"Yes." Hubbard looked grave. "I'll send a boarding officer aboard her to make inquiries. Pardon me, gentlemen."

While the Commander was absent the P.R.R. steamer *City of Washington* passed slowly by on her way to the pier. Shaler laughed shortly. "I wonder what her passengers will say when they find out that they've run slap bang into another revolution."

Soon a cutter was lowered from the warship, and went dancing over the waves to the nearby *Cartagena*. They could see the boarding officer being formally received, by men in the uniform of the Colombian army. After a few seconds' conversation, he and the officers disappeared into

209

one of the upper deck cabins. Before long he was out again, and on his way back to the *Nashville*.

Ten minutes later Commander Hubbard rejoined Shaler and Wesley.

"As you say, colonel, there are nearly five hundred troops aboard that vessel. According to the general in command, General Tovar, they are en route to Panama City to take over garrison duty there."

"Nonsense!" Shaler exclaimed testily.

Hubbard shrugged.

"What will you do to stop them landing, commander?"

"Nothing, sir."

"Nothing! But, good God! man, you must."

"Must!" Hubbard raised his eyebrows. "In the absence of specific instructions from the Navy Department I can do nothing to stop their landing, colonel."

"You have the right, under the treaty of eighteen forty-six, to use all necessary measures to protect the Panama Railroad."

"Protect from what, sir? I have no information that all is not peaceable at Colón, and elsewhere in the Isthmus. Until the revolution breaks out my hands are tied."

"Damn!" Shaler exclaimed explosively.

There being nothing more they could do Shaler and Wesley left shortly, and proceeded to the superintendent's office in the P.R.R. building.

"Sit down, Adam," Shaler ordered. Wesley did so, but the Colonel walked up and down the strip of carpet swearing explosively, and consigning Commander Hubbard and the Navy Department to a destination far hotter than Colón. Presently he stopped by the window, and stared down at the ships riding at anchor.

"Devil take it! Look! The *Cartagena* is getting up steam."

Wesley joined the Superintendent, and watched black clouds of smoke billowing up from the ship's funnel. Further proof of intention to move was given just after he reached the window, for the anchor leaped out of the water, and ran up the bow of the ship as high as the hawser-pipe.

"Is she leaving?" His voice did not sound particularly hopeful. "Perhaps she's taken the hint, from seeing the *Nashville* here."

It took only a few minutes to prove Shaler's pious hopes to be without foundation. The *Cartagena* took a turn to starboard, and headed for the old P.R.R. pier. She was soon docked alongside. A gangway was quickly run up to the top deck, and an advance guard moved down it with arrogant dignity. To judge by the decorations the first two could only be generals, Wesley decided.

"We'll join them," Shaler announced abruptly. "Coming, Adam?"

31

THE OFFICERS WERE formally met by a group of Colombian officials, the Prefect of Colón, General Cuadros, among them. From their window Shaler and Wesley saw much handshaking and excited gesturing; but presently one of the generals drew the Prefect to one side and engaged him in earnest conversation.

"Ha! Their heads are too close together to suit me," Shaler muttered. "We'd better do something before they can put two and two together. Come along, Adam."

The two men hurried out of the P.R.R. offices, and made their way across the untidy dock toward the Prefect and the Colombian General. The Prefect saw their approach; nudged the General, and raised his hat in welcome.

"Good morning, señor. Permit me to present the officer commanding the newly arrived reinforcements. General Tovar, this is my good friend, Colonel Shaler, General Superintendent of the Panama Railroad Company."

The General saluted with a graceful movement. "Good morning, Colonel Shaler," he said with a dazzling smile. "It gives me great pleasure to meet such a distinguished American."

"A pleasure which I share in having the honor to welcome you, General Tovar. I trust you will forgive my joining you, but I have a message for you from General Obaldia."

"General Obaldia!" The General raised bushy eyebrows, and glanced sideways at the Prefect. Apparently he was surprised that Shaler, and not a fellow Colombian, should have been chosen as the bearer of a private message.

Shaler hastened to explain. "Upon being informed of your arrival last night, general, His Excellency instructed me that I was to hold a special car in readiness to take you and your aides to Panama."

The Colombian looked gratified. "That was thoughtful of His Excellency, colonel. At what time does the train leave?"

"As soon as you and your companions are aboard, general. It is already late. I have been holding it for you."

"Then I must catch the next one, my dear colonel." The General waved his hand in the direction of the gunboat. "I must supervise the disembarkation of my troops. Besides, it is necessary that they should accompany me to Panama City. They are wanted urgently."

"Your pardon, general, but His Excellency was very explicit in desiring the presence of you and your staff at the earliest possible moment. To discuss the campaign, no doubt. Your troops can follow by a later train. I am making arrangements for a special train to run at one o'clock."

The General looked annoyed. "I appreciate His Excellency's fore thought, colonel, but I really must protest—"

"I'm sure His Excellency had good reasons for wishing to see you so soon," Shaler's smooth voice interrupted. "I wish I might myself have the opportunity of accompanying you to Panama, but I must remain here to organize the special train. In the circumstances, general, I have delegated Señor Adam to represent me."

Wesley bowed. The General saluted.

"Very well," Tovar reluctantly agreed. "I and General Amaya, and our aides will catch the earlier train in accordance with His Excellency' wishes." He turned and called one of his staff. "Colonel Torres!"

Torres approached.

"General Amaya and I are going to Panama by the train now waiting You will supervise disembarkation of the men, and bring them and thei baggage by a special train which will leave here about one o'clock."

"Yes, general," Torres had keen eyes, a pointed nose, and an aggressive mouth and chin.

"I am at your service, colonel," Tovar said to Shaler. He walked back to the other officers, and after issuing curt instructions to them returned to Shaler. He was accompanied by another general, whom he introduced as General Amaya, and their respective aides.

They entered the special car, followed by Wesley, but no sooner had General Amaya sat down than he jumped to his feet, looking uneasy.

"Do you not think it better that I stay here with the soldiers? As com mander in chief it is you His Excellency really wishes to see."

"Sit down, Amaya," Tovar testily ordered. "Torres is quite capable o disembarking the troops, and I have no particular wish to be left alone."

Amaya remained uneasy: his glance expressed puzzled misgiving. Thi by-play had not gone unnoticed by Shaler. He quickly put an end to fur ther discussion by blowing a whistle. The train began to pull out; with a characteristic shrug Amaya once more resumed his seat.

For as long as the train moved along Front Street the Colombian remained silent, content to look out at the long line of buildings which faced on to the railroad track; but as soon as it reached the outskirt of the town and was gathering speed, Tovar turned to Wesley and courte ously addressed him.

"Have you been long in Panama, Señor Adam?"

The query was the opening gambit of a conversation which continued no longer than politeness demanded. Tovar then turned to Amaya, leav ing Wesley to be entertained by the aides. Both aides were young men who had been told that Panama City was one of the wickedest places in the world, and were eager to know whether their hopes were likely to be

212

realized. When Wesley was able to set their minds at rest they were delighted, and discussed their plans with such zest and frankness that Wesley was almost embarrassed, though he had grown accustomed to hear Panamanians speak of most bodily functions with the same unconcern as they spoke of the weather.

In spite of a disinclination to discuss the more intimate details of his own private life with the two young officers, he knew that he envied them, in a way, the debauches which they were planning with such avidity and minute detail. Since the night he had rescued Ingrid Ericson from Bottle Alley he had managed to ignore the demands of his mounting desires. Unfortunately, the ingenuous eagerness of the Colombians reacted on him by making him more than normally conscious of his own natural urges.

Later, as they neared Bohio, his thoughts turned automatically upon the Perrigots; and in particular upon the time when Marie had tricked him into paying a visit there. Since that day he had seen Anne once, but Marie not at all; for when old man Perrigot had brought his daughters to Colón on the usual half-yearly visit, Anne had called on the Sandersons, where he, Wesley, had met her; but Marie had joined other friends—which both gratified and piqued him.

From Anne his thoughts turned abruptly to Dulcie and Ackermann. After months of indecision he had written to his attorneys in Providence and asked them to trace Dulcie with a view to arranging a divorce. Bob Finnegan had written back, leave everything to him, and in confidence, as one old roommate to another, had he a second in view? If so, who was she? What was she like? And talking of marriage, had Wesley heard that he, Bob, was to marry Betty Summers come New Year's Day?

Wesley had written to congratulate Bob, but he had carefully not replied to Bob's queries because he hadn't reached a decision. Often he felt an overwhelming need to marry. Apart from the physical aspect of marriage, he craved rest and companionship. There was something missing in life when it became necessary to visit other people's homes, and sit in other people's chairs. Of course, it was damn nice to relax in one's own home for a change, with one's own wife to talk things over with. But—once bit, twice shy! He wasn't sure that he wanted to risk a second marriage. He wasn't at all sure.

He was still thinking along these lines when the train reached the outskirts of Panama City, and soon drew up at the terminus. Glancing quickly out of the window at the triangular plaza bordering the station on the west, he saw a vast crowd of people, packed tightly together in the foreground, and stretching away in irregular groups almost to the foot of Ancon Hill in the background. Near the station exit General Obaldia, and Dr. Amador's son, Manuel, were talking with Felix Ehrman, the

United States Acting Consul General. Evidently, the revolution had already broken out.

Now for trouble, he thought, and wondered what the Colombian officers would do when they learned they had walked straight into a hornet's nest. The sight of the Colombian regiment, drawn up in review on the wide street which connected the terminus with the plaza, together with a detachment of Panamanian police standing to what they were pleased to think was attention, suggested that he had mistaken the wish for the deed; it certainly appeared as though both the soldiers and police had paraded in the plaza merely to pay military honors to General Tovar.

His fear that the conspirators' plans must have gone wrong was not allayed by the cheers and handkerchief waving which began as soon as the General stepped down from the coach. Immediately General Obaldia advanced upon General Tovar, and was followed by a number of official personages, some of whom Wesley recognized: the captain of the guard, the military commander of Panama, the U. S. acting consul general, British and French consular officials, Prescott and his son—and Uncle Bill! This reception resembled one accorded to a conquering hero rather than the prelude to an arrest.

To Wesley's astonishment no arrest followed. After General Tovar had expressed his gratitude with a beaming smile, and hearty handshakes, at General Obaldia's suggestion he stepped into His Excellency's carriage, and was driven off to Government House. He was followed by a long line of carriages, each occupied by a citizen of note. The procession was a stirring and brilliant one to watch as it slowly made its way along the winding Avenida Central to the other end of the town. The citizens of Panama thoroughly enjoyed the spectacle, and waved and cheered the gallant Colombian generals who had come to repel the insolent Costa Ricans.

Wesley, sitting in Uncle Bill's carriage, listened to the excited clamor and thought he detected a note of hysteria in the background. When he mentioned the fact Uncle Bill laughed.

"Yeah!" Sure there is, Wesley lad. Rumors have been getting around. People know there's something doing."

"Rumor—or Amador's agents?"

Godwin laughed. "What's the difference?"

"When is the rocket going up?"

"Probably at five o'clock this afternoon. A public meeting is to be held in Santa Ana Plaza. All going well, the new republic will be proclaimed then. You staying overnight here, Wesley?"

Wesley remembered the plans which the young Colombian officers had made for that night. Suppose he were to join them? He was sure they would cheerfully accept his company. Of course, Uncle Bill would naturally expect him, during the earlier part of the evening, but later— Then he recollected that the young aides would not be free to sample the

214

pleasures of Coco-nut Grove. The poor devils would probably be in a cell someplace, or under house arrest—

During the morning public excitement increased until even the most obtuse could scarcely fail to sense the mounting tension. Soon after 1:30 P.M. General Roca called on Tovar, at the Comandancia General, where lodgings had been prepared for the commander of the Colombian reinforcements.

Roca was in a state of great excitement. He barely allowed himself time to exchange the necessary courtesies.

"I think you should be told, General Tovar, that the city is in a state of great excitement."

Tovar stroked his mustachios, and looked pleased. "Well, my dear general, and why not? The sight of our brave soldiers in review is always a stirring one."

"You mistake my meaning, my general. There are rumors that these stupid, pig-headed Panamanians are contemplating another revolution."

"Nonsense! With a battalion of Sharpshooters two hours' journey away? They cannot be that stupid."

"Nevertheless, with the utmost respect, my general, I would suggest that you send orders to Colón—"

General Roca's words of wisdom were interrupted by the entry of an aide.

"A message from Dr. Porras, General Tovar."

Tovar slit open the envelope, and read the contents of the note inside. He looked startled, then angry.

"*Caramba!* This letter gives me the same warning. Will they never learn their lesson, these Panamanians? They had their bellyful of punishment two years ago."

"As I was saying, *mi general,*" General Roca interrupted, "your coming may have precipitated matters." Perhaps he saw anger in Tovar's bushy eyebrows and swelling cheeks, for he hurriedly explained. "They are afraid of your prowess, and possibly hope to strike a fatal blow before you have the opportunity to organize resistance."

Tovar nodded. "You are undoubtedly right, General Roca. I shall at once proceed to military headquarters to assume command." He called his aide. "Fetch General Amaya here immediately."

Amaya soon joined the commanding officer, but before the two men went off to headquarters, at Tovar's orders Amaya sent two aides to the Governor with the request that he should make arrangements for the immediate dispatch of a train to Colón, to fetch the Sharpshooters.

For General Tovar the subsequent hours were busy, as indirect evidence accumulated that His Excellency, the Governor, was not all he should be in point of loyalty. While Tovar was on the sea wall, advising General Huertas how to defend it against possible attack, the Governor's secretary

215

arrived to inform General Tovar that the superintendent of the railroad refused to handle the transport of the troops on the grounds that outstanding debts owing to the P.R.R. by the Colombian government remained unpaid, and that the railroad saw no reason for increasing that indebtedness.

Having been aware, before he sailed for Colón, that the Panamanian national treasury was in a chronic state of penury, General Tovar had aken the precaution of collecting moneys from collectors of customs en route, to the amount of $65,272. He therefore ordered the secretary to return to the Governor with a message that he, General Tovar, held himself personally responsible for all moneys owing, and that the troops were to leave Colón immediately.

In due course aides brought a return message from the Governor, to say that he had been astonished by Colonel Shaler's attitude, for he, His Excellency, had no knowledge of any debt owing to the railroad, but that it was quite certain that the Sharpshooters would shortly be arriving.

Tovar began to feel less sure than His Excellency on that point. Indeed, he began to doubt the existence of the alleged telegrams. When the departmental head of the national treasury arrived, to say that the threat of revolt was beginning to assume alarming proportions, and that when disorder actually broke out, as it might do at any moment, His Excellency could not be relied upon to give the necessary orders to suppress it, General Tovar knew that his Sharpshooters were urgently needed.

He hurried back to the sea wall, where Huertas and his fellow officers were sunning themselves and listening with sardonic amusement to the shouts of a not very distant mob. While Tovar was issuing instructions on how to defend the barracks Huertas asked permission to order out the first patrol, and disappeared. A few minutes later a company of soldiers, armed for patrol duty, marched on to the sea wall and there opened into two files which passed on either side of the astonished generals.

"Generals," said the captain in charge of the company, "you are prisoners."

It was as simple as that.

Uncle Bill and Wesley wandered through the crowded, noisy streets. "Long live the Republic of the Isthmus!" shouted the excited men and women of Panama. "Long live Huertas! Long live President Amador!" And to prove that they meant every word they shouted, most of those who carried firearms fired them into the air. This was unfortunate for the women and children who occupied the balconies overhanging the narrow streets—and there were not many streets without balconies—but who cared? A new republic was in the making. The free and independent Republic of Panama was all but an established fact. Would be a fact,

216

tomorrow. So, why not celebrate? Why not sing and dance and drink and fire off their ammunition?

"Yeah, and those guns are not all that will be firing if those Colombian generals aren't soon released," Uncle Bill said.

"What do you mean?"

"The commander of the *Bogotá* is threatening to bombard the town unless."

"Good God! And the Junta—"

Godwin laughed harshly. "Three quarters of them are scared pink. If it weren't for the Arango and Amador families—and Uncle Sam—the revolt would fizzle out like a damp firework."

"Won't it do that anyway, when shells begin to fall?"

"Are you asking me, Wesley? Because I just don't know. Meanwhile, the battery has promised to stand firm and will return the *Bogotá*'s fire. And so long as the Navy Department don't just sit on their backsides—"

Wesley caught hold of his companion's arm. "Did you see that, Uncle Bill?"

"See what?"

"That flash, beyond the sea wall."

Godwin had neither a chance to reply nor any need to, for Wesley was answered by the wail of a shell, a crash, and the rumble of falling masonry. The shouting in the streets and the small-arms firing ceased abruptly, and were followed by first an uneasy silence and then by whimpering fear from the chicken-hearted. People melted into the dark shadows or else ran for cover to the buildings which lined the streets.

The silence, broken only by an echo of galloping hoofs, lasted for several horrible minutes, which made the next explosion when it came sound louder and more frightening. But with a difference.

"One of ours," Uncle Bill muttered laconically—although what he really meant was, that one of the Panamanian shore batteries was firing back at the Colombian gunboat in the harbor. "We won't sleep good tonight if this goes on."

A chestnut horse came their way, and as the rider passed beneath a street lamp Godwin gave a yell.

"Mr. Prescott!"

Prescott reigned in, recognized the two Americans. "Just the men I'm looking for," he told them. "Do you mind returning to Colón by special train, Adam?"

"Now?"

"Soon as possible. Special orders for Colonel Shaler."

Wesley nodded reluctantly, having little wish to leave Panama at such a moment. Prescott started to say something, but another shell whined overhead. It fell in Salsipuedes Street, and killed a Chinese—who certainly hadn't cared a damn who owned Panama so long as he was left in peace.

32

"LET'S GET DOWN to the station, we can talk there," Prescott said between his teeth, as the chestnut, alarmed by the noise, reared and bucked. "The matter's urgent. Take it easy, my pretty, take it easy," he urged, patting the animal's neck. "Come on, boys."

The walkers were breathless by the time they reached the railroad station, for each explosion made the chestnut shy; and Prescott had need of all his horsemanship to prevent its bolting. He sighed with relief as he leaped off the horse and waited for the other two to arrive.

The station was crowded. People were clamoring for trains to take them into the interior, away from the shelling. The assistant superintendent drew them into a quieter corner.

His face looked grim under the oil lamp. "There'll be a hell of a riot when the people see a special train run for the exclusive benefit of one person. You'd better wait until it's ready to pull away before jumping in. I wouldn't take the risk of running it if it hadn't been for orders from Washington."

"Washington!" Godwin whistled.

"Ehrman cabled them earlier to confirm the uprising, and to say that a government was being organized, that five hundred soldiers had been landed at Colón, and that the situation was serious. He's just had a reply."

The newspaperman chuckled. "Is it hot?"

"Hot enough! But not for publication, Godwin. Is that understood? If it should leak out at home the people may begin looking for scalps."

"Like that, is it? All right, Prescott, it won't get by me."

"Nor you, Adam, except so far as Colonel Shaler?"

"No, sir."

"Good! You understand, of course, that I'm taking the message to Dick, for transmission to Colonel Shaler, but in case of interruption on the lines I want you to take it in person as well. Here's a copy of the message. Read it, and memorize it."

By the uncertain light of the oil lamp under which they were standing, Wesley read the message. It was written on a slip of yellow paper. Uncle Bill stood behind him, and read it over his shoulder.

It was addressed to Ehrman, Panama, and read:

Message sent to *Nashville* to Colón may not have been delivered. Accordingly, see that the following message is sent to *Nashville* immediately: *Nashville,* Colón: In the interests of peace make every effort to prevent Government troops at Colón from proceeding to

218

Panama. The transit of the Isthmus must be kept open and order maintained. Acknowledge. Signed, Darling, *Acting*. Secure special train if necessary. Act promptly. Signed Loomis, *Acting*.

"Jehoshaphat!" Godwin pursed thin lips. "Like you said, Prescott, that telegram's as hot as hell. Suppose there's only one way of stopping the Colombians from proceeding to Panama?"

"The U. S. Navy will have to take that step, if you mean shooting."

"It would mean war, with Uncle Sam as aggressor."

"It would mean war," Prescott agreed soberly.

"If the folks back home could know what was happening! War just round the corner, yet I doubt if there's one person outside the government who realizes the fact."

"They're too busy voting," Wesley pointed out.

"Lucky them!" Godwin commented. "They'll sleep better."

Lucky them to be able to sleep at all, Wesley thought, as the special train steamed out of Panama station and rattled through the outskirts of the city. There had been little time left for sleep the previous night: the immediate prospect looked equally unpromising. It could be any hour by the time he had reached Colón and delivered the message to Shaler.

He had not got away from Panama without causing a minor riot, as Prescott had anticipated. There had been a rush for the train as it drew into the station, and it had taken the broad shoulders of half a dozen railroad men to clear a pathway for Wesley and to keep the people from clambering in after him. The train had to leave in a rush. He smiled wryly at the reflection that, whereas so many wanted to leave the city and couldn't, he could and didn't want to. The sound of the first explosion had awakened a strange, elemental force within him. He felt like a war horse that had sniffed gunpowder, and was rearing to charge. The dangers of war did something to a man; they excited, and created the urge to fight back.

He scarcely knew what was happening to him in these days. If he had not celebrated his coming-of-age he would have suspected that he was growing into manhood. Emotions and desires, which some years back would have shocked him, now seemed an integral, natural part of him. He grinned into the darkness. Perhaps he was only just growing into manhood—developing late, as it were. Or were all men late developers? He knew that women held that opinion of men.

It was a strange fact, he reflected, that every time he reached a genuine decision not to deny himself longer, Fate arranged matters so as to prevent his carrying out that design. Before, when he had rescued Ingrid from the Negro; and now again, tonight. A chastening thought, that brought a perplexed frown to his forehead. Why should Fate demand

219

chastity from him? She didn't from the other men who lived in Panama. Offhand, he couldn't think of one unmarried man in the Isthmus who didn't occasionally find himself a woman. Perhaps it wasn't Fate after all, but just his New England conscience!

He felt too weary to debate that point. He closed his eyes—

Colonel Shaler had not long fallen asleep when Wesley arrived, but he was surprisingly good natured about being awakened. Perhaps he saw that Wesley's need for sleep was as great as his own. He nodded as he took the yellow paper.

"I got the message an hour ago. It came through without trouble, and I've passed it on to Commander Hubbard. But thanks, Adam, for bringing the confirmation along."

"You heard that the Colombians were shelling Panama City, sir?"

"Yes, but it only lasted half an hour. The *Bogotá* broke off the engagement and steamed away—though she hasn't enough coal to go far."

"Any casualties?"

"A Chinese, and a mule."

Wesley knew he should leave, for they both badly wanted sleep. But he was too curious.

"The first message to the *Nashville*, sir. It's funny the Commander never received it—I take it he didn't, otherwise he would have prevented the Colombians landing?"

"He received it too late. In fact, not until after your train had pulled out. Instead of being delivered at the consulate it was given to one of the ship's boats to take aboard at a moment when Hubbard was actually in the consulate. Afterward, he came to me. I told him I had already agreed to do my best to see that the troops were not transported." Shaler yawned. "God! it's been one hell of a day, Adam. That Colonel Torres, who was left in charge of the Sharpshooters, is a fiery-tempered bastard. Persistent, too. I couldn't get away from him. I don't mind telling you I was in two minds about agreeing to his demands. We're responsible to the New Panama Canal Company, Adam, not to Washington, and we daren't do anything which might give the Colombian Government an excuse for canceling our concessions."

"What about tomorrow, sir?"

"Ah!" Shaler nodded his relief. "Transporting the Colombian troops is no longer our affair, thank God! Just about midnight the vice-consul here also received orders from Washington, insisting that in no circumstances must the Colombians be allowed to proceed to Panama. So Hubbard has sent me an official order prohibting the P.R.R. from carrying troops of either party in either direction—ha! ha!—which puts us in the clear."

"What is Captain Torres likely to do when he hears about the General's arrest?"

220

The Superintendent looked grim. "I've been thinking about that, too, and it's worrying me, Adam. Best look out for squalls."

Wesley quickly fell asleep, and slept soundly for two hours. Sometime about dawn he woke up, and knew he would not sleep any more until night. As soon as he had dressed he left the hotel, and wandered over to the beach, where he sat down beneath a palm, and stared, first at the American warship anchored out in the bay, then at the Colombian gunboat warped alongside the old dock.

There was nothing particularly sinister about either ship at that moment. They looked as benign as two Alsatian dogs stretched out in lazy sleep. But at any moment he expected to see them blink an eye at the early sunshine that was turning their shrouds pink, and the underbelly of their guns black. Soon they would be astir with activity; and with the last remnants of their sleep would depart the poetry of their beauty: for all that could remain would be the beastliness of suspicion as they watched each other for the first sign of aggression.

Restlessness soon sent him in search of breakfast; and after he had swallowed cereal and two cups of coffee he wandered back toward the dock area, where he encountered the superintendent.

Shaler looked surprised to see him. "You're up early, Adam. Not wanting to miss anything?" The question was jocular, but the tone of voice was not. Wesley had a feeling that the other man was trying to ignore his own uneasiness.

He responded in the same vein. "That's about it, sir."

The Superintendent's gaze rested momentarily on the Colombian gunboat. "I didn't wake up. I was called. I would have slept until next week if I'd had my way. Colonel Torres was up at daybreak, demanding the transport of his troops to Panama."

"It's the showdown, sir?"

"That's what I'm anticipating. Like to come along? You've been in it from the first." He did not wait for Wesley's reply; he knew his man.

Upon reaching Shaler's office they found not only the fiery-eyed Torres there, but also Malmros, the American vice-consul. Torres looked angry; Malmros, sullen.

Torres wasted no time in formalities. A quick salute, a curt "Good-morning, señores," and then, explosively, "For the last time, Colonel Shaler, I demand that you give immediate orders for the transfer by special train of my troops to Panama City."

The Colonel shook his head. "With my sincere regrets, colonel, no train is available in the yards here, as you saw yesterday, or can see for yourself if you care to look out of that window."

"Where are the coaches? At Panama?"

"The majority are there."

"Then you must telegraph for some to be brought here at once. My men must leave for Panama this morning."

"I cannot do that, colonel."

"Why not?" The Colonel's face was taut with anger.

Shaler drew in a deep breath. "I have received orders, colonel, not to allow your troops to travel over the P.R.R. system."

"Orders!" The slight-statured Colombian nearly jumped into the air. "Whose orders? His Excellency's?"

"The orders of Commander Hubbard of U.S.S. *Nashville,* acting under instructions of the United States Government."

There was a momentary silence while Torres digested this news. Then the storm broke. "You lie, señor," he shouted, banging his hand on Shaler's desk until the ink splashed out of the Superintendent's silver and glass inkwell and spread across the blotting pad in front of it. "You are using the presence of that damned Yankee warship as an excuse—"

The vice-consul pursed his lips. "Colonel Torres, you are going too far—"

The fiery-tempered Colonel refused to listen. "Silence!" he bellowed. "I repeat what I say. I do not believe a word of what you say. You are procrastinating—"

The consul raised his voice. "I must insist upon being heard. I have a letter for you from Commander Hubbard."

"Give it to me," Torres snatched the letter from the Consul's hand, and began to gabble parts of it aloud, his voice rising to a crescendo or falling to an unintelligible mumble as each phrase affected his temper.

> To the General Officer Commanding the Troops, Colón. Sir.
>
> The condition of affairs at Panama, I am advised, is such that a movement of the Colombian troops now at Colón to that neighborhood must bring about a conflict and threaten that free and uninterrupted transit of the Isthmus which the government of the United States is pledged to maintain. I have therefore the honor to notify you that I have directed the Superintendent of the Panama Railroad at Colón that he must not transport on his line troops of either party. Trusting that this action on my part will meet with your cordial acquiescence—

This was too much for the Colombian to accept. "Acquiescence!" he mouthed. "May Our Lady in Heaven never listen to my prayers if I acquiesce." He crushed the offending letter into a ball, which he hurled to the ground. Then he turned to the Consul, and for the first time spoke calmly and with a measure of self-control that added dignity to his martial bearing.

222

"This is Colombian territory, señor, and as such the writ of the United States Government does not apply."

"Your pardon, Colonel Torres, but a treaty in force between your country and the United States pledges the latter to maintain free and uninterrupted transit across the Isthmus in time of trouble."

Torres pounced upon the Consul's last word. "Trouble, señor! This is no time of trouble. The Isthmus is at peace and calm. The Costa Rican troops are many miles to the west of the Isthmus and will be kept there as soon as my Sharpshooters can be transported to the scene of action. Commander Hubbard's letter does not come within the terms of the treaty, and is therefore both illegal and unwarrantable."

Shaler and the Consul exchanged glances. Malmros sucked uneasily at his lips before continuing. "It is apparent, señor, that you have no knowledge of what has happened in Panama since yesterday."

"Well?"

"The state of Panama has recovered its sovereignty, and as a free and independent nation, has seceded from the United States of Colombia. A provisional government has been formed, and a declaration of independence is to be formally read at two o'clock this afternoon."

Torres stood as stiff as a ramrod. The only sign of the shock which the Consul's words had given him was revealed by his twitching nostrils. The others anticipated a violent outburst of disbelief, but to their relieved surprise he accepted the statement.

"In that case I must communicate with my commanding officers for orders—" he began evenly.

"That is not possible, colonel," Shaler pointed out firmly. "They are under arrest."

Torres's face paled. His hands clenched and unclenched. "And His Excellency—"

"Is likewise under arrest."

"By God and all His Blessed Saints, the people of Panama shall be made to suffer for this new outrage!"

"I think not, colonel," the Consul suavely interrupted. "From yesterday the independence of the new Republic of Panama is secured by the United States."

The Colombian drew in a deep breath as, with tempestuous eyes, he surveyed the others in turn. His brown face seemed pale. Presently he swung round on his heels, and faced the Consul.

"Señor Malmros, I am no diplomat, praise the Saints! I am a man of action. Until I have official notification from my government that Panama is no longer part of the United States of Colombia I shall consider Colón as Colombian territory, and the act of holding my superior officers prisoners as an act of rebellion. Unless every officer from the *Cartagena* is released before 2 P.M. this afternoon I shall give orders for the town of

Colón to be bombarded and burned down. Furthermore, my troops will kill every American still left alive—man, woman, or child."

The Consul was shaken. "My God! colonel, you would not dare—that would be murder!"

The burning eyes never wavered. The tight-pressed lips clipped off precise words, one by one. "I shall most certainly dare. Unless Generals Tovar and Amaya and their aides are released before the time stated I shall make a shambles of Colón, and a corpse of every American in it. Good morning, señores." The scabbard of the Colonel's sword struck against the jamb of the door as he marched stiffly out of the room. The men left behind heard the echoing beat of his footsteps grow fainter as he turned a corner of the corridor.

Shaler wiped his forehead. Malmros sucked at his lips and gazed fearfully at the Superintendent.

"He means what he says." Although he put the words in the form of a statement his voice held an undertone of pleading as if he were hoping against hope that Colonel Shaler would contradict him. But the railroad man did not oblige.

"Every word," he confirmed, thin lipped. "The man's unbalanced with rage. He'll act first, and think afterward."

"It would mean war between Colombia and the United States."

"He is a soldier. War is his trade."

"Then what are we to do?"

"We arranged a signal with Commander Hubbard. We must summon him. Adam, go up to the roof and hoist the American flag. You'll find one in the locker at the foot of the stairs leading up."

Wesley hoisted the flag. Within a minute the signal was answered. A few minutes later he saw a cutter round the bow of the warship and make for the nearest pier. He hurried down to Shaler's office, where he found the Superintendent still closeted with the Consul.

"A boat is already on its way here, sir," he told Shaler.

"Good work. Go meet the Commander, Adam, and bring him here."

Hubbard recognized Wesley as he stepped ashore, and saluted with a genial smile. "Am I wanted?"

"Urgently, sir, in Colonel Shaler's office."

"Right!" The naval man turned smartly on his heels.

There was a quick greeting and handshake all around. Malmros wasted no time.

"We've sent for you, Commander Hubbard, on account of the serious situation which is developing here. Colonel Torres, officer commanding the Colombian troops aboard the *Cartagena,* has just been told of the arrest in Panama of his superior officers. He threatens to burn down the town and kill every American in it unless those officers are released before two o'clock this afternoon."

224

Hubbard laughed his scorn. "A bluff, sir."

"No, commander. Colonel Torres is not bluffing. Ask Colonel Shaler." In answer to Hubbard's look of inquiry Shaler nodded. "The man's mad enough to carry out his threat. If he does, it'll be too late afterward to hold an inquest on his sanity."

The Commander's mouth tightened. "Whether you're right or not, sir, and I can't believe that any man could be so mad, precautions must be taken to insure the safety of all American citizens."

"Such as?" In his anxiety the Consul leaned forward and laid a hand on the Commander's arm. "Can you bring a landing party to deal with the Colombian troops?"

"A landing party! I might land about seventy men all told, if I scrape the bottom of the ship."

"Seventy! Good God! There are nearly five hundred Colombians on board the *Cartagena*."

"Exactly!" Hubbard's keen eyes glanced toward the windows. "Collect all women and children, and put them aboard the two ships in dock: the German *Marcomania*, and your own *City of Washington*. Warn their captains to be ready to pull out at the first sign of trouble."

The Consul nodded. "And the men?"

"Tell every foreigner to assemble in the railroad shed. At least that's defensible, being a stone building. As soon as I return to the ship I'll send a landing party ashore to join them; also as many extra arms and as much ammunition as I can spare. Understand?"

"Yes, commander."

"One more thing. Under no circumstances must any man in the shed be the first to fire. There must be no firing unless we are fired on first."

"Of course."

"Right!" Hubbard rose to his feet. "I'll send a signalman with the landing party. Keep me acquainted with what is happening here." He went out, leaving with those left behind an impression of having talked with a man who knew his business and would deal adequately with any eventuality which might arise.

The work of evacuating Colón was quickly completed, save for the refusal of a handful of American women to go aboard either of the two ships. Among them was Madge Sanderson, who refused positively to leave her husband. Another was Ingrid Ericson, who would not leave Madge. Conspicuous among the men who assembled in the P.R.R. shed was Larry. Wesley saw him make a beeline for Ingrid.

Within fifteen minutes of Commander Hubbard's return to his ship a cutter was seen to leave the warship's side and make for the docks. Ten minutes later, a second followed. People on the roof of the shed

225

heard the warship's bugles sounding to quarters, and saw the ship being cleared for action.

A few minutes later forty-two men from the *Nashville*, under the direction of a lieutenant commander and a midshipman, had landed, marched into the shed and taken up defensive positions there, a shout from some civilians on the landward side of the roof gave warning of further excitement. Colombian soldiers were making toward the shed. Just ahead of them, obviously making for the shed while there was still time to enter, hurried an old man flanked by a young woman on either side.

Wesley recognized old man Perrigot and his two daughters.

33

THERE WAS TENSION everywhere. The seamen from the *Nashville* stood stiffly at their posts, rifles at the ready, eyes fixed on the Colombian troops who ringed the building. In the body of the shed the lieutenant commander stood beside a small pile of arms and ammunition, questioning one by one the civilians who clustered about him, pleading to be armed. Outside, the Colombians were equally alert as they sought whatever shade was available and stared contemptuously at the white stone shed as each man selected his own particular target. They had every reason to be contemptuous, the odds were ten to one.

Behind Front Street the town was quiet. For the most part the concrete sidewalks were deserted, but there was plenty of movement behind the shadowed windows above, where dark faces pressed against the shutters, gazing fearfully down into the streets.

Out in the harbor the *Nashville* had weighed anchor, and was patroling the water front, her gun turrets swinging to keep guns turned on the *Cartagena* and the massed Colombians.

The atmosphere was explosive. One false move, one accidental pull on a trigger could mean the signal for an exchange of fire, with consequences so calamitous that Colonel Shaler, the consular officials of several countries, Sanderson, and Wesley hardly dared draw a breath lest it should precipitate the crisis they were trying so sincerely to avoid. The midshipman patroled up and down the shed, warning everyone not to fire first.

Conflict, and maybe war, trembled in the balance as Wesley took his turn to collect a rifle.

The naval man gave him a quick glance.

"Name?"

Wesley gave it.

226

"Ever handled firearms before?"

"Yes."

"Where? How long ago? What kind?"

The answers were satisfactory, and a rifle changed hands.

"Remember, no firing without orders," Lieutenant Commander Witzel barked as a last word before turning to Sanderson. "Name?" he demanded.

Armed, and ready for action should it come, Wesley looked for the Perrigots. He saw them sitting together on some packing cases, Perrigot in the middle, Anne on his right, Marie on his left. Men clustered thick about them like wasps round a basket of plums. He felt immensely pleased to see Madge Sanderson pushing her way through them so that she could join her friends.

"Good for you, Madge!" he chortled to himself. "Chase 'em away."

He stood for a minute in the dark shadow of a crated Cadillac motor car and gazed eagerly at the sisters. It was the first time he had seen them together since his original visit to the Perrigot home.

Time had made them extraordinarily different. Although it was easy to see they were sisters, they could no longer be mistaken for twins. True, they had the same lovely hair, so black, so lustrous that it could almost be the darkest shade of blue—but now they wore it in different styles. Anne's hair was drawn up to form a crown on top of her head. Marie, on the contrary, wore hers pulled back over her ears, to make a chignon at the nape of the neck; a severe style that was in mocking contrast to the sultry expression of her eyes and mouth.

Their faces were as dissimilar in expression as they were physically alike. Everything about Marie suggested the existence within of a consuming fire; whereas Anne looked emotionally serene.

Their figures followed this pattern. Marie with her prominent but shapely breasts was exciting to a man. Her limbs were well covered, rounded, and tempting. Anne's slimness was more spiritual; her lithe grace expressed the poetry of motion whenever she moved. A man might worship at the shrine of Anne's beauty; Marie, he would desire.

Then Wesley looked at Perrigot. Madge had not frightened away the half-dozen men who were ostentatiously standing by in the hope of finding some excuse to talk to the girls. The old man was scowling at them. It was surprising that his fury had not yet scared off the girls' admirers.

Wesley grinned. The scene tickled his sense of humor, especially as he imagined the faces of the other men when he walked up to the Perrigot family. He moved away from the shadow of the crated automobile, and threaded his way through merchandise of all descriptions.

Perrigot was the first to see him, for little escaped those shrewd old eyes. The surprise caught him off guard, and he glared at the American with a malevolence that shocked Wesley even though he was prepared

227

for it. At that instant he recognized Marie's volcanic eyes, and also recognized that Perrigot's gave much the same impression of a seething, eruptive force.

The expression vanished quickly, and was succeeded by a studied air of formal acknowledgment, and a quick nod of open recognition. At the same moment Madge saw Wesley.

"Wesley! I was wondering where you had got to." With a quick flash of intuition she went on, innocently, "Have you met Mr. Perrigot and his daughters?"

"We have met before, Mrs. Sanderson," Perrigot acknowledged. "For one night only, some time ago. Mr.—Mr.—" he hesitated.

"Adam," Madge supplied. "Wesley Adam."

"Ah! I remember. Mr. Adam and a friend were on their way to Alhajeula." He stared expressionlessly at Wesley. "I heard, some weeks later, that you lost your way and reached Indian country. Was that true?"

"It most certainly was, Mr. Perrigot. The Indians were ready to kill us. We were rescued only just in time."

"Tsk! Tsk! After the careful directions I gave you I cannot understand how you came to take the wrong trail." The old eyes searched Wesley's face with veiled intensity.

Wesley shrugged, then grinned disarmingly. "Guess we were too green to be let loose in the jungle, sir." He was sure that Perrigot relaxed. He turned to Anne. "And this is Mademoiselle Anne." He twitched his eyelid at Anne as he bowed to her. "And Mademoiselle Marie." He bowed to Marie. "It's nice meeting you all again. A pity the circumstances aren't more—cheerful."

Madge nodded. "Mr. Perrigot has been telling me that when he heard rumors in Bohio that Colombian soldiers were on their way to Panama he thought it wiser to seek safety in a larger town. He has seen too much of recent fighting to risk staying in the interior. He arrived here only just in time."

"It seems that we have jumped from the frying pan into the fire," Perrigot said.

Marie's eyes mocked Wesley. "When you left us, monsieur, you said that you would come to see us again when you returned to Panama."

He accepted her reproof as confirmation that she had said nothing of his visit. The knowledge embarrassed him. He did not like secrets of that nature. But when he glanced quickly into Anne's eyes, and saw in their serene depths the loyal comradeship of a shared secret, he changed his mind, and decided that circumstances alter cases. Meanwhile, he realized that he had to make some sort of a reply to Marie's mischief.

"It has been my intention for some time to write and ask Mr. Perrigot's permission to call and pay my respects to you all."

"I am sure you are too busy to visit the interior," the old man said

228

positively. He slipped an arm round the waist of each girl, and laughed unpleasantly. "We cannot allow the girls to have their heads turned by too many stories of the big cities, eh, madame?"

"On the contrary, it would be good for them to know there are such places," Madge answered more tartly than Wesley had ever heard her speak.

"Don't worry, Papa," Marie urged. "I am sure that Monsieur Adam has no intention of returning. He is merely being polite."

"I am perfectly sincere," Wesley stated angrily.

"In that case," she mocked, "you will be able to prove that sincerity when we return home—especially if you play chess."

"Hold your tongue, girl."

Marie smiled sweetly at her father. "Not if it means a few hours' pleasure for you, Papa dear. It is so seldom you have a chance of playing. Do you play, Monsieur Adam?"

"A little."

"Well, then!" She laughed. Wesley heard the laughter of a hundred devils underlining the note of triumph.

Wesley glanced quickly at Anne and surprised an expression of pleading in her eyes; but was unable to decide whether she wanted him to take advantage of Marie's stratagem, or was trying to tell him that he would be doing more harm than good in doing so. While he hesitated the wily old fox cunningly avoided the trap Marie had laid for him.

"First things first," he said impassively. He nodded at one of the naval men on board. "We may never see our home again if that Colombian colonel carries out his threat."

Madge Sanderson's hands fluttered. Wesley knew she was thinking of the terrible day, still fresh in her memory, when she had heard volley after volley coming from the direction of the church, and the moans of ravished women— Oh God! he reflected, as for one awful second he saw Madge and Anne and Marie struggling with the roaring, drunken soldiery.

"I'll see what's happening," he announced abruptly.

He went to the nearest window and peered over the shoulder of the sailor on guard. Five soldiers lolled in the shadow of an office doorway, smoking, spitting, and provocatively taking sights at the railroad shed.

The sailor became aware of Wesley's presence. "Bastards!" he growled, jerking his head at the Colombians. "See that one with the ginger mustachios, mister?"

"Yes."

"He's going first, the son of a coyote bitch. I dislike him plenty."

Wesley passed on. Wherever he looked he saw Colombian soldiers, waiting, jeering, waiting— They were ten to one, and knew it. The American sailors knew it, too, and acknowledged the fact with their grim expressions and chewing jaws. Christ! chewed those jaws, if the bastards want it they can have it.

He saw Malmros nearby. The Consul's face was troubled, too. The waiting preyed upon him. He was a man of peace.

Then Wesley and Shaler saw each other simultaneously. The Colonel beckoned.

"Here! Adam!"

Shaler was at the far end of the shed, overlooking the harbor. "Look! What do you make of that?"

Wesley looked. Black smoke was belching from the *Cartagena*'s funnels. The crew were slacking down the breast ropes. On the dock a Negro mooring gang stood ready to cast off.

"She's getting under way."

"She's going to fight it out, Adam. And we have ringside seats. By God!" There was awe in his voice. "What's the *Nashville* going to do?"

The *Nashville* was on the other side of the bay. Apart from the fact that her turrets had swung round to keep her guns trained on the Colombian gunboat she appeared unaware of the movements of her prospective enemy.

The gap between the gunboat and the dockside widened. The water seethed and creamed at the ship's stern. Her bows turned the water over as she nosed forward. Her speed increased as she drew away from the dock and head for clear water. The *Nashville*'s guns traversed.

"History in the making!" Shaler muttered. "Watch out for the first shell, Adam. It may be a signal for the Colombians to attack us."

With hearts beating fast they waited to see the first fatal puff of black smoke mushroom into the clear atmosphere. The seconds passed. The creaming wake of the *Cartagena* grew wider and whiter.

"It must come soon." The superintendent's voice was hoarse from strain. Then "Ten thousand devils! She's broadside on to the *Nashville,* a sitting duck. Why in Hades doesn't the *Nashville* fire? She'll miss her chance. It will be too late."

Too late! Wesley abruptly realized the truth. "She's decamping, sir, heading for base."

Her direction, the belching funnels, the creaming bows and wake seemed to confirm his guess.

"You're right. What do you know? The bastards have deserted their own troops." Shaler was excited. "Now what will Colonel Fire-eater Torres have to say?"

What Colonel Torres had to say was said shortly afterward. Under the protection of a white flag he approached the railroad building and demanded to parley with the American officer in charge. Lieutenant Commander Witzel obliged. Said a much-chastened Torres, he was well disposed toward Americans. It was foolish of them to imagine that he really intended any harm. You know what it is, when you become over-excited. In the heat of the moment you say things you don't really mean. Could he please have the use of a special train to send the Alcade of Colón to Panama, to obtain General Tovar's orders?

Wesley returned to the Perrigots. Madge was no longer there; she had gone, taking Anne with her. But Marie received him with dancing eyes.

"Well, when are they going to attack?"

"The Colombians? Why?" He inspected her with incredulous eyes. "Do you want them to?"

"It will be exciting, thrilling." She stretched her arms into the air. "I've always wanted to be in a real battle. I want to know what it feels like to be afraid, to hear the whine of bullets."

She was acting, trying to impress him, he believed. It wasn't natural for a young woman to find battle and death exciting. Not many men did that; although when the necessity arose most of them bore themselves bravely enough.

Before he could think of a reply, her father rounded upon her. "Silence! You little idiot, there's nothing thrilling about death."

Her mouth was mutinous. "But the risk of it is."

"Nonsense! How could *you* know—"

"That's what I want to find out. I'm sure it is. It must be."

"Then keep such wicked thoughts to yourself, child. Don't let me hear you speak such nonsense. It's thrilling to feel afraid!" His muttering grew unintelligible. Perrigot had lapsed into his native language.

She closed her mouth with sullen decision. Easy to see that she would not speak until her smoldering temper improved.

Perrigot asked, "Well, what about the Colombians? What had that officer to say?"

Before Wesley could reply Madge and Anne returned.

"Is it true, Wesley, that there may not be an attack after all?" Madge asked.

"There's every chance there won't be, now. That excitable little Torres had calmed down and asked to send to General Tovar for orders."

"Mightn't he favor the threat of an attack, in the hope of being freed?"

Wesley shrugged. "He might, but I doubt it. I'm sure he's more level headed and will realize the consequences of any attack."

"You mean, war with the United States?"

"Yes."

"Mightn't there be war in any event? Surely one can't arrest such important men as generals without causing repercussions?"

"Remember, the Panamanians arrested Tovar, not the Americans."

"But—" She indicated the American seamen. "They are Americans."

"Ah! They are protecting American lives and property."

"You men—" Madge laughed. "So long as there isn't to be war!"

231

"I'd say that the chances against have improved no end."

"Shall we be kept here much longer?" Anne asked.

"There are Colombian troops still surrounding the place, but I have an idea it won't be long."

She turned to her father. "Since we're here, in Colón, Papa, shall you be staying for some days?"

"Now that the Americans have the situation in hand, it will be safe for us to catch the first train back."

Was there a mocking note in his voice? Wesley couldn't be sure, but it reminded him of Marie's voice when she was in her most mischievous mood.

Anne's eyes misted as she turned away to hide her disappointment.

Madge said, "Why not stay a few days, just this once, Mr. Perrigot?"

"No, madame. My daughters and I are happier at home. We are content with our own company."

Marie looked at her father and drew back her lips, not in laughter this time. "Speak for yourself, Papa," she snapped mutinously. "Anne and I would like to see a white face sometimes. Why couldn't Mr. and Mrs. Sanderson come and spend a week end with us now and then?"

"Wait until you hear whether they would like to, my girl."

Madge placed her hand on the old man's arm and dimpled. "We'd love to, Mr. Perrigot—if you would have us."

"*Please,* Papa." Anne pleaded with words, eyes, and body.

Her sister was more forthright. "If you won't invite people to visit us, Papa, we will." She challenged him with volcanic eyes.

"You will not dictate to me, *ma fille.* You'll do as I say," Perrigot blustered, and his face grew thunderous as he tried to outstare his daughter. Then despair dulled his aging eyes. Face and body seemed to sag, as if exhausted by the mental struggle, or perhaps because he was realizing for the first time that his power to control his family had slipped away from his selfish grasp, and was being challenged. He looked pathetic indeed at that moment.

Marie was the first to sense her victory. Her eyes turned mocking once more. "Say yes to Mrs. Sanderson, Papa," she commanded. "Tell her that we shall all love to welcome her and Mr. Sanderson."

He turned. "Perhaps Marie is right, madame," he mumbled. "I see so much of them I do not realize they are growing up. We shall be pleased to welcome you and your husband."

"And another week end, Mr. Adam, Papa?" Marie demanded. "He could take us riding."

The old eyes were expressionless, but before he could refuse this new demand Madge added, "Mr. Adam is married, Mr. Perrigot." The glance of warning, and the emphasis underlining the word *married,* was not lost upon Wesley to whom it was directed. He understood its inference, so he nodded back his promise not to forget her warning and advice.

"Very well," Perrigot agreed after a slight pause. "If Mr. Adam cares to pay us an occasional visit, he, too, will be welcome."

The sisters exchanged surprised glances. Anne looked dazed, but the eyes of the younger girl were filled with triumph. The old man won't have much peace after this, Wesley thought as Sanderson hurriedly joined the group.

"Folks, this is a historic moment," he announced. "A message has this moment come through on the only line left uncut between here and Panama. The signal for the canal has just changed to green. The Republic of Panama is now an established fact."

34

TOWARD NIGHTFALL tension had eased sufficiently for Colonel Torres to review the situation, and he was able to appreciate the immediate risk of carrying out his threat to massacre all white foreigners in Colón. After discussions, during which he frequently professed his love for Americans, he agreed to withdraw his soldiers to Monkey Hill, some miles in the interior, if Commander Hubbard would order the American sailors back to the *Nashville*.

The night passed quietly. The following morning, however, brought a renewal of tension when it was learned that Torres had not carried out his part of the bargain. He had moved his troops only as far as the outskirts of the town, and was threatening to reoccupy Colón unless he received contrary instructions from General Tovar. These Tovar steadfastly refused to give, so Commander Hubbard hurriedly landed a small force of thirty men, who took possession of the railroad buildings which once more they barricaded. Fifteen minutes later he sent some marines ashore with two one-pounders, which they mounted on a flatcar behind a shield of cotton bales. Women and children were collected, and sent aboard the *Marcomania*, while their menfolk joined the seamen, and re-formed themselves into an armed party.

At 11 A.M. the Alcalde, whom Torres had sent to Panama to consult with General Tovar, returned to Colón. As a result of his interview with Torres, the Colombian Sharpshooters marched into Colón and surrounded the railroad buildings. Simultaneously the *Nashville* raised anchor, and stood in close to the wharves, from which position her guns could cover the water front and protect the railroad buildings.

Little happened during the heat of the afternoon, but later the attitude of the Colombians grew more threatening. The Vice-consul again approached Colonel Torres, and urged him and his troops to re-embark on the *Orinoco*. Torres refused absolutely and insisted that, in spite of his love for the United States, it was his duty to burn Colón to the ground and massacre all Americans unless his superior officers were released. The Vice-consul was adamant; Torres gave orders to deploy for attack. Commander Hubbard then ordered general quarters to be sounded. Both sides stood ready for action.

"Wait for the first shot," warned Lieutenant Commander Witzel. "At any moment now," he added, thin lipped. "But wait—"

The Americans held their fire. It was a strain to wait, with so many easy and tempting targets in view. There were many itching fingers behind the barricades.

That first shot was never fired. Colonel Torres noticed a smudge on the horizon that grew larger with unusual speed and wondered uneasily if it might not be as well first to make sure that the filthy black smudge wasn't the smoke of another Yankee warship steaming full speed ahead for Colón.

It was. U.S.S. *Dixie* had arrived, with four hundred marines aboard. The Vice-consul hurried across to Torres.

"You have seen?" he asked, pointing to the approaching warship.

"I have seen," agreed the not quite so fiery-eyed Colonel.

"If I were to guarantee the cost of transport to Colombia, and—er—say a little matter of—er—five thousand dollars for yourself—"

"Ten thousand."

"Er—eight thousand. My final offer. That's all the money we have in Colón. You know, my dear colonel, four hundred marines—"

"Eight thousand," Torres agreed.

At five minutes after seven the *Dixie* anchored. At seven thirty-five the Royal Mail Steamer Packet *Orinoco* slid gently away from Pier 3 with two Colombian commanders, twenty-one officers, four hundred and thirty-eight soldiers, and thirteen women aboard, together with two sacks of money.

Oh yes! And two cases of champagne, addressed to Colonel Torres, with the compliments of Colonel Shaler. As one bluffer to another—

As Frederick had said, the green lights signaled a clear track ahead. The Colombian troops had gone, the arrested generals and their aides likewise. A Panamanian government was functioning, and both it and Panamanian independence had been recognized by all the important countries of the world.

Two weeks after the re-creation of the Republic of Panama, a treaty was entered into by the Panamanian and United States governments,

234

whereby the Republic of Panama granted to the U.S. "in perpetuity the use, occupation, and control of a zone of land and land underwater—extending to a distance of five miles on each side of the center line of the route of the canal to be constructed—which the U.S. would possess and exercise as if it were the sovereign of the territory—to the entire exclusion of the exercise by the Republic of Panama of any such sovereign rights, power, or authority."

Now that the Canal Zone was, to all intents and purposes, American territory, the time had arrived for the dirt to fly.

At least, that was what the people back home believed. In their satisfaction they had overlooked the fact that before work can start, a site must be cleared, foundations laid, and materials for the job must be dumped in accessible spots.

A beginning had been made by the French on this preliminary work. Scattered up and down the valley of the Chagres were storehouses filled with materials, a great deal of it of fine quality; repair parts, shop tools, and stationary engines. They had erected large shops at Gorgona, in one shed of which were stored more than one hundred wagonloads of foundry material in addition to old locomotives, excavators, and cranes of varying sizes and conditions. At Empire, Paraiso, and Gatun were other machine shops. One at Bohio, also. There was a marine and repair shop on the Pacific coast, near Panama; a dry dock at Colón. There was also a supply of floating equipment, hopper barges, launches, tugs, and dredges. True, some of this equipment was under the surface of the water, but most of it had been built in Scotland. It was sound and could be floated and repaired.

Then there were more than two thousand buildings, ranging from small huts and laborers' barracks to a fine hospital on Ancon Hill. And more than five hundred workers still on the payroll, most of them at work on the Culebra Cut.

There were also the hospital's death rolls.

* * * *

The white-haired man, who sat at one end of the committee table, inspected his fellow committeemen.

"Gentlemen," he began quietly, tapping the blotting pad in front of him with the tip of his index finger. "I need not emphasize the fact that upon the efficiency of the Department of Sanitation depends the success or failure of our effort to build the Panama Canal. Far more, I venture to suggest, than upon any other department working under the Canal Commission."

The Governor of the Zone cleared his throat. 'Come, colonel, I cannot accept that statement. Without wishing to disparage the work of the Sanitary Department, I cannot feel that the claims of the Engineering and

235

Survey Departments are of less importance than your department. One miscalculation on the part of the surveyors, one error of the engineers might see the whole project ruined by—er—say, flood waters."

Under his drooping white mustache, Colonel Gorgas' lips twitched with annoyance. "Unless there are surveyors to make a miscalculation, or engineers to make an error, nothing can be built for flood waters or any other natural calamity to destroy."

Major General George W. Davis looked puzzled. "I do not follow your meaning, colonel."

"I'll try to make it plain, sir. I'm sure that all of us here have traveled on the Panama Railroad. The railroad took nearly five years to build. Do you know how many of the workers lost their lives during that period?"

"If you are speaking of the myth that every tie cost a man's life—"

Gorgas frowned. "I am not, sir. According to a count made in eighteen sixty, nearly one hundred thousand ties go to make up the railroad. But we do know that more than ten thousand lives were lost from various causes: the greater number from disease."

"That was fifty years ago. Medicine has made great progress in that time."

"Agreed, sir, provided we take advantage of our newly acquired knowledge."

Another committeeman spoke. He had flowing ginger hair, and bushy ginger sideburns and mustache.

"The mortality rate during the French operations has not been so bad, Colonel Gorgas."

"I am coming to that, sir. Though it is bad enough. Between eighteen eighty-one and eighteen eighty-nine the hospital death rolls record nearly six thousand deaths, one thousand and forty-one of those being from yellow fever. Note, please, that I emphasized the words hospital death rolls, for it is known that many more people had yellow fever out of hospital than in it. From inquiries I have made I place the deaths from yellow fever at the figure of two thousand and eighty-two. The total number of deaths from all causes during the years eighty-one to eighty-nine I estimate at more than twenty-two thousand."

The committeeman looked serious. "Those are horrifying figures, colonel."

"They are indeed."

"What about malaria?" asked a third member of the committee. "That's not so serious, I take it, but I suppose it must be reckoned with."

"Not so serious!" Gorgas smiled. "On the contrary, sir. A particularly virulent form of malaria, known commonly in this country as the Chagres fever, is prevalent; and is a worse killer than yellow jack—as our soldiers call yellow fever. This is partly due to the fact that Negroes, generally immune from yellow jack, easily become victims of Chagres fever. We shall have to contend, also, with outbreaks of cholera and dysentery."

"I see what you mean about the importance of the Sanitary Department," commented the red-haired committeeman. "I'm beginning to understand why the French failed to build the canal."

"Nonsense!" exclaimed the Governor. "The French failed because of dishonesty, extravagance, and inefficiency. Why, it was reported to me only yesterday that one storehouse contains torchlights brought here to celebrate the opening of the canal. And there is more than one ton—one *ton,* gentlemen—of rusted pen points in the stationery stores."

"The French may have been all you say, governor, but death from disease was perhaps the greatest single factor which defeated their efforts to complete the canal."

Redhead broke in again. "I want to ask if there's any hope of combating those diseases. We can't afford labor losses of twenty thousand in a few years."

"I agree. Yes, sir, there is hope of combating those diseases—if the Sanitary Department is backed up by the Canal Commission. If I may give this committee a brief account of how the diseases spread—"

"Certainly, colonel," the Governor agreed. "That is what we are here for, as a committee."

"Very well, gentlemen. I will deal first with yellow fever. As you know, a year or two ago, in Cuba, it was my privilege and honor to serve with Major Reed when it was decisively proved that yellow fever was not contagious, but was a result of being infected by a female of the stegomyia mosquito. Since then the following facts have been established: that the stegomyia lives only three months; that it becomes infected with the virus only when, during the first three days of his attack, it bites a man suffering from yellow fever; that it then requires another twelve days before the infected stegomyia can pass on the fever; and lastly, that a man only falls ill with the fever six days after he has been bitten. He thereupon begins a new cycle should he be bitten by a healthy stegomyia during the next three days. Is that clear, sir?"

The Governor nodded doubtfully. "I think so." He looked about him. "Any questions, before the Colonel continues?"

"Yes. Are you telling us, colonel, that if it were possible at this minute to isolate everybody suffering from yellow fever that the disease would die out of its own accord?"

"Not quite, sir, for there are probably some stegomyia mosquitoes who bit a yellow fever victim yesterday, and so will be able to infect a victim in eleven days' time. But if, during the next two weeks we could isolate *every* yellow fever victim, and if there should be no fresh case reported within sixty days after the expiration of that two weeks, it would be safe to conclude that the disease had been eradicated from this country."

237

"Amazing!" exclaimed the redheaded man.

"Too easy," commented the Governor. "If it is so easy to eradicate, why does it still exist?"

"Besides," added another member, "it would be necessary to isolate everyone in the country. The Sanitary Department has control only within the limits of the Zone, and in Colón and Panama."

Gorgas nodded. "That is so, gentlemen, but in dealing with the stegomyia mosquito, man has this advantage: the stegomyia is a town lover: he prefers to breed in sheltered places, cisterns, and tanks—"

"Then he doesn't have to look far for a home in this town, colonel."

"Precisely, sir. And that is one of the ways we shall have to combat yellow fever. Once we have isolated the victims we shall have to concentrate on piping fresh water into every building in Colón and Panama, and installing modern sewerage. When we have done that we can begin on the task of destroying every one of his breeding places."

"We are here to build an American canal, colonel, not rebuild Panamanian cities" Davis interrupted. "I can imagine what Washington would have to say—"

"Unless we rebuild the towns along the lines I suggest, the canal will never be finished," Gorgas retorted. "The Zone must be made safe not only for the workers who have to build it, and afterward for the maintenance staff, but, if it is to become one of the world's highways, safe too for the crews of ships who will be passing through the canal in the years to come."

The red-haired committeeman intervened.

"What about malaria, colonel?"

"Ah!" Gorgas shook his white head. "The anopheles mosquito, the bearer of malaria, is the harder enemy to defeat."

"Why?"

"For several reasons. The Zone is probably the worst malarial strip of territory in the world. Wherever a pool of stagnant water, or a marsh, or swamplands are to be found in the jungle, there you would find an ideal breeding place for the anopheles. Even more difficult to contend with is the fact that a person once infected with malaria remains a potential source of infection to others, not for three days but three years. Moreover, neither the colored man nor the native is immune from malaria. It is probable that fifty per cent of the population are sources of infection."

"Good God, man! Then you can't hope to stop the ana—ano—the What's-its-name, the malarial mosquito from breeding. Ever. Why, you can't even penetrate the jungle more than a few miles. If as much as that in spots."

"The prospect sounds hopeless," echoed another member. "Impossible."

"Not hopeless, gentlemen." Gorgas looked about him with courageous eyes. "Just as nature is said to abhor a vacuum, so nature, I believe, abhors the word impossible. Nearly always she leaves man a loophole if he has the intelligence to find it. The anopheles loophole lies in his dislike of a long, nonstop flight. He can only fly two or three hundred yards. If we push their breeding places back far enough, he will be kept at a safe distance."

"How can you do that?"

"In two ways. By propagating and releasing in the worst breeding areas, insect-eating frogs, fish, spiders, and lizards."

Another of the committeemen was an angler. "Yes, of course!" he exclaimed loudly. "Fish alone would account for millions of the beastly things."

"But what about the millions that are not eaten?" Davis questioned.

"You are doubtless aware, sir, that mosquito larvae, when they hatch out, must breathe to live. If the surface of the water in which they are hatched is covered with a thin film of oil, they will be suffocated and destroyed."

"Do you deny that sufficient will live, must live, in spite of all such precautions? Sufficient to be infected by, in your own words, half the population?"

"I do not deny, governor, that many will survive all attacks," Gorgas agreed calmly. "But suppose they are not given the opportunity of biting the infected half of the population!"

"In the name of all that's holy, how would you prevent that, may I ask?"

"By screening every window in the Zone; making everyone sleep beneath mosquito netting."

The Governor looked doubtful. "That would cost millions. Millions!" His voice was unsteady. "I hesitate to forecast what Washington will have to say when I report on this meeting, colonel."

Every ship reaching Colón which had called at an American port en route brought fresh workers; a trickle of people who would soon become a flood: doctors, nurses, clerks, accountants, dentists, storekeepers, tally clerks, engineer draftsmen, builders, construction engineers, and a host of subsidiary staff, but Wesley saw little of them, for he had been transferred from the railroad to the canal staff, and was away from Colón most of the time. Whenever he passed through, however, he never failed to visit the Sandersons, who remained his firm friends, and there he saw Ingrid, whose fresh beauty seemed to be more blooming with each visit.

One night, on his way back to the Washington Hotel, he encountered Larry. They had not met since the new republic had been proclaimed, for the following night Larry had disappeared.

"Hello, there." He inspected the slender figure, and thought it looked thinner and more pathetic than ever. The face was fleshless and very worn. The mouth drooped with hopelessness. The black hair was gray

239

with dust. The clothes were the same color, and for the same reason. But the black eyes were still mischievous and alert.

"Hello, brother. Just come from the Sandersons?"

"Yes, and you? Haven't seen you since the revolution. Been looking for your mysterious valley?"

"Sure. I used the money you paid me to buy a mule. It died last week, so here I am again."

"Looking for another mule?"

"No, some more money to buy one with. Guess I'll ask Mr. Sanderson to try and fix me a temporary job with the railroad. Booking clerk, or something that won't bother my leg any."

"Why don't you give up your search, Larry? Why not settle down and take on a permanent job? You won't have any difficulty finding one, I can tell you. You'll be able to take your pick."

An obstinate shake. "I haven't covered a quarter of the territory yet. Besides, it's not only a gold mine I'm looking for now."

"Well? Or is that a secret, too?"

"Nope. I'm looking for your friend Olaf Ericson."

"Ericson! I'll be damned! For any reason?"

"Yes. I promised Ingrid. She's breaking her heart for him, poor kid." Larry assumed an air of casualness that was in no way convincing. "I thought I might as well search for two things as one, while I was about it."

"No luck?"

"None. He used to go to the Humming Bird but he hasn't been there for months now, and that means something, according to Mother María. Nor anywhere else within miles of civilization. It's my bet he's not alive."

"Going to tell Ingrid that?"

"I can't." He looked distressed. "She just worships that brother of hers, Mr. Adam. Christ! If I ever was loved like that—" He stopped abruptly. "No fear of that, brother, with this leg of mine. S'long. Be seeing you sometime." He limped off into the darkness.

35

ALTHOUGH HE WAS impatient to visit the Perrigots, Wesley was of two minds about accepting the grudging invitation which Marie had maneuvered her father into giving. In fact, the Sandersons were the first to go. He happened to visit them on the night they returned.

"How did you find old Papa Perrigot?"

240

"Not so disagreeable as I had anticipated," Frederick Sanderson admitted. "In fact, he was almost human."

"Outwardly," Madge added.

"What do you mean, honey? Don't you think he was human inside of him?"

"He was hating every minute we were there. Didn't you see his eyes?"

"Sure, I did. What of it?"

Madge smiled. "How blind you men are. He was seething. If we could have known what he was really thinking—oh, dear! I'm sure we should have been horrified."

"At least he gave us good food. And some good wines, too."

"Of course. What did you expect from a Frenchman? He has a colored cook, by the way. She told me that she had learned everything from her master."

"Was that Dolores?" Wesley asked.

"Yes. You saw her?"

"No. The girls spoke of her."

"She is a fine-looking woman. Shows traces of Spanish blood."

"I suppose he didn't mention the canal."

Frederick laughed. "He scarcely talked of anything else. Seemed disappointed I didn't know more about it." He raised his eyebrows. "You look surprised."

"I am. It's a sore subject with him. He nearly blew up when I first mentioned the possibility of our finishing it."

"Yes." He nodded thoughtfully. "As a Frenchman, he's still sore. Admits it quite frankly. But the engineer in him makes him interested in it in spite of himself."

"But the girls enjoyed your visit?"

Frederick glanced at his wife as if asking her to answer the question.

She nodded. "Every minute of it, Wesley. So long as we were still there."

Frederick grunted. "But as soon as we had gone! You think Papa had something to say?"

"Heaven knows, darling. Maybe he has *some* nice feelings."

"You don't like him much, do you, honey?"

"Not one bit," she answered with a snap.

After hearing the Sandersons' account of their visit to the Perrigot home, Wesley decided to risk going there. He wrote and asked Anne whether he might come in three weeks' time. Her reply was prompt. She thought it would be a lovely idea. Papa had been so different ever since Marie had defied him. Would he write another letter, please, asking whether he might pay the promised visit, and address it to the Perrigot house, so that she could show it to Papa?

He appreciated her reason for wanting the second letter, so he did as

241

she asked. Again, the reply was prompt. Papa had said, yes, Mr. Adam might stay a night or so.

During the next three weeks Wesley's thoughts frequently dwelled upon the coming visit. Most of the time he was excited by the prospect of spending a couple of days with Anne, but there were moments when he wondered whether he had done a wise thing. He had memories of the past which he was unable to forget: for one, the inscrutable expression which had masked Perrigot's eyes when Marie had asked whether Mr. Adam could visit them. That deliberate impassivity was more alarming than the positive reaction of annoyance or dislike; as if the old man had realized that an unguarded expression might betray the violence of his passion.

Nor could Wesley forget that Perrigot had already tried to kill him. For a long while he had refused to believe in Ericson's theory that the Frenchman had deliberately altered the position of the shrine. But since the day of the "siege" he had changed his opinion. He knew that Perrigot hated him.

What reason had Perrigot for hating him, he wondered. Had Perrigot discovered a gold mine, or a cache of Morgen's treasure, and was he protecting it against submersion by plotting the death of the two surveyors? In some respects, it seemed to add up. On the other hand, one thing about the Frenchman was certain: he was a man of intelligence. He must know that the death of two surveyors, the death of twenty surveyors, would not alter the American decision to build the canal.

The same argument applied to the notion of Perrigot's hatred being on account of not wishing his daughters to marry and leave him. By forbidding unmarried men to come to the house he might postpone the departure of two such attractive girls, but it was inevitable that sooner or later they would be enticed away by prospective husbands.

The more Wesley thought the more certain he became that Perrigot had a far more subtle reason for his hatred. He wondered whether he should keep away from a man who bore him such an implacable hate.

There were times when he chuckled at himself for being so melodramatic. It seemed ridiculous nonsense to suspect an old man like Perrigot of being a prospective murderer—until he recollected that Perrigot had already made one attempt. A sobering thought, but not sober enough to prevent his visiting the two daughters.

At Bohio he hired the pinto he had used on his last visit. The journey was uneventful, and in due course he saw along the far end of the trail the now familiar house. In a corner of the porch a figure was crouched in a chair, rocking to and fro. Rock—rock—rock—

Guess he's already seen me, Wesley thought. Probably watching every move I make with those damned uncanny eyes of his. Remind me of a snake's eyes. As malevolent as hell. Ugh! And what's going on behind

242

them, this minute? Walk into my parlor, said the spider to the fly. Can't play the shrine trick on you this time, my poor young fool. But I've other tricks up my sleeve. Watch out for yourself, Wes.

Wesley kicked the pinto into a brisker walk. "Get along there, you," he told the animal. "*You* don't have anything to worry about."

As Wesley moved along the porch toward his host he knew that Perrigot's unblinking gaze had followed his every movement from the moment he had entered the clearing in front of the house. He attempted a disarming smile.

"Good morning, Mr. Perrigot. Nice to see you again."

Not by one iota did the expression of the lined face alter. "Good morning, Mr. Adam. My daughters told me you were coming today."

Wesley flushed. "If it is not convenient, sir—"

"It is as convenient as any other day would be."

A good beginning to a two days' visit. If everything Perrigot said was to be as double edged as the first two sentences, his stay promised to be very enjoyable.

Perrigot indicated a chair. "Won't you sit down? My daughters are not far off."

"Thank you, sir." Wesley sat down.

"So the canal is to be restarted in earnest. Observe that I said restarted, and not built. I have not changed my opinion since your previous visit."

"No, sir."

"Apart from taking over the employees, and work in progress, when will the real work begin?"

"Not for some time."

The old Frenchman looked surprised. "Why not?"

"I think the Canal Commission is anxious to take precautions against disease before laborers arrive here in large numbers."

"Precautions!" The scorn in Perrigot's voice was unmistakeable. "How do your people hope to prevent disease in a country where malaria and yellow fever are more prevalent than in any other country in the world?"

"I don't know." Wesley shifted uncomfortably. "That's not my department. Apart from rumors I only know what is happening on the survey side."

"In that case," Perrigot's voice grew sharper, "you will know whether you have decided to build a sea-level or a lock canal."

"I can't properly answer that. President Roosevelt has left the decision to an advisory board of engineers."

"Then you will certainly not begin for a long time yet," Perrigot sneered.

Happily, for Wesley's sake, Marie appeared. Her eyes shone with excitement. "We're so glad you've come, Mr. Adam. Ever since your letter arrived Anne and I have been praying that it won't rain enough to prevent our riding."

243

"You will make Mr. Adam think you never go riding," Perrigot interrupted in a grating voice.

"Only with Juan," Marie pouted. "We can't talk with him." She turned back to Wesley. "Juan is the colored man who works in the fields at the back of the house."

Perrigot stopped rocking. "Do you then expect me to allow you two girls to go riding unescorted? *Dieu!* How long do you think you could ride without being accosted by the workers at Bohio? You must be mad."

"I wasn't suggesting anything of the sort, Papa." There was a bite in her voice which amused Wesley, for it confirmed his earlier opinion that Perrigot's daughters—or Marie, at any rate—were quickly ceasing to be submissive victims of parental autocracy. "Have you ever tried to talk to Juan for an hour or more, except to give him orders?"

"Why do you want to talk all the time you are riding? If you were to contemplate more and chatter less—"

"Like you, Papa?"

Perrigot frowned. "If you like," he snapped. "Besides, you have your sister."

"Anne." Marie's face turned sulky.

"Well, mademoiselle, and what's wrong with talking to Anne?"

"Nothing, except that after talking with each other for twenty years, we've nothing left to talk about." She went back to the door and called out, "Anne, Anne! Mr. Adam is here." The sharp undertone in her voice made Wesley think that her only reason for calling her sister was to avoid further argument with her father.

Anne appeared. She greeted Wesley with a shy smile. "How nice of you to come, and especially to bring such a lovely day with you after all the rain we've had. If you bring your bag I'll take you to your bedroom."

"I'm coming, too," Marie said. "I want to show Mr. Adam those orchids we picked this morning."

"You don't have to—" Anne began.

"She can go," Perrigot interrupted. "She's just as starved as you for fresh faces," he added with malice.

Anne flushed, but did not argue. She held the door open for Wesley to pass through with his bag. He heard the porch floor creak as Perrigot's chair rocked to and fro.

They went upstairs in silence, and entered the bedroom which he and Ericson had slept in. He was conscious of a change in it, but a quick glance about him failed to identify it. Realizing the trend of his thoughts Anne smiled her delight.

"I knew you would like—" she began.

"Aren't the orchids lovely?" Marie said simultaneously.

Both girls stopped short, and looked at each other.

244

"Don't you think the orchids are particularly lovely?" Marie asked quickly.

"Beautiful. What are they?"

"Lady of the Night. They're called that because they can only be smelled at night." The eyes which glanced sideways at her sister sparkled with triumph. "I didn't know whether to look for Lady of the Night or Spiritus Sanctus. Which do you prefer?"

"I don't think I know Spiritus Sanctus."

"They're very rare, like Lady of the Night. They have a stamen formed like a dove, enclosed in a white bell." She clapped her hands. "I know. Let's try to find one when we go out riding."

"It's an idea," he agreed absently. He looked at Anne. "You were saying, Miss Anne—"

"Nothing important. You'd like to wash—"

"Please. I mean, please tell me."

She colored. "I—I thought you were wondering why the room was looking different."

"I was."

"It's the—the counterpane," she said shyly. "I thought it might remind you of your country."

The counterpane was of patchwork. "It does. It's lovely. Did you make it?"

"Of course she did. You can see that," Marie answered.

"Oh, Marie!" The shadows blotted out the speckled sunshine in Anne's eyes as she turned away.

Wesley looked at Marie; his mouth grew hard. "Certainly I can see that Miss Anne made it. Only an accomplished needlewoman could have matched the colors so exquisitely."

Anger flashed in Marie's eyes. "If you're going to wash before the meal, Mr. Adam, we'll leave you," she muttered. "Don't be long. Papa will be waiting for you. Coming, Anne?" She did not wait for her sister to answer, but taking her by the hand hurried her out of the room.

There were other, subtle changes in the bedroom which Wesley discovered for himself, by degrees. There was a book by the bedside, a new novel, *The Spoilers,* by Rex Beach, which had only been published in New York a short time before: remembering that he had once written to Anne that Beach was his favorite author he believed that she must have bought it especially for the occasion. There was also a pack of his favorite cigarettes.

He glanced at the orchids, and smiled wryly. How indicative of Marie's love of the ostentatious was her contribution to his comfort, he reflected. Especially in comparison with Anne's thoughtfulness. The reflection rather pleased him, for it flattered his own judgment of character. Hadn't he

245

preferred Anne from the first time, even though on that occasion both had been as undeveloped, mentally and physically?

He was still suffused with self-satisfaction when he went downstairs, and found all three members of the family awaiting him in the cool shadows of the porch. There was a gleam of malicious amusement in Perrigot's eyes, otherwise he was in a more amiable humor. Wesley was ready to believe that the old man had guessed what had happened in the bedroom. Later he decided that it certainly was an ill wind that blew nobody any good. The atmosphere was more cheerful, and remained so throughout luncheon and afterward, when they had coffee on the veranda.

Presently Perrigot dozed, still rocking automatically. The other three gathered together at the farther end of the porch and talked disjointedly, for the sultry heat had made them equally sleepy.

Later, as the heat slackened, they discussed where they should ride. Each girl had her own idea, and just when Wesley was realizing with trepidation that he would have to be the arbiter, the old Frenchman woke up and settled the argument.

"You can ride to Bohio."

Marie pouted. "But, Papa, we know the trail to Bohio by heart. The horrible place. I hate it."

"Maybe you do, but there are no stores in the jungle, and there are in Bohio. I need cigars."

"Papa!" There were tears in Marie's voice. "Two days ago I asked whether you wanted any. You said you had plenty."

"I made a mistake," he replied blandly.

"Never mind, Marie," Anne said sweetly. "As Mr. Adam will be coming with me to Bohio, you don't need to."

"I do, too," Marie turned sullen. "If we are going, there's something from the store I need."

"I'll get it."

"No, you can't. It's something I want to choose for myself." She rose to her feet. "If we are going, let's start."

Until they reached the outer fringe of the jungle they rode in single file along the trail, then as soon as they reached the open savannah Wesley moved up beside Anne, before Marie could do so, for Anne was closest to the tobacco fields which bordered the trail. He began talking to her, but Marie quickly interrupted, pointing to a long yellow gash which disfigured the green slope of the hills on the far side of the river.

"Is it true that that cutting is going to be one of the locks of the new canal?"

"Why do you ask that, Marie?" Anne asked. "Papa has told you that it is, again and again. He worked on it."

"He might have been teasing us," Marie answered sulkily.

"He wasn't," Wesley patiently explained. "Bohio occupied quite an

246

important place in French plans. You see that big cutting nearer, with two smaller cuttings on either side? That was intended to be part of the sea-level canal. In fact, it is already deep enough for vessels of light draft. Afterward when they changed over to the idea of a lock canal, they proposed Bohio as the site for the first dam, which was why they sited the locks here."

"Are the Americans going to have a dam and locks here?"

"There's talk of our doing so."

Marie's voice grew eager.

"Will you be working here if they do?"

"Maybe. If I'm lucky."

"I do hope so. Please try to get posted here."

He glanced to his left, at Anne's serene profile. "You bet I will," he agreed.

They reached the village where Marie reluctantly left Anne and Wesley, to make her purchase from one of the Chinese stores.

Anne's eyes, no longer dark pools, were speckled with sunshine as she glanced at her companion. "Did you really mean what you told Marie, that you might be working here?"

"For a time, at least. It all depends."

"On what?"

He swallowed. "Perhaps—on you, Miss Anne," he blurted out. "Shall I —shall I try to be stationed here?"

The last shadows vanished from her eyes. But she had no time to reply, for his question was followed by a cry of amazement from the opposite sidewalk.

"Wesley!"

He turned, startled and apprehensive. Then amazement overcame him. It was Dulcie. A scowling Ackermann stood by her side.

36

WESLEY SLOWLY dismounted, then passed the reins over to Anne. "Would you hold my horse, please, Miss Anne?"

"Of course."

"Thank you. I'll return as soon as I can."

As he walked slowly across the road it occurred to him that he did not really hate either Dulcie or Ackermann. His principal emotion was irritation that they had forced their way back into his life.

"Wesley!" Dulcie exclaimed delightedly as he drew near. "Of all people!" Her naïve attitude was that of an affectionate friend.

"Hello, Dulcie!" He turned toward Ackermann, and decided that it would be amusing to force the other man to meet his own steady gaze; a scowling Ackermann, ill at ease, seemed determined to do his damnedest not to. "Hello, Ackermann."

Ackermann growled something that was unintelligible.

"What in the world are you doing here?" Dulcie continued. "I can scarcely believe it really is you."

"Why? You knew I wanted to come to Panama. The point is, what are *you* doing here?"

"On our way to California," Ackermann said harshly. He took hold of her arm. "Let's get going, Dulcie. The train will soon be due."

Dulcie shook herself free from his grasp. "The train due—but we only just got here, Hector. You told me we should be here about two hours."

The same tactless Dulcie! Wesley chuckled. He was beginning to enjoy himself.

"If you're meaning the next train for Panama, Ackermann, your first guess was right. You've at least two hours to wait."

"In that case, we don't want to spend them standing about on the sidewalk—if you can call it that," he snapped.

"For want of a better name. Of course, it isn't Providence."

For the first time a shadow passed across her eyes. "Don't talk of Providence, Wesley. I'd rather talk about—about you." Her voice was shrill. "Who was that girl with you just now?"

"For God's sake, Dulcie!" Ackermann was actually embarrassed. "That's his business, isn't it?"

"She was very beautiful."

"What of it? Are you coming?"

She stamped her foot pettishly. "Don't hurry me, Hector. You know how I loathe being hurried. I want to talk to Wesley."

"Well, I don't, and that's that."

"Feeling embarrassed?" Wesley asked him sweetly.

"Be damned to you!"

"My dear Ackermann! In front of our wife, too. You should know by now how she hates bad language."

"*Our* wife!" Ackermann choked. "If you were any sort of a man you would have let her divorce you by now."

"Divorce me!" Wesley's smile was not without bitterness. "Isn't the boot on the other foot? Besides, you shouldn't have disappeared so completely. My attorney couldn't trace your address."

"Oh!" Dulcie wailed. "*You* weren't thinking of divorcing *me*, Wesley Adam?"

The two men exchanged glances. Ackermann shrugged. "Look, Dulcie,"

248

he said in a weary voice, "if you can't use a little common sense once in a while, let's leave the subject of divorce out of our conversation."

And Larry had suggested he hate Ackermann, Wesley thought. Good Heavens! he was beginning to feel almost sorry for the poor devil.

Dulcie looked at Ackermann with bewildered eyes. "But you just said to Wesley, if he was a man he would have let me divorce him."

"I know! I know! But that's not to say you should expect it from him as of right."

Wesley grinned. "See here, folks, why not let's settle this question of divorce in a friendly way, right here and now—"

"On the sidewalk?"

"No, Dulcie, not on the sidewalk. There's a sort of café round the corner. You know the French were here, working on the canal. Wherever the French go they must have their cafés."

"You're in a great hurry for a divorce," she snapped. "Well, I'm just not going to discuss our private affairs in one of those French cafés. I'm perfectly sure it would be horribly dirty, and full of insects."

He looked down at her with clouding eyes, for her words made him realize that he was in a hurry to be divorced. He could still remember the way Anne's eyes had glowed when he had spoken of the possibility of his working at Bohio.

"If you know of a better place—" he began.

"Where are you living?"

"Wherever my work takes me. But I'm at the Washington in Colón at least once in every week."

"We'll meet you the next time you are there."

"That's impossible," Ackermann exploded. "Our ship leaves Panama the day after tomorrow."

"Then you'll cancel the booking tonight, and make it for another ship next week," she ordered.

"See here, Dulcie—"

She ignored his protestations, and smiled up at Wesley. "Did you miss me very much, Wesley? I did you, sometimes." Her blue eyes filled with laughter. "It made Hector furious, but for a long time I kept on calling him Wes."

"For God's sake!" Once more Ackermann seized her by the arm, and this time dragged her into the Chinese store just behind. As they passed through the door he motioned to Wesley with his free hand, a gesture which Wesley interpreted as an invitation to take advantage of Dulcie's absence and go. As he walked away Marie came running up after him.

"Who was that, Mr. Adam?" she asked jealously.

"You'd be surprised!" He chuckled. "My wife."

She did not respond to his laughter. "The one that ran away?" she asked in a sharp voice.

249

"Yes. The others all stuck by me."

"You're not being at all funny. What is she doing here? Does she want to become your wife again?"

"The man with her was the man she ran away with, so it wouldn't seem likely."

"Oh!" But she remained unconvinced. "Then why is she here, if she didn't follow you?"

"She happens to be on her way to California. Still honeymooning, no doubt," he added, bitter for the first time.

They saw Anne in the near distance, so nothing more was said just then. Nor later, when they joined her, for she was better mannered than her sister, and asked no questions. He decided to wait until they were alone before telling her what had happened.

He reckoned without Marie. With the co-operation of her father, she succeeded in remaining with Anne and Wesley for every moment of the rest of that day, except when Perrigot was engaging Wesley's attention. This meant most of the evening following the meal; for the old man, with a malicious chuckle, first reminded him that he had promised to play chess, and then, when they did so, proceeded to make a fool of him. The old Frenchman was determined to make Wesley's visit so unpleasant that he would hesitate to repeat it. This thought roused his Stewart obstinacy, and decided him to beat Perrigot at the Frenchman's own game. The more foolish he was made to appear at chess, the more he pretended to enjoy being metaphorically pushed around. He laughed and chuckled with apparent delight at the subtle moves which constantly checkmated him, and gladly extolled Perrigot's skill.

In due course this constant reference to his skill nettled the Frenchman, who knew that it was his visitor's own lack of it which made victory so simple. Observing the effect his tactics were having, Wesley was encouraged to continue. Eventually Perrigot became so exasperated that he made the careless mistake of leaving his king vulnerable to a check which meant the capture of his queen. By good fortune Wesley saw what had happened, and was able to take advantage of it. In the sixth move after capturing the queen he checkmated Perrigot.

He exaggerated his genuine satisfaction. "You see, Mr. Perrigot, your skill is catching. I am improving enormously."

"Mon Dieu!" Perrigot stared at his visitor with incredulous eyes. "You cannot be congratulating yourself on that game."

"But I won it, sir. I must be improving, otherwise I couldn't have succeeded in beating you."

"Through no skill of yours," Perrigot angrily shouted. "If I had not, for once, overlooked the fact that you could put me in check by taking the bishop, I should have checkmated you in five moves."

"Ah! But I gave you no chance of recovering from your mistake, did I?"

"Pah!" The old man swept the pieces off the board, and muttering furiously to himself in French, sat back in his chair. "Go and amuse the girls."

By then the hour was late, so after another fifteen minutes he suggested bed.

The following morning Wesley realized that his host had altered his tactics overnight. Whereas, until then, Perrigot had made sure that his visitor should not be left alone with either girl, now he invented frequent excuses for leaving him alone with Marie. Marie did not hesitate to take advantage of the opportunity: he soon became aware how often he was being maneuvered into gazing into her volcanic eyes, or smelling the strong perfume which permeated her hair.

The knowledge that Marie was trying deliberately to attract his interest was disturbing. In a flamboyant way she was devilishly attractive, and he knew it would be exciting to wrap his arms around her soft plump waist, and feel her snuggling up to him, face upturned, warm lips slightly open, devilish eyes inviting, challenging—

To avoid the possibility of being tempted to experiment he concentrated on remembering Anne. There was something about Anne, even when her physical presence was absent, that was dependable. One would draw more physical and moral strength from the older sister than from the younger. Marie wouldn't give you strength, he believed; she would sap it from you.

The combination of Marie and Perrigot in a conspiracy to prevent his being alone with Anne succeeded. He had to leave for Colón without having had the opportunity of asking Anne to marry him.

In the mornings, the manager of the Washington Hotel usually occupied himself in the little grocery store which adjoined the equally small hotel office. He was there, some days later, when Wesley arrived in Colón. He saw Wesley pass by, and called out.

"Meester Adam, if you please." He was a squat, black-haired Italian who punctuated his words with a variety of gestures. The shrug of his large, square shoulders was known, and copied, up and down the Chagres Valley.

Wesley entered the shop.

"I am sorry, Meester Adam, but I can no longer keep your bed vacant while you are away."

"Why not? I pay regularly—"

"Please!" The manager's shrug was a magnificent effort. "It is not a question of money, but room. Veesitors come here alla day long, and say to me, 'See here, meester, I wanta bed; you must hava bed someplace,' and when I tell them no, they don' believe me, because someone has tell

251

them there are beds here not being slept in. So they say rude things to me. I do not like."

Wesley could believe this story because he knew that the hotel, owned by the P.R.R., was only leased to the man on condition that he would take care of any railroad employees who might be sent there before late afternoon. Nevertheless, he argued with the man.

"Look, you know I'm a railroad employee, and need a room to come back to. You've kept it for me all this time—"

"Times ain't what they was," the manager interrupted in a surly manner. "A dozen hotels wouldn' be beeg enough for all the people coming to Colón. Every day there are more and more."

This, too, Wesley could believe. He had seen for himself that the streets were fuller than ever before.

"See here, meester," the manager went on, with a leer, "Maybe you find some nice woman to offer you da spare bed in her house much more cheap than the hotel does; and maybe she offer a beeg strong man like you more than a bed."

Wesley ignored the suggestion. "Give me a month, Giulio, and I'll see what I can do."

"A mon', eh?" Giulio considered the proposition, then shrugged. "All right, I giva you da mont', because I like you, meester, though I wouldn' do it for nobody else. But no more than da mont', see. Not a day more."

Wesley thought about Giulio's ultimatum several times that day. Each time it made him swear angrily at having been deprived of the chance to propose to Anne. As a married man he could apply for one of the small houses which the Isthmian Canal Commission was putting up for the use of their employees. The prospect of sharing a home of his own with Anne was too exciting to be postponed: he decided to write that night and propose marriage—a hatefully cold-blooded method of asking a woman to share one's future happiness and life, but in his case it was necessary. On second thought he was too impatient to wait for the evening. He stole fifteen minutes from writing out a report on a routine gradient check, and roughed out a letter there and then. When it was finished he reread it, and was very pleased with it. Happily humming a lilting tune he slipped the paper into his pocket. He would read it through in bed; and if necessary touch it up, he blithely resolved.

Time dragged slowly. Later he hurried over his evening meal, not enjoying it in the least, and afterward he went for a walk along Coral Avenue. As he passed by the Sanderson house he thought of paying them a brief visit; but impatience took him past, both going and returning. At a ridiculously early hour he went back to the hotel, and up to his bedroom. Far more quickly than usual he undressed and got into bed.

An hour later he blew out the candle, and extending his limbs in a luxurious stretch, gazed into the semidarkness. The letter, completed, addressed, and stamped was in his jacket pocket. Tomorrow it would be posted: delivery would follow within twenty-four hours at the latest. Allow a day for consideration of the proposal, another for writing her reply, a third for delivery—

The slight snap of the bedroom door latch springing back into the socket made him turn his head quickly. There was enough light in the room to enable him to see the shadowy outline of a woman. He surprised a movement, and she was no longer a black shadow but a white, ethereal specter moving toward him, feet as naked as her body.

He had just time to realize that she was exquisitely built, petite and slim, with little breasts no bigger than pink-tinted apples, then she was on the bed beside him, her face bent over his, her lips seeking his, her hands first clasping his to her breasts, then stroking his shoulders, his chest, his flesh, tantalizing, teasing—

Mad minutes followed. His brain was paralyzed; his conscience; everything. Everything save the fierce, explosive urge to satisfy the suppressed desires of months, years. Who, and why didn't matter. Nothing mattered except the compelling need to accept what the gods were offering—

As soon as his heart had stopped pounding sufficiently for him to speak without panting he raised himself on one elbow and stared at the face beside him. He could see that it was a small face, with a tiny, open mouth, and closed eyelids, but no more: the room was too dark.

"In God's name, who are you?"

The eyes opened. "As if you didn't know, dear?"

"Dulcie!" He must be dreaming, he thought. "Dulcie!" he repeated in a voice that didn't sound like his. "You—*you!*"

She laughed coolly. Her laugh hadn't changed much, he decided. "Well?"

"You! Making love like—like—" He stopped short. Like a whore, was what he meant. Dulcie, of all people. Unbelievable, and damned distasteful.

She could scarcely fail to comprehend what he was thinking, he reflected, but she did. She laughed again, archly this time. "After all, I'm still your wife, legally."

"Where's Ackermann?" he demanded brusquely.

"I've sent him away. He's on his way back to Providence."

"Good God!" His lips twitched in a bitter smile. "Why aren't you with him? Why is he going to Providence, not California? I'm damned if I can understand what's happening—"

"I've come back to you, Wesley dear," she explained. "I'm going to be your wife again."

He freed himself from her grasp with a rough gesture. "I'll be damned if you are. Good God—"

253

"Don't be dramatic," she said calmly. "I realize that I was wrong to leave you and run away with Hector. For your sake I'm sorry for what I did, my dear. But when I saw you the other day I realized where my duty lay."

Her words supplied the answer to the problem that had been tantalizing him. "Your duty? Or the girl with me?"

She gave a careless laugh. "How absurd! A chit like that! A native girl! You insult me." But the shrill undertone in her voice supplied the true answer. She caught hold of one of his hands, and rubbed it against her cheek. "My dear, when I saw you I realized the wrong I had done you, leaving you to live a lonely life here in this barbarous country."

"What about the wrong you will be doing dear Hector, leaving him to live his lonely life alone in Providence?"

She lifted her face. "It no longer bothers me what happens to him. It's you I love, Wesley. You, and only you."

With despair he realized that for once she was speaking from her heart. Jealous she might be of Anne, but that the love she had once felt for him was reborn he could no longer doubt. It proclaimed itself in the soft serenity of her eyes, in the depths of her voice, in the quick rise and fall of her small, compact breasts, in the steady pressure of her hands.

"You'll take me back, my darling. I've nobody else to care for me now. Nowhere to go to." A note of panic made her voice tremble. "You won't desert me now?"

Oh God! he thought. God! God! God! The reiterated oath hammered in his head like the fluttering beat of a sick heart. He no longer loved her. She meant less to him than the pretty daughter of the hotel manager. Besides, there was Anne—

"I'm not going back to the U.S. if that's what you're thinking," he said harshly. "Not until the canal is built."

"Of course not. I'm willing to stay here with you. I've told you, I love you. I'll do anything you say, my darling, if only you'll take me back."

"It's not safe for a woman not born here to remain. There's yellow fever, malaria, cholera— Don't you understand, Dulcie? It's not safe."

"It wasn't any safer when you first asked me to live here with you."

"I didn't know how bad it was. The chance of a non-Panamanian white to survive for more than a few years is only one in twenty. Worse than that, for all I know. You can't live here, Dulcie."

"What about you? It's just as dangerous for you, isn't it?"

"I'm being well paid for the risk. Besides, I'm strong and healthy. I'm becoming inoculated by mild doses of malaria."

"If I'm prepared to take the risk you'll have me back, won't you, my darling? You must. I've nowhere else to go."

He knew she had defeated him. "Those whom God hath joined together—"

254

37

MADGE PROVED her friendship for Wesley in the difficult weeks following Dulcie's decision to remain with him. To begin with, she found them a small house to live in. This was one of those the French had built for the canal employees in the new town of Cristobal, to the south of Colón. It was a stone's throw from the huge two-story building which De Lesseps had built for his headquarters, and which had recently been handed over to the Canal Commission for their use.

Madge also undertook, and successfully fulfilled the even more difficult task of introducing Dulcie to Colón and Cristobal society, and managed to convince her friends that Dulcie and Wesley were really married.

Wesley appreciated most her sympathetic understanding. Sometimes, too, when she glanced at him, he read in her serene eyes an appreciation of the sacrifice he had made. She knew that love, once lost, was beyond recall.

One advantage for him, was the establishment of a home. He also had the satisfaction of being able to return the hospitality of the Sandersons, and of others on the railroad staff who had entertained him. Apart from that, he was immensely glad that he was no longer stationed in Colón, for he was away at least six days out of seven. Had he been obliged to spend more time with Dulcie, her companionship would have been intolerable. Now that he was no longer blinded by affection, her mannerisms, and her inane chatter so grated on his nerves that he had difficulty in remaining reasonably good tempered. He could only comfort himself with the fact that, in a few hours' time, he would be away again.

When he visited Panama again, Uncle Bill had something to say on the subject.

"Heard a strange rumor about you the other day, lad." He seemed ill at ease.

"Well?"

"That you're living with a woman."

Wesley nodded. "That's so. I am. I've married her."

"But—" Godwin looked reproachful. "You didn't tell me you'd got a divorce."

"I didn't because I haven't."

"Good God! You married the woman bigamously!"

"No."

"No!" He was staring at Wesley in frowning perplexity, when he relaxed with a grin of comprehension. "Dulcie is dead! It's no use my saying I'm sorry—"

"No need to either, Uncle Bill. She's not."

"Then I'm damned if I understand."

"Dulcie is the woman."

"Jesus!" His expression was incredulous. "You asked her back?"

"I didn't ask," Wesley explained. "She just came."

"She came here—to Panama?"

"She was passing through—" and Wesley related the story of Dulcie's return. When he had finished Uncle Bill nodded his head with satisfaction.

"I'm real glad to hear the news, lad. Dulcie and you back in double harness. Guess you're happier now—" He saw Wesley's expression, "Aren't you?" he asked sharply.

"I wish I could say I was. But I'm not, Uncle Bill. It makes me feel a skunk to say so, but Dulcie's going off with Ackermann did something to me. I can't explain, but Dulcie doesn't mean a thing to me any more."

"You don't have to explain," Godwin muttered. "I know what you mean. From personal experience."

"I'm sorry—"

"What about Ackermann," he broke in, gruffly. "Did he take it lying down?"

Wesley stubbed out his cigarette with an angry gesture. "I think he jumped at the opportunity. I'm half expecting a present from him this Christmas, in grateful thanks! God! We men are swine about women. How in hell can we love a woman one year, and hate her the next? Are we deceiving her when we say we love her, or ourselves when we think we hate her?"

"Are you in love with someone else? That French girl you've told me about, for instance?"

"You mean Anne Perrigot. I don't know, Uncle Bill. I thought I was, but now I'm not sure what love is. How do I know she'll not mean as little to me, in a few years' time, as Dulcie does? Not that the possibility arises—now," he concluded bitterly.

"How about the girl? Does she love you?"

"I think so."

Godwin's gesture was one of hopelessness. Both men were silent for a while. The newspaperman was the first to speak again, in a more cheerful voice.

"We seem to be going ahead with cleaning up to get ready for the big job. The payroll must be mounting. Come Saturday night and you can't move for the men who've come to spend their earnings on drink and women."

"Colón's the same. There's little sleep before two A.M. for anyone living near the wrong end of Bottle Alley. Men and materials are pouring into the town. Heaven knows where they'll put either if they don't soon build fresh accommodation. Talking about the payroll, I heard the other day that it's already nearing the five-thousand mark."

Godwin nodded. "Near enough, according to official figures. By the way, lad, watch out for yourself. This morning our correspondent in Colón reported two cases of yellow fever there."

"Only two, that's something," he muttered uneasily.

"Two are enough. But they are not isolated, Wesley. In the past two weeks three other cases have been reported, two from Colón, one from Mindi. and one from Gatun. The Mindi victim died yesterday, poor devil."

"Then it's spreading?"

Godwin shrugged. "So it seems."

It had seemed to Wesley that the work of preparing the Canal Zone was going smoothly, but one Saturday night, when the Sandersons, Dulcie, and he were sitting on the porch, enjoying the comparative coolness of the evening, he learned from Frederick that this was not so.

He was watching the lights of an approaching trampship as it nosed its way toward one of the P.R.R. piers.

"Another shipload of material," he commented, indicating the ship with the end of his pipe. Somebody's getting a hustle on."

"You think so?" Frederick chuckled. "Chief Engineer Wallace wouldn't agree with you."

"If he's asking for miracles! But I never come home without seeing something new along the track. Where's all the machinery coming from?"

"Out of the jungle, Wes. Left behind by the French, and thank God for it! Without it, Mr. Wallace would be hamstrung."

"What about new machinery? Isn't it flowing in?"

"Trickling in would be the better word. Work on the canal is the responsibility of the government, not of private contractors."

"Well?"

"You know how governments work. Or don't you? If Wallace needs six washers he has to apply to Washington for them in triplicate—or quadruplicate, for all I know. After some smart guy back home has decided that for economy's sake four washers should be made to do the work of six, he returns the copy requisition for four with suitable comments. Even so, four washers are better than none, so does Mr. Wallace buy them? He does not. He can't buy anything without asking for bids. And speaking of buying, how is the commissariat working with your surveyor?"

Wesley grinned. "Don't mention the word 'commissariat' to a surveyor, Frederick, if you want to remain on good terms with him. The natives live like princes compared with us poor devils. If some of us weren't good shots we'd darn near starve."

"See what I mean? What do you shoot?"

257

"Babies."

Dulcie gave a little scream. "How could you shoot babies, Wesley?" she demanded in a horrified voice. "How wicked! Even if they are colored. Besides, why should you want to shoot poor little innocent babies?"

"To eat."

"Wesley! Oh—"

"Save your pity, Mrs. Adam," Frederick suggested dryly. "He means monkeys, I guess."

She frowned her annoyance. "If that's what you mean, why can't you say so, Wesley, instead of trying to make your wife look a fool?"

Madge tried to appease her. "You see, Dulcie, when a monkey has been skinned it looks horribly like a baby."

"Too darned like one," Wesley confirmed. "A number of the boys can't eat monkey meat for that reason. But they go mighty hungry."

"It's as bad as that?" This was Frederick again.

"Every bit, when we get into the jungle proper."

Frederick nodded. "It's the same all along the line. You know it's Colonel Gorgas' idea to have wire screens over every window and door in the Canal Zone. He can't get enough wire even for the hospitals."

"Speaking of hospitals, what's the latest on yellow fever?"

Sanderson's face was grave, as he glanced quickly at Dulcie. "Bad," he replied in a low voice. "Out of nineteen cases reported last month, there have already been eight deaths. It's spreading quickly, and when the rainy season begins—" He shrugged.

Colonel Gorgas spared neither himself nor his staff in trying to check the spreading fever. Corps of inspectors made house-to-house searches in all the towns and villages along the Chagres Valley. Immediately a suspect was found, or otherwise reported, he or she was taken to one of the isolation hospitals, and placed in a room protected by screening from mosquito invasion, and constantly fumigated. Any house suspected of harboring infection was fumigated. By every mail he sent orders to Washington for the material and equipment to install water mains for every house in Colón and Panama, and screen every window, and drain and pave every street.

But neither Governor Davis nor the Canal Commission could believe in the necessity for such grandiose plans. Instead of supplying in hundreds they sent ones. Nothing Gorgas could do or say made much difference.

The disease continued to spread; particularly among the newly arrived recruits, whose bodies had not become accustomed to fighting mild attacks of tropical disorders. With the coming of the first rains the graph which recorded the number of cases rose in a steep climb.

Away in the mountains northeast of Cruces, Wesley knew nothing of what was happening in the Chagres Valley. Aided by three newcomers to

258

Panama, Richardson, Steinbeck, and Macdonald, he was plotting an altitude map.

"What's this for anyway?" Macdonald asked one evening, as all four of them sat round a campfire having a last smoke before turning in. Macdonald was the youngest. "This survey, I mean."

"The Canal Commission ordered a new survey directly the treaty was signed," Wesley explained.

"I thought the French had already surveyed the country years ago."

Wesley nodded. "They had, and an excellent job they did too. But the Commission naturally wanted a check. That's what we're doing now."

"Yeah, I know, but that's not what I meant when I asked you what it's for. I meant, why are we surveying the mountains? I thought the canal had to be level with the sea."

"Nothing's settled about what type of canal we're going to build."

"For the love of Pete! When are they going to know, then? When they've finished it? Besides, suppose we build a lock canal, Wesley, it won't come anywheres near here by miles."

"It might at that."

"Through these mountains?" Macdonald laughed with a knowing air. "Did you know that pigs were flying in Europe yesterday?"

Wesley grinned, and explained that it was necessary to check the elevation of all mountains within an area of hundreds of square miles to find out how far the water would spread on either side of the prism of the canal proper; and also the highest level an inland lake, created by a dam at Bohio, would reach at any given spot.

Later, when they had completed their assignment, the four members of the survey party, together with their Indian guide and porters, returned to Gorgona, their nearest railroad stop. The station time table and clock between them indicated that the next train for Colón was due in twenty minutes' time. But the booking clerk laughed.

"Mister," he said to Wesley, "ain't you been in Panama long enough to know that the P.R.R. don't never run on time nowadays?"

"It did when I first came here."

"You don't look that old." The man laughed at his own feeble joke. "You fellers look like you been in the jungle."

"So we have."

"You surveyors?"

"Yes."

"Say, is it true the railroad's going to be relocated?"

"Maybe."

"'Bout time, I'd say. It's due to collapse any year now, and the scare ain't helping it any. If somebody don't do something soon, it'll just come to a stop, see."

"What scare?"

The clerk stared at Wesley. "You joking?" Then he understood. "P'raps you ain't if you've been in the jungle some time. You know Chief Engineer Wallace was due back here after a visit to Washington?"

"I read something about it in the *Star and Herald* before we left civilization."

"Well, he gets back here, see, and finds an epidemic of yellow fever is raging. More'n sixty cases this month already. So what's he do? Turns round and gets the hell out of the Isthmus just as quick as the bloody steamer can take him."

"Wallace resigned!" Wesley looked grim. "Not so good."

"Sure it ain't, brother, and there's worse'n that. A lot of the fellers that come here since Uncle Sam took over the canal is hotfooting it back to the States. There just ain't enough ships running to take 'em all back."

"You mean, because of yellow jack?" The speaker was Steinbeck. He sucked his lips.

"No reason else."

"Where's—where's the epidemic worse?"

The booking clerk leered at the surveyor. "Everywheres, brother. Everywheres them skeeters fly, see. You going, too?"

"I—I haven't thought about it."

The clerk winked. "And I ain't thinking of it neither."

The Colón train arrived nearly one hour late. There was very little conversation exchanged between the surveyors. Young Macdonald seemed ready to talk, but both Richardson and Steinbeck snapped back at him, and spent their time either staring at the distant jungle, or waving their handkerchiefs about to keep mosquitoes away.

Wesley was equally silent, because he found himself dreading the thought of returning to Colón, and spending not just one night with Dulcie but several; for his period of leave had come while he had been in the jungle.

They reached Colón in the middle of the afternoon. When Wesley said good-by to his companions and said he would be seeing them sometime, their glances wavered, and they did not reply. Only young Macdonald.

"Sure, Wesley," he said with a cheeky grin. "In Bottle Alley."

Wesley hired a cab to take him to his house in Cristobal. It was driven by a Jamaican Negro who shouted abuse at everyone in his way. It seemed to Wesley that the journey had never been done more quickly.

A man standing in front of the door watched Wesley approach, and did not move.

"Wanting something, brother?"

Wesley's temper rose. "To get in—" he began hotly. "This is my house, so get the hell out of the way."

"Calm down, brother, calm down. You can't go in. Orders, see."

"Orders?"

"Yeah. House being fumigated."

"Oh!" Wesley grew more calm. You don't happen to know where my wife is, do you? I'll look for her."

The man jerked his thumb backward at the house.

"She the lady living there?"

"Yes."

"Sorry, brother." He tried to look sympathetic. "She was taken to hospital late last night. Yellow jack," he added, apparently as an afterthought.

38

ONE GLANCE AT Wesley's serious face told Madge that he knew of Dulcie's illness. She led him into the parlor and made him relax in an armchair. Then she pulled another chair near enough to him to push the wiry, ginger hair from his forehead and stroke it with her plump fingers.

"Poor Wesley!" she soothed him. "If I had known you all were due back today I could have been at the station to give you warning."

"She looks awful," he gulped. "Oh God!"

"You have seen her?"

He nodded. "I went home. It was being fumigated. The man on guard told me she had been taken to hospital. I went there."

"Don't talk now, Wesley dear. Some other time."

"I want to. It might help. I can't keep it bottled up." His husky voice was almost unrecognizable. "She didn't recognize me, Madge. Her face was shrunken and red, and covered with awful patches—and she used to be so pretty—"

"As it will be again, when she's had time to recover."

"She will never be well," he stated flatly. "She's dying."

"Nonsense! Lots of people recover from yellow fever. You've been here long enough to know that."

"Not when it's severe. The doctor warned me. She may not last another twenty-four hours. She had a convulsion while I was with her." He shuddered, as the memory of it tortured him afresh.

She realized that it would be both useless and cruel to talk about recovery, so she comforted him as best she could. When Ingrid brought in coffee and some of Madge's homemade cookies, he ate and drank with appetite, for he had had nothing since early morning.

Presently he made a move to rise. "I must try to book a room at the Washington."

Madge pushed him gently back into the chair. "It would be a waste of time. There isn't a room vacant in the town, Wesley. People are sleeping anywhere and everywhere they can't be rained on."

"Another ship in?"

"Yes, but that's not the cause. Most of the people who can't find beds are not those off the ship, but recent arrivals waiting for accommodation to get away from here."

"The booking clerk at Bohio was telling us. It's a genuine panic then?"

"Yes." There was an uneasy expression in her eyes, but she tried to speak bravely. "Most of us haven't much courage when we are tested, have we? Suppose all the doctors and nurses ran whenever an epidemic broke out."

He shrugged, in no mood to be interested in the heroism of the medical profession. "It won't worry me to sleep out, after weeks of sleeping out in the jungle. Anyway, I'll be more fortunate than most, having a sleeping bag."

"You'll do nothing of the sort," she stated firmly. "You'll sleep right here, in this house."

"You haven't room, Madge—"

"I'm sure Ingrid will be glad to let you have her room for a few nights. She's a sweet girl, and won't mind one bit sleeping on the porch. We have a spare camp bed."

Wesley made an effort, and became more his usual self than he had been since first hearing the news of Dulcie's illness.

"No. I'll sleep on the porch, and be grateful for even that much comfort."

Eventually he gained his point. Later, accompanied by Frederick, he walked over to the hospital for the latest news of Dulcie. The news was no better. But when Wesley suggested remaining at the hospital throughout the night, a harassed doctor informed him there was no necessity. She was not likely to die for another twelve hours at least.

"Come and sleep," Frederick urged. "You can't do any good here."

"And you'll be in the way," the doctor bluntly added. "Come back as soon as you like after dawn, but for Pete's sake get out of here until then."

After leaving the hospital grounds Wesley said that he was going for a walk around the town. "I want to make myself tired enough to sleep," he explained.

"Why not, Wes? I'll come with you. I'm not so good at getting to sleep myself, these nights. When I think of Madge—"

"Why not send her home for a few months?"

"Christ! Do you think I haven't tried to do just that? You know Madge. She won't go without me."

"Haven't you some leave due?"

"Soon. I could probably work it, Wes, but I'm not ratting just when there's a staff shortage."

They walked awhile in silence, but the night around them was far from silent. From every saloon and cantina they passed came sounds of singing and laughing and quarreling. Wesley distinguished a note of hysteria underlying the shouting. When he commented on this fact, Frederick confirmed it.

"It's a form of hysteria sure enough, and it's been getting more pronounced for some time. Ever since the panic began. It's fear driving them to drink, Wes. When they're liquored up they forget about yellow jack. Or maybe they want to sample as much as they can of what life offers before it's too late."

"'Drink deep, for tomorrow we die,'" Wesley muttered.

"That's right, and who can blame the poor devils?" Frederick sounded morose. He added, "I don't say it's all fear. A lot of men drink and whore for want of anything better to do. And that's bad for the canal. Too many hours of work are lost the next day."

They made their way down Bottle Alley, but long before they reached the district where the prostitutes congregated in their squalid rooms Wesley saw justification for his companion's remarks. Two men came reeling out of a saloon and began flailing at each other. They were quickly followed out by a small crowd who encouraged the fight with loud, drunken yells. They had not long been paddling in the mire when one of the men tripped and fell headlong. He was quickly on his knees, but his opponent lashed out with his foot, and kicked the kneeling man on the point of the chin. The man moaned as he collapsed sideways into the mire. The winner kicked the prostrate man in the ribs, and laughed loudly as the loser twitched convulsively.

"See what I mean?" Frederick muttered. "Ten to one that kick broke a rib. Even if it didn't, that poor devil won't be fit for work tomorrow or the next day. There are more than fifteen thousand men on the payroll, but I'll bet you an even dollar there are never more than fourteen thousand at work on a Monday morning."

Farther along the street they saw another man lying unconscious on the sidewalk, face toward a wall. His arm was twisted beneath him into an unnatural, grotesque bend. Easy to diagnose a broken arm. Another twenty yards farther on four men were carrying away a fifth, whose face had a bloody wound down the left side.

"What's the use of prohibiting drink in the Zone?" Frederick asked bitterly. "The men have only to cross the border into Colón or Panama?"

They walked on as far as they could, but when they reached the district of the prostitutes it became too much of a physical effort to thrust their way through the loiterers crowding the sidewalks, so they stood still and watched for a few minutes before turning back.

"Another cause of lost working hours," Frederick went on. "Venereal diseases! I know one isn't supposed to mention such a shocking illness in polite society, but a doctor was telling me in the club the other day that it's rampant in Colón. Not a very pretty sight, is it?" He waved at the street before them; in particular, at one shed where a nude woman was dancing with a young American whose face, although flushed with drink and excitement, was still white enough to show that he was a recent arrival in the tropics.

"Know what, Wes, it'll pay the government to reverse their idea of preferring single men for the work here. The general run of married men won't be interested in that sort of thing. They'll work all the harder for knowing the little woman's at home, waiting with a meal ready. That is," he added, "if Colonel Gorgas succeeds in his boast of stamping out yellow fever. Doesn't look like he's having much luck at the moment."

The remark was an unfortunate one. It wrenched Wesley's thoughts away from Bottle Alley, by reminding him that his wife was dying of that same fever. His few minutes of distraction were over. Time to return to the world of hideous reality: Dulcie might be needing him, calling for him—

"Let's go," he ordered brusquely.

Dulcie died at 4:30 P.M. the following afternoon, and was buried fifteen hours later at Mount Hope Cemetery. When Wesley looked along the hundreds of rows of white crosses, for the first time he had doubts about the success of the canal. If Gorgas failed in his task the whole project could collapse for want of labor. America had the money. America would produce the machinery. America had the driving power to overcome the obstacles. Nevertheless, for how long could America recruit men when it was learned how poor was their chance of survival.

For three days Wesley drove himself almost crazy with remorse. He could feel no genuine sorrow for Dulcie's death, yet he reproached himself for his feelings toward her, and for not having forgiven her for the wrong she had done to him. With the dawn of the fourth day his natural resilience asserted itself, and he began to see matters in a truer perspective. He also began to plan his next trip to the jungle. His first visit was to Mr. Schwartz, who was responsible for posting the survey parties.

Schwartz gave him a sympathetic pat on the shoulder. "Sorry to hear of your loss, Adam." He shook his square, graying head. "A fine homecoming! Must have been a shock to you."

"Yes, sir," Wesley agreed.

"Bloody climate!" Schwartz spat. "See here, Adam, if you'd like a few more days' leave—"

"No, sir. Work is what I'm looking for right now."

"Don't blame you. I'd be the same. Easiest way to forget." He scribbled aimlessly on the blotting pad before him. "What have you in mind? Carrying on where you left off?"

"Yes, sir."

He shook his square head. "There's nobody to go with you. All the assistant staff are away."

"Steinbeck and Richardson are on leave, sir—"

"Yes?" His smile was grim. "They've resigned. So have Curtis, Morgan, Lefevre, and a few more."

"Yellow jack?"

"Of course. Can't blame 'em, I suppose. If I was young, life would mean something to me, too. Not that it doesn't now, but I got responsibilities, and I want the money. Besides, I want to see the canal built sometime. Just now work's more or less at a standstill. You'd better work here until more staff arrive. If they do, before this scare dies down," he added.

So Wesley remained on in Colón, and was depressed by what he saw. Not only was vital preparatory work on the canal being held up for want of men, but all the good work that the Sanitary Department had done to date was being offset by the apathetic attitude of the native Panamanians toward Colonel Gorgas' revolutionary plans for stamping out the dreaded disease. Many of the few precious screens which he had bullied Washington into sending were torn down and destroyed. The sanitary bins which were being gradually supplied to all the houses were ignored: it was so much easier to throw all garbage into the street and let the weather rot down what the crows did not destroy. After all, what were a few deaths here and there? One must die sooner or later. If the Americans were afraid of dying young, let them stay away from the Isthmus until the black vomit had died out of its own accord. It always did, sooner or later.

The superstitious stoutly maintained that there was a jinx on the canal, and that it never would be finished, either by the French, the Americans, the Panamanians themselves, or anyone else. More than a few people, not normally superstitious, agreed with this prophecy.

Exactly two weeks after Wesley's return to work, the new Governor of the Canal Zone, Charles E. Magoon, arrived at Colón. Within a matter of days energetic measures were being taken in support of Colonel Gorgas' plans. Every suspected victim of yellow fever was either transferred to a hospital with screened doors and windows; or, if in his own home, forced to have all his windows and doors screened so that no stegomyia mosquito could enter or leave the building. Immense stocks of wire screening were ordered from the United States, together with the materials necessary for erecting waterworks, constructing efficient sewage systems, making sidewalks, and paving roads, and tons of pyrethrum powder and sulphur. Laws were passed to punish those guilty of damage or destruction of screens already erected. Guards, to see that the law was respected, were enrolled and posted for duty.

The Governor's next move was even more drastic. All work on the canal was practically halted, and every available laborer temporarily assigned to the Sanitary Department. All public buildings and private houses in Colón and Panama were fumigated. Such vast fires were lighted, and fed with the dirt and refuse of centuries, that for days the sun was hidden by a fog of dirty yellow smoke, and the air was black with flying smuts. Sewage and fresh-water pipes were laid. Tens of thousands of tons of ballast material were emptied into the mire on which the biggest part of Colón was built, until the surface was solid enough to support paving stones to be laid. Receptacles were built for the household garbage, and a daily collection organized.

Almost overnight the town of Colón, which had been just over fifty years in the making, bore a changed look. But neither Gorgas nor Magoon was satisfied. Water was piped into every house, and all the tanks which for fifty years had been practically the only means of water supply, were forcibly removed and new ones supplied.

Before long the success of these drastic measures was proved beyond all possible doubt, even to the lethargic Panamanians. The curve of the fever graph took first a slow curve downward, and then, quickly, a steep plunge. Four months after the arrival of Governor Magoon at Colón, his medical officers were in a position to report to him that the epidemic had been checked, only one new case having been recorded during the last two weeks.

Before the year ended Colonel Gorgas knew that he had defeated yellow fever for all time.

The work of remaking Colón kept every available surveyor, including Wesley, occupied in the town. In spite of the Sandersons' invitation to continue making their porch his home he went back to his own home in Cristobal and remained there until he was able to obtain a room at the Washington.

Although the tiring work sent him to bed early every night, he was grateful to the long hours for keeping his thoughts concentrated on his work. At any rate, at first. Later, his thoughts began to dwell more freely on Anne whom he had tried sincerely, but not too successfully, to forget during the months he had lived with his wife. About a month after Dulcie's death he wrote to Anne to give her news, and ask whether he might continue his interrupted correspondence with her. By return mail he received a letter of consolation from her which finished with her permission for him to write again.

From that moment they corresponded regularly. Outwardly their letters were models of decorum, but behind the formal phrases each read into the other's letters the new, more intimate, relationship which had been created in Bohio.

Later, he wrote that as soon as work eased up sufficiently for him to pay another visit to Bohio, he would do so. As it happened, work increased.

266

And the weeks passed without his having fulfilled his promise. But with the coming of Christmas, and the finish of the most important works in Colón, he applied for, and obtained, a few days' Christmas leave.

Accompanied by Madge, he spent an exciting morning before Christmas in and out of the Colón shops buying presents for the Perrigot family. It was fun, but not so much fun as it would have been in the bazaars of Panama, where the East predominated. Colón was more Western than Eastern; and the majority of the shops were filled with American goods. Eventually, at Mueller and Co. in Front Street he bought a Paisley shawl and an anthology of poems for Anne; and from Wing Yuen's, farther along Front Street, an ostentatious piece of jewelry for Marie—a thing of gold filigree work, generously decorated with ruby, emerald, and sapphire chips, which Madge was certain would appeal to her—and last, but certainly not least, a set of ivory chessmen for old man Perrigot. As a matter of fact, the chessmen cost more than the total of the other three presents, which annoyed him excessively, for he would have preferred to spend the largest amount on Anne. But Madge was adamant. So long as he could afford the cost of the chessmen he would be wise to buy them, she assured him. He knew she was right, but he bought them with bad grace.

After Madge had left him to go home for luncheon with Frederick he went along to J. L. Kerr's at Front and 11 Streets and bought a third present for Anne, an engagement ring with a cluster of diamonds. Afterward he collected his bag from the hotel, and caught the afternoon train for Bohio.

Perrigot received him with a coldness that would have chilled him had it not been for the delighted and delightful welcome from the two girls. As it was he concluded—rightly, as he subsequently learned—that Perrigot had heard of Dulcie's death, and in consequence, regarded his visitor as a potential suitor and therefore a potential enemy. However, Wesley was rewarded, when Anne looked up at him with tender eyes, and told him gaily. "This is the first time we've ever had visitors for Christmas."

Anne wept softly next morning when she held the Paisley shawl and the book to her breast.

He was aghast. "Miss Anne! What has happened? Why are you unhappy?"

Her lovely smile broke through the tears. "I didn't want you to find me. Crying always makes a woman look so terrible."

"But you shouldn't be unhappy, on Christmas Day of all days."

"I'm crying with happiness," she explained wistfully. "You see, these are the very first Christmas presents I've ever received from anyone except Papa, Marie, and Dolores. You don't know how much they mean to me."

By a miraculous chance nobody was near.

"I have a third present for you, dear Anne," he whispered. "If you will—

will accept it from me." He slipped the diamond cluster ring on her engagement finger.

She stared down at the ring with momentary bewilderment, then closed her eyes as if embarrassed to reveal the ecstasy in their depths. With a shy gesture she lifted her hand to her mouth and kissed the ring. Before he quite realized what he was doing, he had wrapped his arms about her trembling shoulders, and was gently seeking her lips. Their mouths met in a long, blissful kiss. As he reluctantly lifted his head she kissed him again, this time on his rugged chin.

That was her answer. It made his heart sing.

39

"DEAR, DEAR ANNE," he whispered. "When shall we be married?"

He saw her hand begin to tremble. "Not too soon, dear one. Please, not too soon. My father—" She slipped the ring off her finger, and threaded her handkerchief through it. Then she knotted the handkerchief, which she tucked into her corsage. "Don't tell anyone, please." Her voice sounded urgent. "Not until you hear from me. Neither Papa nor Marie must suspect. Promise."

"Of course." He grew wistful. "But let it be soon, my darling."

"As soon as possible." They heard the sound of approaching footsteps. "I'll kiss your ring every night," she breathed. "I love you so much— Wesley!" In a louder voice, as the door opened: "You will excuse Marie and me until later, Mr. Adam. We must give Dolores a hand."

"Hurry, girl, Marie has already gone into the kitchen," Perrigot snapped. "Do you want her to do all the work?" As soon as Anne had gone he turned to Wesley. "Sit down. I want a talk with you."

They both sat down, Wesley uneasily. There had been an ominous note in the old man's voice.

"That was a beautiful set of chessmen you gave to me, for Christmas. I have already thanked you for them, so that is that. Why did you give them to me?"

The unexpected question confused Wesley. "Because you—you love chess, sir; and as a—I means, in appreciation of your asking me for the— the holiday."

"I didn't ask you. The girls did that. I can find enjoyment in my own company."

"Well, sir—" The words tailed off. He could think of no answer likely to satisfy the old man.

"I am no fool, Mr. Adam. I know an expensive article when I see one. The chessmen are very beautiful—and very expensive. Come, come!" he continued with a snap. "I can add two and two together. You are now a widower. I have two attractive daughters. You give me a well-chosen but expensive present. Am I not right in concluding that you are hoping to ask one of my daughters to marry you?"

There was no friendliness in the harsh voice, and Wesley heard the question with dismay. In the light of his promise to Anne, what answer could he give that would neither betray Anne nor involve him in a deliberate lie? He could think of none, so judging that the truth would serve better than a lie—for surely he would be able to explain his predicament to Anne later on—he resolved to admit his hope.

But he did not have to do so, for his face had already betrayed him. Perrigot's face whitened. "I can see you are. Which one?" he demanded.

"Miss Anne."

It seemed to Wesley that the answer intensified the old man's anger, as though he had been half hoping that the choice would fall on the younger daughter, and was infuriated because it had not done so.

Wesley anticipated an angry outburst. To his astonishment, nothing of that sort happened. Perrigot appeared to master his emotions. When he spoke again both his voice and expression were bland.

"Well, it had to happen one day, I suppose. Perhaps I am selfish in hoping that my daughters would remain by my side until my passing, which cannot be long delayed. You will not be astonished if I do not give you my blessing; but I will give my consent to your marriage on one condition."

Wesley could scarcely believe what he was hearing. For the old Frenchman to capitulate so calmly and quickly was not in keeping with the character of a man who had tried by subtle means to murder one whom he was now apparently ready to accept as a son-in-law without even a struggle.

He was convinced that Perrigot was up to some mischief; but there was a mask over the old man's expressionless eyes, so he could not even guess what crafty thoughts were passing through the shrewd brain behind. Meanwhile, he intended to hold Perrigot to his word.

"What is that condition, sir?"

"That you do not marry her for at least one full year from today."

Wesley's first reaction was to relax, but when he visualized having to wait one whole year before he could take Anne into his arms and call her his wife he realized how hard the condition was. More than that, it quickly rearoused his suspicions. He believed he could guess Perrigot's reason. In a country like Panama anything might happen in the course of a year. A white man could die from any one of half a dozen tropical diseases:

malaria, cholera, bubonic plague, among others. And if not from natural causes, there were ways of ensuring that a man should die. The jungle was full of known and unknown poisons for anyone with the knowledge to extract and use them. The Indians, way back in the unexplored regions of the country, knew and used them. Rumor said that Negro *bocors,* or witch doctors, could and would kill a man by black magic—in other words, slow poison—for the right fee.

The prospect of possibly being under sentence of death for the next twelve months was alarming, but Wesley had all the self-confidence of young, optimistic manhood allied with the natural obstinacy of the Stewart breed. He was capable of looking after himself, especially as he was, in a sense, forewarned. Besides, it might be only a case of giving a dog a bad name— Then he had one more reflection. Maybe Perrigot himself would die in the meantime. He couldn't last forever.

"If you insist, sir, then I won't press Anne to marry me before Christmas Day next year."

Perrigot's eyes filled with malice. Wesley made an inward resolution to watch out for trouble. He hadn't the slightest doubt but that the old Frenchman was up to trickery of some sort.

Within a matter of hours his suspicions were justified. The Christmas meal was in every possible way a merry affair. The Frenchman was in a most affable mood, and his humor set the standard. As soon as the two girls realized what was happening they relaxed, and let themselves act naturally for once. Laughter became more and more frequent. Not least of all from Perrigot himself after he had filled his own glass several times from some special bottles of wine which he brought up from a deep cellar.

At last, the dessert. By that time the four people were replete, and completely happy. Even Dolores giggled uncontrollably as she cleared away the dishes, and brought in clean plates, a bowl of fruit, four champagne glasses, and a magnum of champagne. When Wesley saw the unsteady manner in which she poured the champagne into their glasses he knew that she, too, had been enjoying Christmas out in the kitchen. With native rum, he judged by the smell of her breath.

"And now, *mes enfants,* I'll give you a special toast." Perrigot gazed round the table at each in turn. The old face was wrinkled in a benign smile which contrasted strangely with the masked eyes above.

"To the future Mr. and Mrs. Adam."

There was a gasp from both girls, followed by a reproach "Wesley!" from Anne, a hiss of excitement from Marie which attracted a swift glance from Wesley. He saw her eyes burning with a brilliance he was unable to interpret. For a moment he thought that she was wildly overjoyed, and was puzzled in consequence. He gave no further thought to the matter then, and turned back to Anne.

270

"Your father guessed," he quickly explained. "But he has given his consent to our marriage if we promise to wait until this day next year."

Marie rose from the table and ran out of the room. Just before the door closed behind her he heard the echo of a sob.

"Let her be," Perrigot said. "She'll get over her tantrums. I'll see that she does. Come, *mes enfants,* we'll drink the toast I've already proposed." He raised his glass. "To the future Mr. and Mrs. Adam."

He drained the glass. As he set it down and reached for the bottle to refill it his gaze rested on the door through which Marie had just departed, and his thin mouth parted in a mocking smile.

In the days which followed, Wesley often pondered on the enigma of that smile. Also on the curious wording of Perrigot's toast. Not to Anne and Wesley," or "To you both," but "To the future Mr. and Mrs. Adam." As if, indeed, in his own mind he was by no means sure that Anne would be the future Mrs. Adam. On the contrary, if one were to judge by the way he had toasted the empty chair, he was toasting Marie.

That, Wesley concluded, was the answer to the enigma. Evidently Marie was Perrigot's favorite, and it was she he had been toasting as the future Mrs. Adam.

The thought made him uneasy; more so, because there was nothing he could do to protect Anne from any scheming on the part of the crafty old Frenchman. Sometimes, he assuaged his fears by assuring himself that it takes two to make a marriage, and as long as his choice was Anne, it was difficult to see how Perrigot could hope to substitute his younger daughter as the bride. On the other hand, Wesley had little faith in the reliability of human nature. Although he was sincerely in love with Anne, he was prepared to admit that, failing her, Marie could be very desirable. Although she lacked Anne's slim lines, as well as her serenity, in every other way Marie was as strikingly beautiful as her older sister, and possessed in addition an exciting, disturbing dynamic force.

Before leaving, Wesley had asked Perrigot's permission to write to Anne. This the Frenchman had given, as usual on conditions.

"Providing you also write to Marie," he had blandly replied. "I have always brought up my two girls to share equally. Since neither you nor Anne will wish Marie to share the contents of your letters to my elder daughter, you will be giving Marie a great pleasure, at small cost to yourself, to write her whenever you write to Anne. After all, she will ultimately become your sister-in-law."

At small cost! Wesley found that he had little free time to write to Anne, still less to Marie, but he fulfilled his promise, and had no subsequent cause to regret doing so. Anne's letters were sweet and charming, full of her dreams of the future which she was longing passionately to share with him, and solicitous inquiries as to his health; all the loving tendernesses which are dear to lovers. Marie's letters were trenchant, and filled with amusing news, often of people of whom he knew nothing, but she never neglected to take advantage of the opportunity to tell him how happy she was that she was going to see much more of him in the future; or to say that she was sure that he would prove the nicest brother-in-law in all the world. Always she finished by sending him her love, and a sisterly kiss.

In his letters to Anne he tried to impress upon her never to take risks while on horseback, that she should keep vigilant watch that there were never strange men about when she rode alone with her father's Negro employee, never to allow anyone to persuade her that he did not love her, not to pay heed to Marie's teasing. No letter left his pen without containing some form of veiled hint that she should take great care of herself, but his precautions were in vain. She was too happy in her new-found love to think that anyone else should wish to destroy it. Especially her sister.

The work of preparing the Zone for the intensive work that had to be done there was by then nearing completion. This was most evident in the Colón docks. With the fever no longer a menace to progress, each day saw an ever-increasing amount of goods and material passing through the port. Sometimes it amused him to examine the huge packing cases as they were landed, and in this way he began to learn more of the commercial geography of his country than he had ever learned at Brown.

Dredging engines from A. L. Ide & Son, of Springfield, Ill., lumber from Edward Hines Lumber Co., of Chicago, Ill., wire rope from the Hazard Mfg. Co., Wilkes-Barre, Pa., automatic weighing machines from Pratt and Whitney Co., of N. Y. C., and machine tools from Niagara Machine and Tool Works, Buffalo, N. Y.

Not all goods were directly concerned with actual building operations, however. On one occasion he was amused to see hair tonic landed, from the Herpicide Co., Detroit, Mich. Another time, a case of musical instruments from Rudolph Wurlitzer, Cincinnati, O. And corsets, from Wingarten Bros., N. Y. C. Lastly, a somber reminder of inevitable casualties, a case of artificial limbs from A. A. Marks, N. Y.

He began to appreciate for the first time the colossal organization entailed by the canal. It was necessary not only to buy all the equipment needed for the actual constructional work—and that was legion, ranging as it did from microscopic metal washers to giant triple expansion steam pumps; from candles for the laborers' huts to a garbage destructor furnace, from typewriting paper to vast quantities of rubber boots—but provision had also to be made for extraordinary requirements of an extraneous character. If men were to be kept happy and contented at their work they must have cigars and cigarettes to smoke in their leisure hours; books to read; a clubhouse to visit; billiard tables— And corsets for their womenfolk, diapers and feeding bottles for their children! desks, blackboards, easels, chalks, and other articles for the schools that would have to be built.

The heavy rumble of wheels was almost continuous night and day as long lines of heavily laden wagons pulled out of the docks and moved ponderously along Front Street. As quickly as one warehouse was emptied, ships alongside refilled it.

One day, upon returning to the Washington, Wesley found the bad penny waiting for him. He had been thinking of Larry lately, wondering what was happening to him and how the search for Ericson was going.

Larry had changed little since their last meeting, and Wesley felt glad to see the slender figure, and the smiling, mischievous eyes. For the first time he realized that in spite of mistrusting Larry to some extent, and wholly despising his spinelessness, he had developed an affectionate regard for the other man and had missed his cheerful company far more than he would have believed possible.

Wesley greeted him with a welcoming smile, and a hearty handshake that brought a wince and a protest from his victim.

"Hey, leave me my hand, brother. I've only two."

He chuckled. "Sorry, Larry, but it's nice seeing you again. How's things?

"Couldn't be better."

He believed he distinguished a note of excitement in Larry's voice. "Found El Jaguar's gold?"

"Found Ericson, brother."

He appreciated the reason for Larry's excitement. "And that's good news for sister Ingrid, eh?"

"It will be, when I tell her."

"You haven't told her yet?" He was surprised. Surely Larry wasn't embarrassed?

Larry's expression turned serious. "I wanted to see you first, Mr. Adam. He's in a bad way."

"Ill?"

"He's had just about everything a white man can catch in this country, but he's not ill in that sense. There's almost nothing of him left. He's a walking skeleton. If you were to poke him in the ribs with your finger it would go right through him. *And* he wouldn't bleed, at that. Hasn't enough blood left in him to write your name with."

"So you think it would give his sister too much of a shock to see him?"

"Don't you? Besides, there's something else. I said he wasn't ill. Nor is he, not physically ill. But mentally and morally he's a sick man. He's had the stuffing knocked out of him. He's whacked, defeated, ready to snuff out as soon as may be."

273

Olaf Ericson whacked, defeated, ready to snuff out! Remembering Ericson as he had been when last they had met—robust, vital, aggressive— Wesley wondered whether Larry, never wholly truthful, was up to one of his old tricks. He glanced quickly into the dark, exotic eyes, but for once they were naïvely innocent, even worried.

"Where did you see him?"

"In the Humming Bird. He's sleeping under the stairs in return for help. He'd been there five days when I went yesterday."

"Did you speak to him?" Larry nodded. "And tell him you were looking for him?" A second nod. "And about Ingrid?"

"Yes. Poor devil! He nearly wept when he heard all that she had done to find him."

"It's easy to feel remorseful when it's too late."

"Sure. I'm not trying to defend him, although birds of a feather are supposed to flock together." The old mocking smile appeared for a moment.

"Did you bring him back to Colón with you?"

"He wouldn't come."

"Wouldn't? Knowing Ingrid was here! The swine!"

Larry shook his head. "Give a dog a bad name!" he murmured. "As a matter of fact, he won't come to Colón because he doesn't want Ingrid to see him—yet."

"What do you mean, yet?"

"He wants to see her bad. But not before he's looking more like a human being."

"How does he hope to do that?"

"That's the point. That's why I've come to Colón to see you."

"Well?"

"How is the survey staff? I mean, are you short of men?"

"We're always short, especially among the field parties. The newcomers can't stand jungle life. They go down like tenpins."

"Do you think you could get him a job?"

"Probably, if I wanted to. But I don't want to. He's not to be trusted. As soon as he was fit again, and could jingle some real money in his pocket, it's ten to one he'd give up the job once more!"

"Why should he?"

Wesley was about to remark upon Ericson's gold fever when he recollected his fear that it might complicate matters if either of the two men were to find out that the other was also searching for gold.

"Because, these days, he doesn't like work any more than you do."

"That's where you're wrong. Now that I've found Ericson I'm ready to do anything I can to help in building the canal." Larry leaned forward in his eagerness. "You're working in the Bohio section, aren't you?"

"Mostly."

274

"Could you find a job for me with your party? An assistant assistant, or something like that? And what about Ericson joining you as well? We'd get on well enough, the three of us."

For the second time Wesley's suspicions of Larry's motives prompted him to glance quickly at his companion. This time he surprised a sly expression, and knew that it was not wholly Larry's infatuation for Ingrid that made him so anxious for her brother's welfare. There must be another reason.

Larry's sharp eyes were quick to note Wesley's indecision, but he misinterpreted the reason for it.

"What's worrying you? Think the job's too energetic for me?"

"Isn't it? There is plenty of work in Colón you could do."

"Colón! That shantytown!"

"Cristobal, then? Or Panama?"

"Not Panama," Larry exclaimed sharply. "The farther I keep away from there the better. Only just missed walking into Uncle Manuel the other day."

"Uncle Manuel! Manuel Amador? Are you—"

Larry looked disconcerted. "Manuels are a dime a dozen in Panama," he rasped. "See here, Wes, I'm strong enough, in spite of my foot, to keep up with the average person working in the jungle. I guess you don't believe I want to work, after all the years I've been saying I don't. But I do now. Honest to God! Ever since I saw what the engineers are up against in building a canal across Panama, I've had a new pride in our country which makes me want to give a hand. Give me credit for a decent thought now and again, will you."

With the best will in the world Wesley could not make himself believe it. Pride and patriotism were not part of Larry's make-up. But he could not tell the other man so.

"I was thinking of Ericson. If he's just a bag of skin and bones he'd be no use to us."

"A few weeks of good, regular food would soon put him straight physically."

"And mentally?"

"To be at work with you again will do that. Make him think civilization needs him."

"What's he been doing this last year or two?"

Larry chuckled. "As if you don't know."

"Do you?"

"Yes. When I told him about Ingrid he talked plenty. At one moment I thought he was going to start weeping on my shoulder."

Wesley shrugged. "Perhaps now you'll give up chasing rainbows."

To his surprise Larry nodded. "That's what I've been trying to tell you. I am giving up. That's why I want to work instead. Not that we've been

275

looking for the same thing, Olaf and me. He wasn't looking for El Jaguar's gold, just a gold mine, the poor sap."

"I still don't understand why he didn't come back to Colón with you, Larry. He could have kept clear of the Sanderson's house."

For the first time Larry seemed unsure of himself. "Well, you see, it's not quite so simple as that."

"Why not?"

"He—he didn't say anything about wanting work. That's my idea." He spoke more quickly, as if to prevent Wesley from interrupting. "I thought if you were to go and speak to him, it would make all the difference. He thinks the world of you."

Wesley could not swallow that tall story. "Rot! Ericson and I don't talk the same language."

"Well, even if he doesn't, I do—I mean, think the world of you. That's God's truth."

"So?"

"If you won't go to Panama for his sake, will you do it for mine? If you knew how much it might mean to me?"

"To put Ericson on his feet again?"

"Yes. You see—" Larry swallowed. "It might help Ingrid overlook my foot. Especially if I'm holding down a good job."

Wesley began to feel that he had misjudged his companion; that his former suspicions were unjustified. The possibility of this being so pleased him. When he gave his friendship he gave it wholeheartedly. It had often irked him that common sense had persistently overruled his emotions where Larry was concerned.

His reflection made him feel generous. The effort of trying to restore Olaf Ericson to normal society would cost him little in time or trouble; and if it succeeded in helping Larry along the path to happiness of which the poor devil had probably never dreamed, it would be well worth while.

He nodded. "You win, Larry. I'll do what I can."

40

ON THEIR WAY to Panama Wesley tried to get at Larry's real reason for wanting work. That his love for Ingrid was partly responsible Wesley was sure. At the same time he could not forget the sly expression he had surprised.

Although Ericson might have abandoned his search for a gold mine,

276

he felt certain that Larry intended to continue his search for El Jaguar's missing gold. That might be his intention. Wesley chuckled. If it were, then he was destined for a sharp disappointment. There would be no time off for spare-time exploration. Sunup to sundown was the program among the more conscientious parties.

He glanced at the small brown face opposite. It was sideways to him, and the wide lips were parted in a pensive smile.

Wesley was tempted to force Larry to be frank just for once.

"Larry."

Larry started. "Yes?"

"Touching upon this matter of your being employed by the I.C.C. Wouldn't you prefer to remain at Colón? It wouldn't be such a strain on your foot in the first place, and in the second you would be able to see Ingrid more often."

"Can you see me settling down to an office job? Me, who's been a bum so many years."

A neat evasion; Wesley grinned. He knew his Larry.

"I meant, with one of the surveying parties. There will be work in Colón and Cristobal for years to come. Before long they'll be building new docks there, new storehouses, new hotels, a refrigeration plant, and God knows what else. Probably a breakwater, to make a harborage."

"I'd rather be with your party, if you can fix it, Wes."

"Even if I should be posted to the Panama Division?"

He saw by the dismayed expression that his arrow had found its target; Larry was quick to recover. "I wouldn't care about going too far from Colón," he answered in a casual manner.

"Or do you mean Bohio?"

"Why should I? I was thinking about Ingrid in Colón."

Wesley chuckled. "What was that you said just now, about thinking the world of me?"

"I do, Wes."

"Why not prove it, by being frank with me for once?"

"I don't know what you mean."

"Don't you? All right, I'll ask you a plain question. Isn't your idea to join my party so you can continue your search for El Jaguar's gold?" He held up his hand. "I don't mean, that you don't want work of some sort. I believe you do, because of Ingrid, and I admire you for it, and wish you all the luck in the world with her. But you haven't given up hope of finding the gold, have you?"

Larry stared out of the window at the Black Swamp through which they were passing. Wesley did not press the question, for it was plain to see that his companion was wrestling with the problem of how frank to be. At last Larry sighed deeply, and nodded his head.

277

"Guess you may as well know the truth, Wes. Yes, that was the idea." Then he added quickly, "As well as earning money."

"Of course. Then you still think the gold is somewhere to be found?"

"I'm convinced of it. I can even tell you where it's hidden."

"But if so—" Wesley was puzzled. "Why can't you find it?"

"Promise you won't tell a soul."

Wesley shrugged. "I don't want you to tell. It's your secret. Besides, I still don't believe in its existence, any more than I do in Captain Kidd's treasure."

"All the same, I'm going to tell you," Larry stated doggedly. "And God knows, there isn't another man in the world I would trust with the secret. The gold's hidden in a cave in El Valle Dulce."

"El Valle Dulce," Wesley repeated reflectively.

"Sweet Valley, if you prefer it. That's what Jim Holmes called it to the fellow prisoner in the mines at Veraguas, that I told you about the first day we met."

"There must be thousands of valleys in Panama. You can't hope to visit every one of them, looking for a cave."

"Of course, I can't. I don't have to. Holmes went on to say that Sweet Valley was within a twenty-mile radius of Bohio."

"That's a big enough area to cover quite a few square miles of mountains and valleys. Still, it's something. Did you find your Sweet Valley?"

"That's the point, I didn't." Larry scowled. "I've been to every blasted valley in the radius, not once but several times. Not one of them is called Sweet Valley."

"That man Holmes invented the story of the gold."

"Did your grandfather also invent it? He told you about the gold El Jaguar stole from the California gold trains. Besides, I've checked up on the story, same as your friend Mr. Godwin could do if he wanted to."

"How?"

"Looking through the back numbers of the *Star and Herald*. There were several articles on, 'Where Did the Bandit Hide His Stolen Gold?' and 'Where is El Jaguar's Loot Hidden?' and such like. There's also correspondence to be found. Quite a number of people wrote to the editor to say how he would have hidden the gold if he'd been El Jaguar."

In spite of himself Wesley was impressed by Larry's arguments. "What form did Holmes' message take?"

When Larry heard the note of interest in Wesley's voice he smiled slyly. "Holmes became friendly with a fellow prisoner called Thompson. Thompson had saved Holmes' life one day when he was attacked by another prisoner. They became buddies, and remained that way until his last illness. Apparently he suspected that he hadn't long to live for he called Thompson to his bedside, and a conversation something like this took place.

278

"'You're going to be freed soon, aren't you?' Holmes asked. When the other man said 'Yes,' he went on to tell him about El Jaguar's gold, adding: 'If I should die, Thompson, you can have the gold. I haven't any relatives or friends except you, and a kid I knew long ago but haven't heard of for years.'

"Thompson did all the thinking necessary, and then asked where the gold was to be found. 'Swear you won't touch it if I don't die,' Holmes demanded, so naturally Thompson swore. 'It's in a cave in Sweet Valley, which is within twenty miles of Bohio.'

"'Can't you tell me closer than that?' Thompson asked. Holmes laughed. 'What more can I tell you than more?' When Holmes didn't continue Thompson said, 'Go on.' 'What do you mean, go on?' Holmes asked. 'I can't tell you more than more. Just ask for the valley, and sooner or later you'll find someone to tell you where it is.'

"Holmes died, and later Thompson returned here to look for the gold. He didn't find it, and when he had no money left he became father's valet."

"Why did Thompson pass the secret on to your father?"

Larry shrugged. "Because he was dying. The fool got himself entangled with a married woman. When the husband found out he stabbed Thompson."

"I remember your telling me that your father didn't believe the story."

"He didn't. He made a few inquiries for Sweet Valley, and when he couldn't find it, came to the conclusion that either Holmes or Thompson had been delirious when telling the story."

"What makes you so certain that your father's idea was wrong?"

"Because I couldn't see any reason for a man, who knew he was dying, to invent such a story, especially for a friend who had once saved his life."

He nodded, and Larry continued. "One day when I was bumming in Pennsylvania, a woman gave me an old hat that had once belonged to her father. Behind the band inside was a strip of greasy newspaper that had been used for padding. The strip had been cut from a San Francisco paper, and happened to contain a paragraph about the ingenious way Holmes had bluffed Governor Bigler into freeing him from San Quentin. Reading that finally convinced me that Holmes' story was true."

Wesley chuckled dryly. Larry was doing good work. It might be amusing to try and find the cave!

"Is it certain that the center of the area was Bohio?"

Larry's grimace was disconsolate. "How can one be certain of that? Holmes might have lied to Thompson, or Thompson to my father. But if either man wanted to lie to that extent, why have told the story in the first place?"

"True," Wesley agreed reflectively. "What was that Holmes said, 'I

279

can't tell you more than more?' That doesn't make sense to me. Does it to you?"

"No. My guess is that Holmes had repented of his past life, and had taken to reading the Bible, or poetry, and was talking that way for effect."

"Maybe! So you haven't found Sweet Valley. Do you think the natives won't tell you, because you're American?"

"I've more sense than to let them think I'm American." Larry laughed.

Wesley had forgotten that his companion was half Panamanian. "What's your idea? That the cave is farther from Bohio than Holmes believed, and that we may come across it during our survey?"

"That's what I pray for," the little man muttered.

They reached Panama during the early afternoon, so Wesley went along to see Uncle Bill. He still looked healthy, brown, tough.

He gave a pleased laugh when Wesley said so. "Looking healthy am I, boy? I've never been happier. Life here suits me."

"Aren't you ever ill?"

"Never. Touching wood."

"What about malaria? Don't tell me you haven't had that?"

"I haven't." He chuckled. "Reckon I'm too dried up, or my flesh is too leathery, for them skeeters to bite me. What brings you here?"

"Ericson. Larry's traced him at last. He's at the Humming Bird."

"Mother María's, eh?"

Wesley glanced quickly at the other man. "You know the place, Uncle Bill?"

"I'm not so old that you need look quite so surprised," he smirked. "There's a little baggage there, name of Tina, born in Turkey." He wafted a kiss into the air.

"Uncle Bill, will you do something for me?"

"If I can. What is it, lad? Trouble?"

"No. I'd like to find out what I can about an American by the name of Jim Holmes, who lived in Panama back in the eighteen fifties, when the railroad was being built. Ran Runnels sent him to Veraguas for life. I believe there was some account of him in the *Star and Herald*."

"You would like me to look through past files?"

"Please. And while you are doing that, would you find out what you can about El Jaguar."

Godwin's expression sharpened. "You're not falling for that fable about the missing gold, lad?"

Wesley laughed. "You know what I think. But there might be something in the story that the stolen gold was hidden for a time—possibly in a cave. I'd like to trace the cave if I can. Just for fun."

280

"You think El Jaguar advertised its whereabouts in the *Star and Herald*?"

Wesley returned the older man's grin.

After Wesley and Larry had booked a room at the Gran Hotel Central, they had a meal in the restaurant. Afterward they wandered onto the balcony which the night air had fortunately made cooler.

The scene below was cheerful. Since it was a Sunday night the plaza was crowded with the citizens of Panama who, dressed in their finery, promenaded up and down, talking, smoking, flirting and listening to the Republican Band. As of time immemorial, the colored people used the outside walk which completely encompassed the plaza, while the white population kept strictly to the walk which dissected the square from east to west. Above the promenaders the trees were hung with the recently installed electric lights which brilliantly illuminated the white dresses of the vivacious womenfolk, and the gleaming clothes of their dark-haired, flashing-eyed male escorts.

For the best part of an hour the two men had vicarious enjoyment in languidly watching the gay, colorful scene, but toward nine o'clock Larry suggested that they should make a move. Ericson would be coming on duty at any moment, he said.

They walked along Central Avenue, until they reached the road which led down to the Market. There they turned left and passed out of the populous district into an open area. They could see on their left the dark surface of the Pacific Ocean, alive with the scintillating reflection of the stars, and the lights of ships in the harbor anchorages.

"Here we are," Larry announced.

Wesley glanced quickly at the building in front of them: a large, three-sided stone house that once had been the home of a Spanish grandee. The years had treated it ill by extending the town until it had swallowed up the *rancha,* and surrounded it with the wooden hovels of the public prostitutes. Much of its plaster façade had long since peeled off; its white paint had weathered into a dirty yellow smear; its balconies looked dangerous; its wrought-iron scrollwork was broken and rusty. A large, crude picture of a hummingbird, painted in the gaudiest of colors stretched right across the front of the house. Three lanterns hung from the wall lighted up this monstrosity.

A Negro barker stood outside the main entrance, extolling the comforts to be found inside. He showed his white teeth in a broad smile when he saw the two men make toward him, and he wished them good evening, first in Spanish and then in English.

They passed into the building, and found themselves in a long L-room that ran the length of two wings. The entire wall of the wing facing the main entrance was given up to a bar. The second wing, on the left, contained a dance floor. A small band of five players occupied a small dais at the far end.

Although the bar was comparatively full of men, mostly sailors from the ships anchored offshore, only five couples were dancing. Thus Wesley was able to see that both sides of the dance floor were lined with tables and chairs, several of which were occupied by weary-eyed, raddled women in gaudy clothes.

The rooms were bright with lamps, mirrors, and an inordinate amount of gilt paint. Madre María did not intend any of her clients to complain that the house looked somber or depressing.

"He's not here yet," Larry said. "He serves drinks to the dancers. Will you have one while we're waiting?" He sissed. "But you'll have to pay for it. I haven't any money."

They pushed their way to the bar, where Wesley ordered two beers. On either side of them the visitors to the brothel talked and laughed or pawed some of the girls who mingled with the men in the hope of finding one who would buy them a drink.

Not a few of the girls tried to attract Wesley's attention, for his grim, rugged face with its steady glance and obstinate chin, and his fine robust figure made him an enviable acquisition in the disillusioned eyes of women whom circumstances had forced to become the chattels of pimps and lechers. There was a coarse shoddiness in the whole atmosphere of the place that left Wesley in no mood to enjoy his surroundings.

More and more men were entering the house. Newcomers pounded on the bar and shouted for service, until the noise completely drowned the band. Wesley and Larry pushed their way through the men who were crowding in upon the bar, and looked toward the dance floor. That, too, was becoming crowded. White-coated waiters were waiting for orders, but Wesley could see nothing of Ericson.

"Not here yet," he said to Larry. "What time is he supposed to be here?"

"But he is," Larry protested. "There, by the first table."

Wesley looked with consternation at the prematurely aged, balding man with apathetic eyes, and realized that if Larry had not been with him he would never have recognized Olaf Ericson.

41

WESLEY WAS APPALLED. The blond giant, with his square, fresh-complexioned face and direct eyes, his broad shoulders and fine limbs, his well-built lithe body had been transformed into a travesty of a human being. During the years which had elapsed since Wesley's brief glimpse of him in Bottle Alley fever had robbed him of the blond hair of which he had always been so proud, and had left his pate bald, with a wispy fringe of hair, more like that of an aging monk than of a young man in his late twenties. Successive diseases had wasted his flesh, until it resembled worn leather stretched over a skeleton. His eyes were dead, his arms gangling. His huge frame still remained, but it looked empty, contemptible.

Larry plucked at Wesley's arm. "Coming over?"

"In a minute. I want to get over the shock. God in Heaven!"

"You can't. He's seen us."

The two men shook hands. Wesley had to make an effort not to withdraw his hand too quickly from the feeble grasp.

"Hello, Olaf."

"Hello, Wesley." Ericson's voice was as dead as his eyes. "Ought to have taken your advice, oughtn't I?" he croaked. "So you won. The canal's on its way." He exposed his greenish teeth in what was meant to be a smile. "Sea level or lock?"

"Lock."

He shrugged. "That will please old man Perrigot. He won't be able to mine any more gold."

"Olaf—"

"Still think I'm crazy, Wesley? Don't you believe it! I haunted his damned house for nearly a year, watching him every time he went into the jungle. But he knew I was there, the cunning old devil. Anytime he wanted to lose me, he did. And then he went to Colón or came here to Panama a few days later."

"Oh! come—"

"You're a hard man to persuade, aren't you, Wesley? If you don't believe me, slip that scarred-face clerk at the International Banking Company on Central Plaza fifty dollars. He'll talk. And he'll tell you that old man Perrigot has been selling raw gold to the bank for years."

Wesley admitted wryly to himself that he might well learn the lesson, from both his companions, not to be dogmatic. First, Larry had upset all his convictions about El Jaguar's gold; now Olaf was doing the same about Perrigot's gold mine.

He tried to say to Ericson, "We'll talk about it someplace else," but although he spoke he did not hear his own words for the noise of other, louder voices. While he had been talking with Ericson a group of Italian canal workers had entered the building, and by the sheer pressure of their number were trying to force their way to the already crowded bar. Their onslaught was being resisted by the half drunken sailors already there, and neither side spared their tongues. Bouncers were converging on the rival gangs to prevent the wordy fracas from degenerating into a hand-to-hand fight.

He shouted in Ericson's ear, "Can you take us somewhere?"

In reply Ericson nodded his head, and led the way toward a door which evidently connected with the bedrooms above, for one of the girls was pulling a diffident young midshipman in the same direction.

Although the corridor on the far side of the door echoed with the noise from the bar, at least they were able to make themselves heard.

"You know why we've come here tonight?"

Ericson nodded. "If Larry has had anything to do with you coming it's to offer me a job with the I.C.C.?"

"Yes. We're short of surveyors, especially any hardened to jungle conditions. Interested?"

"Could be, but—" He shrugged. "I can't leave here."

"Why not?"

"I owe Madre María money."

"How much?"

"More than four hundred dollars."

Wesley whistled. "How long will it take you to earn that?"

"At the rate she's paying me, the rest of my life, I'd say." He shrugged. "Two years, at least. Sometimes I get tips."

"Do you want to stay here?"

"Being here has its compensations. And sometimes the girls are kind to me if they've had a slack night." Ericson exposed his green teeth in a grin. "There's a special rate for employees. Besides, sometimes I have fun. Old Mother María gives me the young ones to break in."

Wesley turned away in disgust. "In that case—"

Larry gripped his arm. "Can't you see it's his pride, Wes?"

He turned again. "Is it?"

The dead eyes almost came alive. "If I had four hundred dollars I'd join you tomorrow. God! I'm still a man, aren't I? And this job—" He lifted one of his gangling arms, and with a feeble flourish indicated the staircase along the corridor. "Waiter in a whorehouse!" He turned and spat.

"Besides," Larry murmured, "There's Ingrid."

"Christ!" Ericson exclaimed, looking away.

Wesley studied the gaunt, unhealthy face. Although every cent was

284

precious to him in these days of saving for his marriage to Anne, four hundred dollars was little enough for the price of a man's soul. He felt that he would be glad to sacrifice them if Ericson were a good risk but he was not too happy on that count.

The offer, Wesley presently decided with reluctance, must be made, if for no other reason than to prevent his becoming a victim of his own reproachful conscience.

"Suppose I lend you the money to be quit of this place?" he muttered.

The result was surprising. "By Jimminy!" The old familiar exclamation vibrated with hope. "You won't ever regret it, by God!"

Nothing further could be done that night, for Wesley had only a few dollars in his pocket. So they arranged to meet at two o'clock the following afternoon, when old Mother María might be expected to make her first appearance of the day, and could be paid off in time for Ericson to accompany them on the next train back to Colón.

"Then I'll be going, Olaf. So long." He held out his hand.

Ericson gripped it in his own feeble clasp. "God bless you, Wesley, old friend. Thank you. As soon as I'm fit I'll work like hell."

Wesley detached his hand from the other's grasp.

"Coming, Larry?"

"Not me, brother. Olaf knows just the girl for me—"

As Wesley walked back along the dark streets, his thoughts turned upon gold. He could not understand the fever which drove men almost to madness. Did the answer lie in the lure of get-rich-quick, or in the lure of something-for-nothing? Or in a combination of the two? Or was it an unconscious groping for romantic adventure which blinded men to the realities of everyday existence? Whatever it was, Wesley knew that he was no victim of the fever.

The possession of wealth was attractive. It must be comforting to be able to surround oneself with luxuries, live at ease and yet, as far as he was concerned, it was not sufficiently attractive to make him risk his health, his physique, his future. Why then had Ericson been ready to do so? How had it given Dulcie courage deliberately to defy the social morality which her strict New England upbringing had implanted in her, and to defy convention by living in sin—all for the sake of an illusory dream of a larger, grander home.

His mind was still dwelling aimlessly on the problem when a woman ahead of him turned left into a side street. In doing so she passed under an electric light. To his astonishment he recognized Marie Perrigot.

He grinned at his own idiocy. The Perrigot family were at home. Even had they been in Panama, in no circumstances would the old Frenchman have allowed one of his daughters to be out, unescorted or unchaperoned, at that time of night.

285

Nevertheless, he continued to watch the woman. She certainly was like Marie. So much like her in fact, that presently he began to wonder whether it were not, after all, possible that it was she who was making her way along Avenida Central. Perrigot might have paid an unexpected visit to Panama, and Marie was enough of a madcap, if given the opportunity, to escape from parental control and go exploring on her own account.

In case something of that sort had happened he decided to follow the woman until he had learned more about her movements. He, too, turned into the side street, and closed the gap between them, for already she was attracting the attention of young sparks who were making their way toward Plaza Santa Ana. They began whistling to her, and calling out suggestions which made him angrily embarrassed on her account, but she ignored them except to increase her pace.

As she turned into the illuminated Plaza he again had a good view of her profile, and felt certain it was Marie. He wondered whether she might be going to the Hotel Metropole, or even to one of the two saloons which the French had built overlooking the Plaza. She did neither, but crossed the Plaza diagonally so as to enter Avenida Central again. There she turned left, and proceeded along the Avenue in the direction of the railroad station. He followed, with increasing perplexity, for now she was moving away from the center of the town.

The pursuit continued to the station, and beyond; over the crossing towards the warren of narrow streets on the far side of the track. He grew alarmed, for she was moving into the colored district, a squalid, furtive quarter which he would normally have hesitated to penetrate after nightfall. Convinced that she could not realize what she was doing he thought of calling after her, but while he was still trying to make up his mind she turned to her right, and disappeared around a corner.

He cursed himself for not having stopped her sooner, and hurried after her. He would have sprinted, in the hope of catching her up, but the dark street was too full of lurking shadows whose attention he was not eager to attract. Provided the suspicions of the local inhabitants were not actually aroused, with luck he might be taken for one of them.

He sighed with relief as he reached the corner and detected a dim shadow ahead that might be Marie. Again he closed the gap between them but she turned to her right again—not into another street this time, but into a stinking, unsalubrious courtyard.

He paused there for a moment. What in God's name was she up to? he wondered. The courtyard was dark save for a few narrow shafts of light which escaped through rents in the drawn curtains of the upper story. None of these was enough to penetrate the darkness at ground level. Against the muffled, rhythmic beat of strange music he could hear the uncertain tap-tap of her feet on the cobblestones as she moved, but he

286

could not see her. Then the sound of her feet stopped, and he heard a soft tapping on wood.

A widening shaft of light, as a door on the far side of the courtyard was opened, silhouetted Marie's small rounded figure. Then the door opened wider. To his horror she entered the building. The door closed, leaving the courtyard once more in darkness.

He heard footsteps behind him, and the sound of voices. At least two people were making for the courtyard so he entered and, turning left inside, crouched up against the wooden wall of the building behind him.

He was not mistaken about the newcomers. They, two men and a woman, did precisely what Marie had done. As they passed close to him he heard them talking, and knew by the slurring timber of their voices that they were Negroes.

What fantastic combination of circumstances had brought about Marie's midnight visit to a gathering of colored people Wesley could not guess. Nor in his alarm for her safety, did he try to. His only thought was that, for Anne's sake as much as Marie's own, he must get her away before any harm could come to her—and he could still remember Ingrid's shriek of horror as the drunken Negro in Bottle Alley advanced on her.

He moved cautiously across the yard toward the door which he had seen Marie enter. As he approached the muffled echo of music and the shuffling of feet on wooden boards reached his ears. The sound reassured him, for it robbed the mystery of Marie's visit of its worst implications. He no longer felt that she was in immediate danger.

Upon reaching the far side of the yard he noticed a streak of light that had not been visible from the road. It came from a window. Presently he was able to see, through a gap in the curtains, something of what was happening on the far side.

Against a wall, hung with a cheap scarlet and white striped cotton material, stood a trestle table covered with a jumble of articles. Prominent among them was a crucifix, flanked on either side by crudely painted plaques depicting Christian saints. Before the crucifix and the plaques stood two bottles of rum, a plate heaped with corn, two crossed machetes, a large china bowl, a small mound of fruit, a bunch of orchids, a phallic emblem; and stretched the length of the table, the stuffed skin of a large green snake; and at one end two white doves. Three candles stuck in the necks of empty bottles illuminated what must be a voodoo "altar."

In front of the altar stood an old, old Negro. Underneath the mass of white crinkly hair his face, uplifted, was lined and puckered. His hands were raised up in supplication. They were thin, clawlike. He was dressed in a white ankle-length cotton smock.

Before him stood the worshipers at this pagan ceremony: a Negro congregation dressed in white; the women in cotton frocks, white handkerchiefs on their heads; the men in cotton shirts and cotton trousers. They swayed from side to side, and chanted a soft invocation to the rhythm of barbaric music: the low tom-tom-tom of drums and the warbling wail of a reed.

Wesley had no need to wonder about the ceremony he was witnessing. It was an open secret in the Isthmus that voodoo ceremonies were frequently held in the colored districts of both Panama and Colón; ceremonies at which invocations were made to the ancient gods of Africa. The old Negro in front of the altar was probably a bocor or witch doctor.

The action of the ceremony changed abruptly, as the bocor lowered head and arms. The music stopped; and the congregation stood unmoving as every white-rimmed eye watched the actions of the bocor with mingled fear and wonder. Turning toward the altar he took the bottle of rum, and poured some of the liquid into the china bowl. Then he trickled a handful of corn into the same bowl, threw in an orchid, and several of the fruits. Next he picked up one of the crossed machetes, and having presented it to the plaques, and implanted upon its blade a kiss of homage, he beheaded one of the white doves with a dexterous cut, picked up the still-fluttering bird with his free hand, and allowed the blood from the severed neck to drip into the bowl while he stirred the mess already there with the point of his knife. Lastly, he laid aside the dead bird and the machete, dipped the fingers of both hands into the bowl, and let the liquid trickle from them on to the phallic emblem.

At this there was a shout of jubilation from the congregation, whereupon the unseen musicians began to beat out a new and different rhythm. Immediately, the people swayed their bodies in time to the beat, and with shuffling feet, revolved slowly round the room.

Fascinated by what he was seeing, Wesley wondered what brought Marie to witness what must undoubtedly have been a rite of fertilization and a plea to the gods for fecundity. Through the chink in the curtain he could see bottles of rum circulating, and the rhythm of the dance was already growing faster. He saw, too, for the first time, a door to the right of the altar which had previously been hidden by the cotton hanging. To this door, and through it, the Negro men were frenziedly dragging their partners, doubtless in the hope of obtaining an early answer to their prayers while the gods were still in good humor as a result of their sacrificial libations.

Come on out, you stupid girl, he ordered telephatically. God help you if a rum-crazy colored man sees the color of your skin.

At that moment the door opened and Marie stepped out into the courtyard. He knew it was she because he recognized her voice thanking an unseen person for something—the something being a word he did not recognize. Then he heard her feet crossing the yard again. Immensely relieved, he followed her out and into the street.

288

He waited until she had crossed the railroad track before catching her up, in the station plaza.

"Marie."

She was startled, but welcomed him with warmth.

"Wesley."

"You little fool!" he scolded angrily. "What in Heaven's name tempted you to risk visiting that voodoo ceremony on your own? Don't you realize what might have happened to you?"

"How did you know—"

"I saw you, followed you, looked through a chink in the curtains. My God! When I think—"

"Well?"

"You, a white girl, mixing with Negroes."

She laughed, and drew him under one of the palms. "As if you didn't know."

"Didn't know what?"

"That Anne and I are colored. Everybody knows. So why shouldn't we mix with Negroes as much as we do with white people?"

He was too astonished to do more than gasp.

42

HE WOULD HAVE given much at that moment to be alone, but Marie, laughing excitedly, took hold of his hand and tried to pull him back on to the sidewalk.

"This is too wonderful a chance to waste. Take me dancing please, Wesley. Nobody knows I'm out. It doesn't matter what time I get back."

Instead of yielding to her, he exerted his strength and forced her back under the tree. "You're not telling me the truth, Marie—" he began in a strained voice.

She laughed again. "I wouldn't lie to you, Wesley dear. I like you. Do you realize this is the first time we've been alone since your second visit home? I feel so happy."

He shook her shoulders. "Listen to me, and stop your damned chatter."

The moon was rising. He saw her face looking up into his. "What's the matter? Why are you so cross?" Her voice was artless.

"I want to get this matter straight. Perrigot said your mother was French."

"If you promise to take me dancing I'll tell everything."

"No. You'll tell me now."

"There's no reason why you shouldn't take me out. After all, it will be perfectly decent. I am your future sister-in-law." She laughed softly.

Sister-in-law! A sister-in-law with black blood in her veins! A wife, likewise! And children, if any—God! Maybe coffee-colored, even ebony black.

"Who's your mother?" he choked.

"Take me for a drink. I'll tell you all you want to know."

He realized that he would not get any information unless he did as she asked.

"Come along," he muttered ungraciously. "We'll go to Eddie's, opposite the station."

Although it was past midnight, the saloons near the railroad station were doing a roaring trade—literally—for the noise could be heard from some distance off. They were lucky to find an empty table in a far corner.

"Now," he demanded after the colored waiter had served them.

Mischievously, she gazed sidelong at him. "Now what?"

He was in no mood for delay. He caught her wrist and squeezed it until she whimpered with pain. "Please—Wesley—you're hurting—"

"I want the story from where your father and his French wife arrived in Panama. Or wasn't she white?" he added.

She nodded, and pouted as she rubbed her wrist. "Yes, she was white. I suppose she was. Papa always said she was. She died of yellow fever about a year after they landed."

"Go on."

"Papa couldn't be happy without a woman to look after him, and sleep with. There were so few white women here—so he married a black one. You've met her."

"Dolores? My God!"

"What's the matter, Wesley?" she questioned. "Do you think it worries Anne and me to know we are half black? It doesn't worry me, at any rate. It might, in most countries. But in Panama so many of us are colored that it's you white people who are out of place." She sidled closer to him. "Wesley, it's not going to worry you to have colored children, is it?"

He turned away in the hope that she would not see the horror he was sure was reflected on his face.

It was not as if he intended to spend the rest of his life in Panama. One day, when the canal was finished, he would be returning to New England; there, if Fate were kind to him, to establish a permanent home for his future children. But what sort of a home could New England give to children of mixed color? What sort of a future might they expect? He knew there was only one answer to both questions. Conditions might change before the twentieth century ran its course, but until the spirit of true Christianity had conquered intolerance he could never hope to take colored children back to New England without condemning them to a purgatory of hatred and distrust.

Although the passing years had deepened his desire for children of his own flesh and blood, he recognized in that moment of agony there could be no marriage between Anne and himself. Marie's careless revelation had prevented that as surely as death would have done.

With a shaking hand he lifted the glass to his mouth. The contents tasted bitter, and as the cold liquid comforted his parched throat he seemed vaguely to recall having seen Marie's hand hovering near his glass. The reflection passed as he hastily drained the glass, too damnably thirsty to care what he was drinking.

"Wesley."

"What is it?" he asked flatly as he stared at the bartender. The man's complexion was only slightly chocolate, but his hair had a betraying crinkle. The face was not unhandsome, but its pathos and wistfulness, in conjunction with the drooping shoulders below, tormented Wesley. He sensed something of the man's mental sufferings, and believed that he had lived a lifetime of sorrowful introspection and self-imposed repression. Had he been a white man, Wesley was convinced, he would have achieved a happiness which his mixed blood denied to him.

Marie was speaking again. "Promise to tell the truth if I ask something," she demanded.

He was sure he could guess the nature of the question, but as the truth would have to be admitted sooner or later, he nodded.

"Didn't you really know Anne and I were mestizas?"

"How could I? You don't look it." Even as he spoke he realized that, in the eyes of experience, they possibly did look colored—Marie more than Anne. The dense blackness of their hair, the deep olive of their complexion, their dark eyes—such characteristic offered clear pointers.

"Now you realize the truth do you still want to marry Anne?"

His reply was brutal, and to the point. "No. All the Stewarts have been one hundred per cent white. As far as I'm concerned, they'll damn well remain that way." He shook his head, which was beginning to swim. "You've had your drink. Let's go."

She rose obediently. "You'll take me back where I'm staying, Wesley?"

"I suppose so." A walk might help to clear the fuzz and shock from his brain. "Do me good. My God! the heat of this place!"

Outside he could not feel the sidewalk with his feet. In fact, he seemed to have neither feet nor legs; only a trunk, and a head as big as a balloon, and as buoyant. The one drink seemed to have had a surprising effect.

"What's the matter, Wes?" she whispered.

"I can't walk properly. Anyone would think I was drunk."

"Put your arm around me. I'll help." She did not wait for him to act on her suggestion, but took his arm and pulled it round her waist in such a way that his hand cupped her right breast. Through the thin cotton blouse he felt its firm softness beneath his fingers, so he gently squeezed.

"You're not such a bad kid, Marie."

"Even though I'm colored?"

His mood was changing. He felt reckless. He didn't care what she was, who she was: her body was soft and yielding. For two bits—

He was crazily happy. He was bubbling over with happiness. Not a care or responsibility in the world. Music flooded his memory; a song from *The Belle of New York* which he had seen, one lazy evening, four years ago. He had gone with Uncle Bill, just to celebrate something or other to do with Cromwell's plans for the canal. That had been such a night as this. A highball or so too many had chased away all cares and responsibilities, then as now. They had sung on the way back from the theater. The same songs. Funny thing, the memory, to react like this after so many years, he thought hazily. He hadn't hummed the music from that day to this, yet it was quite clear in his mind—

He was still singing when he realized that Marie was shaking him.

"Shush! We're here?"

"Where?"

"Where I'm staying. See, that's my window."

The building swayed to and fro before his eyes. "Why won't it keep still?" he mumbled. "Which window?"

"Never mind." She shook him again. "Wesley?"

"What is it?"

"Help me to my room. I'm not feeling well."

"*You* not feeling well!" He giggled. "I think I'm drunk. I think we're both drunk. What that man give us? Dynamite or something?"

"Will you see me safely in?"

"Why not? As long as you can find the keyhole. I'm brave enough to go anywhere just now. I'd go and kill and eat a jaguar right now if you were to ask me to, honey. That's me, all over. Hundred per cent Stewart, even if my name is Adam." He chuckled. "If I'm Adam I ought to be in the Garden of Eden. With Eve. Especially with Eve."

She opened the outer door of the building, and led him along a short dark passage into a room at the far end. Inside, enough light entered through the wooden shutters to reveal the simple contents of the room. She led him to the bed, and sat down beside him.

"How are you feeling, Wesley?" she asked in a low voice as she ruffled his hair.

"Good."

"Like you were in the Garden of Eden?"

"Where's Eve? There can't be a Garden of Eden without Eve."

She fumbled with her blouse, then stood in front of him so that she could take his head between her hands. "There's me," she whispered. "Couldn't you love me instead?" Leaning forward she pressed her warm mouth against his.

He was in no mood to resist. His body was trembling with a desire far fiercer than Dulcie had ever made him experience. So violent was the urge, indeed, that the modicum of common sense still left to him warned him that he was not wholly sane at that moment; that he had never loved before; that Marie Perrigot, and only she, was the epitome of desirable womanhood: that only she could assuage the desire that her parted lips were whipping into frenzy.

He must have time for reflection, he told himself, while he still had enough sanity to realize that he was close to insanity. Breathlessly, he freed his head from her grasp and pushed her away. As she stood upright the blouse fell away from her shoulders. In the unreal half light that dappled the small room he saw the translucent sheen of olive flesh, and the firm roundness of pink-tipped breasts. With a sigh of defeat, he slipped his arms about her waist, and pulled her nearer to him so that he could press his lips into the yielding softness of her warm flesh.

"I love you, Marie," he gasped. "I'm crazy for you—"

"I love you, too, Wesley darling. I've loved you ever since you returned to Panama. Loved you more than Anne ever could. Take me, my darling. Quickly, quickly, and afterward we can talk until you take me again—"

They lay on the bed completely and utterly relaxed. Her head rested on his chest; one hand she had intertwined in his hair; with the other she fondly rubbed the side of his cheek, which was rough with a stubble of beard.

"Now do you believe I've always loved you, my darling?" As he did not immediately reply she went on, "Aren't you happy that we love each other so much?"

"Ye—es, but—"

"What is it? Have I failed you?" Her voice quickened. "If so, there's still time." She made a tentative move.

He held her still. "Please. Not even you can work miracles."

"I can try."

"No."

She relaxed. "What is the matter?"

"I was thinking of—of Anne."

She laughed contemptuously. "There's no need to think of her. She could never love you as I do; and you couldn't love her." She stiffened with jealousy. "You don't want to go to her—ever?"

"No."

She moved her head so that she could kiss his chin. "Anne isn't like me. She wouldn't have let you do this, ever, without being married to

293

her. I didn't mind. I wanted you to. For me love is more important than marriage. Wesley, *chéri*—"

"What is it?"

"It's against nature for a man to live in Panama as long as you have without a woman."

He laughed shortly. "I don't need you to tell me that. What of it?"

"You ought to have a woman."

"God damn! Of course I ought. But now—"

"You really mean what you say about not wanting Anne any more?"

"I've told you, I have no intention—" He stiffened abruptly, realizing, now that it was too late, that he had already betrayed his own principles. "Oh God!"

She interpreted his fears. "You don't have to worry about me." She moved slightly so that she could kiss his mouth instead of his chin; and when presently he began to tremble she laughed. "Who said I couldn't work a miracle?" she murmured in triumph.

"You witch!"

"Not a witch, my darling. Just a—a mestiza—"

"I'm sorry."

"There's no need to be. I'm not sorry I'm mestiza. I'm glad. Your white women don't know how to love." Her kisses grew more passionate. "I know you won't marry a mestiza; but take me as your mistress, my darling. Let me live in your home. Please, Wesley."

"What about your father?"

She laughed. "He wants to keep Anne at home, but get rid of me. He's afraid of me. He won't say a word. I'll see to that."

Yesterday, he had thought he loved Anne, but now she seemed far, far away; even his freshest memory of her seemed extraordinarily indeterminate. What matter, he thought, now that Marie was his for the taking, without complications, without responsibilities—

A shaft of sunshine moving across his eyes awakened him early the next morning, and dreamily he wallowed in the exquisitely titillating memories of the previous night.

The mood did not last. As the sweetness ebbed he became increasingly aware of the bitterness which remained—an excruciating conscience epitomized by one word: Anne.

He knew his decision of the previous night had been a right and proper one. He did not try to find excuses for his conduct. To have betrayed her trust with any woman would have been reprehensible. To have done so with her younger sister made him despise his weakness beyond thought.

What had made him capitulate so easily to Marie's insidious suggestions? Shock, bitterness, anger? Could be, he reflected, with contempt.

He knew he was not normally so spineless. In the past he had taken rebuffs and shocks in his stride, and would have to do so again in the future, no doubt. He had fallen so easily, so damned easily, so unnaturally easily. One minute he had been in love with Anne: the next, with Marie. What emotion could have been involved to cause such a complete *volte-face* as that?

He had sincerely believed himself in love with Marie when finally he had gathered her into his arms yet he was no callous student for whom emotional love and physical passion were synonymous. For those few hours he *had* been in love with Marie. Yesterday he had been in love with Anne. He still was in love with her. If prayers could have changed her blood he knew that he would sink on his knees and pray.

He felt the bed move as Marie awoke and stretched. He did not stir. Presently she began to hum a Spanish tune. Unlike many people's, her humming was tuneful and recognizable, he decided. At any rate, she was happy and content. She was not cursed with a conscience—though God knows she should be, he reflected. To betray her own sister—

She rose from the bed, and bending over kissed him softly on his tousled head, then on his cheek. Her lips were as light as thistledown. Then she moved across the room, and he watched her through half-closed eyelids as she went, naked, to the washstand, and began to wash. Since his arrival in Panama he had seen so many naked women that the sight had become commonplace. Nevertheless, in the privacy of the sunshine-dappled bedroom the sight of her nudity excited him. The plumpness, which clothes emphasized and exaggerated, now fell into its proper perspective. He reveled in the roundness of her shoulders, her elbows, and her shapely legs. Nothing about her was angular, nothing sagged. Especially not her breasts. In spite of their size they were as firm as tawny marble.

She must have felt intuitively that his gaze was upon her. She turned abruptly, and saw that his eyes were open. She smiled.

"Good morning, darling. Hurry up, there's so much to be done." She saw his puzzled frown. "You haven't forgotten what we talked about last night? I'm your mistress now. We must find somewhere to live."

The suggestion dismayed him.

"This morning?"

She nodded gaily. "The sooner the better, so I can have your new home all fixed for you next time you come out of the jungle. Where shall it be?"

"That depends where I'm finally posted."

"But meanwhile? Somewhere near Panama. Panama's so much nicer than Colón or Cristobal. We can rent it."

"But, Marie—"

"You do want a home, don't you, darling?"

There could be only one answer to that question. Almost more than

295

anything else in this tropical land of jungle, disease, rain, and hard slogging work, he wanted a home of his own once more, and a woman to welcome him to it—a woman with rounded limbs and passionate kisses. With that to look forward to a man could work with a damn sight better will—

He nodded, dry mouthed.

43

THE DECISION had been made. The majority report of the advisory board, consisting of eight of the world's most famous engineers, convened to decide the "Battle of the Levels," calculated that a sea-level canal could be dug with a total excavation of 110,000,000 cubic yards—half of that amount from the cut through Culebra Mountain—and that the construction of such a canal should be completed within twelve to thirteen years, at a cost of less than $250,000,000, and they had therefore, by eight votes to five, recommended this type of canal to the Commissioners.

This decision not only disagreed with the minority opinion, but also more especially with his own, so President Roosevelt, in his message on the subject, strongly urged Congress to decide on a high-level canal. This Congress did, and instructions were given to Chief Engineer Stevens to proceed along those lines. It was further indicated to this much-harassed man that the time had definitely arrived to make the dirt fly.

A conscientious man, Stevens did his best, but his hands were fettered by red tape almost as much as those of his unfortunate predecessor, Wallace, had been. He had other troubles, apart from bureaucracy in Washington with which to contend. It soon became apparent to Wesley, as it did to the majority of clear-sighted inhabitants of Panama, that all was not proceeding well in the Isthmus.

As he said to Sanderson one day, "More than twenty-five thousand men answered the advertisements for work in Panama, but sixty per cent of them are Negroes from the West Indies who regard work as a boring evil, to be indulged in no more than is necessary for the purchase of their few necessities. Many of them work only four days in a week."

"What do they do with the other three? Sleep?"

"When they are not cohabiting with their women. Any spare time remaining they give up to the cultivation of yams, beans, chickens, bananas, and anything else which requires a minimum of attention."

"Well, all your labor troubles are not restricted to the silver population,"

296

Sanderson pointed out. The colored population was known as "silver" workers because they were paid in silver coinage, in contrast to the white workers, who were paid in gold.

"Your white workers, lured from the States by the promise of high wages, are drifting back there as quickly as they can get berths, and the Sicilians we hope to use are not here in any numbers as yet."

"What makes the whites go back to the States? Scarcity of food?"

"That, and the cost of what they can get hold of. What's the good of high wages, they ask, if it all goes back in food? Fact is, they don't like anything about conditions here."

When Stevens realized what was happening he ordered the construction of a chain of Y.M.C.A. clubs at all the larger communities across the Isthmus; also hotels and messes for both silver and gold employees, where the men would be able to buy food supplies, as cheaply as conditions allowed, by an official Department of Subsistence. In the case of the Negroes, complete meals were sold for nine cents, consisting of cocoa and milk, porridge, bread, and jam for breakfast; soup, meat, doughnuts, rice, bread, and fruit for dinner. Even though these meals were the equivalent of American Regular Army field rations, less than fifteen per cent of the Negroes chose them.

New homes were built at convenient centers, in blocks of four-room flats, with broad, screened verandas, for married employees; and dormitory rooms for bachelors. Theatrical performances were organized; also the showing of moving pictures. Masonic lodges were founded. In fact, everything that could be done to keep the men and their families from brooding upon the eternal sunshine and tropical heat was done.

But one problem had still to be solved. Who, ultimately, was to be responsible for the completion of the work which the American government had begun? So long as the government was the employer, the civil service law applied to work at the Isthmus, and no laborer might work longer than eight hours—a crippling restriction if the canal was to be finished within a reasonable time.

Although the versatile Stevens found a way of circumventing this law to some extent, the Chairman of the I.C.C. was convinced that the canal should be built by contract. Although Stevens expressed a contrary view, holding that the task was too immense for a private firm, President Roosevelt was persuaded to ask for tenders from private contractors, and the bidding opened in October.

Panama was invaded by engineers and surveyors, most of whom were soon intimidated by the magnitude of the task. When the day arrived for opening the tenders, only four had been submitted. Of these, only one fulfilled the conditions previously laid down. In February, 1907, President Roosevelt reached the momentous decision that the only body capable of building the canal was the American Army. Some days later he directed

Major George Washington Goethals, of the Army Corps of Engineers, to supervise operations under the direction of Stevens. When the news reached Panama that civilian and Army engineers would have to work together, Stevens wrote a strong note of protest to Washington which the hot-headed, impulsive President construed as a letter of resignation, and he promptly accepted by cable. When Major Goethals eventually reached Panama it was in the double role of Chief Engineer and Chairman of a newly constituted Commission, the third, of whom the majority were Navy or Army engineers.

Then the dirt really began to fly.

Wesley was not able to forget Anne, in spite of his infatuation with Marie. Night after night, as he lay on his camp bed under the thatched roof of a bamboo house in one or another of the Indian villages of the interior, he spent the first half hour or so of his rest thinking bitterly of the Fate which had robbed him of her loveliness.

He realized, more than ever, how sweet was her nature, how soothing her mere presence. She was, he recognized, one of those rare women in whose company a man could relax in supreme and happy contentment. Madge Sanderson was, of course, such another, and in the past he had sometimes thought himself fortunate in knowing two women of that character.

Not that he had reason to regret his liaison with Marie. They had established a temporary home on the outskirts of Panama, to which he returned each time his period of leave came round. She had never failed to greet him with an urgent warmth that could scarely fail to strike an answering fervor from himself. In fact, he never left the house without experiencing a feeling of smug triumph that he should have the power to stimulate and sustain such volcanic passion. Nor did he depart without eager desire for his next period of leave to come round again soon.

Of two facts he was always sure as the train carried him away from Panama back to the sweating jungle: that few white men were given the opportunity of experiencing such violent proof of physical love; and that no white woman could be so fiercely passionate as an uninhibited mestiza.

Nevertheless, as soon as he was back in his bamboo hut, separated from Marie, he was cursed with a nagging conscience, and sometimes felt shame that he should find such pleasure in cohabiting with a half-Negress.

In spite of Marie's having indicated that everyone knew she and Anne were the daughters of Perrigot's black cook, he had subsequently learned that this was not so. On the contrary, one of Papa Perrigot's reasons for not receiving more people than he had to was, it seemed, the hope that nobody would find out that he had married his cook. Besides, unless one were privy to the secret, it was unlikely that anyone would suspect that his children were half black. To eyes not specifically looking for evidence to the contrary, the glossy black hair, the olive complexion, and the dark eyes could well have been inherited from their European parentage.

One day he mentioned this to Larry, the only person with whom he had so far shared the secret of his affair with Marie. Since the other man had joined the I.C.C. and accompanied the survey party into the interior, Wesley had found himself drawn more and more toward the slight little man with the mischievous eyes and lame foot. Somewhat to his own wry annoyance, Wesley realized he was becoming as much a victim of Larry's charm as the ladies aboard the *Yucatan* had been. Of course, one did not trust him absolutely, but what the heck— Besides, it was stimulating to talk with him. His natural intelligence, his salty humor, and his habit of always regarding events and things with a concept entirely different from, and usually in opposition to, the normal person's gave his arguments and opinions an unusual piquancy.

So Wesley said to him, "Why the devil should I feel ashamed of associating with Marie? I'm not self-conscious about her. I mean, I'm not afraid of being regarded by other people with contempt because I've taken a colored woman for my mistress."

"You're rather proud of your ancestors, aren't you? It means something to be a Stewart?"

"Well?"

"Perhaps you feel that you've blotted the old escutcheon."

Wesley laughed. "Didn't I ever tell you about Great-grandfather Duncan's escapade?"

"No."

"He lived for years with a beautiful pagan creature named Phebe, natural daughter of a slave woman by one of the French or Spanish planters. I've never heard that he was ashamed of having a mulatto mistress. In fact, I'm not so sure he didn't marry her. If he didn't feel shame, why should I? There's not all that difference between the Haiti of French Colonial days, and present-day Panama."

"Oh yes there is. You know, Wesley, we moderns seem to feel physical pain more than people used to in olden days, and we experience more shame. We have more respect for law and order than our ancestors. We drink less, love less, are more gregarious, less individual, altogether more sensitive than the robust hardy pioneers of the eighteenth century."

"In short, we have consciences now?"

"If you want the answer to your question in one word, yes. Centuries ago people had no conscience about keeping mad people in chains, or prisoners in underground cells for life, bleeding pigs to death, torturing helpless animals, flocking to public executions. What your grandfather's conscience allowed him to do without a qualm, yours won't allow you to do."

299

Wesley nodded. "I suppose you're right."

"Wesley?"

"Well?"

"What did Anne Perrigot say when you told her about you and Marie?"

"She didn't *say* anything. I didn't have the courage to tell her to her face that I couldn't marry her on account of her Negro blood."

"That's not like you, Wesley, to be afraid."

"I know." Wesley angrily ground a cigarette butt into the ground with his heel. "But I couldn't do it."

"What did you do? Unless I'm asking—"

"It's a relief for me to have a chance of talking. What did I do? Wrote to her to say that something unpleasant had turned up to prevent our marrying, and that I shouldn't have an opportunity of seeing her for a long time."

"That's the sort of thing I should have done. But you, Wesley—" Larry frowned. "Did she reply?"

"No."

"Does she know about Marie?"

"Not unless she's guessed. Marie just wrote to her father that she had decided to leave home, and that was that."

"Did she write that letter about the same time you wrote to Anne?"

"Near enough."

"Then of course she's guessed. You've made it worse for her, doing it that way. If I were a girl I'd damn sight sooner know a man didn't want to marry me for fear of having colored children, than believe he'd jilted me to go off with my sister. God! How she must despise you."

Wesley said nothing. He knew Larry was justified. Instead, after a pause, "I'm still in love with Anne."

Larry laughed dryly. "Of course you are. We men always are in love with the unattainable."

"But that's not why— Hell! what's the use of trying to explain myself."

"You don't have to."

"Well!" Wesley challenged. "Would you marry Anne—or any other mestiza?"

"If I loved her. But then, I'm me, and not you. That makes a difference. I've no ancestors to worry about; no line that I'd like to see carried on."

"I thought you had. Or was that more of your imagination?"

Larry's eyes twinkled. "No. But there's a break between the past and me that can never be bridged."

"Saying which makes you just as much of a defeatist as I am."

Larry shrugged. "But then I was born one," he muttered. "That's different. It isn't my own fault." He looked up as a shadow moved across his feet. "Hello, Olaf."

With Olaf Ericson, too, Wesley was on better terms than at any time in the past. Since taking employment with the I.C.C. he had slowly put on weight. His health had improved; his eyes were recovering their brightness. His mental health was even better: the fires of adversity had tempered the steel of his intolerance; in every way he was of kindlier disposition, more amenable to the discipline of regular employment. Although gold as a subject was taboo, Wesley understood that it no longer interested him. He seemed to have lost his passionate greed for easy riches. His grandiose ideas had vanished. So had his lust; it had been consumed in the brothels of Panama and Colón, leaving behind not even the ashes of memory.

Their party was a happy one. Olaf and Larry were such firm friends that he smiled at his old fears of the trouble that might result from their meeting. Gold had, apparently, cemented their friendship. That, and Ingrid. For Larry's liking was not solely founded on his pathetic reverence for fine physique; he liked Olaf because he was Ingrid's brother. On his part, Olaf's friendship was part pity for Larry's disability, and part gratitude for the months Larry had sacrificed in searching for him.

Olaf sat down beside them. "There's news in that letter from Ingrid you collected this morning, Larry."

Larry stiffened. "Yes?" he questioned eagerly.

Olaf chuckled. "About the canal I mean." Larry relaxed. "She says that the *Canal Record* is going to publish monthly reports of the best steam-shovel performances."

"What fun! And what for?"

"To encourage the teams to work harder. You know, the spirit of competition."

"Aw!"

"I wouldn't be too scornful, Larry, Wesley interrupted. "Competition adds spice to work, for want of any other incentive. Like when you play college football, or other games. You're no better off winning a championship, but you try like hell to win it."

"I've never played games, brother."

"I'm sorry—"

"There's no need to. I used to have fun other ways."

"If I may be allowed to continue," Olaf broke in, "she says that it's already doing good. Preliminary figures make it look like the shovelers will move a million cubic yards this month."

"A million!" Wesley whistled. "Not bad."

"A million, eh!" said Larry. "That's almost up to schedule, if they're to move a hundred and three million cubic yards in nine years."

"Sure. Here's another piece. The dam's not going to be built at Bohio after all."

"Where?"

301

"Gatun."

"Gatun!" There was a strange note of anxiety in Larry's voice. "What will that make the water level, Wes, or don't you know?"

"Not absolutely. Between eighty and ninety feet above, I guess. Why?"

"Just wanted to know." Then Larry nodded, "Does that mean we'll be shifted from this section?"

"Could be. For a time, at least."

"I like this part of the country, Larry mumbled. He turned to Olaf. "What else does she say, Olaf? Anything to interest us?"

"Not us, but me. She wants to know when I'm going to Colón. Says she's crazy to see me." He looked pleadingly at Wesley. "What you think, Wes? Do I look less like something the cat's dug out of the graveyard?"

Wesley nodded. "I don't see why you shouldn't go."

"Let's all go. All three of us. We'll have fun. Give Panama a miss for once."

"You two go," Wesley told him. "I've seen enough of Colón. I prefer Panama in these days."

Olaf grinned. "Bet you've got a girl there."

"Sure. Didn't you know?"

Larry grinned.

So when their next period of leave came round the three men parted company as usual, but at Bohio station instead of Panama station. Olaf and Larry left first. Having seen them off Wesley wandered round the town to waste time until the Panama train was due in.

Ten minutes later he came face to face with Anne.

44

"ANNE," HE CRIED.

She looked composed. "Hello, Wesley."

"Anne—"

"Well?"

More than anything else at that moment he wanted to remain with her; even if she restricted the time to a few minutes only, even if her chill formality persisted.

"Come with me someplace, the Café de Paris, anywhere, so long as I can be with you."

"Why not?" She looked at her watch. "I can stay with you for fifteen minutes."

302

She would have spoken to her dressmaker with the same lack of emotion. How she must despise him.

In silence they walked the fifty yards to the café, where they sat down. He ordered two coffees.

She was the first to speak. "Why did you, Wesley?"

He could detect no reproach in her manner, only impersonal curiosity. Something of this must have betrayed itself in his expression, for she added, "I'm not hurt any more. I can regard the past with complete detachment."

"I wish I could," he said bitterly. "Did you think me a swine, Anne dear, writing instead of telling you myself."

"Of course. But I am not surprised. A man who could do what you have done is usually a coward at heart."

He winced. The knowledge that he deserved her contempt did not lessen the hurt of it.

She went on, "Why did you have to choose Marie, my own sister? If it had been anyone else—"

He started. "Then you know about Marie and me?"

"Of course. You should have known that Marie would crow over me because you had married her instead of me."

"*Married!* She told you that?"

"Yes." Her eyes expressed emotion for the first time. "Aren't you?" she whispered.

"No."

"Oh, Wesley! Then you're living with her? How could you?" Her expression hardened. He saw a new, an unsuspected Anne. Her eyes began to smolder. "If you're not married, look out for yourself, Wesley Adam." She laughed. The note was discordant.

"What do you mean?"

"I shall fight for you. She robbed me of you. Now it's my turn."

He shook his head. "I love you too much, my darling, to ask you to be, or let you be my mistress."

"I don't propose to be your mistress." She leaned near to him, excited and desirable. "I'm going to marry you."

In spite of his cowardice, the situation he had tried to avoid had caught up with him. There could be no further prevarication. This time he must tell her the truth. For the second time he shook his head.

"It's no use, Anne. I haven't the—the spunk. Or I have too much conscience. I don't know. Call it what you like."

"Call what what?"

"Whatever it is in me that won't have—" He swallowed, and turned away. It wasn't easy to say the words. "Mestizo children."

She was so quiet that he turned, and saw that the shadows had closed down upon the dark pools of her eyes. Her lips trembled. Impulsively he laid a hand on hers. It, too, trembled.

"I'm sorry—"

"No," she interrupted swiftly. "Don't be sorry, Wesley. Please don't ever be sorry. Now I understand. You are right. A thousand times right. It is my fault. I had not realized what it means to a foreigner to have mestizo children. Here only a minority have kept their white blood pure. The rest of us accept shades of color as natural." Then, scornfully, "But you are willing to live with a mestiza, and have illegitimate colored children. They don't count, I suppose."

"Marie promised not to have children."

"How can she promise that?" Comprehension dawned. "Oh!" Her face hardened again. "You have managed matters very satisfactorily for yourself. You have all the advantages of marriage without any of its disadvantages."

There seemed little he could say in response to so obvious a truth.

"How long had you been making love to Marie before deciding not to marry me?"

This stung him. "Not at all, Anne. I'm not that much of a swine, to make love to two girls at the same time."

"That's comforting to my self-esteem."

"Please, Anne," he pleaded. "Please try to understand. Even to this day I still don't understand how it happened. I suppose I was knocked flat by hearing from Marie that your mother was a—a—colored woman. I didn't know what I was doing. Just as if I was drunk."

She stiffened. "Did you say that Marie told you about our mother?"

"Yes."

"Didn't you know before she told you?"

"No. Should I have known?"

"It was supposed to be a solemn secret between the four of us, Marie, Papa, Dolores, and me. Were you drunk when she told you?"

"I was dead, cold sober. It was hearing the news that made me want a drink."

"Poor Wesley! I can understand that. What happened next? You got drunk? Both of you?"

"I didn't say so. I said I felt like I was drunk. We only had one drink each."

"And then?"

"She took me back to the house where she was staying and asked me—I mean, I suggested seeing her safely to her bedroom—"

"Wesley." She placed her hand on his. "Please tell me the truth. Was it Marie's suggestion or yours? It means so much to me to know."

"Marie's," he answered gruffly.

"And then?"

"Good God!" He swallowed with embarrassment. "You can't want to know any more?"

"But I do. Was that the—the first time?"

"Yes," he mumbled.

"You'd never even thought of making love to her before that night?"

"Damnation! It's you, I love, Anne. To me she was just your sister— sometimes a damned nuisance."

"It was to spite me. But that—that night, when she took you to her bedroom?"

"You make me feel every kind of a cad, Anne—"

"On account of Marie, me, or yourself?"

"All of us. Just put two and two together. My head was swimming, I felt drunk—"

"On one drink?"

"On one drink. Don't forget the world had kind of dropped away from under me, hearing about you. So it just—happened."

She clenched her hands, but that was the only sign of emotion she betrayed. "How did you come to meet her?"

"Well—" He hesitated, disliking the idea of giving Marie away even to Anne. But he had gone too far.

"Please," Anne demanded imperiously. "I have a right to know how Marie succeeded in stealing my happiness."

Fair enough, he reflected. Except for one word. "You can't put all the blame on Marie, my dear. I did my share of stealing."

"Did you? Can't I?" She smiled wistfully. "I know Marie far better than you will ever do, my dear. She has always hated me."

"Why?"

"I don't know why. How can you ever explain why one person in a family should hate another? Perhaps because I was the elder, and more attractive to a white man. Your friend Olaf Ericson is the only man who ever showed preference for her."

"That's because she was young. Olaf always liked them about that age."

"Oh!" Her mouth twitched as if the information about Olaf's perverted tastes had distressed her. "But you haven't told me yet how you came to meet Marie."

"Funny you should have mentioned Olaf Ericson. I had just left him, and was returning home when I saw someone ahead of me on the street who looked like Marie."

"Wesley! She hadn't just left Olaf?"

"Good grief! I hadn't thought of that." A short reflection: a shake of his head. "I don't think so. Not then. Olaf was dead on his feet."

Her eyes expressed horror. "You said—*not then*. You mean—some other time?"

"Oh God! What the hell am I saying—"

"Was there another time?" she interrupted.

"I don't know. How could I know? How could there have been? Your father has always watched you like a lynx."

"There could have been, Wesley. Papa isn't at home as much as you believe. Sometimes he is away for several days at a time. She used to visit a friend in Panama. Or—so she used to tell me."

"I still don't know. It was just an impression. No more than that."

"Where a woman's concerned, a man's intuition is sometimes to be trusted. You saw her in front of you?"

He nodded, and continued. "I knew she oughtn't to be out alone—it was at night. A Saturday night, so the streets were filled with canal workers on the spree. Because she was your sister I followed her in case of trouble."

He gave her an account of what happened up to the moment when the bocor killed the dove.

"Dear God!" she interrupted. "Marie—there—"

"She wasn't there long. As she came out I heard her thank someone for something—" He saw by her stricken face that she was upset. "What's the matter, darling? You're ill. Let me order you something."

"No, dear. I'm not ill, physically." Her voice became urgent. "Then what happened?"

He told of Marie's revelation. "I felt glad when she suggested a drink," he continued. "I didn't realize the damn thing would almost knock me out."

"It didn't."

"What do you mean?"

"What Marie put in it affected you. Don't you know that bocors practice black magic?"

"Black magic! I've heard stories, of course—Anne—you don't believe—"

"Don't ask me to say what I believe and what I don't believe, Wesley dear. I can't be certain. But I do know that Negroes believe implicitly in the power of witch doctors to perform black magic. And some of the things that happen here, and in Haiti, and in Africa—how can one begin to explain them? What Marie must have bought at the voodoo ceremony was a—a love philter which she may have dropped into your drink."

"Damnation! The idea's crazy, Anne. A charm couldn't have made me fall for Marie, just like that."

"Then what else did, my darling?" she asked quietly.

What else indeed? The repulsive idea that his affections were seduced by some filthy concoction supplied a reason for his experiencing the extraordinary floating sensation which he had put down to intoxication. Also the readiness—the frenetic lust, in fact—with which he had accepted her invitation to possess her. It was common knowledge that the African

306

pharmacopoeia, inherited from generations of witch doctors, contained secret preparations of herbs and drugs, some noxious, some healing, of which the white man had no knowledge.

In fact, Great-grandfather Duncan had written in his *Diary of a Haitian Doctor,* which had been published in Boston almost one hundred years previously: "The *bocor,* as some call the witch doctors, will manufacture a charm, or as they are called in Haiti, *ouangas,* for every imaginable eventuality which the applicant desires to bring about. I myself witnessed a *bocor* prepare a love *ouanga* for a young soldier of Christophe's Royal Dahomeys. Dahomey supplied a dead hummingbird and the witch doctor, the while he droned an incantation to the god Legba, first ground the dried body of the insect into dust, then added to it the pollen of certain jungle flowers I was not able to identify, and a few drops of the swain's blood, extracted from the left armpit, together with his semen. The whole, when ground down to a fine powder, he poured into the scrotum of a goat, which he gave to his client. The following night the Dahomey threw the powder into the maiden's face; whereupon, greatly to my astonishment, the maiden gladly yielded to her swain's caresses.

"Few white men will be ready to believe in the efficacy of *ouangas* and philters, yet one should not overlook the fact that Negro witch doctors have extensive knowledge of the medicinal properties of herbs, leaves, and the bark of tree, which we white doctors do not even suspect...."

He also recollected an article he had read in *Harper's Weekly,* which dealt with the effects of various drugs. If Marie had dropped in his drink cantharides or some local substitute comparable in its effects: added to other, secret drugs it might well act on the cerebral nerves, not only producing the effects of partial intoxication, but also causing excessive and urgent sexual desire. The entire idea was obscene.

After he had parted with Anne he caught the Panama train—but not for Panama. He alighted at Culebra, to stay there for the period of his leave. Frederick Sanderson also alighted.

"Frederick!" The sight of Sanderson's homely face restored Wesley to a sense of reality: he had never been more glad to see anyone. "You old scoundrel! What are you doing here?"

"Major Goethals has called a conference to discuss ways and means of shifting the dirt. The shovels are digging it out more quickly than we can carry it away. Come to that, I thought you were in the jungle."

"So I was, a few hours ago. Just starting a few days' leave. Going to stay here for a change, to have a look-see at what's happening."

"There's plenty happening, believe me. But I thought you would be spending it in Panama."

"Not this time. By the way, you must have passed Larry on his way to Colón."

Frederick chuckled. "Then there will be smiles and songs at home.

You know, I believe Ingrid has fallen for that chum of yours. Not a bad little fellow. Intelligent, too, when he wants to be."

"He's taken Olaf with him this time."

"Has he, by heck! Then there certainly will be smiles. Wish I was there. Ingrid's smiles make one glad to be alive. You did us a good turn, Wes, bringing her into our lives. She's more like a daughter to us than Madge's companion. On second thought, I won't be so pleased if Larry takes her away. I suppose it would have to be someone else if not him. How is Olaf?"

"Making good progress. Staying any place?"

"Nothing fixed."

"Come with me. I'll be here overnight, probably longer."

As they walked out of the cool shadows of the station into the brilliant sunshine, Sanderson went on talking. He seemed wound up. He waved his hand about him.

"This place grows overnight, Wes. When I first saw it the population of the village was about the seven-hundred mark—but you saw it for yourself; you remember it. Now look at it. In less than three years it has increased nine times in size. Nearly five thousand five hundred souls live here, and more are on the way, I hear. By heck! there must be many worse places in the world to live in."

Wesley agreed. No matter which way he looked his eyes were delighted with a panorama of green, undulating country bounded to the east and west by mountains which rose higher and ever higher until their snow-capped peaks were lost in the dim, illimitable distance; and to the north and south by descending valleys, with glimpses of the rivers which had made them, and small, isolated native villages nestling among the fringes of the jungle.

Here, on the western slopes of the hill which was to make one bank of the canal, the village of Culebra was built. It was a compact mass of buildings divided into four distinct sections: the American district, contiguous with the principal streets; one occupied by local merchants, and native and Chinese workers not employed on the actual construction of the Canal; the Negro settlement; and lastly, a camp occupied solely by European laborers.

The houses of the American section were typical of the hundreds that had been, and were still being erected at the various centers. For the members of the executive there were large airy houses, two stories high, of wooden construction, on concrete piers high enough to allow space below the lower floor to be used as a playground for children—and as a garage, too, for the few lucky ones able to afford automobiles. Broad, screened verandas, back and front, could be, and mostly were, used not only as sitting rooms, but were especially built to allow every possible puff of air to flow through the house and keep it reasonably cool.

For the lower-paid workers there were smaller houses; one-story bungalows with only a front veranda, two living rooms, dining room, kitchen, one bedroom, bath, and toilet. Alternatively, there was similar accommodation in any of the apartments of a four-family house. Electric light was available in all houses.

The Negro quarter comprised barracks to house between forty and eighty men; and a kitchen where three meals for twenty-seven cents could be bought.

The merchants and noncanal workers lived in the oldest part of the town. Some of the houses had been standing there since the railroad builders had made the place a temporary terminus in the 1850's. This move had attracted hotels, where one could stay overnight for exorbitant prices. The remainder of the buildings were three-room cottages which the French had built. "Doghouses," the Americans called them. The opprobrium was justified when they were compared with the American frame houses.

In addition to homes for workers, nearer the summit of the hill were a number of official buildings—the homes of the chief engineer, the president of the railroad, the Governor of the Canal Zone, the resident member of the fortification-board, and many other officials. On the extreme top of the hill was the administration building, an ugly two-story edifice.

Wesley had not seen this building. It was new since his last visit to the town. Remembering the fear of slides which had obsessed the French builders he thought the choice of site an unfortunate one.

45

ALL THE TIME they walked—and Wesley noticed that they appeared to be making for the summit of the hill—Frederick talked of this and that. He seemed buoyant and his conversation flittered from one subject to the next. Wesley had never known him to be more gay, and wondered why.

They reached the far limit of the town; and Frederick was silent, awed by the magnificent scene which had opened up below them. With their backs to the administration building they stood on the edge of a canyon seven hundred feet wide, a dirty, muddy canyon of loose shale and rock; a canyon that lacked any natural beauty; a canyon which stretched away for several miles on either side of them until its distant ends wriggled and twisted their ways through distant hills; a canyon that had straightened out many of the curves in the Pass which had given it its name of Culebra the Snake, but which still retained enough to justify its old name.

A man-made canyon not even nature in her most freakish mood could have fashioned. Beneath the flurry and seeming chaos, beneath the white plumes of steam huffed out by thirty or more steam shovels, beneath the dirty black smoke of the dozen dirt trains which chugged up and down the canyon, beneath the sudden eruptions from exploded dynamite charges, beneath the throb of engines, the rumble of wheels, the clatter of drills, the shrill blast of warning whistles—beneath the camouflage of confusion, the pattern of progress could be seen by a professional eye.

"If you can make head or tail of that!" Frederick gasped.

But of course Wesley could. "Well?" he chuckled. "What do you want to know?"

"Just what's happening down there? What's the idea of all those shelves?"

" 'Benches' to the engineers, Frederick. It was a French idea to expedite excavation, and it's good enough for us to carry on along the same lines. After they had removed the peak of the divide, together with any other summits which were situated in what ultimately will be the prism, they excavated their first ditch, which ran the length of the Cut. This was to serve a double purpose. First, to carry off surplus water, which naturally became an increasing menace as the depth increased. Secondly to act as a track for the side excavators when they started on the next stage of the work.

"As soon as that first pilot cut was completed—when it met in the middle after having been started from either end—the excavators were hauled back to their starting points, and restarted to make a new pilot out on the bench, or shelf if you prefer, immediately above the original cut. Meanwhile a railroad track had been laid along the original pilot cut, along which loading cars were shunted immediately below the excavator. Thus the excavators could dig out ahead of them, swing around, and deposit their spoil into the loading cars below them. Do you follow?"

Frederick nodded.

"Later, as the ends of the cut in turn mounted the side slope of the hill they were cutting through it became possible to cut a series of shelves at the same time, and excavators were enabled to move forward in echelon."

"As they are now?"

"Yes, but the difference between French days and the present time is that all the old French side excavators have been discarded in favor of steam operated shovels which scoop up several tons of dirt with every hoist. Also, we are no longer dealing with surface clay. The mountains are rock, with a substratum of clay, so the rock has to be broken up by dynamite before the shovels can shift it."

310

Frederick stared down into the canyon, and could begin to see the pattern of things. "It's colossal!" he muttered. "How deep is it now? Hundred and fifty feet, or I'm a Dutchman!"

"More than that. The French cut was nearly that when I first surveyed Culebra. Seeing the way these Bucyrus shovels are biting into the ground I'd say its present depth is all of two hundred by now."

"And how much more to go?"

"At this point? Maybe half as much again."

"And it's taken twenty-five years to dig this much? God, Wesley! It'll never be finished. I mean, the deeper you go, the wider you'll have to make the bottom, I suppose, if you don't want overhanging sides?"

Wesley nodded. "Of course. The French estimated a bottom width of seventy-four feet. It's double that already. But don't overlook the Bucyrus and Marion shovels, and the hundreds of well drills, tripod drills, hand drills for blasting purposes, the hundred-ton locomotives, capable of pulling twenty-seven large dump cars, each capable of carrying seventeen cubic yards apiece. You know the equipment end better than I do. With their obsolete equipment, those poor French devils could only scratch at the surface compared with what we can do."

"I know that, Wes, and perhaps I can tell you something. There are more than fifty miles of track in this Cut alone. I didn't believe it when I was first told. I do now. All the same, it'll be a miracle if the Cut is finished in another—how many—say eight years from now."

"Sometimes I think it will be a miracle if it's ever finished."

Sanderson was surprised by the unexpected somberness of his companion's voice. "What's worrying you, Wes?"

"Something that's worried me from way back." He pointed to the opposite bank. "See where those shovels are working down there on the bed?"

"You mean, where the work stopped short all the way up to the top? Opposite that dump of dirt? What's that been left there for, by the way? It stops the water draining away?"

"It wasn't left there, Frederick. It's been pushed up from below."

Sanderson laughed unbelievingly. "Now you're joking! Who pushed it up? Old Nick himself, because he doesn't like his territory being invaded?" He chuckled at his own witticism.

"If so, he hasn't done much good to that steam shovel that's lying on its side; nor the track that's twisted into a corkscrew."

"Been dumped there with the dirt, I suppose."

"Dump nothing! They want to get rid of dirt, not dump it. That part of the bottom was as flat as the rest a few days ago. It's been forced up by the weight of a slide which displaced laterally the material lying directly below it. Much as one part of a rubber ball bulges out when you press another part in."

311

"Then all that rock and stuff over there, where I thought the shovels had stopped short, that's a slide, is it? Christ! Then all that rock will have to be shifted, too?"

"Naturally. And that's only a small slide. A matter of two or three acres, I'd say, looking at it from here. You can imagine what a big slide means. One at Cucaracha, started in 1884, and hasn't stopped."

"What a headache for the executives." Sanderson was silent for some time, watching the activity two hundred feet below him. It was like observing a colony of ants at work: the figures of thousands of men looked very little larger. Then he nodded his head several times, and said, "I reckon you and I, Wes, are looking down on one of the wonders of the world. Kind of makes one proud to be connected with it, doesn't it?"

Wesley nodded in agreement. He had thought that several years previously.

From Colón to Panama the work of dividing a continent in two continued unceasingly. At Colón, where new docks were rising to handle the ever-increasing volume of shipping; and a breakwater was extending a curving arm out into the bay. At Gatun, where three pairs of parallel concrete locks, capable of lifting the largest vessels afloat from sea level to eighty-five feet above, were slowly taking shape: where, close by, an immense dam was being thrown a mile and a half across one of Panama's narrow valleys. At Culebra, where mountains were being slashed in halves. At Pedro Miguel, where one pair of twin locks were under construction, to drop vessels from eighty-five feet to fifty-five feet above sea level. At Miraflores, where two more pairs of locks would, in stages of twenty-seven and one-half feet each, restore ships to their native sea water. At Balboa, where a new dock town was in the making. At Ancon, where a breakwater, built of the spoil from Culebra, was connecting the mainland with Naos Island. At a dozen other places where the Panama Railroad was being relocated.

From Colón to Panama the restless army of thirty-thousand workers toiled and sweated and grumbled and swore, and fell ill. Unable to stand up to the gruelling test of being alternately scorched by tropical sunshine and drenched by thunderous cloudbursts, some died; and many others moved on to more equable climes, or returned to their native country. The movement was constant. Men came, worked for a year, and went. The Service personnel remained, because they had orders to do so. The colored folk remained, because they were hardened to tropical conditions and were not affected by them. Of the rest, only a handful stayed on year after year.

To that handful time ceased to mean much. To some extent the endless days of hard slogging work dulled their senses. They worked the daylight hours through, slept the unmoving sleep of the exhausted, and were up again at daybreak, to work through another day. When they wanted con-

312

solation it was supplied by the knowledge that their bank balances were steadily mounting; also that they were each playing their part in a magnificent achievement. There could be no doubting its magnificence. It was more apparent to the workers at that time than it was ever likely to be to the rest of the world, once it was completed. For the rising waters of the great lake that was in the making would allow future generations only a bird's-eye view of the result, and a bird's-eye view is seldom accurate, for it sees only the flattened, foreshortened surface above, and little of the tremendous depths below.

In the jungle Wesley wrestled with his problems.

"When are you going back to Marie?" Larry asked.

"God knows! I don't. Perhaps never. Would *you* go back?"

"You still love Anne, don't you?"

"Yes."

"Are you going to marry her then?"

"No."

Larry shrugged. The explosive, emphatic reply left him in no doubts on that score. "Are you ever likely to make her your mistress?"

"Damn it!" Wesley began angrily. "I told you I love her."

"Well, then, what's the harm in carrying on with Marie?"

"Because the whole idea's too damn degrading. How would you like to think you had been tricked into a woman's bed by drinking a witch doctor's filthy brew?"

Larry hissed. "I wouldn't mind what tricks were played upon me to get me into the beds of some women I know."

"In spite of Ingrid?"

"You're right," Larry's reply was abrupt. "It makes a difference when you love someone. But if you're positive about not marrying Anne—"

"And possibly having mestizos?"

"Again, you're damn right, Wesley, for their sake as much as your own. More, perhaps, if you think of returning home."

"Of course I do. When the canal's finished. I want to see it through."

"So do I. So does Olaf. We're three of a kind. Funny, isn't it? All of us being so different, and all keen on the same ends. But about Marie now. As you can't have Anne, for God's sake, why not have Marie? At least, she's second best. I know this. If I don't marry Ingrid— By heck! I'll go to bed with every woman who'll have me from Colón to Panama.

"Look, Wes," he went on earnestly. "We're all of us proud to be doing this work, but that doesn't make it any less one hell of a job. If a man doesn't have something to look forward to in between bouts of work, he'll crack up. Like all those others who go rushing home again after a few months here. You nearly cracked up once or twice, didn't you?"

"Yes."

313

"The work you were doing then was peanuts compared with what we're doing now."

"I know. And there are times—" Wesley looked up at his companion. "You and Olaf always come back from Colón looking happy enough, and you don't—at least—"

"I still have some decencies left. As for Olaf, he hasn't a woman there if that's what you mean. He's still burned out. He's happy just to have his sister. You wouldn't care to see Anne sometimes, I suppose? Just in a friendly way. For the sake of companionship."

"It wouldn't be fair to either of us."

"I suppose not," Larry agreed. "All the same, if I were you I'd think of going back to Marie. Yeah, and before it's too late. She's not the kind to be without a man for long."

"How could I explain to Anne?" Wesley asked with scorn.

Larry smiled. "Guess you wouldn't have to do any explaining. Just so you're honest and tell her what you plan to do."

So Wesley went back to Marie, and was soon congratulating himself on having done so. Her strange allure still held him in spite of himself whenever he was with her. She rushed into his arms and embraced him with such abandon that he found himself returning her kisses with no less passion. He could not have asked for a more exciting welcome. Before he could properly realize what was happening he was relaxed in an armchair, hastily trying to invent excuses for having remained away so long. She sat curled on his knees, head on his shoulder, lips pressed against his neck. Of course, it was too hot to remain like that for long, for the sun was still high and the oppressive heat clung to their flesh. The welcome was too much like his dreams of marriage not to react upon his emotions. He tried to overlook the fact that it had been brought about by some sort of mumbo-jumbo, and did so without too much effort.

Later, he reproached himself, both for his own weakness in becoming too easy a victim of her charms, and also for his enjoyment in doing so. Although he had returned to her for no other reason, he should, he reflected, have had a little more respect for his pride—to say nothing of his love for Anne. What was the value of his love, if he could enjoy sleeping with one woman while loving another? Why were men made differently from women? A woman was more constant in her love. She could not so easily divorce the physical from the spiritual. Her body was the servant of her heart. In that case—he smiled—Marie must love him very, very much to have gone to the witch doctor for his damned aphrodisiac.

When he returned to his temporary headquarters at Frijoles, for they had been working southward, he found a small parcel waiting for him. In it was a letter from Anne, together with the anthology of poems he had given her for a Christmas present.

314

The letter was sweet, and made his eyes prickle. Of course she understood, she wrote. It was not natural for a man to live without a mate, especially in the tropics. For herself, she would go on loving him forever. Although circumstances made their physical separation necessary, perhaps they might meet in their dreams. So she was sending him the anthology of poems he had given her. She had read some of the poems every night until she had come to learn them by heart. If he would do the same, perhaps their thoughts might bring their souls together in closer communion. Although her heart was bitter at the bar which had separated them, she thanked God for the great joy he had brought to her life, and would pray nightly for his health, his safety, and his everlasting happiness.

So each night, after going to bed, he read the poems for fifteen minutes or so, usually by the light of a candle. He began to learn some of them by heart, so that he could repeat them to himself after blowing out the candle, trying at the same time to visualize Anne's sweet face in its lovely serenity. Sometimes it seemed to him that in the few seconds before sleep encompassed him, he was in communion with her. The thought gave him ineffable peace.

Beyond that peaceful half hour in bed there was very little rest for him, or for any of his party. The tempo of work was increasing. The Commission was pressing for quicker results. Costs were rising as nature fought back tooth and nail against the bold men who were striving to change her face. Nowhere else was the battle more in evidence than along the length of Culebra Cut. Again and again the despondent workers saw weeks of slogging, heartbreaking labor ruined by fresh slides. The estimated total of the spoil to be excavated was raised, torn up, and raised again, as tens of thousands of cubic yards slid into the Cut, wrecking locomotives, spoil cars, miles of track.

Strange stories of the fantastic antics of these slides were circulated across the Isthmus by amazed beholders. Stories of a ninety-five-ton steam shovel carried halfway across the Cut, and gently set down again, unharmed; of what another slide did to three parallel sets of track, sinking the one nearest the bank by several feet while the farthest one rose by the same amount, leaving the middle track undisturbed; of a third slide which moved forward so gradually that a steam shovel made more than one hundred trips across its bottom end without once moving its track; of steam shovels in the bottom of the Cut being completely submerged as flood waters swept through it; of fissures, blasted open by dynamite gangs, which gushed smoke and steam, and sent the superstitious Negroes running for their lives in fear of a volcanic eruption.

If nature could fight, so could man. Encouraged by the indomitable chief engineer—"The only way to overcome the slides is by unremitting excavation," said Colonel Goethals—the digging went on. Each month showed an average increase in the number of cubic yards excavated from

315

the Cut. One million cubic yards a month—1,150,000—1,210,000—1,280,000. The total of the original estimate was reached, yet nearly as much again still remained to be shifted before ships could hope to pass through. Greater depth had still to be reached, and because of the slides more shelving banks had to be allowed for, and that meant more spoil to be shifted. The running of the spoil trains was speeded up. They followed one another out of the Cut at intervals of four minutes.

In spite of slides and breaks accounting for an additional eight to ten per cent of material to be excavated and removed, the work kept up to schedule, went ahead of schedule. The Cut would be completed on time, before time.

But one day brought news of a new disaster. Seventy-five acres of mountaintop had started to slide into the Cut, carrying with it part of the town of Culebra.

46

THE NEWS OF the fresh slide reached Wesley and his companions in a letter from Godwin, which Wesley found waiting for him when they returned to the valley from the hills. Godwin's main object in writing was to ask Wesley to look him up on the next visit to Panama. He had been going through old files of the *Star and Herald,* he wrote, and it looked as if he were on the trail of a very interesting story about which he did not want to say more at that stage in case the trail led to a dead end. Trouble was, he added, he didn't have much time to spare, these days. The canal—"I often think of it as *our* canal, lad. Do you remember how we spewed out our guts to put the Panama Canal on the map?"—was taking up so much of his time there wasn't much left for anything else except an occasional visit to the Humming Bird.

I suppose you've read about the new slide at Culebra. I've just come back from there. It's the worst yet, if you except Old Man Cucaracha who's been with the workers so long they would miss the big feller. This new one is not only bigger, it's immediately opposite Culebra; its summit is actually within the limits of the village, of which quite a sizable part has begun to slide as well. It's fortunate that it was a slide and not a break, for although it's still moving slowly forward, there will be time to move the threatened buildings before they land at the bottom of the Cut. The joke is that one of the buildings is the administration building, so I can't help appreciating the rough justice of the new slide, though I doubt whether the poor old Colonel sees it in that light. Another of the bigger buildings which will have to be shifted is the Y.M.C.A. clubhouse. Another is the hotel next to it. Was that the one you've stayed at in Culebra?

The latest slide will mean more of a holdup than usual. I understand that the Colonel has given orders that no shovels are to be used on the slide until a large part of Culebra has been moved away from the danger slope, in case it develops à la Cucaracha. These are mighty interesting days; and I thank my guardian imp—not being eligible for an angel, I guess—that I had the chance of coming here. I'm only sorry I didn't come years ago. I must be one of the few white people who prefer living here. I wouldn't go any place else.

Olaf Ericson grimaced when Wesley read this passage aloud.

"By Jimminy! He's nuts, preferring to live here."

"It's not so bad as all that," Larry protested. "Ingrid likes it here."

"That's so," Olaf agreed. "But Ingrid's easy. She likes any place where she likes the people. Me, I can't get back quick enough to the U.S.A. Jimminy! Just to feel cold again, and see snow sometimes."

Larry smiled. "There's nothing stopping you, brother."

"You mean, there won't be when the canal's finished."

Wesley glanced at the speaker. Olaf was looking more like his old self, for he had filled out and his shoulders were square again. He was once more a fine figure of a man.

"Then you've changed your mind about the canal, Olaf? You fought against it, remember?"

"I'm still against it in principle. That village where we stayed last night. What was wrong with it?"

"Nothing. Nice view. Close to the river. Close to a savannah. Everything within reach, you might say. In fact, I thought it rather a pretty little place."

"So did I. That's the point. How much longer will it remain nice?"

"Why shouldn't it?" Larry asked.

"Because its elevation is only thirty feet above sea level, that's why."

"Oh! You mean, it'll be at the bottom of the lake one day?"

"Sure it will. Even if you were only an Indian, if that home had been yours all your life would you like to see it disappear under the rising waters, and know that you would be forced to live someplace else, perhaps not half so nice?"

"They'll be well paid—"

"Of course they will, but money isn't everything—" Olaf paused, and glanced shamefaced at Wesley. "I'm a fine one to talk, after the years I've wasted searching for gold. Guess I'm older than I was."

"I wonder."

317

"Well?" Olaf challenged.

"Suppose you sniffed gold tomorrow, wouldn't you go after it like a cat after fish?"

Larry and the Scandinavian exchanged quick glances. Olaf shrugged, then grinned. "Suppose so, Mr. Prosecuting Attorney. A leopard, that's me."

"But, gold apart, you'll continue with the I.C.C."

Olaf nodded. "I'm a damned fool, but it's got me like it's got most of us. It's the challenge, I suppose, and the idea of not being beaten. To cut the bloody Continental Divide in half so ships can sail through it. Can you imagine it? Ocean-going ships steaming over a range of mountains."

"Anything more in the letter about the slide?" Larry presently asked.

"That's all."

The slide was bad. It grew worse. The men in the Cut were disheartened by seeing how much of their previous work had been wasted, and how much more they would have to do again. The job began to look as if it never would be finished. Goethals, impervious as always to disappointment—at least, outwardly—whipped them on to fresh efforts. He ordered the removal of the heavy material at the top of the slide, so as to lessen the weight which was exerting a downward pressure and forcing up the bottom of the Cut. Six weeks later the weight had been eased enough for three shovels to work at the bottom of the slide, lowering the center cut there so as to promote fresh drainage.

Although Colonel Goethals had bad trouble at Culebra Cut, this was compensated by the fact that at almost every other point work was up to and even ahead of schedule. At Gatun the huge mile-and-a-half dam which was to be the key, as it were, of the entire canal, was rapidly nearing completion. It was announced that the locks of the spillway would be closed at the end of the year. From that moment the Chagres River would cease to empty itself into the Caribbean, and would pile up against the walls of the dam and flow backward from whence it had come.

Back in the foothills, every elevation had been checked and rechecked. In the headquarters of the I.C.C. there already hung on the walls a map showing the area of the lake as it would exist in three and a half years' time, when the waters had risen to the height limit of eighty-five feet. New villages were being built, on a higher level, to replace those which were destined to sink forever below the rising waters, but in the remoter valleys the doomed villages were still occupied, and would remain occupied, until it was too late for personal belongings to be removed, for it was beyond the imagination of the simple Indians to realize that a lake would come where no lake ever had been in the history of the world.

In the larger villages of the Chagres Valley, where the white and colored population lived, preparations were being made for the inevitable move,

318

for many of them, too, would disappear during the next three years: notably, Ahorea Largarto, Tabernilla, San Pablo, Mamei, Gorgona, Matachin.

Bohio would be luckier; and Perrigot's home, too, for both were above the ultimate water level. For this mercy Wesley felt pleased. Although there was no love lost between him and the old Frenchman, there was Anne—but of Anne's reaction he was less sure. There were occasions when he gathered from her letters that she would have welcomed a move to either Panama or Colón, that she was more lonely than ever, and wanted company and gaiety and other interests.

She never put these wishes in actual words; still less the reason for them. He had several times to check himself from hastening to her: to tell her that he still loved her, and would always love her. Each time only the one thought held him back: the possibility of her bearing him mestizo children. Sometimes, he was made so crazy by his love that he contemplated asking her to marry him and promise that she would have no children. But this thought he dismissed almost at once. He realized that marriage with Anne under those conditions would be no marriage. It would be no more than a degrading union that would ultimately turn their love to ashes. He might live with Marie on such conditions, but not with Anne. He loved Anne.

So the months passed. It could not be said that life was monotonous for Wesley's small party, for the jungle could never be monotonous. It supplied too many surprises. One dark night, for instance, Wesley had seen a pair of burning eyes glowing above him. He had fired, hoping for an ocelot, but the body which crashed down had been that of a goat-sucker bat. Another time, they found the entrance to a cave, and decided to investigate. After advancing nearly twenty yards along a sloping corridor filled with dripping stalactites they entered a large, limestone chamber. The moment they did so the cave began to fill with a wind that had ruffled their hair, and instilled in them a fear which might have degenerated into panic if Larry had not pointed to the roof to indicate the hundreds of bats that were circling over their heads. Then there was the alligator that had snapped at Larry's hand as he stupidly trailed it in the water while they were crossing the river in a cayuca. And on one famous occasion Olaf had been involved in a jaguar's pursuit of a peccary. First of all the big-boar peccary, in its panic-stricken flight from the great cat, had cannoned against Olaf, nearly knocking him over. No sooner had he recovered his balance than he had found himself face to face with the roaring, menacing pursuer. Larry had fired, missed Olaf's head by inches, and the jaguar by a greater margin. Fortunately the shot had frightened the beast away.

Their lives alternated between work and sleep. Whenever one of them could relax sufficiently to contemplate the date, it was nearly always a surprise to find how quickly time had passed.

319

One day Larry sprang a surprise of his own. "Ingrid and I are going to be married three months from now," he announced with startling abruptness.

Wesley's first reaction was to glance at Olaf. When he saw the blond giant puffing away at his cigar with composure he knew that the matter had already been discussed, and had met with the brother's approval.

"Congratulations," he muttered, but he could not put much warmth into it.

Larry smiled. "That's what I like about that guy," he said to Olaf. "He's always so god-damned enthusiastic." Then to Wesley, "You're thinking of Ingrid?"

"Kind of."

"Don't blame you, Wesley. In fact, I wish I were as sure of myself as she is of me. I'm a poor specimen of manhood for any woman to accept, but bless her sweet soul, she swears she's contented and happy."

Olaf chuckled. "She waited so long for the poor fellow to say something that she got tired, and proposed to him instead. She said it's Leap Year, so why not?"

"Is it? God! Nineteen twelve. That makes—aw, what the hell! I'll soon be looking for gray hairs." He spoke with bitterness, thinking of Anne. All this time they might have been married. He could easily have been a father.

"Olaf's told the literal truth, Wes. I wouldn't have asked her, ever. It isn't only my damned foot, it's me. Do you approve, Wes? It will mean a lot to me if you can."

"I'll approve if you never let her down, Larry. Can you be trusted?"

Larry looked somber. "God knows! But I swear I'll try hard. Besides—" A mischievous grin brought the old cheeky expression back to his face again. "I know what Olaf will do to me if I let her down."

"By God! I will, too, if you do." There was passion in his voice. Then he, too, grinned, and shook his head. "You won't, little man. Ingrid will mother you so as you won't want to let go her apron strings. You're a nicer guy than you think you are."

"Thanks, Olaf." Larry looked sideways at Wesley. "But Wes knows me better than you do, Olaf. Do you think I'll make it?"

Wesley reflected. "It's a fifty-fifty chance, and that's about all any marriage is. I should know. I had faith in myself, once, until I let Dulcie down."

"*You* let *her* down!" Larry added one more word: it was short and to the point.

The imprisoned Chagres began to creep across the countryside, except in the vicinity of the locks and other points where temporary dams kept the

320

slowly rising waters from flooding the works and so interrupting the erection of huge concrete chambers, and the installation of the electrical machinery that would ultimately open and close the massive 700-ton gates.

One morning, after a week's incessant rain, the inhabitants of the Chagres Valley looked out of their doors and windows, and saw that the river had vanished beneath the surface of a vast spreading lake.

In spite of the rains for months its average depth did not rise above the soles of one's feet, for it had to cover a total area of 164 square miles. Larry had married and settled down to a blissful life long before the waters rose to ankle depth. For one complete period Wesley and Olaf had had to carry on work with substitute help, and were miserable in consequence. As Olaf said one night, "Now the little guy isn't with us we begin to appreciate what his company means. Do you know we haven't cracked a smile for three god-damned nights, Wesley? And haven't talked about anything more interesting than how to make money from running a blasted delicatessen on the East Side in New York. I think they're going to be happy, the two of 'em."

The waters continued to rise. Valley bottoms changed their appearance, as narrow river beds were transformed into shallow lakes which grew infinitesimally wider and longer with every rain. As the waters penetrated the jungle, there was a constant movement of livestock retreating from the lapping waters. Not all the animals moved in the right direction. Many found themselves marooned on small islands in the center of the spreading waters. It was no uncommon sight to see jaguars, ocelots, sloths, armadillos, and monkeys slowly dying from starvation, still clinging desperately to the tops of isolated trees. Drowned bodies of tapirs, iguanas, and snakes often floated slowly northward on the impulse of a sluggish current that had once been a leaping, unfettered torrent. Crocodiles and swamp alligators spread farther afield, the fish population increased enormously.

Canal employees discovered a new and delightful way of spending Sundays, holidays and periods of leave. Where once an impenetrable tangle of undergrowth had prevented hunting and exploration, now the ubiquitous water had opened up easily negotiable highways into distant parts of the jungle hitherto unexplored. Many new kinds of boat made their appearance on the spreading lake, especially the gasoline launch, and even house boats. Sundays were noisy with shotguns. As a consequence, any territory that could be easily reached by cayuca was quickly depleted of anything shootable, even nongame birds and animals. On the other hand, the population of heron and egret, and other swamp-loving bird life increased enormously, for like the crocodiles and alligators, the area of their natural habitat had been increased a thousandfold.

And still the waters rose and spread.

One day Godwin turned up out of the blue. "Just felt like coming to see the three of you at work," he explained blandly, as the four men sat round a campfire and smoked contentedly.

Wesley chuckled. "Get rid of it, Uncle Bill. I can see the gleam in your eyes that you've important news. Another slide at Culebra? Gatun dam collapsing?"

"Nothing like that, lad. Something personal."

Larry looked up. "Like me to leave you, Uncle Bill?"

Godwin shook his long, gray head. "Nothing that nobody here needn't know. It's history."

"By Jimminy!" Olaf exclaimed with horror.

"I've got through all the *Star and Herald* files at last," Godwin went on. "As far back as eighteen fifty, when Judson Ames sold the *Panama Herald* to the *Panama Star*. That's far back enough for what you want to know."

"Guess so," Wesley agreed. "The California gold rush didn't start much before then. Go on, Uncle Bill."

" 'Course, you all know about the gold strike, and what happened to the gold, so I'll go—"

"Not me. I don't," Olaf told him.

"There's not much to tell, Ericson. At that time it was safer, and cheaper, to dispatch the gold to New York by way of the old Spanish trail which ran from Panama to Cruces or Gorgona, and then by canoe the rest of the way to the town of Chagres.

"It wasn't long before the express agencies began to operate gold trains across the Isthmus. It wasn't long after that before bandits began *their* operations. In August, eighteen fifty, masked men held up and robbed a Howland and Aspinwall gold train of thirty thousand dollars' worth of gold.

"Other robberies followed. More than one hundred thousand dollars' worth in December; another hundred thousand a few weeks later. These were followed by other organized robberies, and individual holdups, culminating in a loss of quarter of a million in gold the following September." Godwin looked up abruptly. "Maybe you know all this?"

"Wes gave me an outline of it years ago. You elaborate, Uncle Bill. I'm interested."

"All right, son. By then it was practically an established fact that the bandits were organized by an American known locally as El Jaguar. Well, the express agencies became a little tired of all these losses, and decided that it was high time somebody did something to end them. So they sent to the U.S. for a Texas Ranger called Ran Runnels. The old timers here tell me he was a little runt of a man with chestnut hair.

"Almost the first person this here Runnels spoke to was Wesley's grandfather, Henry Stewart. They sort of liked each other from the start, so Runnels persuaded the P.P.R., who Henry was working for, to release him

322

so he could help establish a secret police force. So the two men went to Panama together, and the next thing you know had enlisted forty men for the Isthmus Guard.

"For weeks nothing happened. That is, the people back in Colón didn't think so. But Runnels' men weren't just standing about. They were working underground gathering information and assembling a list of names of known bandits.

"One night Runnels, Henry Stewart, and their forty Guards rounded up thirty-seven suspects, marched them to the sea wall, and hanged the lot of 'em as a warning to any remaining bandits that gold trains weren't to be held up any more."

Ericson looked at the speaker.

"My God! Without a trial?"

"Sure. That was Texas justice in those days, Ericson. Rough and ready, but ninety-nine per cent effective." He looked back at Wesley. "You knew all this?"

"Heard it a hundred times from Grandfather."

"Thought so, but I wonder if you know something else, lad? The name of one of the men your grandfather helped string up?"

Wesley grew taut. "Spill it, Uncle Bill?" he demanded, tight lipped.

"Edouard Perrigot—old man Perrigot's father. Does that answer some of the questions?"

"Jesus!" Ericson gasped.

47

"SO THAT IS WHY he hates me," Wesley murmured at last. "He wanted to avenge his father."

Ericson looked savage. "What about me? He had no reason for hating me, but he didn't mind me going along with you to die in the jungle, the rat."

Wesley tightened his lips. "It's not easy for us Americans to understand that kind of hate."

"*I* can understand it." Larry was hard, bitter.

"I know." Wesley relaxed. "So all our deductions about old man Perrigot trying to protect a gold mine were so much poppycock?"

"Were they?" Godwin asked.

The flames leaped up and illuminated Godwin's crooked grin. Wesley chuckled. "He's holding out on us, boys. What else, Uncle Bill?"

"Perrigot's buddy, at the time of the hanging, later adopted young Perrigot—I don't mean legally, but as good as. That buddy was El Jaguar's partner, and his name was—"

"Jim Holmes?" Larry shouted.

Godwin nodded.

"By God!" Larry's face looked sharper than usual in the firelight. His lips were tight; his eyes, angry with disappointment. "As Holmes knew where the gold was, the chances are that he told young Perrigot. And Perrigot lives near enough to Bohio. It adds up, blast their god-damned hides!"

"What adds up?" asked Ericson, slow witted.

"Use your brain, brother. Don't you see? It wasn't a gold mine Perrigot's been living on all these years. It was El Jaguar's cache."

"Damnation!" Ericson exploded.

Wesley studied each man in turn, and realized that his old suspicions, that they had become allies, instead of enemies, in the search for gold had not been without justification. No wonder they had not been anxious to move away from the Bohio district. True, other interests had superseded their frenzied search for gold—his own self-respect in the case of Olaf; love, in Larry's case—and no doubt they had resigned themselves to the inevitable. But the old excitement was still there. Both men were revealing obvious signs of agitation.

He grinned as he took a deep puff at his cigar. "If Perrigot knew where the gold was, why did he leave the country and return to Europe?"

"If he ever did," Ericson answered. "He said so, but what does that mean? He's an old bastard anyway."

"At any rate, he worked for years with the French company as an engineer. Frederick Sanderson knows that as a fact. He met a man who had worked with Perrigot."

"Well?"

"If you knew the whereabouts of a quarter of a million in gold would you work as an engineer for peanuts?"

"Suppose he found it while he was working as an engineer?" Larry suggested. "Don't forget what the cashier at the bank said about Perrigot selling gold to the bank regularly twice a year."

"And what about those mysterious disappearances in the jungle?" Ericson added hotly. "What has he been living on for the past twenty years?"

Wesley shrugged his shoulders. "Maybe there's something in what you say, fellows, but if he's been helping himself to it for the past twenty years, how much gold do you think is left?"

"Still a picking," Ericson claimed. "He's not been spending at the rate of twelve thousand dollars a year."

"He might have been saving at that rate."

Ericson angrily threw another log on the fire, scattering sparks in all directions, and muttered, "God-damned miser!"

324

When Godwin continued on his way to Colón he took with him, unwittingly and unknowingly, something of the genuine comradeship which had developed among the three men. Or perhaps, it was less something taken away than something left behind: a restlessness, a reserve. For months past they had been able to, and had, discussed both El Jaguar's lost gold, and gold mining in Panama, with a complete frankness underlined with wry humor about human frailties. Fortunately, for all the I.C.C. white workers had vague hopes of striking gold. In Culebra Cut particularly, shovelers, loaders, and blasters alike had kept a sharp eye open.

Gold became, by unspoken but mutual agreement, a forbidden subject, at any rate, whenever all three men were together. Sometimes, when Wesley saw his two companions muttering in an undertone he suspected that the missing gold was their subject. The bar between him and them was up again.

Apart from this difference, life went on much as it had done for the past months. Work and sleep continued to alternate with monotonous regularity. There was so much to be done, and quickly, and too few people to do the work. There could be no easing-off for them, and there was none. They were always on the move in the Central Division to which they had been allocated, under the Division Engineer, Lieutenant Colonel Gaillard, on detached duty from the Corps of Engineers, U.S. Army. The I.C.C. was bringing civilization to the Isthmus of Panama. So every day brought new amenities to the Chagres Valley, which had to be constantly surveyed: the relocation of the P.R.R., the diversion of rivers, the siting of temporary railroad tracks, the siting and subgrading of new roads and culverts, the siting of new machine shops, routine checks, the construction of new plant, many miles of trail to be surveyed for cleaning and draining, a new bridge over the Mandingo River to be constructed, the siting of new pumping stations and waterworks— The work was endless.

The waters continued to rise. Already the area of the lake was bringing new problems to the Indians who for centuries had been accustomed to sailing, paddling, or poling their cayucas along swift narrow waterways, and over rapids. Now they found themselves having to face the hazards of storming winds and buffeting waves, and without the knowledge or the necessary technique there was sometimes loss of life when a canoe was overturned perhaps a mile or more from the nearest land.

Wesley still traveled to Panama from time to time. He and Marie were still occupying the same house on the outskirts of the city, and had settled down to a normal routine.

In many ways the frame dwelling had become a home to him, and often he had to remind himself that he was not a married man again. Except when Marie kissed him in passionate welcome upon his arrival, and later proved only too conclusively that she looked upon her marital duties

325

as those of a mistress rather than a wife—except for these occasions his liaison had settled down to the ordinary humdrum of marriage.

Every time he entered the house and relaxed into one of the oversize rattan chairs which Marie favored, he did so with a feeling that was as close to contentment as any emotion could be that did not involve love. He did not love Marie. He did not hope that he ever could come to love her as he would have loved Anne, but she did her best to make him comfortable. She kept his clothes cleaned and mended; she fed him with all the usual skill and inventiveness of the French. Occasionally she snapped at him, but he noticed that whenever this happened she would stop abruptly, and glance at him with a nervousness which he believed indicated that she did not mean to give him any excuse for breaking up this liaison.

Yet with the years his longing for a family had deepened. There had been occasions, soon after Marie and he had moved into the house, when he had leaned back against the mass of gaudy cushions with which Marie had insisted on filling every chair, and tried to picture the room peopled with his children: two boys, at least, to carry on the Steward-Adam traditions, and of course a girl. Before long, however, he found it necessary for his peace of mind to make a rule not to indulge in introspection, for he realized that if he did not strictly obey it, he would grow to hate Marie because she could never give him the sort of family he wanted. And he did not want to hate her. She was much too exciting a person not to have around. As well expect a drug addict to give up drugs, or a gourmet not to eat.

For Marie was completely uninhibited. From African ancestors she had inherited unreasoning recognition of the old, barbarous concept that a woman was the slave of her lord's desire. She was proud of her body, and constantly used her nakedness as a means to inflame his passions. To the music of a phonograph which she had bought in Panama City from an American seaman, she would dance a variation of the seductive dances of the Congo, until he was well-nigh intoxicated with desire. When he had reached that state she would use every artifice and wile to reward his patience, and extend his pleasure, until he was sated with sensation and physically exhausted.

Even then she remained unsatisfied. Sometimes he had to use what little will power remained to resist further efforts on her part to rouse him to wakefulness. This always made her angry. His last glimpse, as he fell asleep, was often of pouting lips and eyes sparkling with fury. Then, one day, he chuckled at her ingenuous expression. The sound roused her to impulsive action. She smacked his face. A moment later she was crouching at the end of the bed, whimpering at the threat in his eyes.

"Please, please, Wesley—"

326

He mastered his temper. "Don't you ever do that again," he warned thickly.

"No, never, I promise," she gasped, then sighed with relief as he relaxed back on the pillows.

Sometimes he was worried by sensing mysterious depths in Marie, which he seemed unable to plumb. Sometimes she seemed almost to hate him, despite her passion for him, but he put this down to her hot African blood. He could never hope completely to understand the way her mind worked, he consoled himself. Sometimes, too, he was puzzled by an unusual lassitude which often overcame her, but as she seemed always to recover quickly, he did not worry overmuch. In every other respect she seemed well enough. So, in spite of occasional moments of tension, they lived together as contentedly as the unusual circumstances allowed.

One day Wesley's party was ordered back to the Bohio region, for some grading work on a proposed new road. On the third day after their arrival, as they took their siesta under the cool shadows of an umbrella tree, they were astonished to see Anne hurrying along the trail which led to their temporary camp. They quickly scrambled to their feet, greeting her, but she had eyes only for Wesley.

"Wesley, I'm terribly worried. It's Papa—"

"Ill?"

"I don't know. I'm afraid. I mean—he's disappeared."

He made her sit down, motioned to Larry. "Coffee." Larry nodded, went over to the fire.

"Now, Anne, tell us what happened?"

"Ten days ago he told me that he was going orchid hunting the next day, and to prepare rations for six days."

"Six? I thought you told me once that he never left the house for more than three days at a time."

"At any rate, never more than four. I was surprised when he said six."

The three men exchanged significant glances. "Making hay while the sun shines," Larry muttered, tight lipped. Then he nodded in the direction of the door, where the rain was still teeming down. "Except it ain't shining," he added.

"Go on."

"I was surprised, especially in view of the weather. But you know Papa." Her eyes pleaded for understanding. "Old as he is nobody can argue with him, or make him alter a decision."

"We know. Go on."

"He went off early the next morning. I haven't seen him since. I didn't worry the seventh day, and only a little the eighth. But yesterday—" Her agitation supplied its own proof. "I didn't know what to do. I wanted to let somebody in Bohio know, so a search party might be sent out, but I was afraid to."

"Why?"

She moistened her lips. "Papa always loses his temper whenever people interfere with his private affairs. Last night when Juan heard you were here, I knew what to do. Please, please help me find him." She glanced quickly at each man in turn.

"Can we, Wes?" Ericson asked. "I mean, can you fix it?"

"I'll try. Are you sure, Anne, that it's necessary to find him? Mightn't he have gone on somewhere else?"

"I'm sure he would have let me know. You see, in spite of his—his awkward ways, he was meticulous in his courtesy, even to his daughters."

"I'll say," Larry muttered.

"What do you think can have happened to him?"

"I daren't think. Suppose he—he is lost. Dear God! He may be starving. Or perhaps he has hurt himself, and can't move." She swallowed. "I heard a jaguar roaring last night—"

"Anne!" Wesley covered her hand with his own. "There's no use your imagining the worst. I'll telephone through to Culebra and ask for temporary leave for the three of us to look for your father. Have you any idea which direction he took?"

She shook her head. Her eyes were filled with misery. "He could only go one way to begin with. He would be out of sight by the time he arrived at the first cross trail."

"He went alone, of course?"

"Yes. He always went alone."

"On foot?"

"On a mule."

"The mule hasn't returned?"

"No."

"How much food did you give him? Only enough for six days?"

"Perhaps seven, no more." She clenched her hand. "I didn't think he might want more, Wesley. He's always been so punctual, always been proud of doing exactly what he said he would do; no more, no less."

"You don't have to blame yourself, darling." The endearment slipped out. He had not called her darling since the broken engagement, not even in his letters. "The jungle covers a large area. Can't you give us any idea where to begin looking for him? Has he ever said that this mountain or that valley was particularly rich in orchids?"

"No, never." Her voice rose slightly. "He never told Marie and me anything. He was always so secretive."

Wesley glanced helplessly at his companions. Ericson shrugged. Wesley knew the other man would willingly do everything he could to help Anne, although he would not be greatly upset if his efforts were wasted. In fact—

and here Wesley thought he detected a sardonic grin on Ericson's face, and an avaricious expression in the ice-blue eyes—it was easy to see that he was not overlooking the poetic justice of Perrigot's dying the death he had once plotted for Ericson. Perhaps, too, Olaf was already anticipating a renewal of his search for gold.

And Larry? Wesley turned, but as he did so Larry spoke. "Any Indian guides or trackers you know of within reach of your home, Miss Perrigot?"

"Oh!" A suspicion of hope manifested itself. "Do you think an Indian could pick up the trail?"

"A nine days' old trail, and raining every one of those nine days? I don't know, but it's worth a try. God knows! there's nothing else I can think of."

"Can you start now, please?" she pleaded.

Upon Wesley's explaining the circumstances leading to his request for special leave of absence, it was immediately granted. Within three hours all preparations had been completed. With an adequate supply of food, arms, and ammunition, the three men accompanied Anne back to her home. There, Anne sent Juan, her father's colored servant, to comb every village within reach to find an Indian who would agree to accompany the Americans on their search for old man Perrigot.

No sooner had Juan departed on his errand than the clouds rolled away. Before long the blazing heat of the afternoon sun was transforming the afternoon into a sweltering inferno.

Ericson mopped his forehead and face. "By Jimminy! I can't ever decide which is worse. Rain which never stops, or sunshine which makes you feel like a fried egg."

"Tell you something," said Larry. "The rain we've had this last week will raise the lake plenty."

Wesley nodded. "I wonder if the old man is bogged down someplace."

Ericson angrily stubbed out the butt of his cigar, and mopped his throat and chest. "I've decided," he declared. "Rain's cooler. Bloody heat!"

Within the hour Juan had returned with an Indian on muleback. García, he told the Americans, knew the district like the back of his hand, and was willing to try to trail the missing man.

"The point is, is he any good at following a trail?" Larry asked sharply.

"Wait a minute, Larry. I've got me an idea." Wesley turned to the Indian. "Which way did the señor start off?"

The Indian turned and pointed silently to the northeast.

"How do you know? Did you see him starting off on his journey, nine days ago?"

The man shook his head; the dark sloe eyes void of any identifiable expression.

"Did the señor always start off in that direction when he was looking for orchids?"

This time the Indian's reply was in the form of a slight nod. Wesley glanced at his companions.

"These chaps don't miss a thing. I'll bet he's known for years where Perrigot went."

"You're right, Wes," Ericson eagerly confirmed. "Don't know why I didn't realize the fact before, but whenever I followed him he started off in a northeasterly direction. Suppose I thought he did so purposely, to put me off the scent."

"When I've arranged terms with the man we can say good-by to Anne and be off. I doubt whether we'll get far before nightfall as it is."

Anne was waiting for them on the veranda. Her face was pale, but she gave them each a grateful smile, and a "Thank you," in turn. Dolores stood in the background, but Wesley did not look at her, afraid that his eyes might reveal his distaste for her and his disappointment because she was Anne's mother.

"God keep you, darling," Anne whispered in his ear as he turned away from her.

The four men mounted their mules, and started down the well-remembered trail for Bohio. Presently they reached the first cross trail. There was a tree in the middle of the clearing, from the trunk of which was suspended a small, weathered shrine. Wesley called Ericson's attention to it, and they grinned wryly at each other.

"To think we never made the old man eat dirt for what he did," Ericson grunted.

"What would have been the use?"

"And now *we're* trying to *save* his life!" Ericson shrugged. "We're nuts."

The Indian turned into the left-hand trail.

"For Alhajuela?" Wesley asked him.

The man nodded, and heeled his slow-moving animal.

"He sure keeps us entertained with his lighthearted chatter," Ericson muttered.

Later, they turned left off the Alhajuela trail, but all three men noticed that the Indian never once glanced at the ground to look for footprints or droppings, nor turned his head to left or right. Sometime later they turned into a trail on their right. It was overgrown, and the Indian had frequently to use his machete to free the path from whipping branches, festooning lianas, suckers. To the eyes of the three Americans the trail had not been used for months. Ericson spoke for them all when he voiced his doubts.

"I don't know what you fellows think, but this trail don't look like Perrigot came along it nine days ago." He called out in Spanish, "You, there, García. You sure the señor used this trail?"

The Indian turned. For a moment his expressionless gaze rested on the caller. Then he turned again and continued on his way, ignoring the question.

Larry chuckled. "Now you know, brother."

Ericson was angry. "I'll flay his blasted red hide off him," he spluttered. "What the hell—"

"Leave him be," Larry counseled. "Time enough to get rough when he gets us nowhere."

"Which he's doing fast."

But Ericson was wrong. Less than a minute later the Indian held up his hand to halt the men behind him. When they stopped he pointed to the trunk of a tree bordering the trail.

"What is it?" the suspicious Ericson called out from the rear.

Wesley looked. "A small P cut in the bark. Freshly cut."

"Perrigot!" Ericson exploded.

"Yes. Perrigot, his mark!" Wesley waved his hand. "Lead on, Macduff."

The Indian heeled his mule, but not before Wesley had detected a ghost of a smile on the brown, flat face.

48

THE FOUR MEN slept that night under a tarpaulin the Indian had erected in a clearing he had made close to the trail. During the night they were awakened by the thudding of heavy rain on the tarred canvas roof of their shelter.

"*Santa María!*" Wesley heard Ericson exclaim, turning over. "More damn rain." But the sound of his snoring soon afterward proved that he was not losing much sleep on account of it.

Wesley remained awake for some time. He was uneasy, a feeling for which he could not account. Maybe the constant rain was depressing him.

Certainly, his depression was not caused by any trouble old man Perrigot was in, save vicariously, on account of Anne's distress. He reached the conclusion that the trouble was with Ericson and Larry. From the start the two men had betrayed an unnatural excitement. Each had tried to disguise the fact, but not very successfully.

Easy to read what was in their minds. They were hoping that the Indian was leading them straight to El Jaguar's cache. What was to happen if their hopes were realized, probably neither man had stopped to think, for they were not robbers. Yet Wesley was convinced that sooner or later his companions would argue themselves into maintaining that Perrigot had no more legal or moral right to the gold than the next man. Therefore, they would divide what was left of it. With himself, as a third partner, of course. He had that much faith in their integrity.

It was not easy to blame them, yet he wanted no share of the gold himself, nor did he want his friends to have any of it. It was tainted gold. Too many men had already died for it. Nearly a hundred, if one included the thirty-seven brigands whom Ran Runnels and Grandfather Henry Stewart had hanged from the sea wall. And two attempted murders, if one included Perrigot's treachery of a few years ago. It was best forgotten, where it could do no more harm to the souls of men.

Rain was still falling when daylight awakened them early the following morning. Fog enclosed them, and gave to their surroundings an eerie nightmarish appearance. Ericson's language was lurid and unrepeatable. He was not normally a loose-tongued man, but his nerves seemed edgy.

They ate beneath the comparative shelter of the tarpaulin, but after that they had to break camp. Within seconds they were soaked to the skin. They folded and tied up the tarpaulin, and stood ready to move. By this time the fog had dispersed, so the Indian looked up at the clouds, studying them. Then he waved his hand toward the trail, and moved forward.

"Bet he could tell us what the weather is going to do," Wesley commented.

"Ask him," Ericson told Larry. Larry was the only one of whom the Indian took any notice. Wesley wondered whether the Indian guessed that Larry was partly a countryman. Larry's flawless Spanish? Hardly. Instinct, then?

Larry spoke to García in Spanish. García replied, shortly, and in monosyllables.

"He says you won't see a cloud in one hour and ten minutes from now," Larry told the others in English.

The Indian's forecast was amazingly correct. With five minutes to go before the expiration of the hour and ten minutes it was still raining. Five minutes later every cloud had vanished. For once, the Americans were inclined to wish they could stand directly in the sunshine, so their clothes might dry quickly; but the trail they were passing along was narrow, and they were in deep shade. However, it was not long before the steamy heat, plus the heat of their own sweating bodies, dried them.

Presently, "Is it my fancy, or isn't our pal quite so confident as he was?" Ericson asked.

Wesley nodded. "He's looking about him more than he was, and not going so quickly.

"Ask him, Larry."

Larry did so. After half a dozen sentences, "García says he's still on the right trail, he'll point out Perrigot's blaze, but this is new ground to him so he's being more careful."

332

"We're a hell of a way from civilization."

"Yes," Larry agreed. "A hell of a way."

García carried out his promise to point out the next blaze. When he did so the others saw it plainly: a P with a crude circle round it.

"Looks clear enough when it's pointed out," Ericson grumbled testily. "Bet I wouldn't have seen it otherwise. No wonder I lost him."

The jungle grew noisier as they penetrated it more deeply. Bands of monkeys in the treetops easily kept pace with them, leaping from branch to branch with a graceful ease that made Larry remark with envy, "I wonder why we humans troubled to develop our feet. If I could move like that little feller just ahead of us—"

Toucans scolded them from a safe distance; parrots and parakeets screeched from the treetops; the chachalacas sang their strange choruses. Here there was no hint of the solemn silence of northern forests, which had grown accustomed to human intrusion. The jungle of Panama resented the invasion of man, and proclaimed the fact with angry voices.

García brought his animal to a halt, and held up his hand for the Americans to do the same. They saw a cross trail in front of them. It was barely distinguishable, but they were not surprised. They realized they were in a part of the country which even the Indian rarely visited. They watched García slide off his animal, and move from tree to tree seeking a blaze. He completed a circle without having done so, but with the ingrained patience of his race he repeated his search, more slowly this time.

Again he was unsuccessful. "Wait here," he said to Larry, and disappeared along the trail on their left.

Ericson looked uneasy. "That bastard isn't deserting us, Larry? Wesley and I have had a bellyful of being lost in the jungle. As far as I'm concerned, anyone else can have that fun."

"He's left his mule," Larry pointed out.

"So? He could walk back home from here."

"Why should he desert us?" Wesley asked reasonably. "He's nothing to gain, and his hire to lose. Besides, we could probably find our way back with the help of Perrigot's blazing, if the worst came to the worst."

The Indian returned, then investigated the other two trails. When he reappeared for the third time he shook his head and spoke to Larry.

Larry translated.

"Perrigot never got this far. We must retrace our steps."

They returned along the trail for nearly a quarter of a mile, then once again García halted them.

"He came as far as this," Larry explained, after a conversation with the Indian. "García can't understand where he went to from this point."

"Is he sure this blaze is a recent one?" Wesley asked.

Larry nodded. "I asked him that before. Apparently Perrigot reblazed

333

the same mark each time. Probably he knew the trail by heart, but wasn't taking any chances of being lost."

"Then if anything happened to him it was near this point?"

"Between here and the next cross trail."

"Then—" For the first time Wesley felt sorry for the old man. "Poor devil!" he muttered. "God! I wouldn't want to die out here, all alone."

"For God's sake! Who said he was dead?" Ericson demanded.

"If he isn't, what happened to him?"

"If he's dead, where are his remains?"

"A jaguar could have carried him away. Or unfriendly Indians perhaps. A raiding party—"

Ericson looked unusually upset. "God-damn jungle!" he exclaimed harshly. "Does the Indian think he's dead?"

"*Quién sabe!*" was García's reply.

There was a long pause. The Indian remained impassive and unmoving. Larry and Ericson glanced questioningly at Wesley.

"Do we go back?" Larry asked at last.

"Let's go on to the next cross trail again," Wesley suggested. "Tell García to keep an eye open for some evidence of—of something, anything. A button, maybe. A torn piece of clothing."

The Indian nodded agreement, slid off his mule, and leading it, moved along the trail on foot.

He had proceeded two hundred yards or so when he held up his hand for a halt. The undergrowth on his right was a tangle in which giant ferns, vines, swinging lianas, clumps of bamboo, and the roots of trees struggled for existence and formed a green wall splashed with a cataract of scarlet flowers, and spangled with red bunches of parasitic capsules. Giant butter-flies fluttered up and about to make a living kaleidoscope of ever-changing color and pattern.

As soon as the Americans had caught up with him the Indian indicated the dying ends of some bush twigs. Larry looked closer.

"He's pointing to some broken twigs," he told the others. "Something's pushed its way through."

"An animal," Ericson muttered.

Evidently the Indian must have realized what had been said, for he bent down and picked up a piece of twig from the ground, and showed the end of it to Larry.

"This one's been cut with a steel edge. Look." He passed it over to Ericson.

Suddenly the Indian pushed his way into the curtain of undergrowth. It gave way before him, closed in behind him. He disappeared from their sight.

Larry hissed. "Like a secret door."

A few moments later the Indian reappeared. "Come," he said in Spanish.

334

He took hold of the mule's bridle, and pushed his way back into the green wall. As before, it seemed to wrap itself around him and swallow him up. After a moment's hesitation Wesley dismounted, and followed suit. As he passed through the thick belt of greenery he realized that all the vegetation at that point had been kept carefully pruned of all thickening twigs and branches, and that only the extreme tips of twigs touched his face and shoulders, doing little more than brush against his flesh with a caressing softness.

He had moved along this green tunnel through the undergrowth for a distance of about ten yards when it broadened out into a proper trail. García, already mounted, was waiting for him. By the time he, too, had mounted, the other two had joined him.

"What do you know! Another trail!"

Larry spoke to the Indian. The others understood a word here and there, but not enough to comprehend everything. So they waited for an explanation.

"García thinks this trail once joined the other, until somebody deliberately blocked it up by planting bushes."

"Perrigot?"

"Perrigot, or even El Jaguar. He thinks we'll probably find that this trail leads directly to Perrigot's destination, with no other trails crossing it."

"Weren't these trails originally Indian?" Wesley asked.

"Of course."

"Then how was someone able to block one off without the Indians finding out?"

"I asked him that. He said that if any particular trail was not often used it might have been possible to plant bushes across it, they would have grown up in a matter of weeks."

"Who cares how?" Ericson muttered irritably. "If this trail's likely to lead us to the old man let's get moving."

They started off along a trail so narrow there was barely enough room for them to pass along it in single file. The tips of branches brushed against their arms and legs. Overhanging lianas constantly threatened to brush off their hats. On the other hand, it was plain to them all that the trail had been cut back at intervals.

The trail rose until it reached a high point from which much of the surrounding countryside was visible. They were standing on a ridge separating two narrow valleys, one of which they had just traversed; not a very high ridge, for in all directions save behind them the country rose in a series of ever higher, green-felted peaks. Both valleys were thickly wooded, and in neither was there any evidence of human occupation. A boa constrictor stared at them from a distant tree, its beady eyes frighteningly evil. Wesley unslung his gun, but the movement startled the snake, which hissed and slid down the far side of the tree into the undergrowth.

335

There was one difference between the two valleys. The bottom land of the one before them was covered with a wide expanse of water which wound out of sight behind a high peak, and beyond the far side of the valley was a much larger expanse of water stretching away toward the Chagres Valley. It was evident that they were above one of the many lagoons which the rising Chagres waters were creating everywhere. Moreover, there were at least three waterfalls in different parts of the valley.

The Indian spoke. Larry translated. "García remembers this valley. He passed through it years ago, before the bottom land was flooded. Three rivulets met here, so it is known as El Valle de Aguas Vivas—the Valley of Lively Waters. Apparently even the Indians thought it beautiful."

" 'There is not in the wide world a valley so sweet, As that vale in whose bosom the bright waters meet,' " Wesley quoted in appreciation of a valley that was still beautiful.

He felt a hand grip his arm so fiercely that the finger tips dug into his flesh and hurt. He turned, startled.

"Wes—what was that—"

"What was what? What's the matter with you? Are you nuts?"

"That quotation—"

"Something from Burton Stevenson's *The Home Book of Verse,* which Anne sent to me—*The Meeting of the Waters* by Thomas Moore. What of it? And what about my arm?"

"Madre de Dios. This is it, Wes. Holmes's valley." Larry's voice was hoarse with excitement. "Sweet Valley!" He saw that Wesley did not comprehend. "In God's name, Wes, don't you see? A valley so sweet—where the bright waters meet. And—and—and—" He swallowed, tried to speak coherently. "That crack about, 'What more can I tell you than more?' Holmes was punning on Thomas Moore—and this is where Perrigot has come. It all adds up—"

Yes, it added up, Wesley was forced to agree.

"Do you know how to find the cave—if you're right?"

"I know I'm right. The trail will lead us near enough, then we can fan out and search—" Larry did not wait for comments; he turned to García and spoke rapidly. The Indian turned and started off down the descending trail.

They reached the water's edge. "Well, Larry?" Wesley queried, for the green walls either side of the trail not only reached the edge of the water, but actually entered it, going down to the bottom of the valley, doubtless, now covered by twenty feet of water.

Larry's face expressed despair, but he turned to García. The Indian listened, shrugged.

"Looks like we're too late, old son," Wesley said, placing a sympathetic arm round Larry's shoulder. "If there was a cave here, it's gone for all time, under the water."

"Where's Perrigot?" Larry shouted, choking with disappointment. "He wouldn't have come here if the gold was already under water."

"That's true!" Ericson exclaimed abruptly. "He wouldn't do that. Where is he?"

"Señor!" the Indian touched Larry's arm.

They realized that he was listening. For nearly a minute the Americans stood quiet and unmoving, watching the brown, impassive face uplifted toward the sky.

"What's he listening for?" Ericson asked at last.

"Shut up," Larry ordered.

García listened another twenty seconds, then cupped his hands round his mouth and shouted. The sound traveled across the valley, where it was echoed. The sound startled a flock of herons which rose into the air from the water's side, and went wheeling away into the more peaceful distance.

The Indian repeated his call, waited, and then reached a decision. He began to examine the left hand wall of the trail, and almost at once disappeared through it as he had done elsewhere, before. The others crashed through after him, and found themselves on another hidden trail. As they moved forward the sound of a waterfall grew louder.

Presently they emerged into a clearing immediately by the foot of the waterfall. García shouted. After a moment or two they heard a muffled answer.

"It's behind that rock by the waterfall," Larry called out in excitement. He hurried forward toward a huge rock which looked as if, centuries ago, it had rolled down the mountainside above. Its toe was in the water, but Larry waded in. Before he had taken six steps forward he was shoulder deep. Wesley followed close behind, for fear Larry's unstable foot would pitch its owner under the surface. But Larry clung to the rock, and somehow managed to retain his balance. As the two men rounded the toe of the rock they saw before them, no more than eighteen inches above the level of the water, what was apparently the arch of the narrow entrance to a cave.

Larry clutched Wesley's arm. "Oh God!" he whispered. "If he's inside he's cut off. He can't get out. There's not enough room."

"He got in, didn't he?" Wesley moved nearer the cave, but as he did so the water reached his chin. He began to think that it would not be possible to walk into the cave. He would have to swim.

He turned around to Larry, whose drawn expression and trembling mouth told their own story.

"Can you swim?"

"No, Wes, and even if I could—" He swallowed. "I couldn't go in there. I couldn't. There's no room even to swim."

"Stay where you are, or go back. Call to Olaf to stay until I tell him different."

"You're not going in—you can't—you don't know what's inside—"

337

"Perrigot's in there. Here, take my coat and trousers." He undressed as best he could, and threw the clothes to Larry. He turned again, and began to swim. He reached the entrance to the cave. There was barely enough room to go forward without hitting his head against the roof. He hesitated, treading water. Ahead he could see nothing but darkness. There might be alligators inside, a boa constrictor, a jaguar: Heaven alone knew what perils. Then he remembered that the muffled echo of a shout had come from somewhere near. Where one man could go another could.

"Perrigot!" he called. The echo of his voice traveled before him, rebounding hollowly until its last whisper died away in the distance. "Perrigot!"

"*Au secours!* Quickly, for God's sake! Quick! Quick!"

Quick! Quick! The despairing call revived Wesley's flagging courage. He swam forward into the black tunnel.

49

AS HE ADVANCED along the narrow tunnel Wesley found that it was not so dark as it had at first appeared; when his eyes had become accustomed to the gloom, he noticed an eerie green radiance which he presently concluded was projected along it and into the cave ahead by the reflection on the water of the brilliant sunlight outside. He was gradually able to distinguish the rock formation of the roof, and in particular a dangerous spur against which he might easily have struck his head.

Presently the roof took an upward slope. After a few more strokes his feet touched a solid surface, and he found he was able to stand up. He moved up the sloping floor until the water barely covered his knees. He felt something pluck at his arm, and only just stopped himself from giving a startled yell.

"I'm here. To your left," a weak, trembling voice announced.

Wesley turned, and was able to distinguish the vague outline of a body lying on a shelf of rock several inches above the level of the water. The light was not bright enough to see the face, but he had already recognized the voice as Perrigot's.

"Perrigot, what the hell are you doing here?"

"Who is this?" the Frenchman quavered. "Who?"

"Wesley Adams."

"Wesley!" Perrigot's laugh was incredulous. "Of all people," he muttered. "Of all people." His voice turned vaguely stronger, sharper. "How did you get here?"

Wesley echoed Perrigot's laugh, but there was no underlying humor in his. "Aren't you going to thank me, old man?"

"How did you get here?" The Frenchman's voice was weak, but the old vicious hate was still distinguishable.

"Thanks to Anne, if you must know. She heard that I and my companions were camping near your home, so she called on us yesterday morning, told us you had been missing for nine days, and begged us to try and find you. Funny, isn't it, the ways of Fate."

"What do you mean?"

"Two of the people come to rescue you happen to be the very two you tried to kill in the jungle. God! it would serve you right if we left you here." It occurred to Wesley at that moment to wonder why the old man had remained where he was. "Why are you still here, anyway? Don't feel like swimming any more?" he questioned with contempt.

"I slipped and broke my leg." Perrigot clutched at Wesley. "How are you going to get me out of here with a broken leg?" He groaned with agony. "If I don't get out soon it will be too late."

"You won't die from starvation yet awhile—"

"I don't mean starvation. I haven't eaten for three days, but I don't need much. I'm an old man. But I'll drown. *Mon Dieu!* The waters are rising steadily. I've watched them creep up and up—"

Wesley shivered. Compared with the heat outside, the cave was damnably cold. For the first time in years he longed passionately to step into the sunshine. God! he thought. Having to lie helpless while the water rose higher and higher—

"I'll go back for Ericson," he announced harshly. "Let go of my arm, old man."

"Don't go, Wesley. Don't leave me," Perrigot pleaded.

"Do you want us both to die, you old fool? How am I to get you out without help?"

"You'll come back? You won't leave me here to die, like a rat in a trap—"

"Don't judge others by yourself, Perrigot. Though it's to be hoped that the two of us and the guide can get you out, at that."

"You brought a guide?" The weak voice sounded angry.

"Yes. An Indian. He followed your trail, in spite of your having done your damnedest to hide it. How much of El Jaguar's gold have you spent, old man?"

Perrigot's gasp was evidence enough of the shock the question had given him. "Who told you?"

"Have you forgotten that my grandfather shot El Jaguar dead?"

"Forget! May he and Runnels live in everlasting hell-fire—"

"Keep your curses to yourself," Wesley curtly interrupted. "Unless you want to be left here."

"Wesley! I'm an old man—you couldn't desert an old man."

339

"An evil old man—but don't worry, Perrigot. I'm not your judge, thank God. I'll fetch Ericson."

He had to use force to release his arm from Perrigot's grip, and was astonished that so old a man could have so much strength left in his fingers, especially after a week of nervous strain, and three days' starvation. He swam back through the tunnel-like entrance of the cave, and was never more glad to see the sunshine ahead of him. As he emerged into daylight he felt the heat strike against his chilled head and shoulders, but for once it was like a gentle caress.

He waded around the toe of the intervening rock and joined his companions, answering their inquiring eyes.

"He's there. Leg broken. Can you swim, Olaf?"

"Yes."

"Enough to help bring him out?"

"How?"

"Float him out. There's just enough room."

"What about the gold?"

"Hell! If we don't get him out he'll die. Isn't it more important to save life?"

"Not his, the bastard. Didn't he try to have us killed? What sort of fools does that make us, trying to save his life?" But all this time he was stripping off his clothes. Soon he was naked. "I'll have my head examined when I get back home," he grumbled. "What about the Indian giving a hand?"

But the Indian said he could not swim, so Wesley and Ericson went by themselves. Perrigot welcomed them with a pathetic gasp of relief.

"Can you swim?" Wesley asked him.

"No."

"Then you can't float, I suppose. But you must. Just lie flat on the water, and trust to us to pull you through. For God's sake don't struggle, or stiffen, or double up, or anything of that sort or you'll sink to the bottom. If you do, by thunder, we'll leave you there."

Perrigot was plainly terrified. For all his years life was still precious to him, however, and he nodded in agreement, and prepared to get ready to leave. In the vague light they saw him reach for a bulky haversack, and clutch it tight to his chest.

"Hey! You leave that behind," Ericson growled. "What do you want to do? Sink?"

"No. I—I can't leave it. I want it," the old man quavered.

The Scandinavian guessed his reason. "Gold!" he exploded. "What do you know! Rather sink than risk losing ten cents' worth."

"You'll leave it," Wesley ordered. "And your outer clothes. I'll come back for them."

He expected opposition, but the old man was unexpectedly amenable.

340

"Very well, Wesley. It is heavy," he muttered. "The result of five days' mining."

"Mining!" Ericson shouted. "What did I tell you?"

"I thought this was El Jaguar's cache," Wesley said.

Perrigot chuckled. "It was both. He had a peculiar sense of humor, to hide stolen California gold in an old Panama gold mine."

"Where's his gold?"

"Spent. Years ago." The Frenchman spoke scornfully.

"You god-damned thieving old bastard—" Ericson began stormily.

"Shut up, and help me get him out," Wesley ordered. "Take off his trousers."

All went well until it came to the point of floating him. The moment the water met under his chin he began to struggle violently. In consequence all three went under, and he was not quiet again until Ericson knocked him unconscious with a punch on the jaw.

"For that," Ericson announced viciously to the unconscious man, "I'll mine the rest of your gold if I have to swim under water to get to it."

"You will, in a few days' time," Wesley told him. "I'll take his shoulders, you push his foot. Ready?"

With Wesley floating and Ericson swimming they swam the old man, heavy with the fat of age, toward the outside world. Halfway through the tunnel Wesley's shoulder bumped against what looked like a short log. There was a flash of white, the sound of crunching bone, a heavy tug at Perrigot's body which nearly pulled the old man from his grasp, a thrashing of water—

"In God's name—" Ericson shouted.

"Swim like mad, thrash your feet about—"

Somehow they thrashed their way out of the cave, and round the rock, leaving a red trail of blood behind them. As they scrambled out of the water they saw that Perrigot's right arm had been severed at the elbow.

It was obvious to them all there was no hope of his living long enough to get him home. They manufactured a crude tourniquet and succeeded in stopping the bleeding, but it was too late. Too much had already been lost in the water from the severed artery.

He never properly recovered consciousness, and died two hours later.

Two days later Wesley, at Anne's request, called at the Perrigot home. She was dressed in conventional black, but her eyes were serene.

"I can't really sorrow for Papa," she told him. "I couldn't love him. I don't mean he was cruel to me. Not physically cruel. It was as if he resented my having been born."

"Perhaps he did, on account of—of your mother—"

She nodded. "I'm sure you are right."

"And Marie?"

341

"I don't think he hated her so much as he hated me, but although he often favored her in order to spite me, he had no real liking for her; no affection. It seems horrible to speak badly of the dead, but I don't think he loved anything in this world except gold."

"You knew about the gold?" Wesley was surprised.

"Not until you told me, but now I know I can understand so much of what has puzzled me all my life." She shivered. "Let's not talk about Papa any more, my dear. I want your help."

"You have it. Doing what?"

"Going through Papa's papers. I have found a tin box full of documents. I scarcely know what one of them is about."

Wesley examined the papers one by one, and as he went through them he realized that Perrigot had died a rich man. Year after year the total of his bank deposits had averaged fifteen thousand dollars, a large part of which had been transferred to France and there invested in property. One bundle of documents in the box consisted of nothing but title deeds—a small block of apartments in Paris, a house in St. Cloud, a *buvette* in Calais, a small farm in Normandy—and that all had been purchased at bargain prices was proved by a schedule of properties, dated the previous year, with purchase price in one column and latest estimated value in another, showing that not one property had depreciated. The smallest gain was as little as eight per cent. Three had appreciated by as much as twenty per cent.

It soon became apparent that Perrigot had been miserly by nature. There was a ream of loose memoranda sheets filled with figures and calculations based on his financial worth; all dated, and showing that not one month had passed without an increase in his capital. Capital which he had never spent, so far as could be seen. It seemed to the American that he could almost read into each successive calculation Perrigot's gloating joy.

Halfway through the box Wesley pulled out a square, sealed envelope. Delicacy prompted him to pass it over to Anne, but she passed it back.

"You open it, my dear. I have no secrets from you."

He opened it. Inside was a certificate of marriage, signed by the Mayor of the Seventeenth Arrondissement of Paris, between one Gabrielle Henriette Marie Fouchard and Félix Edouard Jean Perrigot, dated October 15, 1879. Attached to it was a Panama death certificate dated November, 1880, for Gabrielle Henriette Marie Perrigot.

"That was Papa's first wife," Anne explained sadly. "He told Dolores that she died of yellow fever."

He was about to put the envelope on one side when he felt a small square of pasteboard at the bottom. He pulled it out. It was a photograph of a dark-haired woman with a baby in her arms. The face was vaguely familiar to him, but as the fashion was of three decades ago, he gave it no more thought. Besides, he felt embarrassed, as if he were peeping through the keyhole of a man's private room. He passed it over to Anne without a word.

342

She shook her head, apparently reading a question into his gesture. "I wonder who she is," she said. "He had no sisters or brothers." She turned it over. "There's a name written on the back. It's—oh! the ink's almost rubbed off. It's Gabrielle and—"

A long silence made him glance up. The hand which held the photograph was trembling.

"Anne! What is it?"

She passed it back to him. He stared down at the faded writing.

"Gabrielle Anne—God Almighty!" He swallowed. "Anne—you—"

She caught hold of his hand. "Wesley, if it's me, then—then I'm white."

"And Marie—no, by God! she couldn't be. Gabrielle died one year after marriage."

They gazed at each other, not daring to think or hope.

"Call Dolores." His voice was husky with excitement.

Dolores came. Fat, swarthy, black Dolores.

"Listen to me," he began sternly. "We want the truth. Who was Miss Anne's mother?"

The cook's eyes grew afraid. "Me, señor. You know I am. Marie, she tell you Dolores was Señor Perrigot's wife."

"You lie, woman—"

She grew more afraid, looking about her as if expecting Perrigot to enter the room at any moment.

"Before the good Jesus Christ I swear I suckled Anne at these breasts," she answered in bastard Spanish, displaying her ample breasts with her large black hands.

He rose to his feet, angry and threatening.

"The truth, damn you. The truth, do you understand? Look at that." He thrust the photograph before her white-rimmed eyes.

She sank on her knees in an attitude of supplication. "Forgive, señor, forgive. Señor Perrigot, he force me to swear I never tell the truth about Anne's *mamacita.*"

"He is dead. You tell the truth now or I'll curse you by all the saints in Heaven."

"No, señor, no." Her voice rose in a terrified wail. "Me tell truth. Anne was the señora's *niña.* A white child," she added, looking at Anne with contempt. "When the señora die, señor look for wet nurse, and find me, because my niña die, too, same day as Señora Perrigot."

Wesley dared not look at Anne lest his joy and hers should spoil this moment of revelation.

"Why did the señor make you swear that?" he demanded.

"Because he hate Anne for killing her mother. He love the señora so much her death nearly break his heart. He never want any more to do with her niña."

"And Marie?"

343

Her expression grew immensely proud. She nodded her big head, and her mouth opened in a happy smile.

"Yes, yes, señor, Marie really mine. *Mi querida,* my dear child by Señor Perrigot. Her very fine woman, mi María, Spanish also from my *abuelo.* It make Dolores very happy to know her daughter marry white man. Marie too good for Negro men."

Wesley saw that Dolores was looking at him with the benign expression of a woman regarding her son-in-law with marked gratitude and affection.

He turned away, unable to look any more at the face of Marie's mother, but as he prepared to tell her to go a new reflection occurred to him.

"Marie knows that Anne is all white?"

Dolores nodded, proud as a peacock. *"Sin duda.* I love my child too much to tell her lies. Besides, I want her know she has the whole of my love. She alone her mother's angel."

Marie an angel! Marie, who had deliberately wrecked his marriage with Anne.

"You can go," he ordered harshly.

Dolores clambered to her feet with marked relief. With a contemptuous glance at Anne she hurried from the room. As the door closed behind her he turned to Anne. For a few moments they stood still, gazing at each other as if to make sure they were not dreaming. Then a smile spread across his rugged face, dissolving the sick distress contorting his features. He held out his arms, and she moved trustingly into their strong shelter.

"It's all right," she sobbed with happiness. "All right forever, my dearest, dearest, darling."

It was easy to be wise after the event.

"Now we know why your father encouraged Marie to tempt me away from you," he said presently. "He wanted to revenge his father's death by tricking me into marrying Marie. God! How he could hate. And of course he also meant to hurt you."

She nodded absently. "You know, darling, we have misjudged Papa in one respect. He hated me, yes, but the measure of his hatred for me is probably the measure of his love for Mamma. I think he must have worshiped her. Strange, isn't it, that we thought he was only interested in gold." She frowned. "What did you mean when you said that Papa wanted to revenge his father's death by hurting you?"

"Because of what my grandfather did to—" He stopped, aghast to realize what he had been on the point of saying. It wasn't likely, he thought, that she could possibly know that her grandfather had been hanged as a brigand. She must never know.

"You probably don't know," he continued hurriedly. "I only found out a short while back. My grandfather was indirectly responsible for your grandfather's death." He was sure he would be forgiven the slight devia-

344

tion from the strict truth. What was an adjective more or less when the future happiness of two people was concerned? "That's why he hated me," he added.

"Poor Wesley," she comforted him. "But, now—" She faltered.

"Well?"

"What about Marie? You and she."

He laughed harshly. "She had no conscience about robbing you of me. Why should I have any conscience about deserting her?" He kissed her hungrily. "You do want me?"

"More than anything else in the world."

50

AS USUAL MARIE received him with passionate kisses. He had to use force to free himself from her embrace.

"What's the matter with you?" she asked sharply.

"Sit down, and keep quiet."

"Wesley!"

"Sit down."

She did so, mutinously, glowering at him. He saw Perrigot in her eyes.

"I've several things to say to you, Marie, so try and listen without interruption. First of all, I have bad news. Your father is dead."

"Dead." She mulled the news over in silence, then shrugged. "He had to die sometime. He was old enough to die."

He looked at her with disgust. "Is that all you have to say?"

"What do you want me to do? Cry? He had outlived his time, hadn't he? Am I supposed to make myself unhappy because he can't live forever? You can't think I was fond of him, or ever have been. Damn his soul!"

"Marie!"

"Damn his soul," she viciously repeated. "That's what I said, and I meant every word. It was his fault that I'm mestiza, a half-breed, something to be sneered at, insulted, treated like dirt. Besides, what sort of life do you think he led Anne and me? It wasn't until he found I could be of use to him that he ever said a soft word to me."

"You mean, when he encouraged you to steal me from Anne?"

She drew her lips back in her old familiar smile. "Yes—not that I needed any encouragement. I wanted you, so I fought for you. I would have done the same even if it had meant fighting him too."

"For love of me, or hatred of Anne?"

Her answer was a careless shrug.

345

"Why do you hate your sister?"

She scornfully smiled. "Is it so unusual for sisters to hate each other? How did Papa die?"

He told her. After all, that was her right. He went on, casually, "Yesterday your sister asked me to help her examine and sort your father's papers."

Her temper flared. "What right had she to do that? Why didn't she wait until I was present?"

He ignored the question, not an easy one to answer.

"I made a duplicate list of the papers. Here it is." He handed an envelope to her. "Your father died a rich man."

"Who gets the money? Me?"

"He died without a will, apparently. I imagine you'll share the inheritance equally, but I don't know."

"How much am I worth?"

"You'll find that in there, too." When she began to open the envelope he snatched it back from her. "There'll be enough time for that when I've gone. Which will be in another five minutes. Meanwhile, you can listen to me."

"Going where? You've only just come. Aren't you on leave?"

"Only until tomorrow."

"Well then . . ." The lips drew back. "There's tonight."

"Will you listen to me? There's one thing I found among your father's papers which is not on that list."

"What is it?"

"A photograph of Gabrielle Perrigot, and her two-weeks-old baby. A *white* baby named Anne. Now are you interested?"

A long silence. "Perfectly," she said at last. "So you don't want your half-black mistress any more now that you can marry another of your insipid white women, and breed children by her. Fool!" she exclaimed explosively. "That's all you will do. Use Anne as a brood mare for a lot of puling white brats. How long do you think you'll be satisfied with her milk-and-water embraces? It won't be long before you'll be remembering what I was to you, and cursing the fact that you have her instead of me in bed with you."

"Is that all?"

"Almost." She shook with laughter. "You poor fool, Wesley, you stupid, conceited white fool. Do you think I ever had real satisfaction from you, or any other white man for that matter? Your friend Olaf Ericson taught me years ago to expect nothing from a white man. I only took you from Anne, and kept you, because I hated her as much as ever Papa hated your grandfather."

He looked at her with growing horror and suspicion. "What are you implying?" he asked.

"You understand well enough," she mocked. "Whenever you were in the

346

jungle, then I really enjoyed myself. In your home, and in your bed. That was the best joke of all. In your bed, and your sheets."

"With whom, damn you, woman. With whom?"

She laughed at him, white teeth showing between her drawn-back lips. "You haven't enough fingers on your hands to count them all. And all of them men, too. Not weak, spineless, two-minute white men, but men with virility and power, capable of satisfying even me. Colored men, do you hear me, Wesley Adam? Colored men. Full-blooded Negroes, some of them. . . ."

Her voice rose as he turned and walked blindly out into the burning heat of midafternoon, away from her scornful, contemptuous revelations. . . .

The waters of Gatun Lake had risen to their controlled level. The last dike holding back the sea from Miraflores had been blown. Miraflores and Gatun locks had been filled and tested. The Gamboa dike had been blown, allowing water to surge into the great cut at Culebra. The old enemy, Cucaracha slide, had fought to the last moment to defeat man's efforts to join two great oceans. As if determined to prevent the waters reaching Pedro Miguel locks, its toe had never stopped creeping forward. After one and a half tons of dynamite had made less impression upon it than a colony of ants, engineers had begun to despair of ever checking it by normal means. So it had been decided to let the Lake water flow as best it could around the obstruction, in the certainty that the counteracting weight of water would prevent further sliding; and that once the depth permitted of dredging operations dredgers would clear the bottom, and keep it cleared.

The engineers' forecast had been justified. The slides were being mastered. Everywhere along the length of the Canal, from Cristobal to Panama, the way was open for ships to pass from ocean to ocean.

At her berth at Cristobal, the cement-carrying steamer *Ancon,* especially furbished for the occasion, was waiting to make the first official trip through the Canal, thus opening it for commerce. The time was 7:15 A.M., and two hundred distinguished guests were aboard. Across the world, on the far side of the Atlantic, Europe was in flames: the German Kaiser's army had rolled across the Belgian and French frontiers. The awful holocaust had begun. But for the moment the people aboard the *Ancon* had only one thought: the greatest engineering feat of any century had been successfully completed.

Mr. and Mrs. Wesley Adam stood in the bow, and watched the waters slide gently past them as the vessel slowly nosed its way toward the entrance of the Canal. Wesley had been silent so long that Anne's sun-speckled eyes glanced shyly upward at the strong brown face above her. Wesley's hair fluttered in the early breeze, and she felt an absurd impulse to lift her free hand and pat the unruly red locks into place. She desisted, only because she thought that the other one hundred and ninety-eight guests might

347

think that the couple in the bow were on their honeymoon, whereas they had been married long enough for the first of a new generation of the Stewart breed to be already stirring within her.

"Happy, darling?"

He lowered his glance, which had been fixed upon the line of distant foothills through which they would shortly be threading their way.

"Incredibly."

"You don't begrudge its having robbed you of your country—our country —for so many years?"

"Robbed me!" He laughed happily. "It's robbed me of nothing. It's given me everything: increased pride in the achievement of mankind, added pride in our country, a background. Memories to last a lifetime—and an adequate bank account for next year when I take you back to your new home in New England. Above all, my darling, it's given me—you."

"Come out of the clouds, you lovebirds," Frederick Sanderson called from behind them. "Remember, this is a great day. Isn't it, Madge?"

Madge and Anne smiled at each other in secret understanding.